Sergeant Barker awoke to a blinding light in his eyes...

and a thundering voice in his ears. When he emerged from the fog of sleep, he saw that the shouting came from Lieutenant Morris. Morris stood just inside the door to Barker's quarters and was speaking in a loud but normal voice. The blinding light was just the yellow flame from a lantern in the lieutenant's hand.

"Sergeant Barker, Sergeant Bell," Morris was repeating. "We have to assemble on parade at once!"

Barker threw back his mosquito net and swung himself out of bed.

"What's up, sir?"

An eager excitement lit the young officer's face.

"It's happened, Sergeant! The Bengal sepoys have mutinied! They murdered their English officers and made off for Delhi. And the entire Ganges valley is in flames!"

SWORD OF THE MOGUL

Empire And Honor 3

HAROLD R. THOMPSON

ZUMAYA YESTERDAYS   AUSTIN TX

2015

This book is a work of fiction. Names, characters, places and incidents are products of the author's imagination or are used fictitiously. Any resemblance to actual persons or events is purely coincidental.

SWORD OF THE MOGUL

© 2015 by Harold R. Thompson

ISBN 978-1-61271-276-5

Cover art © François Thisdale

Cover design © Tamian Wood

"Zumaya Yesterdays" and the phoenix colophon are trademarks of Zumaya Publications LLC, Austin TX.
Look for us online at
http://www.zumayapublications.com

Library of Congress Cataloging-in-Publication Data

Thompson, Harold (Harold R.)
 Sword of the mogul / Harold R. Thompson.
    pages ; cm. -- (Empire and honor ; 3)
 ISBN 978-1-61271-276-5 (print/trade pbk. : alk. paper)
-- ISBN 978-1-61271-277-2 (electronic) -- ISBN 978-1-61271-278-9 (epub)
1.   Great Britain--History, Military--19th century--Fiction. I. Title.
 PR9199.3. T4668S96 2014
 813'.54--dc23
                                        2014024084

For 2/JBF

CHAPTER 1

He had forgotten the green of England.

The quilted fields nestled amongst the hedgerows, the dark stone houses seeming to grow out of that fertile soil— he was almost home. The familiar lane was firm beneath his feet, and there beyond the trees rose the square stone tower of his uncle's church, the slate rooftops of the school. Beyond that, surrounded by ancient oaks he remembered well, stood the house. The leaves of the oaks shone bright emerald, luminescent in the early summer sun.

It was strange to walk here again, to see this place. This was the land of his childhood, where he had conjured romantic dreams of soldiering, dreams that had been twisted by the blood, filth, horror and valour of the war with Russia.

Now, he had returned. His regiment, the Royal Hampshire Fusiliers, had been among the first to arrive in England from the Crimea, the voyage under steam having taken less than two weeks. When they had landed in Portsmouth, the regiment had paraded up from the docks, the band

1

crashing out "Cheer, Boys, Cheer," the townsfolk lining the streets to greet the conquering heroes.

It had been a triumphant moment, but William Dudley had only half-shared that sense of victory, so heavy was the burden he carried. The burden of fear that he was no longer welcome in his uncle's house.

I betrayed him, he reminded himself, *betrayed his wishes. He did everything for me, raised me as his own upon the death of my father, secured for me a position at St. John's College, Cambridge, and I turned my back on him, ran off to enlist as a soldier. A common soldier in the ranks.*

Yet here he was to seek forgiveness.

The previous night he had roomed at the Black Horse Tavern; from there, he had sent word of his arrival, a letter explaining he had secured four weeks leave away from his regiment, four weeks before he would have to depart for his next posting in India. He wondered now whether he would spend those four weeks here, or whether he would need to return to the tavern, seek his old lodgings there, the room he had kept when he had served as a tutor for the Wilkes family.

The latter was a possibility he was prepared to face. His aunt would receive him warmly, that much he knew, for she had maintained a steady correspondence with him throughout the war, as had his cousins. But if his uncle, who had never sent or returned a letter, would not have him, he could not remain.

He reached the end of the lane and halted at the gate. He stared at the house, the simple Georgian box of dark slate. The shutters and window frames were painted a bright red that matched his tattered uniform, his scarlet coatee with its faded bullion epaulettes. He had worn the uniform in the hope it would help demonstrate his success as a soldier, his improbable promotion. He was now *Ensign* William Dudley, a commissioned officer, a rank befitting his social status. He was a gentleman, and a veteran of war who had been wounded twice and survived.

Survived thanks, in part, to Miss Florence Nightingale's nurses, in particular a young woman named Elizabeth Montague he had met in Scutari Hospital. She, too, was from Hampshire, and she, too, had returned to her family's ancestral house outside Winchester. Dudley had promised to visit her and would, when this was done with, one way or the other.

So much had happened in the past three years. Three years since he had run off—"gone for a soldier." So much.

"He's here!" someone cried, and he started. He had been lost in his thoughts, had not seen the front door open, the small figure emerge. Running toward him was a dark-haired and bright-eyed boy, a boy Dudley realized must be his little cousin Phillip, grown three years older. Behind Phillip came a beautiful young woman, her face a perfect heart framed by a mantle of golden curls. Cousin Jane, his closest childhood companion. Dear Cousin Jane.

Dudley snatched off his forage cap as Phillip opened the gate. Jane was smiling at him, crying, "Oh, William! William! It is you! You're home! You're home!"

She threw her arms around his neck, almost knocking him backwards, and he let out one sharp bark of laughter. Phillip was tugging at his sleeve, asking, "Can I see your sword? Can I see your sword?"

Dudley let the laughter take him, and for a moment, his fears were forgotten, his cousins' joy was so sincere, so infectious.

"Oh, my dears! It's so very fine to see you both. I will show you the sword later, Phillip! Later!"

Then he spied his Aunt Bronwyn, waiting on the steps. With her was Agnes, the housekeeper, looking the same as always, stern features hiding her jolly interior. The sight of them brought the expected pleasure but also a twist in his heart, for it reminded him of the confrontation that awaited.

"Let me take your satchel," Phillip insisted, and Dudley did not resist. Jane took his hand and led him forward. A few paces from the step he halted, his cap in his hands.

"Well, Aunt," he said, "I'm back."

She was smiling, a smile as warm and inviting as he could have wished. Then she descended, arms raised, and embraced him as well.

"It has been too long, William," she said, and she stood back. "Your uncle is waiting for you in his study."

***

The Reverend Robert Mason stood behind his vast oak desk, facing the windows, his head wreathed in pipe smoke. The air was heavy with the scent of his tobacco, the leather of his books. Dudley stood at attention, as if awaiting an interview with his colonel.

His aunt's words had been reassuring, and he found further solace in the old drill. It released him from thoughts and worries, although he took a moment to survey the room. He found it unchanged, and thought it strange how he had always been comfortable here. The bookcases, the framed maps, the globe in one corner, and the stuffed birds on their stands had all contained mysteries for him. He had played here as a child, his tin soldiers battling on the carpet with invisible foes. Here, he had formed his desire to seek adventure in the far-flung corners of the empire.

The tin soldiers had played their role as well. They had been a gift from his father, a last gift before Thomas Dudley's foolish accident, before he had toppled into the River Test in a drunken stupor, still mourning the passing of his beloved wife. With both parents gone, Dudley had come here to live with his mother's brother, bringing with him dim memories and the box of soldiers.

Only one of those soldiers had survived. As a boy, Dudley had named it Wellington, after his hero, and now he wore it on a chain around his neck, inside his uniform as a charm of good luck and a connection to his past, to his family. It had helped him maintain his sense of home when he had found himself in such places as Gibralter, Malta, Turkey, the Crimea. He realized now that family and home had never been far from his thoughts; he had constantly been sending back gifts with his letters. Turkish slippers for Aunt. A Russian helmet for his uncle.

He stared at his uncle's cluttered desk. There sat the Russian helmet, the *pickelhaube* he had captured and shipped home the previous year. Next to it stood the photograph of No. 3 Company he had ordered from the photographer Roger Fenton.

He would not display such things, Dudley thought, *if not for pride in me, in my accomplishments.*

His uncle cleared his throat. Dudley fixed his eyes on the window opposite and straightened his shoulders, which had begun to slump. His uncle at last turned to face him.

Robert Mason was an imposing man even when in the best of tempers. He stood over six feet, his piercing eyes passing judgment upon whatever they saw. He did not tolerate wrong-doing as he saw it, not in friend, family, or foe. And yet Dudley knew him as an honest man, a man of honour.

The pipe he smoked was the one Dudley had purchased as a gift for him in Constantinople.

"You have grown, my boy," Uncle Robert said. "You are thinner. Though you have done well for yourself. Well, indeed, winning a commission. Most extraordinary."

"You always taught me to strive to do my best, sir," Dudley replied, although, in fact, luck had also played a part in his success. He had survived the hard-fought battle of Inkerman, a desperate struggle against overwhelm-

5

ing enemy numbers, a battle fought for the most part in a dense morning fog that had blown in from the Black Sea. The queen herself had been so impressed with the conduct of her soldiers that she had issued a Royal Warrant authorizing the granting of an ensign's commission to one sergeant from every battalion engaged. Dudley had been chosen for the Royal Hampshire Fusiliers.

He was proud of that achievement, for merit had played its part. He had led his company in the capture of a battery of Russian guns near the end of the fighting. But his social standing had also played a part, elevating him beyond other sergeants who had performed equally brave and daring deeds that day. Dudley had been known as a "gentleman" ranker, an educated man who would have little trouble surviving in the society of the officers' mess.

"Yes," his uncle said, "it seems I taught you well in some things, though your impulsive nature was one trait I have been unable to curb. An inheritance from your late father, I can only assume."

"I did not know my father well," Dudley replied. "You were always a father to me, and Aunt is the only mother I have ever known."

Uncle Robert eyed him for a moment, puffing on his pipe. Then he moved to his leather chair and sat. He held the pipe clamped between his teeth, one hand on the edge of his desk.

"You cannot conceive the depth of my shock, my boy," he said, "when I received your letter explaining that you had enlisted in the army. Enlisted in the ranks as a private soldier!"

Dudley swallowed. Three years ago, he had sent that letter from the Black Horse, just hours before he had been required to follow the recruiting sergeant north to the regimental depot at Fairbridge.

"Uncle, I know I have wronged you," he blurted. "You did your best for me, and I cast away your gifts. I felt I had to choose my own course in life, and I cannot apologize for that, but the manner in which I made the decision was abominable. I should have discussed it with you and Aunt. Yet it was the right choice for me. I can only hope that you can find it within yourself to see that, and to forgive me."

His uncle let a curl of smoke seep from the corner of his mouth.

"Humility and defiance all at once. That was ever the way with you, my boy. Though I believe Miss Wilkes also played a part in your rash decision to follow the drum?"

"Yes, sir, she did." Dudley had been engaged to marry Martha Wilkes, the elder sister of his single pupil. One day, he had discovered her in the arms of another man—the day he had enlisted.

"You discovered that she did not return your affections as you originally thought?"

"Yes, Uncle."

"And in your state of despair you thought to run from it." Uncle Robert nodded. "I have given much thought to those events. I was a boy once, too, you recall, and understand the passions of the young. I also understand that, once you had taken the Queen's Shilling, you were bound by your decision. There was nothing I nor anyone else could do to change that.

"However, you must also understand that what you did was an act of rebellion, that by giving in to your passions, you betrayed my judgment and my trust."

Dudley faced the window, trying to find a suitable reply. He had rehearsed something for just such a statement, but he found it eluded him.

"Yet you have done well for yourself," his uncle continued. "As well as the circumstances allowed."

Dudley sighed with relief. "The war with Russia provided many with opportunities for advancement, sir."

"A concept part of me finds difficult to accept, for I do not approve of war, not as a rule. Yet Britain's interests must be protected."

Dudley gripped his hands together behind his back. The interview was going better than he had hoped. Far better.

"I agree, sir."

"Perhaps soldiering does suit you. I remember you and your books of battles, your play with wooden swords. I had hoped that you would lose interest and, in fact, dreaded the day you would come to me, declaring your intention to seek a commission. Of course, I never dreamed that you would join the ranks! I understand now that I misjudged you, that I was in error to establish a trust to enable you to attend Cambridge."

Dudley bowed his head. "I no longer deserve such a gift, Uncle."

"I am happy that you think so. I am glad that you are capable of observing that fact. But you are home now, safe and sound. I shall give you this gift anyway, as a token of your return, in the manner in which the Lord no doubt intended that I give it to you."

Uncle Robert rose from his chair with a creaking of leather then moved around to the front of his desk. Dudley stared at him, astonished by his last statement.

"I have given you much consideration, my boy," Uncle Robert said. "In many ways, you were the primary occupant of my thoughts. I would not speak of you and did not return your many letters—that you know. And yet I thought of you. I believed that you would be killed, that all my work in raising you would be cast away on some foreign battlefield. I did not expect to see you in this room again."

"I understand, sir. It was a reasonable fear."

Uncle Robert took hold of Dudley's left forearm with one broad hand, gave a gentle squeeze.

"I have played no small part in what you have become, William. Somehow, I did not understand the strength of your wishes, and now I will have to accept my lack of perception. Perhaps it was selfishness on my part to expect you to follow in my footsteps. You see, I, too, can admit my errors."

"You always taught me to do the same, sir."

"Yes, and you have done so here. It would be unchristian of me not to admit mine then not accept your apology." He drew back his hand and chewed the stem of his Turkish pipe, brows knit in thought. "The question remains, if you are to follow your own path, what shall you do now?"

Dudley's answer was obvious.

"I must return to my regiment, sir. As I explained in my note, I have four week's leave, then we are off to a new posting. Madras, sir. India."

"Indeed, you must return, but in what capacity?" Uncle Robert smiled for the first time that afternoon. "I am not a rich man, you know, my boy, but I have done my duty by your elder cousins, and I have not wavered from that intention where you are concerned. I have simply modified the specifics."

"I don't understand, sir."

"It is simple. The funds which I had intended for St. John's will go towards the purchase of a lieutenant's commission in your regiment when you are eligible. I understand that you are required to first serve for a certain period of time at your current position?"

"That is so, as an ensign raised from the ranks." Although such rules were flexible, as necessity dictated. Indeed, Dudley's promotion to sergeant had been sooner than regulations allowed, coming in the field after the Alma.

"Then I will have fulfilled my duty to you at last. After that, you must keep your independence. I trust you will accept this gift?"

"Of course I accept, Uncle," he cried, for this was no true choice at all. "And gratefully!"

"Good. I pride myself on being a just man, William. Just and fair. I am happy to have you returned to us, safe from the war."

He extended his hand. Like a man, not a mere nephew, Dudley shook it. He felt the strength there.

"That is all," his uncle said by way of conclusion. "I will see you for supper. I believe Agnes has prepared something special in celebration of your return."

***

Dudley's happiness seemed complete, the fear that had haunted him for three years gone. His family had at last accepted the life he had chosen for himself, and now all he must do was live it. And live it as a lieutenant, when he was eligible! He had never dreamed of such a possibility so soon!

He had one regret. His uncle had spoken of duty; and although Dudley had demonstrated his competence in his chosen profession, he had failed in his first duty to those who had raised him. He could never undo that action, but he vowed he would never make such a mistake again. He would observe his responsibilities to his family, just as he did for his regiment.

For now, he would enjoy his furlough, bask in the simple pleasures of home. Although, he had one more promise to fulfill.

That promise saw him, five days later, making his way south to the outskirts of Winchester, to the house of the

Montague family. He had sent word ahead of his arrival, and the response had been welcoming. Miss Elizabeth Montague, just having recently arrived home from the war in the Crimea, where she had served as one of Miss Nightingale's nurses, would see Dudley at two o'clock in the afternoon.

At precisely that hour, Dudley stood waiting in another hallway. Elizabeth's father, who sat in the Commons as a Radical pledged to reform, was not at home. It would just be a moment, the maid had told Dudley, and Miss Elizabeth would come down.

He waited. For some reason, his hands began to tremble, and he thrust them into the mule-ear pockets of his civilian trousers. He could find no reason for the trembling, for his heart to suddenly quicken with anxiety. When he had last seen Elizabeth, it had been a happy occasion, a surprising reunion in Gibraltar on the voyage home.

By coincidence, her transport had also been there to re-coal; Dudley had stumbled upon her in the street. Their exchange had been brief, he going up the town and she coming down, but they had agreed to see each other at home, in Hampshire. And now he had nothing but good news to tell her.

"Why, my dear William!" her voice chimed, and there she was, sweeping down the stairs. At once his anxiety vanished, for she was more beautiful than he remembered, far more so than when he had first met her in Scutari. There, she and the other nurses had dressed in simple attire of brown and gray, their hair plain and pulled back. Here she was in a spring dress of pink-and-white, with white ribbons in her hair and a smile brighter than any she had ever managed during the war.

"I'm so glad you came," she went on, taking both his hands, her flesh warm. "So glad! Come! We will have tea in the back garden!"

The late-spring day was warm, the sun beaming and the air fresh after a morning rain. They sat on either side of a little iron table, a tray of tea and pastries between them. Small birds danced and chased each other through the hedges as Dudley related the story of his meeting with his uncle.

"That must be a great weight lifted from your shoulders," she said.

"Greater than I understood." He laughed. "I feel as light as a feather. I don't know what could bring me down now." He leaned back in his chair, grinning as he took in his surroundings—the solidity of the house, the long stretch of green lawn—and breathed in the scent of the rose bushes. "It's a long way from the stink of war, isn't it?"

This was not the sort of thing a young man said to a lady, but Elizabeth had been there, buried in that stink. She had been there during Dudley's darkest moments, when he had been wounded at the Redan. It had been then their bond had formed, a bond first of gratitude on his part, then of friendship.

Later, that friendship had begun to grow into something more, although Dudley had never felt comfortable, had never been certain of that something. Neither of them had been willing to face it, to put a name to it. He had never been able to understand why that was. He had always been forthright in his dealings with women he found attractive, but not Elizabeth.

She placed her tea cup on the table and shaded her eyes.

"It is a different world here, one of blissful ignorance. I love it, and I shall miss it."

"Miss it? You mean you did miss it."

"I did, but that is not what I mean. You see, I mean to go to America."

"America?" Dudley said. "Indeed. For how long?"

Elizabeth said nothing for a moment. Her eyes flickered to her teacup before again meeting his.

"There is a new hospital in Boston, an experimental hospital."

"You mean to visit it, to study it?"

"No, I mean to offer them my services, my experience."

Dudley sat forward in his chair. His buoyant mood, so assured a moment before, was suddenly forgotten. He did not like the thought of her leaving for another continent an ocean way.

At once, he reminded himself that to fear such a separation made no sense, since he was for the East in three weeks, and he had no idea for how long. What did it matter that she was going to America?

"I suppose…" he began, but his voice cracked. He cleared his throat and tried again. "I suppose I should not be surprised. You have claimed it's in your nature to continue moving, to…continue seeking."

She smiled. "God has more work for me to do, my dear William. I'm glad you understand that."

"Yes."

He did understand. It made perfect sense. She had never been one for the domestic life, to remain in her parents' house until the right gentleman came along. It was something they had discussed many times.

"You may continue to write me, of course," she said. "Write me here, for I will not leave for another two months. I cannot wait to hear of your adventures in India!"

"Of course I will write you," he said. He did not wish to break the thread that bound them, whatever else happened.

His chair creaked as a he again leaned back. His shock at her news was subsiding, and his contentment was beginning to return. There was only the future now, stretching before him. Three more weeks of rest, then the steamer for India. India—exotic land of princes and adventurers. He had always dreamed of one day going there, of walking in the footsteps of his military heroes, men like Wellington and Clive. What would that country hold for him? What new wonders?

And of course, India was at peace, so there would be time to see the sights, the land and its people in harmony, untouched by war.

CHAPTER 2

Madras
April 1857

Sergeant Brian Barker peeled a ripe orange and let the scraps fall where they might. The famous Madras surf pounded the beach to his right, the broken waves receding with a hiss. Gulls and terns swooped and screeched among the fishing boats pulled up on the sand. A native girl, a clay jar perched on her head, moved along the promenade, and the sergeant touched his cap in greeting. She seemed surprised by the gesture and stared with suspicion for a moment, but at last, she smiled. Barker saw the flash of her teeth as she passed.

A pretty thing, he thought, *and like as not good to go.*

He began to whistle, a random series of notes. He studied the almost empty stretch of road. Save for the gulls and terns wheeling overhead, the girl was one of only two things moving in the heat. The other was a solitary rider, his mount loping along the line of lampposts that separated the promenade from the beach. Barker recognized the horse, the chestnut gelding that belonged to Mister Dudley.

The horseman drew closer. Barker let the last piece of orange peel fall to the dust then touched his cap again, this time in a proper salute. Mister Dudley slowed his horse to a halt, lifting his wide-brimmed straw hat in return, revealing a head of sweat-soaked golden curls.

"Good afternoon, Sergeant," Dudley said. "I did not expect to meet the likes of you here."

"I could say the same for you, sir. Funny time of day to be out riding. The heat is at its worst, sir."

Dudley leaned back in his saddle.

"Yes, but at least it's quiet with no one else about, no choking crowds, for once. Peaceful, and I, for one, cannot get enough of peace."

"I agree, Mister Dudley."

In the evening, the beach and promenade would become crowded with members of Madras society, out to stroll or ride, the cooler air a welcome relief from the oppressive heat of spring in southern India. But Barker loved the early afternoon for its silence, its promise of solitude. It was a chance to get away, to think while everyone else slept in the shade.

And he needed to think, to find a solution to a growing problem in the company, the problem of Private Geary.

The regiment had been here for nine months now, and in that time, Geary had gone from a good soldier to a mediocre one, then to nothing but trouble. Barker did not understand why.

"Well, it is good that we agree," Dudley said. "Not like the old days, eh?"

"No, indeed, Mister Dudley. No, indeed."

Dudley nudged his horse forward.

"Well, I must be off. I wish to feel the wind in my face, cool myself off a bit."

Again they exchanged salutes, and the brief meeting was over. That was the extent of their social involvement.

They had been friends in the ranks, were still friends, Barker reminded himself, but Dudley was an officer now. For the sake of discipline, he kept the society of the officers' mess and none other.

It was enough that they exchanged words now and then.

The sergeant tossed the dripping orange from hand to hand. Ahead of him loomed the Madras ice house, a great stone cube with a round turret jutting from one corner, a little flagstaff on its pointed roof. Farther north lay the sprawling masonry walls of Fort St. George and the twisting and crowded streets of Black Town. West lay the suburb of Vepery and the cantonments where the Royal Hampshire Fusiliers had its new quarters.

There was a sudden pounding of hoofs behind him, too fast for the promenade at any time of the day; and he stepped aside, looking back in alarm. Two more riders were thundering along almost at a gallop, another officer and a European woman in a pale yellow habit. They hurtled towards the native girl with the jar, doing nothing to check their pace. The girl leapt aside, crying out as her jar fell with a splintering crash. The riders simply laughed.

"Bloody aristocrats," Barker muttered.

The mounted officer reined in hard when he came alongside Mister Dudley, the dust rising in a small cloud. His companion did the same, squealing with delight.

"Hello, William!" the officer cried. Barker knew the man, another young gentleman from his regiment, Lieutenant Tom Carlisle.

"Afternoon, Tom," Dudley replied, and Barker saw him glance at the native girl as she gathered the pieces of her shattered jar.

"Will you be attending tiffin at the colonel's later?" Carlisle asked.

Barker did not linger to hear more of the conversation. The social life of Mister Dudley's mess did not concern him. He had an orange to eat, and a problem to ponder.

He wandered a few yards to the left of the promenade, making for a grove of pagoda trees, their spreading branches ablaze with white-and-yellow blossoms. A number of native men lay in slumber at the base of each trunk, some clad in white robes, a few naked in the heat. Beyond the trees, a flight of wide stone steps led to the ice house. Barker chose a step and sat.

The position offered a view down the length of the promenade, and he saw Carlisle and his companion leave Dudley and resume their ride. Barker expected them to pass by his nook, but they turned off the road as he had done, coming to a halt to the left of the stairs. He could see them through the intervening blossoms, although they had not noticed him.

Lieutenant Carlisle dismounted and helped the woman do the same. Barker noted her slim figure and fine features. She had all the appearances of a true English lady, with a dainty mouth and pale complexion. Something twisted in his gut, and he thought of the native girl again, relived her hesitant smile.

There was certainly no shortage of beautiful women in India. Some of the lads took temporary wives to sooth their spirits, but such arrangements only lasted until the regiment shipped out to its next station; and unless a man could afford to pay for passage, the wife would remain here.

That was a situation Barker did not wish to find himself in. He had been married before, to a horrible meanspirited lass who had died of a fever in Turkey before the Crimean campaign. He missed her sometimes, but he did not think he would like her much now. He had been a bitter, mean-spirited fellow himself then, and she had suited his mood.

"There, now," Carlisle was saying. "It is nice and shady in here. Never mind the few niggers lying over there. They won't bother you."

"You are most thoughtful, Lieutenant," the woman replied. "Though I must chastise you for not introducing me to that young gentleman just now. Your friend William?"

"Ah, yes," Carlisle said, and Barker thought he saw the man's suntanned face turn a deeper shade. "Well, that young gentleman, Miss Edwards, is Ensign William Dudley, and he is not properly a gentleman at all, in my opinion."

Barker stifled a snort of disgust. Some of the subalterns still delighted in revealing Mister Dudley's humble origins, as if it made them better officers by comparison. Mister Dudley was twice the gentleman any of them was.

"He's an officer, is he not?" the lady asked.

"Yes," Carlisle admitted, "but he was promoted from the ranks, like our quartermaster, our paymaster! He may have the bearing of a gentleman, and some of the manners, but he has neither family, money, nor connections. His parents are deceased, their lineage unknown. He is, or was, the ward of a radical clergyman—his uncle, the Reverend Robert Mason. And the Reverend Mason is a fellow of scandalous notions, indeed!"

Miss Edwards glanced back to where they had encountered Mister Dudley, although he was now nowhere in sight.

"Why, I have heard Mister Dudley's name mentioned several times since I arrived in Madras, and that was just the day before yesterday. He must be the most talked about officer in the regiment!"

Barker chuckled to himself. Carlisle appeared to have sparked the lady's interest rather than dampened it.

"Dudley is, indeed, notorious," the lieutenant stated with a note of disapproval. "He enlisted as a private soldier, fleeing broken marriage vows or some such scandal. A private soldier, mind you, in the ranks! In the recent war with Russia, he gained a promotion to sergeant, then won his commission at Inkerman. He led some of his fellows in a charge against some enemy guns."

Carlisle paused, as if realizing he was making Dudley sound more impressive by the word. Perhaps to add to his discomfort, Miss Edwards exclaimed, "That all sounds rather heroic!"

"Save for the fact that the Russian guns had pulled back by the time he finished his charge, so really, it was nothing at all," Carlisle asserted. "Nothing at all! As for his commission, it came by Royal Warrant, so they had to choose someone, and I suppose the colonel thought Dudley would fit in better. Nothing to do with him being the most deserving.

"And he was by no means a popular fellow at first in the mess. He still isn't popular with some, for a supposed gentleman who enlists as a common soldier is always suspect. That is a desperate act. Who would choose to live in the gutter? Yet, Dudley has his friends and supporters, including Captain Norcott of our Grenadiers. But really, it seems a wonder that a fellow like that is kept on. Don't you think?"

"I think he sounds most intriguing," Miss Edwards said. "*Most* intriguing. And you seemed very friendly with him just now. Really, Lieutenant, is it fair to be friends one moment then speak ill of him the next?"

"Oh, but we *are* friendly," Carlisle stammered. "That is to say, we're not friends exactly, but…no sense in being rude, you see. A proper gentleman remembers his manners. We must have harmony amongst the officers, at least in public. For the good of the regiment, you understand."

"Well, then," said the lady, touching his elbow, "you must grant me a proper introduction to Mister Dudley later."

Carlisle's smug grin had disappeared.

"Of course, Miss Edwards." He patted her hand. "Of course. I would do anything for you, you know."

Barker crouched low beneath the stair railing, clamping his hand over his mouth to keep from laughing out loud.

CHAPTER 3

Madras
April 1857

Dudley turned off the promenade, heading west along an avenue of tall ornamental palms. The hot breeze rustled the fronds high overhead, and a gentle scent of orange blossoms drifted from the garden enclosures. He drew in a deep breath.

"A fine afternoon," he remarked to his horse Akbar. It was a habit of his whenever he went riding alone. "Not too hot for you, I hope, old fellow?"

The gelding snorted, and Dudley rubbed its neck. He missed Bill, his little Crimean pony, but Akbar was of similar temperament, calm without being lazy, spirited when it counted. The horse had only cost two hundred rupees, a price Dudley's comrades had insisted was more than reasonable.

He had been reluctant to spend the money, but a horse was essential in India, and he had no reason to complain. He had purchased his saddle at a discount from a captain of the 1st Madras Fusiliers, while his spurs had been a gift from a friend in his own company, Lieutenant Trevor Morris. He could not have done better for the sake of frugality.

Riding into the Madras suburb of Vepery, he saw the British cantonments just ahead. This was his new home, an expanse of dusty parade ground between wide roads and a series of brick barrack buildings. At one end of the barracks stood the junior officers' quarters, the mess, the theatre, the library, and the billiard room. Nearby were a dusty racecourse, a tennis court, an icehouse, the Anglican church and a Catholic chapel.

The compound was home to most of the Madras garrison, one Queen's Regiment and two regiments of the Madras Native Infantry. A fourth regiment, the 1st Madras Fusiliers, one of the East India Company's European battalions, made its home within the walls of Fort St. George.

Dudley headed for the junior officers' quarters and veered toward the stables in the rear. When he halted, a native syce rushed forward to take Akbar's bridle. Dudley dismounted, removed his saddle valise and nodded to the syce.

"Thank you."

The man nodded but said nothing. They were unaccustomed to courtesy.

The journey from the stables to Dudley's bungalow was not more than a dozen paces. The bungalow was a narrow building of pukka brick, its clay tile roof shading two wide verandas, one in front and the other in back. On the front veranda, Dudley found Captain Norcott of the Grenadier Company perched in a rattan chair reading a weeks' old edition of the *Times*. Beside him stood an ancient native wearing nothing but a white puggaree on his head and a dhoti about his thin waist. The native held a fan on a long pole, which he swept back and forth to provide the British officer with a cooling breeze.

On the other end of the veranda stood Kesab Bardai, Dudley's principal servant, a middle-aged Brahmin with a graying beard and a mustache upswept at the tips. A black patch of cloth covered Kesab's left eye socket.

"Did you enjoy your ride, Dudley Sahib?" he asked, stepping forward.

Dudley climbed the veranda steps.

"I did, thank you, Kesab."

"Allow me to take your valise, sahib."

"There's nothing in it, I'm afraid," Dudley said, passing the leather case to the servant. "Matter of habit, I suppose, in case I stumble on a souvenir."

Kesab bowed. "I will put it in its rightful place, sahib."

As the Brahmin disappeared inside, Dudley sighed and sank into another rattan chair, a twin to Norcott's. He swept off his hat and undid the collar of his tunic, aware of the greasy sweat that had pooled around his neck.

The tunic was of fine doeskin wool, part of the new uniform he had purchased from a London tailor while on leave. It was made according to the new regulations, with an even hem that hung to the upper thigh. With it went a whitened leather waist belt and a silk sash that draped from the left shoulder to the right hip. Rank insignia came in the form of twisted golden shoulder knots in place of the old fringed bullion epaulettes that had still been in vogue during the Russian war.

It was a smart garment but not practical for India. Dudley's only concession to comfort was the straw shade hat, a nonregulation item that was tolerated by the garrison.

Norcott glanced up from his paper.

"Collecting flotsam from the beach, were you?" the captain remarked.

"No, sir, just out for a ride. I didn't feel like a lie-down."

"Neither did I, though I believe I could now, tiffin or no tiffin."

The bungalow door squeaked open a second time, and Trevor Morris emerged. He yawned and stretched.

"Thought I heard voices," he said. "Back from your adventures, eh, William? Conquered the Mahrattas again, did you?"

Dudley smiled. "Actually, I was just off having a bit of a think. I was thinking I might write a memoir of my adventures in the Crimea."

He had been toying with the idea for some time to organize his reflections of the war on paper as a fitting tribute to his comrades, men who had shown such devotion and sacrifice in the face of horror and misery. And, if the book sold, it would provide him with a private source of income.

"You're just trying to rub it in, aren't you?" Morris said. "To remind me of what I missed."

Morris had joined the regiment only about six months ago.

"If I wanted to truly rub it in," Dudley said, "I would end all my war stories in the mess by saying, 'You know, chaps, Lieutenant Morris wasn't there.'"

Morris dragged a third chair towards Dudley's. After seating himself, he leaned back and hung one leg over the chair arm.

"Well, I *wasn't* there, but I'm here now, in this most wretched of countries." He ran one long hand through his lank blond hair. He was a slender man, pale and blue-eyed, the youngest son of a prominent Irish Protestant family. "I suppose I can always hope for war, some petty monarch rising in rebellion. I envy you, Dudley, you and your luck. Here I sit with five years of active service, all of it in garrison without a chance to distinguish myself. Just a chance, that's all I ask."

"You may get your chance if the Bengal Army rises in general mutiny. Then you might have your rebellion."

The Bengal Army was one of three standing armies in the pay of the Honourable East India Company, the mercantile body that governed India on behalf of Britain. Morris rolled his eyes towards the veranda ceiling at its mention.

"It will never happen," he said. "Why should the Bengal Army rise? Because the men are paid more than regular British troops? Because they've never been flogged in the whole long history of the East India Company? These mutinies in the north will come to nothing."

Captain Norcott at last tossed his newspaper aside.

"Quite true. Native troops are a finicky lot, always upset over something, always threatening mutiny over some imagined outrage. Fifty years ago, the sepoys of the Madras Army threatened to rise because they did not like our English uniforms. Nothing was done, and it all blew over. Now it's the Enfield cartridge. Next year it will be something different. It's the same old story."

"What's not to like about the Enfield, anyway?" Morris said. "It is a fine weapon, the finest in the world."

"It is," agreed Dudley. The British Army had first received the new .577-calibre Enfield rifle during the second year of the Crimean campaign. It was a light, well-balanced, and accurate rifled musket, quick to load and with a maximum range of more than a thousand yards.

"But, as the captain says," he continued, "it's the cartridge, not the rifle itself, to which the sepoys object."

The ammunition for the Enfield was a type developed by Captain Claude Minié of the French army. It consisted of a conical bullet attached to a prepared cartridge of rolled paper. The paper was greased to increase the ease of loading, and it was this grease that had caused trouble when the Enfield had come to India the previous winter.

The rumour that the grease was made from cow and pig fat had spread fear and outrage amongst the Hindu and Muslim sepoys of the Bengal Army. The cow was sacred to the Hindu and the pig unclean to the Muslim, and the standard loading procedure for any musket called for the soldier to bite the cartridge open. For the sepoys, biting into this grease would mean defilement.

"Whatever the reason," Morris said, "it would be absurd for me to wish for a such a disaster, a mutiny of our own troops."

And "such a disaster" it would be, Dudley thought, although perhaps Captain Norcott was right. Despite the fears and rumours, the troubles had been going on all winter, and still nothing had come of it.

The first incident had been in February, at Barrackpore on the Ganges River. The 2nd Bengal Native Infantry had refused the new cartridges. In response, the commanding general, Major-General Hearsey, had paraded the entire Barrackpore garrison. He had assured his men there was no plot to convert them to Christianity, which had seemed their greatest fear.

They had appeared to listen to him, but a month later, on March 29th, a more serious incident occurred in the same garrison.

A Brahmin sepoy of the 34th Native Infantry named Mangal Pande had donned his uniform, loaded his musket, and called upon his comrades to assemble on the parade square to defend their religion. Pande had been intoxicated on bhang, a distillation of native hemp, and had wounded both his adjutant and regimental sergeant-major when they had tried to disarm him.

At last, General Hearsey himself had come to deal with the situation. Under his stern gaze and loaded pistol, some of Pande's comrades had moved to arrest him. The enraged sepoy had then turned his musket upon himself, pulling the trigger with his toe. The bullet had dug a furrow in his chest and the muzzle flash had burned his skin, but he had lived to face a court martial. His sentence had been to hang, and hang he soon did.

After the Pande affair, the men of the 19th Bengal Native Infantry, like those of the 2nd, had also refused the cartridges. Their lieutenant-colonel had been less accommodating than General Hearsey and ordered the regiment disbanded—an outrageous overreaction, in Dudley's opinion.

Since then, a new drill had been developed in which the sepoys could tear open the Enfield cartridge with their hands; but not every garrison had adopted the procedure, and rumblings of discontent continued in the north. Some army and East India Company officials feared a general mutiny, a violent rising, but such rumours had circulated for years. Most officials agreed that, in time, the troubles would pass.

There had been no trouble in the south. *All is quiet here in Madras*, Dudley had written in one of his frequent letters home.

He realized he didn't fear a rising of native troops, that the rumours had done nothing to spoil these last splendid months. Since the interview with his uncle, his life had been nothing but unending pleasure. He had found the acceptance in the officers' mess, at least from most of its members, that he had feared he would never receive as an ensign promoted from the ranks; and India itself had held nothing but fascination for him.

The first six weeks had been difficult, that was true, when his regiment had languished in the entry depot in Poonamalee, a cooler location twelve miles south of Madras. There they had done nothing but try to grow accustomed to the climate, and in that Dudley had been successful. Now he relished the mere fact of being here, in this famous and exotic country.

He enjoyed wandering the bazaars in Black Town just to take in the sights, the heady smell of the spices, the chatter of the people. On some days, he liked to ride west into the country, past the fields of indigo and sugar cane, through the mango groves and into the brown hills. He meant to embrace India as he had embraced the army, to understand its history and its strange and often shocking customs. He longed to get out of Madras with its flat monotony and see more. He longed to see the Assaye battlefield, where Wellington had won his favourite victory.

"Perhaps I merely need a diversion from this garrison monotony," Morris was saying. "The Enfield, I hear, is an excellent elephant gun. Perhaps we could arrange a hunt or some such excitement."

As he spoke, he sat up in his chair and reached forward with one leg, stretching his leather boot toward the native servant with the fan. Some time during the conversation, the old man had faltered in his task, sunk to the veranda floor, and gone to sleep. His head rested against the wall, his eyes closed, his fan across his skinny knees.

Morris pursed his lips in disgust then gave the man a sharp kick in the shoulder, crying, "Wake up, you old blackguard!"

The servant yelped, his eyes springing open, but at once he heaved himself to his feet. Without a word, he raised the fan and began to wave it with added vigour.

Dudley's brow creased in disapproval.

"See here, Trevor, a little kindness goes a long way, you know. The old fellow is tired, standing here listening to us prattle."

"I would agree, were we dealing with European servants," Norcott interjected. "But you have to know how to handle these people, Dudley. They are a lazy lot and require a firm hand, like children. It is a simple fact that the contempt in which we hold them is what has led to our maintaining this empire."

"I don't know if that's so, sir," Dudley said. "We won this empire through their cooperation. Clive had no contempt for the Indians. Quite the contrary. And that is what led to his success."

"Oh, here he goes again." Morris sighed. "Always on about his precious heroes. Clive. Marlborough. Wellington—I suppose you think you'll join their ranks some day?"

Dudley was unabashed.

"Shouldn't we all wish to?"

Morris laughed. "In truth, I do! Though I suppose you have a better chance at it than I. Father thought me a wastrel, and he may have been right. The army for Trevor, he declared. Thought it would do me some good.

"But then I missed my chance by missing the Crimea." He leaned forward, clasping his hands before him. "You're the sort to reach those ambitions, for you do your duty and more. You have the strength and the ideals even to see some good in the Indians. I'm afraid I do not share those strengths."

Dudley never quite knew how to take Morris's compliments, unclear whether they were meant as flattery, mockery, or spoken with sincerity.

"You could at least try."

"Yes." Morris stared at his hands. After a moment, he added, "Though perhaps your capacity for tolerance comes from having served in the ranks. I can't imagine how you stood it. Quite the experiment, I imagine."

Dudley shrugged. "It wasn't so bad as you would think. Some of our men are good and honourable fellows, as you well know. There were rough characters, for certain, with rough language and rough habits. But with stout hearts."

"Rough habits! Yes, I can imagine them trying to drag you off to a bawdy house, kicking and screaming all the way."

"That was, indeed, one of their habits, but I never partook. Sorry to disappoint you."

"You do disappoint me! Were you not even tempted?"

Dudley paused before answering. The temptation had been there, but the establishments the lads in his company had frequented had seemed seedy and repulsive.

"Not even once."

Morris seemed about to say something else, but there was a sudden flurry of hoofbeats as two riders came pounding up the road towards the officers' quarters. Tom Carlisle had at last returned from his outing; in a whirl of dust and laughter, he and his fetching companion came to a halt on the edge of the parade ground.

"Quite right," Morris said at length, and as if reading Dudley's mind, he added, "I can understand how the quality of the houses in question would turn you off. Filthy places, of course. Not the standard that a gentleman would insist upon. But I know you, William. A pretty face and a whiff of perfume are your greatest weaknesses." He stared as Carlisle and the young woman walked their horses towards the stables. "I wouldn't mind taking that little filly for a few laps around the course. Would you?"

"Well, now that you mention it…" Dudley replied. He had noted the young woman's beauty when he saw her on the promenade, and suspected that Carlisle had not introduced her on purpose. That would be just like Carlisle, trying to keep the attentions of such a creature to himself.

"Afternoon, gents!" Carlisle called as he passed.

"Afternoon, Tom," Norcott returned, but Morris was frowning.

"Do you think," Morris said to Dudley, "that he will bring his charming companion to the colonel's?"

Dudley reached into his tunic to pull out his watch. It was an inferior instrument, purchased in the Madras market, but it served him well enough.

"I suppose we'll soon find out," he said. "It's almost two o'clock. Time for tiffin."

CHAPTER 4

Madras
April 1857

As with tea in England, tiffin was an integral part of an officer's day in India. Under the shelter of an awning in Lieutenant-Colonel Willis's garden, Dudley and his companions found a table spread with lightly curried dishes and chutney, plain and candied fruit, biscuits, and cakes. Someone had asked for hot tea with cream and sugar, but Dudley preferred the lemonade, cooled with ice imported from America.

Willis had been named lieutenant-colonel just after the regiment arrived at its new post. He had succeeded the old commanding officer, Lieutenant-Colonel Freemantle, who had decided to retire a full colonel before the War Office could promote him to brigadier-general and so deny him the privilege of selling his commission. Dudley had welcomed the change, for although Freemantle had been much loved he had also been old, having served under Wellington in the Peninsula, and somewhat inattentive to the needs of the regiment.

Willis occupied a Georgian house of grey stone on the outskirts of Madras. To Dudley, the house and garden appeared to have been transplanted whole from England. The only indications this was India, apart from the heat, were the complexions of the servants and the cluster of tall coconut palms rising beyond the garden wall.

It was, still, comfortable and pleasant, and both the colonel and his wife insisted on having guests every afternoon when they were in residence.

With Dudley and Morris, Lieutenant Carlisle and Captain Norcott had also come, as had the new commanding officer of No. 3 Company, Captain Reed. As Morris had hoped, two recent arrivals in Madras were also present. These were Mrs. Grace Edwards and her daughter, Charlotte, Tom Carlisle's riding companion.

Dudley could not help sneaking glances at her, for she was striking, her eyes a deep brown that matched her lustrous hair. It was no wonder Carlisle had latched onto her so quickly, no wonder that he now made certain he sat next to her at the table. Dudley sat opposite, next to Morris.

As the dishes passed from hand to hand and the servants poured lemonade, Colonel Willis opened the conversation by lamenting the fate of his beagles. He had transported an entire pack from his home in Sussex, but they had been unable to survive the Indian climate.

"The entire pack, gone," he explained, absently twisting one end of his steel-grey moustache. "It's the heat, of course. They were suffocating in their kennel. I did my best to ease their suffering, charged their keepers to maintain their supply of water and take the survivors for walks in cooler weather.

"The walks themselves almost proved disastrous, for one evening they caught the scent of some wild beast, and the fool who was supposed to control them let them get away. We managed to round up all save one. That was the first loss. The rest expired one-by-one, safely at home. The poor things simply could not live in this climate."

"You did all you could, my dear," his wife consoled, patting his shoulder.

"Yes, the heat is most distressing," agreed Mrs. Edwards, although she appeared to have taken no precautions against it. She wore a dress of dark, heavy material, a silver-mounted cameo at her throat. She was a stout woman with a firm, square jaw, but Dudley could see the reflection of her daughter in her eyes.

"Charlotte and I have also suffered terribly since we arrived," she added. At her back, a servant did his best to cool her with his long fan. "But suffering is what builds character, and I do not fear it. Did our Lord not suffer for us all?"

"You are bearing up nobly, Mrs. Edwards," Captain Norcott complimented.

"Thank you, Captain, but I fear we have far to go yet." She sipped her lemonade.

"You are going on a journey, ma'am?" Dudley asked.

Charlotte turned towards him.

"Mama and I are going north, to Cawnpore. From there we will journey into Oudh. That is why we have come to India, to join my uncle at his mission."

"Your uncle is a missionary?"

"As are we," Mrs. Edwards explained. "As the Kingdom of Oudh is a recent acquisition of the British government, its people need guidance. They are heathens one and all, Mister Dudley, Hindus for the most part. Idol worshipers."

Dudley glanced at the waiter who stood near Mrs. Edwards's shoulder, but the man appeared not to have heard her words. He and the other servants held fixed stares, like idols themselves.

"The missionary," Mrs. Edwards went on, "will remake India, guide it into the modern world. Even now, we are struggling to bring about the fall of Hinduism, to awaken these people to the light of our Lord and Saviour."

Dudley had heard this sort of talk many times before, usually from friends or colleagues of his uncle's. Yet Robert Mason had never been convinced of the value of spreading Christianity to foreign peoples. Converts, he said, merely gave lip service to their new faith, all the while continuing to practice their old in secret.

"We all come to the Lord in our own way," he often stated, words that sometimes had him being accused of leaning towards unitarianism and away from the official Church.

"Forgive my impertinence, Mrs. Edwards," Dudley said, choosing his words with care, "but are you certain that the natives will agree to be so converted? I know, for one, that the Hindu sepoys of the Company armies are very much attached to their faith."

Mrs. Edwards narrowed her eyes and tilted her head back.

"You are the nephew of the Reverend Robert Mason, are you not, Mister Dudley?"

Dudley wondered how she had come by this information but held steady under her stern gaze.

"I am, ma'am. Do you know him?"

"I know of him, of course. He is the author of 'On the Evils of Slavery in America,' is he not?"

"Yes, ma'am," Dudley replied, wondering what point Mrs. Edwards was about to make.

He thought of the pamphlet in question, one of his uncle's earlier works. Its front page depicted a kneeling black man, a West African, his chained hands held out before him, beseeching the heavens. Under the picture ran the words *Who shall deliver them? Who shall do the Lord's work?*

"Then you must agree with our great task in India," Mrs. Edwards concluded. "Have we not abolished domestic slavery in this country? Have we not banned the barbaric practice of suttee, the burning of innocent young widows on the pyres of their deceased husbands? Have not the values of Christianity led to these reforms, young man?"

"I do not dispute you, ma'am," Dudley declared, feeling his face at last begin to flush. He darted a glance at Charlotte, but she was busy nibbling a bit of cake.

The conversation drifted on to other topics. The tragedy of Colonel Willis's hounds arose again, while Captain Norcott described the excitement of a recent tiger hunt. Dudley gradually turned away, examining the garden wall and the palms beyond.

He hated to be on the losing side of an argument, no matter what its nature, and the brief exchange with Mrs. Edwards had soured his mood. The notion of Christianizing India, in effect turning it into a hotter, drier England, did not appeal to him. He believed in reform, of course, and that India benefited from British rule. Britain had brought a unified language, the railway and telegraph, had eliminated corruption, had built schools and homes for orphans.

Yet none of those things would have been possible without some cooperation from the natives, and there lay the foundation of Britain's empire. Dudley worried that the forceful spread of Christianity would erode that foundation. It might even change the things that made India interesting.

He heard Charlotte laugh, a bright musical sound. He glanced again in her direction, and she caught and held his gaze. There was a trace of haughty mischief in her wide brown eyes, and in the gentle curve of her lips. His irritation began to subside, and he smiled.

Charlotte smiled back then took another small, dainty bite from her cake.

After tiffin there was nothing to do but rest in the shade for an hour or so, waiting for five o'clock when the air would begin to cool. Dudley whiled away the time daydreaming and jotting notes for his proposed Crimean memoir.

Dinner in the officers' mess was at seven. After that, there was another gathering at the colonel's house, this one for music, dancing, and charades; Willis often held parties and invited his subalterns. Dudley suspected the colonel liked to keep his officers happy. He seemed to approve of games and dancing for his young gentlemen as much as he approved of musketry practice for the men.

There were civilians present in the spacious parlour, including several daughters of East India Company officials. The young ladies had come decked out in their best pale silk dresses, on the lookout to capture a young officer, a griffin of John Company's regiments or of the Queen's troops.

Charlotte Edwards was there among them, with her mother as chaperone. Dudley spied Mrs. Edwards perched in a corner with Mrs. Willis, sitting with a stiff back, her face set with apparent disapproval, although she did not object to her daughter taking part in the first dance.

The dance was the usual quadrille, with two groups of four couples going through the forms. Charlotte's partner was Tom Carlisle. Lieutenant Morris provided the music, banging out a jaunty tune on the piano. Dudley did not take part. He stood next to the sideboard, watching.

Morris concluded the number with a flourish, running his fingers along the keys, eliciting laughter and applause. Dudley applauded along with the others, crying, "Well done, Trevor."

When the applause had died, he discovered Charlotte standing at his side. Morris was already preparing to perform a second tune, and she stood with her hands on her hips. Dudley noticed the way the candles reflected from her hair, which she wore parted in the centre and dressed on the sides in a series of ringlets. Her dress was pale turquoise.

"You simply must dance with me, Mister Dudley," she said.

The other dancers were assembling for an old-fashioned line dance, the gentlemen on one side of the room and the ladies on the other. Dudley managed a lopsided grin.

"I would be honoured, Miss Edwards."

"Oh, you must call me Charlotte, please," she insisted as she reached to take his arm.

The dance began; Morris played a slower tempo this time. The dancers moved together, the gentlemen and ladies approaching, joining hands, twirling, and breaking apart again. Dudley enjoyed the warmth of Charlotte's flesh, felt her squeeze his fingers. And there was something else.

There was no mistaking the look in her eyes, the slight mischievous smile. With mounting surprise, he realized she fancied him. He was certain of it. Tom Carlisle might have gotten to her first, but she preferred another, and that other was William Dudley.

When the dance and the applause had ended, he took Charlotte's arm. She leaned against him.

"Would you like some punch?" he asked. It seemed a sensible question.

"Certainly, Mister Dudley," she replied. "That would be lovely."

He left her and returned to the sideboard. Morris surrendered the piano to Captain Norcott, who at once began calling for requests in a loud voice and with much laughter. As Dudley filled two glasses from the punchbowl, Morris appeared at his side.

"Madras has a new belle," Morris said. "The new prettiest girl on the station."

Though mere seconds had passed, Dudley noticed that Charlotte was already surrounded by other young men, Tom Carlisle included. Carlisle stood on the edge of the circle, his features sagging.

"Indeed," Dudley said. "She is proving popular."

"Ah, such humility." Morris chuckled. "You forget I know you, William. You can see as well as I that she has it in for you. She knows of your fame. It's a case of hero worship. You have nothing to worry about from those others."

Dudley held the two glasses of punch.

"I'm not looking, Trevor."

"But I think she is. You had best watch yourself." Morris nodded towards Mrs. Edwards. "Someone may be trying to find a husband for her daughter."

Dudley shook his head.

"Unlikely. They're going north in a few days."

Morris gave him an exaggerated wink.

"Then enjoy it while you can. Perhaps she is the adventurous type."

"Are you questioning her virtue, Trevor?"

Morris shrugged. "This is India. Virtue has a different meaning here." He chuckled. "At least, that is what I tell myself."

Dudley sighed. He had made an effort to avoid this game. The young officers of the garrison were forever trying to conquer the young ladies who appeared on the station. Some became ensnared, finding themselves with a wife at a young age and no means to support a family. That had been Dudley's greatest fear.

He was no longer naïve enough to think he was prepared for marriage, not as he once did, before his enlistment in the army. He could not afford a wife, and he had feared that any sort of momentary tryst would risk his reputation, which was already precarious due to his once having been a private soldier.

And, of course, there was the shadow of Elizabeth Montague lurking in the background.

I have had very little luck in love, he thought.

But luck came to those who acted, fortune favouring the brave. Elizabeth was in America now, and there, it seemed, she would stay. Why should he not take this opportunity? A brief fling, as Morris suggested. What did it matter if others talked? Terrible things had been said about him—were still being said—and he had survived.

"Maybe I shall enjoy it," he said to Morris.

"That's the spirit. Though I suggest you take care."

"My plan of attack will be foolproof, and my withdrawal orderly."

Morris chuckled and slapped him on the back. Armed with his cups of punch, Dudley advanced upon the circle surrounding the new belle.

CHAPTER 5

Madras
April 1857

Another day dawned like all the rest, the bugles pealing out across the broad maidan, waking the garrison. Sergeant Brian Barker dressed with quick efficiency before making his way to the parade. With him went Sergeant Bell, with whom he shared quarters, and Colour-Sergeant Aiden O'Ryan.

The Indian sun was still low on the horizon as the old Royal Hampshire Fusiliers formed in two ranks, each man touching the elbow of his comrades in close-order dressing. O'Ryan took the right flank of No. 3 Company, in the rear rank behind Captain Reed. Barker made his way to the dispersed third rank where the sergeants and subalterns served as file closers.

"Good morning, Sergeant," Ensign Dudley greeted, and Barker touched his rifle sling in salute.

"Good morning, sir," he said, and then he took his position near the left flank. Ensign Dudley stood a few paces to his right, then Sergeant Bell, then Lieutenant Morris.

Barker relaxed and let the military routine carry on around him. Sergeant-Major Maclaren placed the rear rank at open order, and the officers fell out to take new positions in the front. The sergeant-major then relayed command of the parade to Lieutenant-Colonel Willis.

Willis returned Maclaren's salute and walked his horse along the long line of the front rank. He smiled, nodding at the occasional man, pausing to speak to others. On the edge of the parade square, the regimental brass band played "Over the Hills and Far Away."

Barker glanced at the dispersed line of officers, swords sloped on their shoulders, sweat stains already forming on some of their tunics. They wore the new dress cap— the new pattern of shako that had been issued near the end of the Russian war. With its tapered crown and slight forward cant, the cap resembled a French kepi. For service in India, it was fitted with a white cotton cover and a curtain to protect the neck, the only concession to the heat Willis allowed.

Barker believed it was altogether proper the gentlemen should have to suffer so in the morning heat. It served as an example to the lads, a demonstration that the officers did not place their welfare above that of the men. This was thanks to Lieutenant-Colonel Willis, who allowed the men in the ranks more comfort.

Under his battalion standing orders, the men did not wear the shako at all, and the new tunic was reserved for special occasions. Willis preferred his soldiers to employ a service dress that consisted of a white cotton frock and cotton trousers. The headdress was the round forage cap, fitted with a visor and wrapped with puggaree, the excess cloth forming a neck curtain. It was a sensible rig, tailored to the climate. Some complained that it made the regiment look like a crew of sailors, but no one denied that light cotton was more comfortable than wool.

Unfortunately, in the dust of India, the white frock and summer trousers turned a dull tan colour, what the Hindus called "khaki." The colour would not wash out. If not for the bright scarlet tunics of the officers, Barker thought, the regiment would have blended into the parade square.

Parade lasted almost an hour and concluded, as always, without event. The men were dismissed for breakfast, to wash the dust from their throats and sate their hunger. Barker and the other members of the sergeants' mess feasted on mutton chops and beer, the usual fare. The meal finished, he reclined in his chair and put a match to his pipe.

O'Ryan joined him. O'Ryan was the senior sergeant in the company, a small wiry fellow with flaming red hair and a merry glint in his eye. He smoked in silence for a few minutes, and then said, "So, ye'll be wanting to take the lads out for another drill parade, then?"

"Aye, that I will."

Morning parade was the only mandatory assembly of the day, but company and squad drill was an option. Barker knew it was not popular, but he wanted to keep the lads sharp and had requested the duty of leading company drill every so many days. O'Ryan had agreed and had asked Captain Reed to approve the proposal.

"It's an easy thing to become complacent here, in particular during a time of peace."

O'Ryan studied the smoldering bowl of his pipe.

"You know my agreement on that subject, Brian."

"And I want to keep an eye on Private Geary."

O'Ryan looked up. "Aye, he's been troubling of late."

Barker stood and wandered toward the open doorway. Pipe smoke made a wreath about his head, and he pulled at his heavy black moustache.

"I blame myself. I was a poor example to him."

"That was almost three years ago. Ye went through a bad spell, that's all. That's all behind ye! Ye're now senior sergeant in this company, second only to meself."

Barker grunted. He appreciated O'Ryan's words, but he knew the truth of the matter better than anyone.

It is my fault, he thought. *Whatever is going through the lad's head, it's the result of what I put there first.*

Geary was sixteen when he enlisted just before the war with Russia. Barker had been an embittered veteran, a former sergeant who had lost his stripes to a court martial. Neglect of duty had been the charge, and absent from parade. Barker had tried to help a comrade, retrieve him from an awkward situation. The fellow had been drunk in the arms of a married woman, away without leave.

Barker's plan had been to fetch the man back to barracks before the woman's husband returned or the man's absence was discovered. But the task had taken longer than anticipated, and Barker had missed roll call himself.

It had not seemed like a very serious matter at the time, especially with his record of good service, but Barker's open disdain for certain officers—officers he considered poor leaders—had made him some enemies. He was charged and had lost his rank.

The injustice of it had been too much for him, and in his anger, he had changed, become all he had been accused of being—a man of bad character. He had started bullying the other men in the company, in particular the recruits.

With his towering six-foot frame and broad shoulders, his menacing dark eyes and black hair, he had been a terror to many. He had provoked fights in the barracks almost every night. He had been a poor orphan who had grown up in a workhouse with dreams of one day becoming sergeant-major and owning a silver-tipped cane, but those dreams had disappeared along with the chevrons on his arm. His life, he decided, had been a failure, all his achievements come to nothing.

Barker suspected now that, deep down within his heart, he had been hoping to get himself drummed out of the service, but that had not happened. In time, the members of No. 3 Company had become divided into two camps—those who supported the troublesome Private Barker and those who did not. Those who did not got the worst of it. For his own survival and well-being, the green Private Geary had become Barker's staunchest apprentice.

The war with Russia had intervened, and it had been Mister Dudley who had brought Barker back to his duty. Dudley had reminded him that true honour and glory lay in how a man treated others, how he worked for the betterment of his comrades despite the fools who might stand in his way. There would always be fools. One need not surrender to their vision of the world.

Barker had remembered his dreams, remembered he had earned his first promotion to sergeant for valour during the Second Sikh War back in '46. In his shame, he had struggled to regain his former reputation. Amid the muck and blood of the trenches before Sevastopol, he had at last earned a second promotion to sergeant, and his healing had begun.

But once he had returned to the sergeants' mess, Geary had no longer been one of his companions. His direct influence was gone, and Barker knew that there lay the problem. He had been present to steer the lad onto the wrong path, but he had not been present to steer him back.

"Unfinished business," he muttered. The boy was still his responsibility, and he would have to find the answer.

Barker held company drill at ten o'clock, for in the afternoon it would be too hot. He took the men through the manual exercise, a series of basic arms movements. He shouted each command in its prescribed order: "Company, port...arms! Company, charge...arms! Company, shoulder...arms!" The men executed each movement with near-perfect timing, rifles crashing against their shoulders in unison.

"That's it, lads," he cried. "Show the sepoys what an Englishman can do with an Enfield rifle."

He considered the sepoys' complaints about the Enfield foolish, for he knew the weapon's superiority to its smoothbore predecessor and had used it to great effect in the Crimea. The rifle was also well-balanced and sleek, resembling a French musket with its three iron bands binding barrel to stock.

He preferred the standard model to the sergeant's pattern, which was shorter and somehow heavier. The muzzle of the standard model was made to fit the seventeen-inch three-sided bayonet; the sergeants' rifle, which had only two reinforcing bands, was made for use with the twenty-three-inch "yataghan" sword bayonet. The yataghan had a flat blade and textured grip and doubled as a sergeant's sword. Barker thought it might have its uses, but when fixed as a bayonet it felt awkward and ungainly.

He gripped his heavy rifle in his right hand as he marched along the front of the company.

"The drill is shaping up," he stated.

Now and then, a few men lagged behind or rushed a movement, but the overall display pleased him. The men kept their shoulders square and their heads steady, and no one had made a glaring mistake. Even better, when he had given them a brief rest between some of the exercises, no one had complained.

On other days, Geary had been the most vocal in his resistance to the extra drill, but this morning he had not uttered a peep.

Not yet.

"Not long now," Barker continued in an attempt to encourage a little extra effort. "Think of your dinners awaiting you at one o'clock. Then it's nothing but a novel in the station library, a game of chess or draughts, or a trial in the gymnasium."

Although more than likely, he thought, it would mean long hours in the barrack canteen. Perhaps it was time to organize another football tournament with the other companies, with the winners challenging the best from the other regiments on the station. It was worth pursuing, to keep the lads out of mischief.

Meantime, there was drill. Barker shouted commands as he walked a slow beat.

"Company, advance…arms! Company, order…arms! Company, advance…arms!"

The men moved and slapped their rifle slings as one, and he grinned. That was the sound of discipline.

There was a crash behind him, and someone muttered a curse. He snapped his head around, his eyes at once falling on the shape of a rifle out of place. The rifle lay on the parade square, at the feet of Private Dick Geary.

Well, it was *about time*, Barker thought.

He turned and walked with deliberate steps towards the unfortunate private. Geary stood empty-handed, his eyes darting here and there. Sweat, whether from the heat or humiliation, ran in rivulets down his narrow features.

Barker stood over the fallen rifle.

"Do you wish to fight the enemy with your bare hands, Private Geary?"

"No, Sergeant," was all Geary could say, his voice weighted with mortification.

At least he had the decency to feel remorse.

"Then there's no reason for you to bloody drop your rifle, is there, Private?"

"No, Sergeant," Geary repeated, although this time the mortification held an edge of anger.

"That rifle is an extra limb, my boy," Barker shouted. "Treat it like a part of you, like your bloody mother's life depends on it, which it may! And never drop it on my parade square!"

"Yes, Sergeant," Geary said, chin puckering.

"Corporal Johnson!" Barker shouted.

"Sergeant?" another voice answered from the ranks.

"Private Geary will fetch water and cook breakfast in your mess for the next seven days."

"Aye, Sergeant," Johnson replied.

"Now pick up your rifle," Barker said to Geary.

With jerking movements, the private stooped and retrieved the fallen weapon. Barker stormed away. He had been lenient, for a soldier had to value and respect his weapons above all else. Barker suspected Geary hadn't meant to drop his rifle, but it had been a careless mistake. *Another* careless mistake.

Yet, as he pondered the matter, he was suddenly uncertain. Geary was young, not yet twenty years old, but he was a four-year veteran of the army and a survivor of the war in the Crimea. He was not just making mistakes. He was becoming sullen and listless, and was often unresponsive to corrections.

I'll have to speak to him, Barker told himself, *man to man, not sergeant to private. Man to man, as we once did.*

He pulled a watch from a small pocket he had sewn to the left breast of his frock. He snapped the timepiece open. The face showed almost half-past eleven. It was time to dismiss the parade.

He replaced the watch and gazed at the sky. Another day of searing temperatures. A small flight of vultures circled in the west. He wondered what prey they had found.

CHAPTER 6

Madras
April 1857

The routine of garrison duty continued, but Dudley had found something new to occupy his mind. In fact, it occupied his every waking thought.

After breakfast, he joined Morris on the veranda. Captain Reed had left them some recent newspapers, and Morris sat in a rattan chair to read. Dudley had brought his sword and scabbard, and he rested them across his knees. The sword was a 1796 pattern light cavalry sabre, a dying gift from a fellow officer who had been mortally wounded at Sevastopol.

"What shall I do to pass the time this morning?" Morris wondered aloud. He folded his newspaper and set it aside.

"Are you looking for suggestions?" Dudley asked.

"Do you have something in mind?"

"Not really," Dudley admitted then added with a grin, "I'm afraid that I'm busy this morning. You will have to amuse yourself."

Morris raised an eyebrow. "Busy, are you? Does Miss Charlotte Edwards have anything to do with your being busy?"

Dudley stood and fastened his scabbard to the slings hanging from his waist belt.

"I promised to call on her at half-past nine."

Morris chuckled. "So that's why you have the sword. Trying to impress, eh?"

Dudley felt his face flushing, for that *was* the reason. His grin widened.

"Worth a try."

"Good boy, William. Grab hold while you can, as I always say."

"Nothing will come of it, of course," Dudley insisted. "In a week or two, she will be gone, and we'll never see each other again."

"Grab hold while you can," Morris repeated. "I envy you, as usual. She's a bold one, if I'm any judge. You *should* take advantage. Women can be a pleasure, like a fine Turkish cigar. They're not all purity and goodness, as some think."

Dudley stared at him, thinking perhaps he should protest, but such a protest would be for form only. It *was* mere pleasure he sought, after all.

"Women are not cigars, my dear Trevor," he said at last. "And Miss Edwards is the niece of a clergyman."

Morris chuckled. "The best sort, my dear fellow."

Dudley called upon Charlotte at her hotel in the city. When they emerged into the sunlit street, she said, "Why don't you show me your regiment? You must be very proud of it."

"I am," he confessed, "though that does not seem very exciting, just looking at the regiment."

He saw the glint in her eyes as she twirled her parasol.

"I think it is. Show me your men, the ones who helped you capture the Russian cannon!"

He offered her his arm.

"Very well, then, if you insist. I'll hire a hackney to take us back."

This was not what he had in mind, but he supposed it would do. Barker would be out with the company by now, and if Charlotte wished to see them at drill and to hear about his exploits, he would oblige her.

Soon they arrived at the cantonments. Barker was there, as were two other companies under the direction of their sergeants. A single officer was present, the duty officer of the day, standing alone and uninterested on the edge of the parade.

Dudley pointed to No. 3 Company.

"There they are. Some of the same lads who were with me at Inkerman are still with us. At one time, they were my friends and comrades, though now I feel very removed from them, especially since it is peacetime."

"Tell me their names."

"Their names? Well, Private Geary was there, and Corporal Johnson, who was a private at the time. And the sergeant instructing now, the big fellow with the black hair and whiskers, is Sergeant Barker. He was a great help to me and must take some of the credit for our success in the Russian war."

"How noble of you to say so! So many young officers would keep the glory to themselves."

Dudley struggled not to demonstrate how effective was her flattery.

"Here I am prattling on about my adventures," he said. "It is very selfish of me. You must tell me more of yourself. Tell me why you have decided to join your uncle and become a missionary."

Charlotte laughed and shook her head. He noticed how her hair bobbed, how it reflected the light.

"It is Mama's notion. She thought I should come to India for the education, to see it before it is changed forever."

"Then you are also here to see the sights?"

"Yes, and hear the sounds and smell the smells. I am so looking forward to going north! We plan to tour along the Ganges and then go to Agra to see the Taj Mahal. And I do so want to see a tiger in the wild!"

Her enthusiasm impressed him. Perhaps here was some common ground between them.

"I have also looked forward to visiting the north, the land of the old Mogul emperors."

"Ah, yes!" she cried. "But who were the Mogul emperors?"

"The rulers of much of India," he explained, "before the Europeans came. The greatest of them was perhaps Akbar, for whom I have named my horse."

Charlotte took his arm with tight little fingers and leaned against him as they walked the edge of the parade ground.

"Tell me about them."

He said nothing for a moment, distracted by her touch. *This is going very well*, he thought. If only Tom Carlisle and the others could see him now!

"The Moguls," he began, "were the descendants of Genghis Khan and Tamerlane, Mongol warlords who conquered most of Asia. The first Mogul was named Babur. At the beginning of the sixteenth century, when Henry VIII was our king, he marched south into Afghanistan then through the Kyber Pass to Delhi.

"With the strength of his armies, he established an empire in the north of India. Akbar was his grandson, and it was Akbar who first opened trade with Britain—with Queen

Elizabeth, in fact. Not very long after that, Britain founded its first Indian trading station. Bombay, on the west coast."

"This is all *very* interesting," Charlotte said. She rested her head against his shoulder then just as quickly pulled it away.

Dudley carried on with his subject, trusting that someone who had made the effort to travel to India would be as enthusiastic about its history as he.

"That was the beginning of the Honourable East India Company, which rules British India on behalf of our government. The Company was already in place when the Mogul Empire began to decline.

"The last Mogul, Aurangzeb, died with seventeen sons and a score of other relatives. As you might imagine, they began to bicker over the inheritance.

"Soon, the empire had splintered, making way for other powers, like France, to invade. The East India Company began to raise its own armies to protect its trade. That's why the Company has troops—to protect its three presidencies, Bombay, Madras, and Bengal.

"Most of the troops in the Company armies are sepoys—native soldiers—though there are a few European regiments as well. And the officers are almost all from Britain."

"But yours is not an Indian regiment, is it? I thought it was English."

"Indeed, it is. The Royal Hampshire Fusiliers is one of the few Queen's Regiments in India now. The rest are all with John Company."

"You know so very much!" Charlotte exclaimed. "Perhaps you should come north with me as my guide."

He patted her arm where it still encircled his.

"I wish that I could, Miss Edwards," he said.

On the parade square, No. 3 Company continued to drill, responding to the boom of Sergeant Barker's voice.

CHAPTER 7

Madras
April 1857

"Well," Sergeant Barker said, "I'll be on my way, now."
Dinner was long over, and he had decided that today he
would speak to Geary.

O'Ryan did not agree with this course of action and
shook his head.

"This ain't necessary. You're not his bleedin' mother,
Brian. If he don't do his duty, he must face the consequences."

"I believe this to be my duty," Barker insisted. "Geary
is a special circumstance. I'll go now, before I put it off
again."

O'Ryan shrugged. "Well, then, good luck to ye."

Barker nodded and stepped down from the veranda
of the sergeant's quarters. He had dressed to emphasize his
appearance of authority, setting aside the white frock for
his scarlet undress shell jacket, its three white lace chevrons prominent on the right sleeve. His sergeant's sash of
red worsted wool hung from his right shoulder to his left
hip, the tassels dangling over the hilt of his long yataghan

bayonet. His brass buttons and waist belt locket gleamed, as did the polished leather of his bayonet scabbard. On his head perched his covered forage cap, and under his left arm, he had tucked a slim bamboo drill cane with a silver head.

With his back rigid, he made for the No. 3 Company barracks, his shoes crunching on the seashells that covered the path. When he reached the building, he mounted the three short steps to the outer veranda. Three more paces brought him to the enclosed inner veranda where the married soldiers lived with their families.

This inner veranda was meant to remain empty, to allow for the flow of air, but too often the quartermasters insisted on utilizing the space for housing. Barker wrinkled his nose. The place was stuffy and squalid, a few blankets hanging from the ceiling offering the only privacy for the women and children. A reek of urine rose both from the wooden tubs set out for nighttime convenience and from the surrounding floorboards. Too often, the sweepers who were charged with emptying the tubs spilled the contents in their carelessness.

Barker ignored the harsh chatter of the few wives present and pushed through to the barracks proper. Here, twenty-two men lived and slept in two rows of iron bunks. The bunks were folded in half now, as they had been for the morning inspection. The men, in shirt sleeves, were tidying up after their dinner, dismantling the trestle tables. Their feet shuffled through the dried cow dung that covered the floor to keep away fleas and crawling insects, and the close air stank of sweat and curry. *Tatties* covering the tall open windows kept out some of the midday heat, but the slight breeze from the four swinging *punkahs* did little for the room's comfort.

Barker hovered in the doorway, staring about the room for sight of Geary. He noticed a skinny native servant collecting the dirty tin plates, arms heaped. As the servant moved to the last standing table, a stocky private, a ruddy-faced man with thinning copper hair and a massive pair of side whiskers, stuck his foot out. The skinny Indian fell with a crash, the dirty plates clattering in all directions. The men roared with laughter.

The servant stood. Without a word, he began gathering up the scattered plates.

"It's as I said, lads," the copper-haired private said to his companions. "Not a scrap of backbone in the lot of 'em."

Barker's anger rose. With two long strides, he crossed the floor, grasped the private's shirt collar, and jerked him backward. The man fell, sliding on his backside across the dung-strewn floor.

Shock and anger contorted the man's face as he glared at his attacker, but his expression quickly changed to one of startled recognition. Scrambling to his feet, he stiffened to attention. The room had gone dead silent, save for the rattle of plates as the servant continued his thankless task.

"Now, then, Private Marten," Barker began, "that was nothing but the actions of a bully, and a man who assaults someone who cannot fight back is a coward. Are you a coward, Private Marten?"

"No, Sergeant," Marten sputtered. "We was just havin' a bit o' fun."

"A bit o' fun?" Barker repeated, keeping his voice low and menacing. "If I catch anyone else having what you call fun again, there'll be hell to pay. We're the Royal Hants. We're fighting men, not bullies."

Marten's face coloured, but he said nothing.

Barker surveyed the other men in the room, remembering why he had come.

"Where's Private Geary?"

"Gone to Black Town, Sergeant," said a lance-corporal.

Barker turned to him.

"What for?"

The man shrugged. "A bit of amusement, Sergeant. Some doxy, we think. Spending his pay, like. He's gone this time nearly every day."

Barker sighed. Nothing wrong with visiting the local colour, if one did not mind the risk of getting the pox.

"Carry on, then," he said, although he gave Marten one last glare of disapproval before he left.

On the edge of the cantonments, he found an idle hackery waiting behind its fat bullock. He climbed aboard and said, "Take me to Black Town."

The driver, a boy of about ten, grinned and cracked his whip. The hackery lumbered forward on its two wheels.

Barker idly tapped his leg with his cane. The hackery wound through the twisting streets, past cramped houses of mud, wood, and simple sun-dried brick. The city here stank of cesspits, of the open sewers that flowed along the edge of the streets. Everywhere lay the dung of horses, camels, oxen and buffalo. Pariah dogs, their ribs showing, huddled panting in the shade, while the human population crammed the doorways and narrow alleys, brown hands and faces contrasting with their light-coloured clothing. The crowd came and went, on foot, in ox-drawn carriages, on horseback, and in hackeries like his.

"Turn right here," he told the boy, for he knew exactly where to go. "Right. Right!" He pointed with his cane, and the cart turned into a wider lane, the entrance to a bazaar.

The fetid air was suddenly loud with the sound of haggling and the whine and jangle of native music. Shops and stalls lined the street, the shopkeepers squatting on mats out front. Hindus mingled with Christians, Muslims, Arabs, Jews, and Chinamen. Barker saw men he knew to be sepoys of a native regiment, although they went about in civilian dress. He also saw sailors in white cotton duck and straw sennets, another fixture of an eastern port city.

"Stop here," he commanded, but the crowd had already slowed the hackery to a halt. Barker dismounted, passing the boy a few annas without a second look.

He pushed through the crowd towards the end of the street. No one tried to bar his passage. Two men in blue tunics, privates of the Madras Fusiliers, steadied to attention as he passed them.

At the end of the street lay the prostitutes' quarter. Many of the brothels were just shabby stalls, little more than squalid tents, but one was a proper building of sun-dried brick. The women stood outside dressed in bright pantaloons, their breasts bare, their arms covered in bracelets, noses and ears pierced and heavy with golden bangles. This was a favourite haunt for the soldiers of the Royal Hants and other European regiments.

Barker halted before the brick house and stared up at the shuttered second-story windows. He did not wish to waste time going inside, so shouted over the noise of the bazaar, "Private Geary! Private Dick Geary, get your bloody arse out here!"

There was no reply. An aged woman, her pendulous breasts hanging to her sagging belly, smiled at him and said in English, "Only three annas, Sahib Bahadur."

"Do I get a blindfold, ma'am?" Barker remarked, then laughed. The woman hissed at him, but he ignored her and cried again, "Private Geary, this is your favourite sergeant! I know you're bloody well in there, boy, so come out if you know what's good for you."

Again, there was nothing. Barker wondered if perhaps Geary was not here. He reached for the door handle. He would have to make certain.

"That you, Sarge?" came a thin tremor from above. Barker stepped back and stared up at the windows. A shutter had creaked open, and Geary's head just showed above the sill.

"Get down here this instant, Private," Barker commanded, although as he spoke he wondered if perhaps this was the wrong approach. Perhaps he should speak less as a sergeant, more as a friend.

Geary hesitated for a moment, his lower lip jutting in defiance. At last, his head ducked back into the darkened room, and a minute later he emerged from the door. He was buttoning his red dress tunic, which the men of the regiment were required to wear when off-duty.

"I need to talk to you, lad," Barker said, forcing some kindness into his voice.

Geary adjusted his whitened waist belt.

"What about?"

Barker sighed. "Not here, boy. We'll head back to the compound."

He turned and began pushing through the crowd in the street. Geary trailed behind him.

"Some of the lads say you've been off to the bazaar every day," Barker commented.

"They go, too," Geary protested. He hunched his shoulders as he walked. "That what you want to talk about? You angry about that?"

Barker shook his head.

"No, no, lad, that's not it. You've been...preoccupied lately. That's it—preoccupied. Your mind's not on your duty. You make too many mistakes. And you don't take correction well." He paused then added, "It seems almost as if you're doing it on purpose, and that I don't like one bit."

"I ain't doing it a-purpose," Geary cried. "You're always on me, Sarge!"

Barker halted. He took Geary by the arm and turned him so they stood face-to-face. Geary looked startled for a moment then pursed his lips and drew himself up.

"Always on you?" Barker repeated. "I said you make too many mistakes! That's why I'm always on you."

"We used to be mates," Geary stated.

"Oh, aye, we used to be mates, but what of it? That give you the right to let go of your rifle on parade? Make a right turn instead of a left, and complain when I correct you? Well, does it?"

"No, Sarge," Geary admitted.

"Then tell me what's troubling you," Barker insisted. "There's got to be something."

Geary looked down at his feet then back at Barker.

"Tell me, boy!" Barker cried.

Geary pushed his fingers under his forage cap to scratch his scalp. At length, he stammered, "Remember I told you about my da? How he was strict, like? Didn't take no guff from me? I guess that's why I joined the army."

"Aye, you told me so, lad," Barker said.

"Well, I got a letter. From my sister. She lives in London. She's a seamstress, but she can write."

"And what was in the letter, lad?"

"I couldn't read it, so Corporal Johnny read it for me. It said my da was dead, Sarge."

Barker softened his tone. Perhaps this was it. He had discovered the source of the discontent.

"Well, then. That's hard, so it is."

"No!" Geary cried. He was clenching his fists. "You see, that ain't it. I was glad he was dead. Glad, Sergeant! He was never like a da should be!"

Barker nodded. "So he was an old mugger, then. Now you're rid of him."

"And glad of it, too, Sergeant!" Geary repeated.

Barker nodded. Well, perhaps he was not so glad as he thought, or maybe filled with guilt over being glad. It must be something of the sort.

"That's it, then? That's why you haven't been attending to your duty?"

Geary shrugged then looked at his feet again.

"Listen here, Dick." Barker almost never used a man's given name, but it seemed appropriate in these circumstances. "I never knew my dad, but I reckon he was no good, or I would have known him, see? I grew up in a London workhouse, but now I'm sergeant. Maybe next in line for colour sergeant. Do you get my meaning?"

Geary still stared at his shoes.

"We used to be mates. You used to say that sergeants didn't know nothing. That it was the privates who did all the work."

"Aye, I did say that. And I was wrong. Dead wrong. Are you trying to follow my former example instead of my current? A good sergeant is worth ten privates. That's why he gets to be sergeant."

Again, Geary raised his shoulders and let them fall.

"Do you want to amount to anything?" Barker demanded. "Do you want to make something of yourself? Dying on a battlefield would be fine for a soldier, but you may never see another war, boy. Then one day you'll be a discharged private. Or maybe there will be war, and you'll be discharged with wounds, unable to work another day in your life. That what you wish for? To die penniless in the gutter? Or do you want to work, do your duty and one day make corporal?"

Geary's lips trembled. "You said…you said the corporals all kissed the officers' arses. The ones who didn't never got to be sergeants."

"To hell with what I said! That's what I'm trying to tell you, lad! I was angry with the world. Can't you see that I'm trying to admit my past sins? My pride is not so great. Listen to what I'm saying now."

Geary looked away. "I don't know what you want me to do."

"I want you to do your duty," Barker stated, gritting his teeth in frustration. He studied Geary's thin face. The lad seemed fit to start bawling any minute.

There has to be something else to this, he thought. Perhaps the boy lamented his no-good father and wanted some attention, some direction. Well, Barker would give it to him.

"Listen here, Private," he began. "This is what you will do. Starting tomorrow, I want to see you in front of your barracks at one o'clock in the afternoon. Full marching order, fully shone. And I'll want to see you every other day after that, until you stop bloody mucking up my drills. Do you get me?"

Geary's head snapped up as if his neck were a spring. His face had gone white.

"But…"

"I'll hear no protests, d'you hear me? One o'clock tomorrow afternoon."

Geary's body slumped.

"Yes, Sergeant."

Barker nodded. He had said what needed saying. They would take it from here.

Without another word, he turned and marched away through the crooked streets, leaving Private Geary alone in the bazaar.

CHAPTER 8

Madras
May 1857

Dudley hummed a jaunty tune as he shaved by lan-tern light, something the regimental band often played, although he did not know its name. He had seen Charlotte every day for the past week, and today would be no exception. When the usual routine of morning parade and breakfast was finished, he would join her for an excursion on horseback. She had asked him to take her beyond the confines of the city, and he had agreed.

She had let him kiss her again yesterday evening on the promenade. Just one kiss, but he could still feel it, like the burning hint of something greater yet to come.

Behind him, Kesab was making the bed. It was a simple lattice of ropes stretched across a wooden frame, with two cotton quilts serving as a mattress. Kesab had tied the gauze mosquito netting back against the headboard and was now folding one of the quilts. Dudley watched him for a moment, then glanced at the eastern windows, at the brightening sky.

A turquoise glow flooded the room, new light bathing the washstand with its brass pitcher and basin, the two basket chairs in the corners, the landscape prints on the white-washed walls. Another glorious day.

He rinsed his razor in the basin, noticed the light glint from a length of fine chain curled on the washstand. Wellington, his tin soldier. He did not know how long it had been lying there, for he had not been wearing it much since coming to India. The war with Russia was long over, and he no longer seemed to need the charm's reassuring presence.

He finished shaving and wiped his face with a clean towel. The tin soldier seemed to stare at him, and for a moment, he considered wearing it for the morning parade; but at once he changed his mind. It made an unsightly lump under his tunic. He prided himself on keeping his kit in fine order, and the little toy would only spoil the line of his buttons.

Kesab opened the trunk at the foot of the bed and began laying out Dudley's uniform. The servant then helped him don a clean white shirt, although Dudley pulled on his white summer trousers and braces unassisted.

The glow from the windows had turned to pale gold, and the air was already warm. Sweat beaded Dudley's forehead as he sat to lace his shoes. He continued to hum to himself, grateful for the light breeze from the *punkah* swinging back and forth overhead, although it troubled him to think of the poor punkah wallah who endlessly kept the machine in motion. The *punkah* was a long wooden frame covered in canvas, worked by a rope that led across the ceiling and through a hole in the wall. The punkah wallah sat on the back veranda, pulling on the rope to keep the fan swinging.

Kesab held Dudley's dress tunic.

"You are very cheerful this morning, sahib," he said.

"Yes, I am. I see no reason not to be."

"Those are true words of wisdom, sahib."

Kesab prepared to slide the tunic over Dudley's arms, and Dudley complied with his usual mild embarrassment. It still felt strange, even absurd, to have someone dress him, but he wanted to behave as an officer should. That included employing and using servants, and he had hired as many as he could afford. Besides Kesab, he kept a tailor to mend his clothes and do his laundry, a *bhisti* to fetch and carry bathing and drinking water, and two *punkah wallahs* to operate the fans and run petty errands.

It would have been easy for him, a former sergeant, to mend his own clothes and fetch his own water, but an officer did not do such things. Dudley had vowed to embrace the officer's life, to maintain the habits of a gentleman, and servants in India were not expensive. At the same time, he treated his servants well, even if sometimes they did not understand why.

Morris had once said to him, "Don't be afraid to beat them, William. It's the sort of thing they're used to, what they expect. The arrangement was here long before the British arrived, and none of them will ever acknowledge or thank you for kindness."

Such was the common view in India, but Dudley did not agree. His uncle had taught him that one did not give kindness simply to receive thanks or praise but because it was the right thing to do. He could hear his uncle now, telling the students at his boarding school, "The Golden Rule is the blessed rule of our Saviour."

Along with the Golden Rule, Dudley reasoned, there was also British policy to consider. If natives of low station were accustomed to ill treatment, British justice should work to change that. Otherwise, British rule amounted to nothing more than the control of Indian trade. He felt that Britain needed to demand a higher standard of behavior from its subjects, a standard of fairness. That was the duty of the empire.

Of all his servants, Dudley had a particular fondness and respect for Kesab. The Brahmin was an old soldier, something Dudley had recognized at once on their first meeting. Kesab reminded him of another old soldier he had known—Private Daniel Oakes, a good steady man who had possessed the honour and practical wisdom of a veteran.

Like Kesab, Oakes had been missing an eye, the result of a wound taken at Inkerman. Dudley had employed him as a batman, but soon after he had been killed during an assault on a Russian redoubt at Sevastopol. His widow, Hester Oakes, had been the unofficial matron of No. 3 Company. She had since married another veteran who had later paid off, retiring on his pension to Hampshire. There, he had opened a public house, the soldier's dream.

Kesab had told Dudley he had been a *havildar* in the 53rd Bengal Native Infantry.

"You are from the Kingdom of Oudh, then?" Dudley had asked. Most of the native troops in the Bengal Army had come from Oudh. Until its recent annexation, the kingdom had been an independent state, its soldiers professionals, mercenaries fighting in foreign service.

"I am from Oudh, sahib," the old soldier confirmed. "Like my brothers in the old regiment."

"Please, call me Mister Dudley," Dudley had insisted. "May I call you Kesab?"

"That is my name, Dudley Sahib," Kesab had quipped. "I am not ashamed to hear it spoken."

"You were wounded in action, I take it," Dudley had then stated, and asked, "Why have you not retired on your pension? Why seek employment as an officer's servant?"

At this, Kesab had been silent, and Dudley had quickly added, "Forgive me. It's none of my business, really."

"There is a reason, Dudley Sahib," Kesab had said at last. "The new laws will not allow me to retire."

"Ah."

Dudley had again felt foolish. Like the Enfield cartridge, the General Service Enlistment Act, not even a year old, had caused resentment and anger in the Bengal Army. One clause of the Act required native regiments to fight overseas on foreign service, which meant they would have to board naval transports. Although the Madras and Bombay regiments already did this, the Hindus of the Bengal Army maintained that they could not perform the daily ablutions required of their faith on a cramped wooden ship. Nor could each man prepare his own food to prevent its defilement.

Another clause was even more contentious. It stated that those men not fit for active service could no longer retire with invalid pensions. The law now required these men to serve out the remainder of their enlistment on cantonment duty.

"Well, if it's any consolation," Dudley had said, "I'm glad to have you." He wished to make Kesab feel welcome. It was the least an old soldier, a havildar who had served the Sirkar and been wounded in action, deserved.

"Thank you, Dudley Sahib," Kesab had said. Then he had looked Dudley in the eye, a rare occurrence between a British officer and native servant. Dudley had seen inherent confidence there, humour, and pride.

Since then, they had grown familiar with each other. Kesab knew much of Indian history and was always willing to answer Dudley's persistent questions. And he was an efficient and professional valet.

"Thank you," Dudley said as Kesab fastened his sword belt for him. Dudley then attached the scabbard to its slings, took his cap from Kesab's waiting hands, and adjusted the cap and its cover.

"Well, I'm off. Good morning, Kesab."

Kesab bowed. "Good morning, Dudley Sahib. May you have a fine parade."

The morning ritual between master and servant was done. Dudley moved from the bedroom into the sitting room he shared with Morris. He paused to appreciate the light from the window, a brilliant patch of it falling over a rack holding three birding guns. The guns belonged to Morris, as did the playing cards that lay strewn upon the floor under the table. Dudley's things included the books and the bookcase, the small writing desk with its inkstand, and a collection of pictures for the walls. One picture, an engraving entitled "The Fall of the Tippoo Sultan," was a favourite.

When Dudley at last stepped out onto the front veranda, Morris was already there and gave him a cheery, "Good morning."

"Another fine day in paradise," Dudley said. The air smelled of dust and blossoms from the cantonment gardens. The sun was now a blinding sliver on the horizon.

Morris pushed back his cap. "Shall we be seeing Miss Edwards again today?"

Dudley grinned. "Well, I don't know about you, but I certainly shall."

"Good boy." Morris slapped him on the back. "You are driving Tom Carlisle to distraction, and that is a service to the regiment."

They stepped down from the veranda and walked towards the parade square, where the bugles were calling Assembly.

———————

Hours later, Dudley and Charlotte rode west, away from the cantonments. Charlotte wore the same yellow riding habit he had seen before, when she had been with Tom Carlisle. She let Dudley lead, and he took her away from the dusty road, away from the travelers and the muddy trace of the

Cooum River. It was, perhaps, not advisable to take a young lady too far into the countryside, but he had a place in mind, a secluded spot he had discovered on one of his solitary journeys.

It was a place where he was certain they would not be disturbed, where they would be alone.

"There," he said, pointing to a grove of date palms. In their midst stood the dark outline of a wall, a square enclosure, the stone covered with vines and bright flowers.

"Oh, it's wonderful!" Charlotte exclaimed. "A ruin from antiquity."

"Not so ancient, I think, but it was a garden enclosure, the sort you see everywhere in these parts. Abandoned now, it seems."

He led her through the open gate. Inside there was shade under the trees, and the fragrant jasmine and oleanders had run wild. He dismounted and helped Charlotte do the same. She smiled and unlaced her hat.

"It is a tiny bit of paradise," she said.

"There was a house there," Dudley said, indicating another ruin adjacent to the back wall. "There must have been a fire or something. Obviously, no one lives here now."

She looked at him. "Why don't you spread your blanket? We can sit and enjoy this together."

"Your wish is my command, my lady," he said with a grin.

He undid the straps on the blanket roll in front of his saddle, unfolded the blanket, and spread it over a patch of thick and tangled grass. Charlotte knelt, smoothing her skirts, and Dudley sat cross-legged beside her.

He suddenly realized he was trembling, vibrating inside. He hoped Charlotte did not notice.

"I will miss you when you're gone," he said, and wondered why he had brought her here. What did he wish for?

Perhaps another kiss, to see her off? Or something more? For a moment, he felt a pang of remorse. It was a game after all.

"We leave the day after tomorrow, you know," she said, her voice soft. "I will not see you after today. Tomorrow, we will be too busy getting ready for our journey."

"You will have a wonderful adventure in the north, I am certain."

"A wonderful adventure, yes," she said. "And I do want adventure. I want to travel the world and see all its wonders!" She breathed a great sigh and tilted her head back, revealing her white throat. Dudley's eyes played across the rounded contours of her shoulders, the swell of her bosom.

He made himself look away. Taking a bit of grass, he rolled it between his fingers.

"I would like to have adventures like you have had, William," she said. "You have fought in battles, and you have traveled to many places."

"A few places. With the army. Gibraltar, Malta, Turkey. Russia, of course."

"Has your regiment gone on marches through the Indian countryside?" Her eyes blazed with sudden excitement. "I have heard that the women bathe naked in the rivers, standing still in the sun for everyone to see!"

Dudley felt his face flushing.

"I have seen them, yes."

She leaned towards him and placed her hand on his arm.

"Do you like the Indian women? Or are English women prettier?"

He sat still, relishing her touch.

"Each has a different sort of beauty, though none is as pretty as you, Charlotte."

She smiled, and for a moment, she placed her head on his shoulder, running her hand up his back. Without thinking, he reached for her, encircling her with his arms. His pulse quickened.

"Would you like to kiss me again, William?" She stared up at him. There was dark mischief in her eyes.

He did not hesitate, for this was what he had wanted, devious as that may have been. He cradled her cheek in one hand, tilting her face, pulling her lips to his. She responded with vigour, her arms encircling his neck as she drew him down, down onto the blanket.

"There's no one here but us," she murmured. "And the horses."

He felt her unlatch his belt buckle, the leather belt with its empty sword slings slipping away. He sat up in surprise, but she had already undone the bottom button of his tunic. He took her hands, held them, but that dark look was still in her eyes.

"I want to see your scars," she said. "From your battle wounds."

"My right arm," he said. "My leg. There is a scar on my side…"

"Show me."

She pulled her hands away, reaching for the bodice of her dress, began unfastening the hooks and eyes.

The blood was rushing in his ears, the desire strong. He knew this was wrong, that his uncle would truly be disappointed, but he did not care. He knew he would not stop now, no matter what rational and moral objections he might conceive.

Damn scandal, he thought, *and damn the consequences.*

He pulled off his tunic and cast it aside then kissed her neck, her hair. The rules of England were not relevant here. *This is India*, he thought. *This is India.*

CHAPTER 9

Madras
May 1857

Dudley was restless with anxiety the next morning. He fidgeted on parade, for once impatient with the daily ritual as he waited for Lieutenant-Colonel Willis to complete his inspection.

He relived his last moments with Charlotte, astonished by the depth of his disappointment and regret that he would not see her again. That, he realized, was a reality he could not avoid.

He wandered in a daze when the parade concluded, unsure of what to do with himself. Breakfast, of course. He wondered how he would feel when he saw the others, when he saw Tom Carlisle. Would he feel victorious? And if so, over what?

Halfway to the officer's mess he came upon Captain Reed. Reed was a lanky fellow with a stiff and humourless manner who had transferred to the Royal Hants from the Green Howards. He wiped at his prominent nose with a handkerchief and said, "Ah, Mister Dudley. I was com-

72

ing to find you. Lieutenant-Colonel Willis wishes to see you in his office at once."

"The colonel's *office*, sir?" Dudley repeated. Although Willis kept an office next to the compound orderly room, he was seldom in it.

"That is what I said, Ensign," Reed repeated, knitting his brows in weary irritation before turning away, not waiting for Dudley's salute.

Dudley stood frozen for a moment, wondering what this could be about. He could think of nothing, good nor bad.

He made his way to the office bungalow. At least here was something to rescue him from his sense of displacement. He reported to the colonel's secretary in the office anteroom.

"Ensign Dudley to see Lieutenant-Colonel Willis."

"Come in, Lieutenant," the colonel called from beyond his half-open door. Dudley entered and stood at attention in front of the dark mahogany desk.

"Be at ease, Lieutenant," Willis said, somehow forgetting that Dudley was still officially an ensign. "I have a special assignment for you. Just the sort of thing you will appreciate, I should think."

Dudley relaxed. "A special assignment, sir?"

"Yes." Willis leaned back in his chair. "As you are no doubt aware, a friend of my family's, Mrs. Grace Edwards, has been visiting the garrison with her daughter. They are to proceed to Cawnpore tomorrow morning. She has requested a military escort, just in case there is trouble in the north. The garrison lacks cavalry, so infantry will have to do. It's last-minute, but the general has approved it. You will lead the escort."

Dudley said nothing for a moment. He was to escort Charlotte and her mother north?

"Very good, sir," he said then cleared his throat. A smile fought to overtake his features, but he held it at bay.

"Take a sergeant to assist you and twelve men from your company. Your choice. You must be ready at first light tomorrow to board the coastal steamer. When you reach Cawnpore, you are to report directly to General Wheeler, who is in charge of the garrison."

"Yes, sir. General Wheeler."

Willis smiled. "Not exactly a danger-filled escapade, but you were the first fellow who came to mind when I received the request. It will afford you the opportunity to see more of India, and I know you are an enthusiast. Your duty is simply to protect Mrs. Edwards and her party from all manner of trouble along the way. Wild animals, bandits, that sort of thing."

Dudley thought of the threatened mutinies. There had been another incident on 23 April, when members of the 3rd Native Irregular Cavalry had refused the greased Enfield cartridges. Several men faced courts martial.

"What of the troubles, sir? The unrest with the native troops?"

Willis gave a dismissive wave of his hand.

"I admit that the troubles are one of Mrs. Edwards' concerns, but it's nonsense, in my opinion. Utter rubbish. A few men have refused the new cartridge, but there have been no repeats of this Pande affair. Native troops are always threatening to mutiny. You may rest easy, I assure you. Most of your trip will be by ship, train, and postal *dak*. Maybe you can take a river steamer part of the way, though the upper Ganges is low this time of year."

"That seems sensible, sir."

"And feel no obligation to hurry back, Lieutenant. Take a bit of leave while you are there. I know you are curious to tour the north. As I have said, now you may take the opportunity."

Dudley was only half-listening, already anticipating more time with Charlotte. He could not believe his luck.

"Thank you, sir. That is extraordinarily generous."

"Perhaps," Willis said. "But things are quiet here. We have no particular need for every officer."

"Then I will go and prepare my things, sir. And thank you again for considering me for this assignment."

"You are welcome, indeed, Mister Dudley," Willis said. "My secretary will pass you your official orders on the way out."

Dudley turned and almost skipped out of the office.

CHAPTER 10

Madras
May 1857

Barker perched on the edge of his cane chair, his accou-
trements spread upon the table before him. He had polished his shoes and draped a cloth over them to keep off
the dust, and now worked on his two cartridge boxes. His
old sixty-round main box already gleamed, but his new
expense pouch needed a fresh base coat of blacking.

The expense pouch was smaller than the old version,
a black leather box with a curved flap or lid. It could hold
up to twenty rounds and was worn on the waist belt, just
to the right of the locket. Barker liked it for its ease of use.

He whistled while he worked. He could have employed
a servant to clean his kit for him, but there was something
satisfying about making dull leather and brass come to
sparkling life.

Setting aside the expense box, he turned to the locket
of his waist belt, working a tiny brush amongst the letters
in the circlet that spelled "Royal Hampshire Fusiliers." The
gleaming brass made him think of Geary's inspection
that day.

Geary had stood at attention, not concealing the look of furious resentment on his face. His kit had been spotless, and Barker had been pleased. The lad was trying. Barker hoped that, in time and with more simple army discipline, Geary would come to pay extra attention to all aspects of his duty. Then the inspections could end.

A bead of sweat dripped from his brow onto his belt buckle. He swore under his breath and wiped the drop away with a rag, then ran the rag over his forehead. He hated the heat of India. The army was always trying to burn you to death, he thought, or freeze you, as in the Crimea.

He heard a soft patter behind him, like a gentle rain, and he glanced toward the open door. A small dog stood on the threshold staring at him. He stared back in surprise. The dog was a scrawny thing, it ribs protruding, its fur matted with brown dirt, but there was no mistaking its pure breeding. This was not one of the mongrels that roamed the streets, but a beagle, its coat white with black and brown spots. Its feet were golden, and a patch of black covered its right ear and eye.

Barker set down his belt and leaned forward.

"Well, little fellow," he said, "where did you spring from?"

The dog did not run but took a few cautious steps before sitting back on its haunches, its tail slapping against the floor. Barker rose and went to it. It whined and let him rub its back and scratch its neck.

"I know who you are, now that I think of it," Barker cried. "You belong to Colonel Willis, the one they couldn't find, I reckon. They were asking if anyone had seen you. You must be a tough little bugger to have withstood this climate."

The dog must have survived on rats and insects, Barker decided, but it had not lived well. It leapt up on its hind feet, pawing at him, and he scooped it up in his hands. It was much lighter than it should have been. As he carried it outside, it rested its head in the crook of his arm and closed its eyes.

"Poor thing," he murmured. "Thought you'd like a life of freedom, eh? Now you've come back, looking for the pampered existence you missed."

He carried the dog along the path to Corporal Johnson's No. 3 Company barrack room, thinking to leave the creature there until he could contact the colonel. Private Geary also made his home in that room, and Barker wondered if the boy would fancy looking after the dog until things could be sorted out. A little responsibility for someone other than himself might do wonders.

The barrack room was quiet, although a few of the men were there, engaged in kit maintenance and other menial activities. Private Geary sat on his bunk, staying away from the brothels for one day, at least. He was polishing his main cartridge box.

"What you got there, Sarge?" Corporal Johnson asked when he saw the dog. Johnson was a short and powerful man with a mean face like a rat's, his narrow eyes locked in what appeared to be a chronic sinister sneer. Barker considered him one of the best men in the company.

"Found this little fellow wandering about half starved," Barker explained. "Private Geary, clear the way there."

Geary had his bunk unfolded, his kit items arranged on its cramped surface just as Barker had done on his table. Geary pushed aside his belts and Barker set the dog down in their place. The men crowded round to see.

"Here, give 'im some air, boys," Barker said, "give 'im some air. This mutt belongs to the colonel. He'll want to know it's safe and sound after all."

Geary reached out and began to stroke the animal's back. The dog rolled onto its side, its tongue lolling.

"Clean the little fellow up," Barker told him. "I'll go and see if any of the young gentlemen are about."

⚓︎

Barker waylaid Captain Reed in front of the officers' mess, and together they fetched Lieutenant-Colonel Willis, who still occupied his office. The officers followed the sergeant to the barracks, where a bathed and brushed hound awaited them.

"You have nursed him back to health, by Jove!" Willis cried in astonishment.

"Boys just cleaned him up a bit, sir," Barker explained. "He'd been getting along all right on beetles and such, it seems."

"Well, one beagle hound is not much use to me, I'm afraid." Willis scratched his chin and turned to Captain Reed. "I shall make of him a gift. Your men may have him as a company mascot, Captain. If they wish, that is. As a sign of my gratitude that they have found him and saved his life."

"What do you think, Sergeant?" Reed said to Barker.

Barker nodded. "The lads will like that, sir." The regiment had kept other animal mascots, most recently Blacky the raven, who had perished from overindulgence in drink.

"Well, then, that's settled," Willis said. "Captain?"

Reed turned to Barker and said, "Carry on, Sergeant."

The officers left the barrack room, picking their way across the inner veranda. Barker stood next to Geary's bunk.

"We'll name him Lazarus," the sergeant declared. "The beagle who rose from the dead. And, Private Geary, I have another task for you."

"Yes, Sergeant." Geary stood at attention, as if fearing further punishment.

Barker chuckled. "It's all right, boy. From now on, the extra inspections are cancelled. I have something better in mind."

A flicker of mingled relief and confusion crossed the private's face.

"Cancelled?"

"You bloody heard me." Barker knelt and stroked the beagle's scrawny back. "You're to be Lazzy here's keeper. Keep him fed, trained, and out of trouble. I expect him to be in the peak of health in a week."

Geary looked down at the dog; it was licking Barker's hand. The creature seemed starved for friendship and affection. The private's narrow features crumpled in a smile, the first smile Barker had seen in some time. He turned back to the sergeant.

"I'll look after him, Sarge."

Barker lifted the dog and placed it into Geary's arms.

"Then he's yours. And don't be feeding him anything improper in the barrack canteen."

Geary's grin widened. "I won't, Sarge."

CHAPTER 11

Madras to Cawnpore
May 1857

Dudley chose Colour-Sergeant O'Ryan to lead his de-tachment of twelve men. At dawn, they marched to the Madras docks, and there they met Mrs. Edwards and her daughter.

When Dudley saw Charlotte, he gave her his most charming smile, but she did not return it. Instead, she looked away, her mouth a firm line, as her mother declared, "We are very glad to have you, Mister Dudley. Charlotte, in particular. She tells me you have been a most gracious host this last week."

"I am happy to hear it," Dudley replied, but he was puzzled by Charlotte's behaviour. He had expected her to squeal with delight, but she behaved as if she did not want him here at all.

She cannot appear too eager in front of her mother, he told himself. Yes, maybe that was it.

The coastal steamer set out at eight o'clock and for two days paddled north to Calcutta. In all that time, Charlotte Edwards remained close to her mother. Dudley stayed with his men and did not speak to her.

In Calcutta, the party boarded a train, and soon they were rolling west along the lower Ganges valley. Dudley enjoyed gazing through the open window at the fertile fields of corn, rice, and sugar cane, the spires of mosques and the terraced towers of Hindu temples rising above the villages, the river lying low and brown in the dry season.

The rail line covered more than a hundred-and-twenty miles before its terminus at a town called Ranigunj. There, the travellers spent the night at the wooden train station; Charlotte and her mother shared one room while Dudley and Kesab took another. Kesab had been willing to stay outside in the tents with Colour-Sergeant O'Ryan and the men of the escort, but Dudley insisted his servant remain with him.

In the morning, Dudley joined his charges for breakfast in the train station mess as the men ate their rations. The conversation was polite, although there was a tightness to Charlotte's smile, a coldness in her eyes. After breakfast, the travellers waited while the stationmaster gathered enough Dak *gharis*—postal conveyances—to accommodate them.

Dudley stood a few yards apart from his men. Charlotte's continued aloofness was wearing on him, and the depth of his hurt surprised him. He was beginning to believe it was not an act, that she had expected their time together to cease and was irritated by his presence. Of course, he had never intended their dalliance to carry on this far, either; so why, he asked himself, should he be sorry when she felt the same way? Or surprised? She had given up on Tom Carlisle quickly enough.

Another aspect of the game, he thought.

To her, William Dudley had been nothing but an idea, the Crimean hero everyone talked about. As Morris had said, she was the adventurous type. Whatever hurt he felt now, Dudley decided, he had brought it upon himself, for he, too, had been false. He, too, had simply wanted her attention, the pleasure of her company, and for others to see him with her.

So now, if she meant to discourage him from further advances, he would oblige her by not making any. He would do his duty as commanded and see that she and her mother arrived safely in Cawnpore. That was all.

The *gharis* were ready. Each was a large wooden box on four carriage wheels, like a police wagon or photographer's van, hitched to a team of six horses. The sides slid open and inside were cushioned seats, shelves, and lockers for baggage and mail. The driver of the lead *ghari*, a tall man in white puggaree and pale blue caftan, blew his post horn, the signal that it was time to board.

Dudley helped Mrs. Edwards mount the vehicle, then did the same for Charlotte. The touch of Charlotte's hand brought vivid memories, and he stifled a rush of bitter anger as he climbed in after her, taking the opposite bench with Kesab. O'Ryan and the men piled into the three following gharis.

Each *ghari* driver was accompanied by a small boy. The boys cracked their whips, and the vehicles started off, the yellow dust rising as the teams launched at once into a gallop. Charlotte squealed in delight at the speed. Her excitement rekindled Dudley's anger, but he forced himself to smile.

"We're on the grand trunk road, on our way to Oudh, Miss Edwards," he said, shouting over the noise of hoof and wheel. "Think of it!"

"Oh, I am!" she cried. "Can we go faster, do you think?"

"Heavens, child!" Mrs. Edwards exclaimed. "You must show some restraint." She reached into a pocket of her dark skirts and drew out a silver flask. She eyed Dudley as she uncapped it, adding, "For the heat and dust, Mister Dudley. It aids my breathing."

"It must be indispensable in this country, ma'am," he replied.

Kesab stared at the opposite wall of the *ghari*, now and then turning his head to watch the countryside. Dudley also kept his eyes on the rushing landscape, trying not to look at Charlotte. He even dared to lean out to gaze forward, past the racing horses.

The trunk road, with its pavement of carbonate of lime, stretched across the land like an undulating white ribbon. On the right, the low river glistened in the sun. A few small boats rode on the water, but there was a great deal more traffic on the road. Merchants led strings of camels piled high with goods, oxen pulled carts filled with cotton bales, and pedestrians marched along in their pointed slippers. All leapt or moved out of the way as the four *gharis* approached.

All day the *gharis* roared along. Stages set every five miles allowed the drivers to change the horses, and when evening fell, the travellers stopped for the night at one of the Dak bungalows that lined the post route. The bungalow was large, with a central courtyard and several suites of rooms. Dudley shared a suite with Kesab, but his men elected to pitch their tents rather than pay the eight annas—an entire shilling—charged for every traveller.

Dudley prepared to take a bath before turning in, glad the day's journey was over. He could not have borne another moment in Charlotte's presence, with her uncaring gaze and tantalizing beauty. He would try to enjoy the journey for its own sake; and he certainly could not complain, for they had encountered no trouble, they did not have to march, and now they were lodged in comfort.

Like his quarters in Madras, the suite featured a bathroom paved in smooth bricks with a central drain. Waiting on a shelf were three earthen jars of cool water. With great satisfaction, he scrubbed away the sweat and dust, humming a series of marches. Somewhat refreshed, in body if not in spirit, he went straight to bed.

After breakfast the next morning, he and Mrs. Edwards signed the station guestbook, recording their time of arrival, departure, and the amount they had paid. They then boarded the *gharis* and were off again at breakneck speed.

The journey by Dak continued for four more days, and in that time, Charlotte kept her cool distance. On the fourth day, they at last reached Allahabad, where the rail line resumed, a new stretch that would take them about halfway to Cawnpore.

While the men of the escort, like the native passengers, rode on open flat cars, Dudley rode in the forward passenger car with his two female companions. As the passenger car rattled and swayed, he tried to concentrate on the passing countryside, watching it change from green fields to wide sandy plain. Bushes sprouted at intervals on the burnt soil, and once he noted a herd of grazing antelope. There were fewer villages here.

The rail terminus was at a place called Khaga, the station consisting of a small collection of tents in a grove of shading trees. A flock of green parrots perched overhead in the branches as Dudley's party waited with the other passengers, both European and Indian, to continue the next leg of their journey. After an hour, four more *gharis* were ready, and then they were off again; they did not have to go far. Just after five o'clock in the evening, seven days out from Madras, they arrived in Cawnpore.

Dudley knew the town as a once-vital military post for the East India Company, the halfway mark between Benares and Delhi, although its strategic value had diminished since the annexation of Oudh. Its still extensive cantonments lay in a long strip along the western bank of the Ganges. A wide canal, its head at the eastern perimeter of the cantonments, ran at right angles to the river for about a mile before turning north. Cawnpore itself lay sandwiched between the canal and the cantonments.

The *gharis* turned right off the grand trunk, taking a secondary road towards the river. Dudley noted a group of unfinished buildings on their left, what looked like new barracks under construction. Ahead, beyond the canal, lay the city proper, which from here seemed a disappointing collection of low nondescript structures built of stone, brick, and plaster. It had the utilitarian appearance of many garrison towns.

The river drew closer. It was wide here, more than five hundred yards across. Close to the shore rode a multitude of small river craft, their thatched awnings like so many rooftops. A bridge of boats gave access to the far bank and the province of Oudh. The bridge marked the beginning of the road north to Lucknow, the ancient capital city of the kingdom.

The *gharis* stopped at a station close to the head of the canal, and the travellers dismounted as Colour-Sergeant O'Ryan formed the escort squad into two files. As the *ghari* drivers piled the military baggage in a hired ox-cart, Mrs. Edwards described the location of her brother's house and invited Dudley to dinner that evening.

"I regret he is not here to meet us," she said. "Though I suppose, since we have arrived with the post, there was no way of announcing our imminent arrival."

"You will be a pleasant surprise for him," Dudley suggested. "And I would be honoured to accept your invitation. Though I must apologize in advance if I am late. Since I have brought you here safe, my next task is to find billets for my men and to report our arrival."

"Certainly, Ensign, certainly." Mrs. Edwards sniffed. "Now I must have the post drivers hire us a carriage or some other transport. Until later this evening, Mister Dudley."

Charlotte followed her mother into the station. She did not look back.

Well, damn her, Dudley thought.

He and O'Ryan marched their squad to the cantonment headquarters, the ox-cart and its boy attendant lumbering behind them. Dudley at once reported to the orderly room. The orderly sergeant on duty gave him directions to available barrack space in the European quarter.

"We been expectin' you, sir," he said. "Quartermaster set these aside for you." He gave Dudley a map drawn in pencil.

Dudley had not expected such an efficient welcome, and he was pleased. The barracks were not hard to find, and soon the squad had settled in and O'Ryan was assuring Dudley the lads would be comfortable enough. Satisfied, he bid them goodnight and parted company.

He decided General Wheeler would be getting ready for dinner about now, so he could not report to him, as Lieutenant-Colonel Willis had insisted, until tomorrow morning. At least the orderly room knew he was here. There was nothing left for him to do but go to dinner himself, and that he was dreading.

He and Kesab made their way on foot, each of them carrying one of Dudley's leather satchels. They moved along Cawnpore's wide main avenue, the Chandni Chowk, or "Street of Silver." Here was something worth seeing, for the street was famous as the place where one could find the finest silver- and goldsmiths in India, the finest leather workers and shoemakers. Unfortunately, because of the late hour, the shops and stalls stood closed, and Dudley noticed small groups of men lounging about in the mouths of alleyways, smoking pipes, tossing dice, and muttering in low voices. By their squalid appearance, he did not take them for smiths or merchants.

"There are many *badmashes* in this city," Kesab commented. "Many rascals who come up the river, looking to make trouble."

Something about the loitering men made Dudley uneasy.

"We should have taken Mrs. Edwards straight to her brother's doorstep," he said, and wondered why he had not. That had been a mistake. He had been too eager to report his arrival, too eager to get away from Charlotte.

He rested his hand on the hilt of his sword and quickened his step.

In the western end of the city lay the suburb of Nawabganj. Unlike the native sector, the houses there stood on wide, tree-shaded lots. Charlotte's uncle's house was no exception, a large square bungalow with a central courtyard, its tall arched windows covered with slatted shutters. Behind it lay several outbuildings and servant's quarters.

Dudley and Kesab climbed to the veranda and approached the front door. Dudley pulled the bell rope, and a moment later, a thin and solemn native butler appeared and beckoned them inside. The butler wore a large wooden crucifix around his neck.

They waited in a narrow hall as the man disappeared through a door to their right. Dudley could hear voices, and soon the butler returned in company with a thin middle-aged Englishman dressed in an old linen frock coat. The Englishman had large eyes, and spectacles perched on the end of a long, proud nose. Dudley assumed this was Charlotte's uncle, the Reverend George Teecher.

"Mister Dudley!" he said. "Welcome! Welcome to Cawnpore, and welcome to my house. It is so unfortunate that you had to arrive in these circumstances."

"What circumstances are those, sir?" Dudley asked. "Is Mrs. Edwards all right?"

Reverend Teecher's eyebrows shot up in surprise.

"Oh, she is quite all right." He seemed to notice Kesab for the first time and gestured to his butler, saying, "Jaideo here can show your man to the servants' quarters out back. Will you, Jaideo?"

Dudley passed Kesab his second satchel, saying, "Thank you."

Teecher watched as the two Indians moved through to the courtyard, then turned to Dudley.

"All of the servants here, from the stablemaster to the maids, are converts to the true faith. When I embark on my mission into Oudh, I will be sorry to leave them."

"I see," Dudley said. "But what is this unfortunate circumstance you just mentioned, sir?"

"Ah, yes." Teecher led him to the doorway. "I am referring to the mutinies. But of course you haven't heard. You were with my sister and niece the entire time."

Dudley followed his host and found himself in a cluttered parlour. Paintings of horses, dogs, and Indian landscapes completely covered the walls. Mrs. Edwards was there, sitting near a window in a wingback chair. Charlotte was curled in a settee opposite.

"Mister Dudley has arrived," Teecher announced.

To Dudley's surprise, Mrs. Edwards's face twisted in anguished fury.

"Oh, horrible news, Ensign! Horrible news!"

"What news, Mrs. Edwards?" Dudley asked, his confusion mounting.

Reverend Teecher motioned him to a chair.

"I apologize profusely for this most shabby of greetings. Please try to make yourself comfortable. I will do my best to fill you in."

Dudley sat waiting as Teecher collected his thoughts. A moment later, the missionary began his extraordinary tale.

A general mutiny in the Bengal Army, feared by some and discounted by many, had come at last. The courts martial at Meerut, site of the most recent protests over the Enfield cartridge, had seen eighty-five members of the 3rd Native Light Cavalry sentenced to ten years of hard labour. Native officers had conducted the proceedings, but the divisional commander, Major-General Hewitt, had decided to make a public example of the convicted men. On May 9th the general had paraded the prisoners before their regiment. They had worn leg shackles, and their officers had ordered the buttons and insignia cut from their uniforms.

The punishment parade had been the spark for revolt. Indignant over the treatment their comrades had received, that night the sepoy regiments of the Meerut garrison had at last risen against their commanders. They had released the prisoners and then run riot, setting fire to houses and official buildings. They had also killed any European they could find, including women and children.

Dudley listened to the clergyman's story with stunned disbelief. An entire garrison rising in mutiny? It seemed so improbable, so outrageous.

"The most awful atrocities," Mrs. Edwards interjected. "Foul murders!"

"It was unfortunate," Reverend Teecher continued, "that the general decided to humiliate his already disgraced men. Insult upon injury, I suppose. Most unnecessary, I should think."

"Indeed," Dudley said, his throat thick.

There was more to the tale. The mutinous regiments had left Meerut and marched for Delhi, thirty-six miles away. Perhaps because of shock and disbelief, the European troops at Meerut had received no orders to pursue, an oversight that had sealed Delhi's fate. There had been no European troops stationed there at all, and when the rebels reached the city, its sepoy garrison joined them. Some of the British occupants had escaped, and a few young Company officers had succeeded in firing the gunpowder magazine; but many others had become the victims of a second massacre.

"So, Delhi has risen against us," the Reverend Teecher concluded. "The mutineers have found a figurehead to rally round. They have returned the aged Bahadur Shah, the last surviving heir to the Mogul Empire, to his ancestral throne. Some now fear that this will encourage other discontented princes to rise in rebellion."

"But what of Cawnpore?" Dudley asked. The Company maintained a large native garrison here. Three regiments of infantry—the 1st, 53rd, and 56th Bengal Native Infantry—lived in the cantonments alongside the 2nd Cavalry and a company of artillery. The sepoys outnumbered the few European troops ten-to-one.

"General Wheeler insists his men are loyal," Teecher said. "But this catastrophe at Delhi is only days old now. We shall have to wait and see."

"There is no question of our leaving, George," Mrs. Edwards insisted. "To abandon our dream before it is even realized? We are here to do the Lord's work, to open a new mission in Lucknow! Until then, there is also your English congregation and the Orphan's Relief fund to consider. We will not flee at the first sign of danger. Not when General Wheeler says it is safe."

"You are right, of course. Like Job, we must persevere." Reverend Teecher stared at the wall. "I find the situation difficult to comprehend. Why did this happen? Were we not diligent enough in pursuing our great and important task?"

Dudley remained silent. He noticed that Charlotte had pressed herself into the settee as if trying to hide. At her mother's brave declaration, she had covered her mouth with her hands and closed her eyes.

Supper that evening was a gloomy affair. Charlotte remained silent throughout, and for Dudley the enormity of the situation had begun to sink in. There had not just been a mutiny. War had suddenly come to this land. The usually warm light of the table candles seemed strange and lurid.

"You see, Ensign," Teecher was saying, "aside from my servants, I have as yet no native flock. I minister to a portion of the European population only, here in Nawabganj. But now that my dear sister Grace is here, I may begin my great service. Cawnpore will be the staging area for the advance of Christianity into the old kingdom of Oudh."

"You are a pioneer, then, sir," Dudley said, to be polite, for he did not agree with this man's work.

Teecher smiled. "You have found billets for your men?"

"I have," Dudley replied. "There is plenty of available space in the European barracks."

He did not add that this was due to the lack of non-native troops.

"Good, then. You must stay here with us." The missionary's smile broadened.

Dudley considered the offer. He did not wish to stay here, so far from his squad, but he had come as an escort to protect Charlotte and her mother. He had already made one mistake for the sake of his own feelings, and he would not make another. They might need him if there was to be trouble with the native garrison.

"That's very kind of you, sir," he said. "I accept your invitation."

"Good, then. I will have Jaideo ready the spare room for you. And I will have a courier take a message to your sergeant."

With the meal concluded, the ladies withdrew, and Teecher proceeded to keep his promises. Dudley wandered outside onto the front veranda alone. The evening sky was a deep velvet blue sprinkled with stars. It filled him with a profound sadness.

The door behind him opened, and there was the rustle of skirts. He turned to face a dark silhouette. He recognized Charlotte. She stood in silence.

"I thought you had retired for the night, Miss Edwards," he said. He tried to keep his tone light, but to his ears it sounded harsh.

Charlotte shook her head. "Mama has been sipping her 'medicine.' She is quite drunk."

"I see." He shifted from foot to foot. "Is there something I may do to help?"

"I want to leave," she whispered. "I don't want to stay here with all of these…black heathens surrounding us!"

"It will be all right," he said. Her fear astonished him. He had thought she would relish the prospect of danger. "This is not Delhi or Meerut."

"But what if they mutiny here as well?"

It could be disastrous, he thought but said, "We must put our faith in cooler heads, and in General Wheeler."

She moved to the edge of the veranda, arms hugging her shoulders, fingers clutching her sleeves. The air was filled with the whir of insects. Dudley searched for something to say.

"I am sorry if I have offended you, Charlotte," he said at length then sighed. Yes, that was true. He was sorry, a sorry fool.

"You have done nothing to offend me," she said, although there was anger in her voice. "My mother knows nothing of us. She believes you were my chaperone, by order of Colonel Willis. I would like for her to continue believing that to be so."

He nodded, but his anger was quick to rise.

"I did not ask for this mission, Charlotte. I did not do this to pursue you, though by your words and actions I had every right to do so. In Madras, you expressed a wish that I should come here with you, but now that I am here by pure chance, you have decided to shun my company. I believe that I understand your reasons, but that does not justify your behaviour."

Her hands had risen to her face, covering her mouth. When her shoulders began to quiver, his anger at once changed to remorse. That had been a bit much, perhaps.

"I am sorry, Charlotte," he said. "Perhaps you have a right to be angry. I have been confused myself. Please accept my apology."

"I could never marry a soldier," she suddenly cried, choking back a sob. "My father was a soldier."

"Yes, you told me. A friend of Colonel Willis's."

"He died when I was very young. Mother tried to raise me. I have not always been…agreeable to her. It is true that she has a fondness for her whisky, but she is strong in other ways. And worthy. I would do nothing to harm her!"

"I understand." He moved closer to her, hesitated, then took hold of her shoulders. She did not resist but fell against him.

"Can we not at least still be friends?" he said. "While I am here with you?"

She pulled away, breathing deeply.

"Of course we must be friends. Of course."

A weight lifted from his shoulders, and for a moment, the danger of mutiny was forgotten. He reached into his tunic, fingers fumbling for the inside breast pocket. At last he found what he sought, the little tin soldier, Wellington, bundled with its chain. He had brought it with him on the journey for luck. He held it out, letting the chain unravel, and pressed it into Charlotte's hand.

"Take this. It isn't much, but it will bring you luck. It brought me through the war with Russia."

Charlotte examined the tiny figure as it lay in her hand for a moment; then she looped the chain over her head.

"Thank you, William."

"You are welcome. Now let's go inside. The mosquitoes are becoming unmanageable."

He held out his arm, and she took it. Together, they entered the house.

CHAPTER 12

Cawnpore
May 1857

Dudley ate a breakfast of eggs, bacon, tea, jam, and hot *chupatties* before setting out to report to General Wheeler. As he made his way through the cantonments on foot, the morning parades were just finishing. Groups of sepoys sat on the ground in front of their huts, clustered about their *tulas*—their cooking places—preparing and eating their breakfasts. They laughed and chattered, not seeming at all like troops ready for rebellion.

In front of the general's headquarters, a sepoy sentry stood at ease before a wooden sentry box. At Dudley's approach, he snapped to attention and shouldered his musket. Dudley paused to study him. He wore the usual native uniform—sandals, a white cotton dhoti instead of trousers, an old-fashioned red coatee, standard accoutrements, and a plain round forage cap without visor or cover. A brass number 53 gleamed on the front of the cap. At the sepoy's side was not an Enfield but an 1842-pattern smooth-bore musket.

Dudley glanced back at the sepoys at breakfast. They might have been John Company troops and natives, but they were still British soldiers, trained in British arms and tactics. They knew all the British ways, all their tricks. Were they to turn against the Sirkar, they would make a formidable enemy.

He carried on into the headquarters building. Perhaps, he thought, the general could reassure him that this station was secure.

General Sir Hugh Massey Wheeler was a slight man of sixty-seven, his face kind and his voice touched with a hint of Irish lilt. He did not appear irritated in the least at meeting with this mere ensign and was calm and composed as he read Dudley's orders.

"So, you have brought the sister and niece of our Reverend Teecher," he said. "Members of the Propagation Society, here to spread the gospels."

Dudley thought he sensed a hint of disapproval in the general's tone and was unconvinced when the man added, "I look forward to meeting them. I have had Mister Teecher to supper on several occasions. Most unfortunate timing, bringing his relations from Madras now, but I suppose it can't be helped."

"Will this delay their expedition into Oudh, sir?" Dudley asked.

"I believe it must, to err on the side of prudence. The same goes for your return to Madras, Ensign. There has been trouble in some of the towns you passed through since. Going back to Calcutta may not be safe."

This was more alarming news.

"There have been further mutinies, sir?"

"Small incidents only," Wheeler insisted, "and a few local *badmashes* taking advantage of the situation. It will remain quite safe here. You must tell your charges that they may rest assured Cawnpore is the most secure station in the valley. I know my men, and they know me. They will

97

remain loyal. The rebels in Delhi will be contained soon, and I have asked Lord Canning in Calcutta for reinforcements. European troops. I am certain he will be as good as his word."

Dudley nodded, wanting to believe this man. But others had insisted no mutiny would come at all, including Lieutenant-Colonel Willis; and they had all been wrong.

"However, one can't be too careful," Wheeler continued. "I have given orders to fortify part of the European barracks. Some of my officers have suggested that, in the event of an uprising, we should make a defensive stand in the powder magazine."

The main magazine was a bomb-proof stone building with a sturdy outer wall.

"Unfortunately, that would mean relieving the sepoy guards there, and they may take that as a sign of disloyalty on our part. We have made too many mistakes already. The regiments in revolt now were unduly provoked by their commanders. I shall make no similar mistake."

Dudley's confidence had not improved when he left the office and made his way to Colour-Sergeant O'Ryan's barracks. There the red-haired Irishman fed his concern with a bleak assessment of the situation.

"This city is a powder keg, sir," he said.

They stood on the edge of the dusty maidan. A *naik* was taking a squad of sepoys through a series of bayonet drills, shouting his commands in English. Like the sentry, the sepoys all wore British red coats. Dudley wondered how long that would continue.

O'Ryan jutted a thumb at the squad at drill.

"None too pleased to see us, sir. And not very keen to become our friends, neither."

"General Wheeler insists his men are staunch," Dudley offered. "And they seemed in high spirits this morning."

"Not to contradict the general, sir, but they don't look staunch to me. Shot us plenty o' dirty looks. I think it would be in our interest to turn back for Calcutta, if ye don't mind me sayin' so."

Dudley sighed. His position here had become very awkward. Willis had told him to stay for his amusement, Wheeler for his safety. At the same time, although he had brought Mrs. Edwards and Charlotte here without mishap, their safety was still his concern.

"You know I trust your judgement, Colour. But if there is to be trouble, we can't abandon this station so quickly, running off to save our own hides. There are so few Queen's troops here. We must do our duty, and our duty is here."

O'Ryan pushed back his covered cap and scratched his freckled scalp.

"Aye. My apologies, Mister Dudley. I forgot about the wee Miss."

Dudley narrowed his eyes, but he could see by the Irishman's expression he had meant no disrespect. Like Barker, O'Ryan had once been a friend, a fellow sergeant until Dudley's commission had created an unbridgeable gulf.

O'Ryan glared at the sepoy squad.

"And if they do give us trouble," he added, "they'll bloody regret it!"

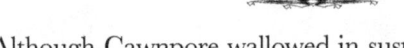

Although Cawnpore wallowed in suspense, its citizens did their best to carry on as usual. Trade and traffic continued on the roads and river, and the sepoys maintained the daily routine of garrison troops.

Like everyone else, Dudley tried to pretend all was well and normal. He spent his hours in mundane activities, guesting with the officers of the garrison, composing a long letter home, even making further notes for his memoir. He also volunteered his squad to help with the construction of General Wheeler's fortified barracks.

The entrenchment was east of the city, at the far end of the European section of the cantonments and a mile back from the river. It did little to inspire Dudley's confidence when he marched his squad through the gap that served as a gate. The surrounding ground was open maidan with a few clumps of trees that would offer an enemy cover. The fortification was a rectangular compound enclosing two new but completed barrack buildings, the larger with a thatched roof, the smaller with pukka shingles.

Between the buildings sat a pukka well with a wooden *chabutra*, or seating platform. Outside the compound stood several unfinished barracks, bamboo scaffolding still leaning against their bare, unplastered brick walls. Dudley recognized the unfinished structures as the same buildings he had seen from his *ghari* upon arriving in Cawnpore. They too would offer an enemy cover.

With his squad waiting in their files, Dudley approached the first two officers in sight. One was a captain of infantry dressed in a covered forage cap and a plain tunic the colour of ash. Dudley assumed the man was a member of the Cornwall Regiment, Her Majesty's 32nd, which had served in India for more than a decade. Most of that regiment was in Lucknow, but two companies, many of them invalids, were here in Cawnpore.

Dudley saluted, saying, "Good morning, sir. I wonder if you could direct me to the person in charge?"

The captain's round face was tanned almost as dark as a native's.

"I would," he said, "though damned if I know who that is. I'm here under orders from my colonel, who I must assume is under orders from General Wheeler. But I'm the senior man here, so far." He extended his hand. "Captain Morrow, Thirty-second."

Dudley shook the hand. "William Dudley, Royal Hampshire Fusiliers."

The second officer present was a lieutenant of the Bengal Artillery, Lieutenant Charles Delacourt. Delacourt wore a blue tunic and a bullet-shaped sun helmet. He, too, shook Dudley's hand, and Dudley pointed to where his squad stood easy.

"I came to Cawnpore as an escort to some civilian travellers," he explained. "Now I feel I should stay and help out however I can. Whatever you need done here, sir, we are at your service."

"Damned fine of you, Dudley," Morrow replied. "We need whatever scrap of help we can lay our hands on." Then he muttered, "Whole thing is a bloody shambles."

Soon, O'Ryan's men had stripped off their tunics and started in on a new section of trench and parapet, side-by-side with men of Morrow's regiment. So far, the completed sections of trench were only about two feet deep, with the parapet adding another five feet. The earth was dry and crumbling, making it difficult if not impossible to raise the parapet higher.

Dudley examined the works, kicking at the loose soil. He did not think it would give much protection from artillery fire. He also noted the number of nearby houses that offered positions overlooking the entire entrenchment.

"Riflemen in those houses could easily shoot over this wall," he said to O'Ryan. "And the flat maidan offers an excellent field of fire. An enemy could put cannon in those topes."

The colour-sergeant shook his head. "I agree, sir; it's untenable. We should try to defend the powder magazine. There's plenty of room there, a good stone wall, and positions for guns. This is no place to make a stand."

"Hopefully, we won't have to," Dudley said.

"We'll have to build magazines," O'Ryan commented, as if he had not heard, "and bring in plenty of provisions."

———✦———

The work on the entrenchment continued. Although rumours of an imminent revolt persisted, the days passed without incident. Dudley's squad concentrated on the work and stayed away from the sepoys. O'Ryan even asked permission to move the men out of their barrack and pitch their tents close to the fortified area. He believed the rumours, feared the increasing tension in the city, and expected a mutiny any day.

Dudley agreed to the move. Mutiny was certainly possible under these circumstances, but he still thought it could be avoided. He said as much to Charlotte and her mother, trying to reassure them that the situation was under control.

"We will put our trust in God," Mrs. Edwards insisted, "and in British reason."

Charlotte was still fearful, had not set foot outside the house since their arrival. Dudley suggested that she would feel better if she ventured out and saw firsthand that all was business as usual. He had borrowed a pair of horses from the 32nd and asked her to accompany him. Mrs. Edwards urged her to accept, and to Dudley's delight, she did.

Their route took them southeast along the riverbank. The sky was a heated blue, a few wisps of cloud hanging on the northern horizon. After a few miles, they halted in a grove of tamarinds, the slender leaves like green feathers. Charlotte dismounted and walked towards the sparkling river. Dudley let the horses graze for bits of dry grass and followed her.

"You are trying to make me feel better," she said, "but I am not blind, William. Many people are trying to get out of the city. Some have tried to hire small boats to escape by river, but the heathen boatmen tell them the river is too shallow." Her exquisite face twisted in a sneer, an expression Dudley had never seen it wear. "The river does not look too shallow to me!"

"There are shallows and sand bars farther down," he explained. Even here, he thought, the river looked unnavigable. The banks sloped down to the water like the sides of a clay pot, brown and smooth.

"And they also say there are too many bandits on the road," Charlotte went on. "No one is able to escape that way, either."

"How do you know this?" Dudley asked. "Has your mother considered leaving after all?"

Charlotte pouted, her lower lip quivering.

"No, she still stubbornly insists upon remaining here. Against all the indications! Something horrible is going to happen, I know it." She turned to him, eyes blazing. "Your men are still here, William. They could defend me against bandits on the road!"

Dudley could understand her desire to leave, but it astonished him that she would contemplate abandoning her family.

"Are you suggesting that we take you out of Cawnpore alone? Leave your mother and your uncle?"

She said nothing for a moment, then turned back to the river.

"No, of course not. I wish you could talk some sense into her, that's all."

Dudley agreed that Charlotte's point was valid, but the decision had already been made. Mrs. Edwards was resolved to stay, and as he had explained to O'Ryan, his duty was here. He could have made an argument that he needed to return to his regiment, but his own conscience would not allow him to give that any serious consideration.

"There's little point in my leaving," he said at length. "I'm sorry, Charlotte, but General Wheeler may need my men. He expects reinforcement from Calcutta if the sepoys mutiny, so he will only have to hold out for a few days. My thirteen men could make a difference in such a case. I'm a soldier, Charlotte. I must do my duty. Part of that duty is to keep you safe, but it is to keep others safe as well."

"I suppose you must play the hero," she said, but there was a hint of derision in her words, where once there had been admiration.

"I will protect you and your family, Charlotte," he told her. "I will do my best in this. You have my solemn promise."

She nodded but did not smile. He hoped that she understood.

She began walking back toward the horses.

"Take me back, please, William. I have had quite enough of this wild open country."

CHAPTER 13

Madras
May 1857

Sergeant Barker awoke to a blinding light in his eyes and a thundering voice in his ears. When he emerged from the fog of sleep, he saw that the shouting came from Lieutenant Morris. Morris stood just inside the door to Barker's quarters and was speaking in a loud but normal voice. The blinding light was just the yellow flame from a lantern in the lieutenant's hand.

"Sergeant Barker, Sergeant Bell," Morris was repeating. "We have to assemble on parade at once!"

Barker threw back his mosquito net and swung himself out of bed.

"What's up, sir?"

An eager excitement lit the young officer's face.

"It's happened, Sergeant! The Bengal sepoys have mutinied! They murdered their English officers and made off for Delhi. And the entire Ganges valley is in flames!"

Morris disappeared, and Barker snatched off his nightcap. He could hear bugles now, calling for assembly.

"What did the little blighter say?" Sergeant Bell grumbled from his bunk. He was a rough and vulgar man but a stout soldier, in Barker's estimate.

"He said rise and shine, Oliver," Barker said, reaching for a clean shirt.

Within ten minutes, Barker and Bell had dressed in their white frocks and were running for the parade. Men were streaming from the barracks and forming in line by company. Barker saw Private Geary emerge from his barrack room with his rifle in one hand and Lazzy's lead in the other. Barker grinned at the sight of the little dog scurrying along with the men. Geary had already become a steadier soldier since taking on care of the beagle. Every day he brought the creature to Barker's quarters to show off some new trick.

The dog bayed at the sound of the bugles, as if anticipating a fox hunt.

With O'Ryan absent, Barker was senior NCO in No. 3 Company and took his place on the right of the rear rank behind Captain Reed. Sergeant-Major Maclaren dressed the ranks then took post in the rear of the assembled companies, his cane under his arm. In front of the regiment stood the adjutant, while behind him Lieutenant-Colonel Willis sat on his horse. That day's quarter guard had fallen out and formed near the colonel, the nine members of the detachment holding lit torches.

The adjutant took the roll call, shouting out the name of every man not on the sick-and-invalid list or on detached duties. Several men were absent, and their names would go on report for punishment.

When the roll was complete, the adjutant faced about, saluted, and made his report to the colonel.

"Stand them easy, Sergeant-Major," Willis commanded.

"Sir!" Maclaren barked then shouted, "Battalion, stand at...ease!"

Every man bent his arms at the elbows, bringing his right hand up to his chest, palm down, and his left hand to his waist, palm up. After a beat, every man brought his right hand down to strike his left, making a resounding clap. At the same time, each man dropped his right foot back six inches, bent his left knee, and let his now-folded hands hang just below his waist. When Maclaren followed up the command by shouting, "Stand easy," the men of the battalion relaxed. They scratched, stretched, or leaned on their rifles but kept silent.

Willis stretched his legs to stand in his stirrups.

"Men of the Royal Hants! A great task awaits you! Mutiny, foul and murderous, has erupted in the north!"

He went on to describe the events at Meerut and Delhi, emphasizing the cruel slaughter of women and children. Barker listened with sinking spirits as the colonel then described other mutinies in Oudh, at Bareilly, Aligarh, and Ferozepore. There had even been a small rising in the Bombay Army. Garrison commanders had disarmed Native regiments at Agra, Lahore, Mardan, and Peshawar. There had been no mutiny among the Madras sepoys.

"The mutiny is general," Willis said. "No native regiment in the Bengal Army can be trusted."

The Royal Hants would embark for the north that afternoon. Most of the regiment would go to help recapture Delhi, but a small detachment would proceed to Calcutta.

Willis concluded his speech with the usual, "I know that every man will do his duty."

The battalion dismissed by company. The men would have an early breakfast and begin packing.

The companies broke off, and Barker made his way back to his bungalow.

"Sergeant Barker!" someone shouted behind him, and he turned to see a stern Captain Reed approaching with Lieutenant Morris. Morris still carried his lantern.

"Sir!" Barker said, coming to attention and saluting, his right hand flat against his right eyebrow.

Reed returned the salute.

"As you were, Sergeant. You are to report to my quarters in half an hour to receive orders."

"Yes, sir."

Reed moved off, but Morris stood there grinning.

"It's to be war, Sergeant! Ain't it thrilling?"

"Aye, sir," Barker said sadly. "I suppose to some. But a war against our own men, sir."

"Oh, stuff. John Company may trust sepoys to guard its trade, but they aren't like us, Sergeant. We'll have to teach them a lesson."

Barker nodded. He had little more than contempt for officers like Morris. Untried, naïve and stupid, they needed good sergeants to undo the damage they wrought.

"Aye, sir. I'm sure some lessons will be learned in the next few months."

"That's the spirit." Morris suddenly grew thoughtful. "I do hope William Dudley is getting on all right. Though there was no news of mutiny in Cawnpore."

Barker gritted his teeth. He had not thought of that, but Mister Dudley and O'Ryan both were stuck in the middle of what was now hostile country.

"Let's pray there won't be, sir."

"Yes." Morris seemed deflated. "Well, I must be off. Carry on, Sergeant Barker."

Barker hurried to the sergeants' mess. By the time he had consumed three lamb chops and several *chupatties*, it was already time to report to Captain Reed.

Reed was fussing with his native batman, trying to buckle on his sword belt, when Barker entered his room.

"Ah, Sergeant," he said with his usual peevish tone, "I have the orders for No. 3 Company." He nodded towards a folded piece of paper sitting on a side table. "We are to embark for Calcutta with the Grenadier Company. Captain Norcott will command the detachment. We must be at the docks by two in the afternoon. Our steamer is the *Zenobia* and leaves at three."

"I'll see the boys are formed and ready by one, sir," Barker said.

Reed straightened his belt.

"See that you do, Sergeant. See that you do."

Barker made his way to the barracks. He would have to make sure the lads packed light.

CHAPTER 14

Cawnpore
May 1857

Dudley returned to his room after supper, expecting to find the lamps lit and Kesab waiting, as on every night. Instead, he found the room dark and empty. He lit a lamp himself and removed his tunic, wondering what had caused the delay. He assumed Kesab would arrive soon. He waited.

After fifteen minutes, he went out to the back of the house to the servants' quarters. He knocked on the door to the room Kesab occupied, but there was no reply. Undoing the latch, he pushed the door open. There was no one in the room.

He returned to the house and found Teecher's butler in the process of snuffing the lamps in the parlour.

"Jaideo," Dudley said, "have you seen Kesab, my servant?"

"No, sahib," the butler replied. "I am sorry, but I have not seen him since this morning."

A light still burned in the Reverend Teecher's study, an orange sliver at the base of the door. Dudley knocked, and heard Teecher say, "Come in!"

Teecher sat with his window open, reading his Bible. He shook his head when Dudley asked after Kesab.

"Your great hulking manservant? No, I'm afraid not." A moth fluttered into the light of the lamp, hovering above the chimney. Teecher swatted at it, crying, "I must get these window screens repaired!"

Dudley bade the reverend goodnight and returned to his room. He settled onto his rope mattress with growing unease, trying to formulate an explanation for Kesab's absence. He remembered the man had friends amongst the Bengal sepoys, that he was also a native of the province of Oudh and his home was doubtless somewhere across the river. Were mutiny imminent, he might have run off to join his old comrades.

Or he could be trying to dissuade them, Dudley realized. Perhaps they were holding him against his will. Or perhaps he had urgent personal business somewhere. There was no way of knowing.

He turned down the lamp and tried to sleep. His mind drifted back over the events of the day, searching for a clue to explain Kesab's behaviour. The old sepoy had been here in the morning, as on every morning, to help Dudley shave and dress. He had said and done nothing out of the ordinary. Dudley had then eaten a quick breakfast and left for the entrenchment.

As he passed the sepoy lines, he saw nothing to indicate trouble. A work party was busy giving one of the public buildings a coat of whitewash. A *havildar* took the relief sentries from post to post. Nothing unusual, although he later wondered why he had expected unusual activity to precede mutiny. Maybe there would be no warning at all.

In the fortified entrenchment, he watched a group of gunners from Lieutenant Dalacourt's battery position three 9-pounders in a section of the perimeter. The entire compound was in a flurry of activity. Men of the 32nd Regiment were removing part of the thatch roof of the larger barracks to replace it with pukka tiles. Other detachments were throwing up earth over the new underground powder magazines. The men worked in their shirt sleeves, trouser braces dangling.

Captain Morrow and Lieutenant Delacourt stood in the rear of the 9-pounder battery. Dudley made his way toward them.

"Good morning," he greeted them, examining the guns. They stood in a gap in the trench. The trench stopped on their right and continued on their left, leaving them no protection. "Thing is rather exposed, isn't it, sir?"

Lieutenant Delacourt was smoking a cheroot; he exhaled a casual jet of smoke and said, "We shall be all right here, I think, in the event of an emergency. My men are stout fellows. Good enough to hold for a week or two before reinforcements arrive."

"We can't appear to be in a panic, Dudley," Morrow added. "If the sepoys think we expect them to mutiny, and that we fear them, that may just push them over the edge."

"The very fact we have dug this entrenchment, sir," Dudley replied, "means that we expect them to mutiny."

He looked at the two barrack buildings and knew Delacourt was wrong, that they would not be all right there. The buildings were large, with flat roofs and rows of rectangular windows in all four sides. There were five barrack rooms in each building, each designed to house twenty men. The walls were of ordinary brick. Round shot would go through those walls, into those crowded rooms, like musket balls through paper.

It was one thing not to panic, Dudley thought, but quite another to be so unprepared.

Now, he shifted on his rope bed, staring at the gray shadow of his mosquito net, and suddenly he understood just how unprepared they were. He thought of the mistakes in the Crimea. The government and army were making similar mistakes here.

The mutinies and fall of Delhi were the result of mistakes. In one sense, General Wheeler was right—the sepoys had responded to provocation. Dudley had seen Indians mistreated, had seen his fellow officers and people like Mrs. Edwards display a callous disregard for native traditions.

He did not dislike Mrs. Edwards, and even considered her a strong woman of firm convictions. But in some ways she was blind, just as others had been blind.

He remembered Lieutenant-Colonel Willis, one evening in the mess, saying, "India's not like it used to be." A distance had developed, the colonel had lamented, between the British and the natives. They no longer behaved like partners in a common endeavour but more and more like master and servant.

Master and servant, like Dudley and Kesab. The master was a man from a foreign land, with different customs and a different religion. Now the servant was in revolt.

With these thoughts, he drifted into a fitful sleep.

He awoke with a start. Sitting up, he brushed aside the mosquito net, holding his breath to listen. He heard a thump, then the voice of Mrs. Edwards. Another voice responded, raised in panic. Charlotte.

He climbed out of bed in the darkness, stumbling to the shelf where his clothes lay folded in a neat stack. He threw on stockings, shirt, trousers, and shoes then hurried out to the front hall to see what was the matter.

The Reverend Teecher was just coming in through the front door. As the door swung shut behind him, Dudley caught a glimpse of movement in the streets, people and vehicles rushing along.

"What's happening?" he asked.

"Come into the front parlour," Teecher said.

Dudley followed him into the room. Jaideo was there, and Charlotte, immodest in her nightgown with her hair hanging loose. Mrs. Edwards sat in a chair with a fowling gun across her knees. A silver powder flask lay on the table beside her.

The Reverend Teecher rubbed his hands together.

"A fellow in the street said that there are fires burning in the sepoy lines. Rumours are flying about again. People are fleeing to your fortifications in the European barracks."

"We must go at once, Uncle!" Charlotte cried, voice trembling. She squatted in her chair, seeming to sink into herself. "We aren't safe here."

"But there is no confirmation of mutiny?" Dudley asked.

"All I have seen is panic in the streets," Teecher replied, "and I have been up all night. I did not leave my study."

"So, we don't know what is happening." Dudley glanced at a clock on the shelf that read five o'clock.

"How much better protection than this house do the barracks offer?" Mrs. Edwards asked. She was priming both barrels of her gun with percussion caps.

"Not very much," Dudley admitted. "But there are armed men there, while there are plenty of *badmashes* in the city who will take advantage of any trouble. If you are caught here you will be surrounded."

Teecher rubbed his chin.

"We should go as a precaution. We mustn't be caught here. We will take the buggy. Jaideo, will you prepare it?"

The butler bowed and left the room. Mrs. Edwards stood, the shotgun cradled under her arm.

"Charlotte, you will get properly dressed. I will pack a few things."

"What of the house servants?" Dudley asked. "Will any of them be coming with us?"

Mrs. Edwards snorted. "It is the whites who are in danger, Ensign! The servants will be all right here."

Twenty minutes later, Teecher, Mrs. Edwards, and Charlotte had crowded into the little pony-drawn buggy. Dudley followed on his borrowed horse as they started for the canal. Carriages, bullock carts, and people on foot thronged the streets, all moving in the same direction—towards the entrenchment.

They found the fortifications in a state of chaos, with vehicles of all descriptions jammed together outside the perimeter. A mob of frightened citizens representing every colour, profession and sect had crowded into the compound. Dudley saw Company employees, clerks, writers, and tradesmen, all with their families. Mothers carried infants, while children clung to their ayahs. To his dismay, he even saw officers from the native regiments.

Bloody fools, he thought, abandoning their men, displaying their lack of faith. Did they not realize that betrayal bred betrayal?

Soldiers from the 32nd stood at the parapet, dressed in khaki shell jackets and leaning on their smoothbore muskets. The artillerymen had loaded the 9-pounders and stood at their numbers. Dudley noticed the gunners still wore their nightcaps, although they had found time to don their bayonet belts and sling their carbines over their shoulders. There were no friction primers for the guns, so linstocks wrapped in slow match burned next to the limbers.

"Oh, the barracks will be crowded!" Teecher exclaimed. "We can't stay here."

Dudley wanted to disagree, to argue that this was safer than the house, but of that he was uncertain. Here was the panic Captain Morrow had warned against. The scene before them was one of weakness, and the sepoys respected only strength.

"I'll find my squad," he said. "We came here as an escort, to protect you. We will serve as a guard on your house. We will only come back here if it is absolutely necessary."

Teecher nodded. "I would appreciate that, Ensign. Thank you."

"Do you mean we're going back?" Charlotte cried.

Mrs. Edwards's face showed her disgust.

"I think it's for the best, my dear. What an utter shambles! Where is General Wheeler?"

Dudley spurred his horse forward, guiding it through the mob. Inside the entrenchment, he dismounted next to the well and tied the horse's reins to the winch. He went in search of O'Ryan, at last finding him in one of the barrack rooms. The Irishman was attempting to assign space to the new arrivals.

"These buildings were built to hold a hundred men, sir," the colour-sergeant said when he saw Dudley, "not three hundred, and most of 'em civilians accustomed to their luxuries."

Dudley saw a beautiful young woman, perhaps an officer's wife, sitting at a trestle table. Her face was pale with dread, eyes wide and staring. A baby cried, and an ayah tried to comfort it. The room was foul with the close air and stench of fear and mingled sweat. The open windows did little to improve the atmosphere, instead letting in the acrid scent of the slow matches, the scent of war.

"We're getting out of here, Colour-Sergeant," Dudley said. "Round up the lads."

"Amen to that, sir," O'Ryan replied.

Dudley accompanied the squad back to the city, riding as they marched. The buggy went ahead of them. As they passed near the sepoy lines, all seemed quiet. There was no sign of any fires.

With the rising sun, the city became as quiet as a tomb. By noon, there had been no mutiny. Dudley's men waited with loaded rifles, some at the windows in Teecher's house and two positioned in the back garden. Still no enemy showed itself.

After a quick lunch, Dudley decided there must have been no foundation for the panic.

"I want to go out," he announced. "Mister Teecher, will you accompany me?"

The buggy again bounced along the dirt streets. To their relief, Dudley and Teecher found normal traffic and saw that the merchants in the bazaars were opening their stalls again. The crisis seemed to have passed.

Near the Government Treasury, they at last found a column of native soldiers, although these were not sepoys. Riding at the head of the column was a short, plump man with a dainty pointed moustache. The man was richly dressed in a silk tunic, with a tiara of diamonds and pearls on his turban and a jewelled sword hanging at his side. Behind him followed a squadron of lancers in bright native dress and a company of infantry carrying ancient matchlocks and blunderbusses.

"Lord above," Teecher said as the incredible procession went by. "That is the Nana Sahib."

"Who is the Nana Sahib?" Dudley asked.

"He is the Maharajah of Bithoor," the missionary explained. "The rightful heir of the Mahrattas."

"Ah, yes," Dudley said, nodding.

The Mahrattas had been a strong and warlike people who had ruled much of northern India after the Mogul Empire's collapse. The British, under Sir Arthur Wellesley, the future Duke of Wellington, had begun the destruction of Mahratta power at the battle of Assaye in 1803.

"His title is a courtesy only, I'm afraid," Teecher continued. "British authorities in Calcutta don't recognize it. Yet he has professed support for the British cause."

The Nana's procession steered for the Treasury. The British sentries at the door presented arms, and then General Wheeler himself came out of the building to meet the little nobleman.

"I think by this we can rest easy today," Teecher said. He wiped his brow with a handkerchief. "I must go to my church, sound the bells. A prayer of thanks may be in order."

"Yes," Dudley agreed. "Perhaps a bit of prayer will do us some good."

He did not think they could rest easy. The Nana's appearance did not make him feel any more secure; it had only deepened his concern. It was these dispossessed princes who had everything to gain from a rebellion.

They turned the pony around and made their way back to the house.

Dudley bent over the table in his room, writing a letter to his uncle and aunt by candlelight. His watch lay next to him, its face proclaiming the early hour. He had been up all night with O'Ryan for the third day in a row, sitting on the roof and watching for signs of trouble.

Things had been quiet for a week, ever since the Nana Sahib's arrival, although most of those inhabitants loyal to the British had remained huddled in crowded quarters at the entrenchment. Reverend Teecher and his household were among the few who had kept to their homes. General Wheeler was another, along with a small number of Company officials.

"This anxiety has been a terrible burden on us all," Dudley wrote.

> Day after day we wonder, and yet I feel that
> something must happen. Several times the
> shops have been closed, only to reopen
> later. It is almost as if we hope there will
> be a mutiny, to ease this tension. We take
> turns sitting on the roof, waiting for a clue
> that will tell us it is time to flee to the en-
> trenchment. Colour-Sergeant O'Ryan has
> the watch now, as I write.

There was a tapping on his door. He stood and pulled it open. O'Ryan was in the hallway, as if summoned by Dudley's pen.

"Something to report, Colour?"

"There's fires and noise, sir," O'Ryan explained, "in the direction of the Treasury, right here in Nawabganj. Sowars riding about. It's the Second Cavalry, sir."

Dudley rose from his chair.

"Do you know for certain what's happening?"

"Of course not, sir," O'Ryan said, his eyes sunken with fatigue and worry. "I don't know. But I feel it. The storm's about to break."

"You feel it?" Dudley repeated, even though he knew O'Ryan would not exaggerate.

"Yes, sir. The boys are all primed and loaded. Much as I hate the place, sir, I think it'd be best if we got the wee Miss and the others to the barracks. Ye know as well as I that we can't defend this house if we're surrounded."

Dudley sighed and scratched his hands through his hair. He still did not like the thought of returning to the entrenchment, but there *was* strength in numbers. If it was another false alarm, they could always come back here.

He moved to the shelf on the wall, took down his sword and laid it on the bed. Then he began to pack one of his satchels.

"Get them ready, if you would, Colour."

O'Ryan nodded. "Aye, sir."

The colour-sergeant moved off. Dudley finished packing then went out into the hall. Charlotte was there, face white as bleached bone. Mrs. Edwards stood clutching her fowling piece.

"George and Jaideo have gone to get the buggy ready," she said.

O'Ryan appeared in the front doorway.

"Streets are clear, sir. I took the liberty of ordering one of your horses saddled. But we'd better hurry."

As Dudley nodded, from a distance came a sudden popping sound. He felt a chill flutter up his neck and along his scalp. The sound was musket fire.

The others listened in silence. Amid the musketry, they could hear shouting.

"Dear God," Dudley said, "it's no false alarm. We'd best go now."

They filed outside. A fierce red glow coloured the sky in the direction of the Treasury, only a short walk away. The sounds of musket fire and raised voices emanated from the same vicinity.

Soon the buggy and horse were ready, and they all mounted. Within minutes, the buggy was wheeling up the Street of Silver towards the canal with Dudley riding behind it. The squad double-marched on either side.

When they passed near the sepoy lines, they could hear drums and bugles.

"Sounds like any early morning parade, sir," O'Ryan called.

"Maybe it's just the cavalry," Dudley suggested.

When they reached the entrenchment, the depth of his relief surprised him. The men of the 32nd were again lining the parapet, muskets ready, and Lieutenant Delacourt stood with his guns. There seemed to be much less panic than before, although Dudley found it disconcerting to see General Wheeler sitting on his horse just outside the low earthen wall. Standing below Wheeler's horse was Colonel Ewart of the 1st Native Infantry, one of the officers Dudley had met in the mess. Ewart's uniform was dishevelled, his cap missing.

"I spoke to them in Hindustani, sir," Ewart said, voice and eyes hollow, broken. "I pleaded with them not to take part in such wickedness. But they've joined the rebels, sir. Their last honourable act was to let myself and the other white officers go unharmed."

"I pray we shall still be spared the fate of Meerut and Delhi," Wheeler said.

"The other native infantry regiments have not joined in the mutiny, but they may...they may." Ewart began to sob and covered his face with his hands. "My poor regiment," he managed to croak, "lost to me...lost..."

So, Dudley thought, at least one infantry regiment had mutinied.

He beckoned to O'Ryan. When the colour-sergeant approached, Dudley leaned close to him.

"Get Reverend Teecher and the ladies settled, Colour-Sergeant. I'm going to stay here, near the general."

O'Ryan saluted then gave Dudley a nod. Behind him, the Reverend Teecher was wheeling the buggy into the entrenchment, entering through the gap made for the guns. O'Ryan advanced on the buggy as his men took positions along the wall.

Dudley rode towards Delacourt. The artillery officer had ordered three of his guns limbered. Drivers were bringing the horse teams.

"Where are you going?" Dudley asked.

Delacourt peered out from under the rim of his helmet.

"Who's that? Ah, Mister Dudley. General's orders. We're to advance the battery to the sepoy lines. They're forming up over there. One regiment has already gone off with the rebels. We don't know what the others will do."

With the teams ready, the limbered guns rattled towards the road, trace chains and harness jangling. General Wheeler, a pair of aides trailing him, followed. Dudley spurred after them.

The sun was a brilliant arc on the horizon when the guns neared the river. In the amber light, he could see long lines of infantry formed on the parade. The 53rd and 56th Native Infantry stood in ranks as if this were any other day, their officers and NCOs in position.

The guns halted within five hundred yards of the formed regiments and Delacourt shouted, "Action front!" The gun crews unlimbered their cannon, spinning the muzzles so they pointed at the sepoys.

Dudley reined in next to Delacourt and demanded, "What are you doing? Those men are still loyal!"

Delacourt stiffened at Dudley's tone.

"General's orders, and none of your business."

Dudley knew he did not have a right to question another officer under orders, but Delacourt's tone and the absurdity of the situation were too much for him.

"It *is* my business, damn you! Why don't you just order those regiments to mutiny and have done with it?"

Delacourt turned his back and shouted at his men, "Load with round shot!"

On the parade, commands rang out as the regiments dismissed for breakfast. The sun was climbing, the sky changing from amber to a searing blue. General Wheeler sat his horse apart from the battery, watching the sepoys through his field glasses. Far away, the popping of musketry continued. A column of black smoke rose into the sky from the Treasury.

The sepoys were squatting on the ground in front of their row of huts, readying their cooking fires, pots and kettles. A few stared at the guns, at the black muzzles facing them.

The gunners loaded the field pieces; General Wheeler waited. Dudley wiped sweat from his eye and glanced at Delacourt. The artillery officer was ignoring him.

At last there was a stirring amongst the sepoys. Wheeler again raised his field glasses, and Delacourt raised a small telescope. Dudley wished he had not left his spyglass in his quarters at Madras. He strained to see what was happening.

A few sepoys appeared to be taking up their arms. Small clumps of men drifted away from the huts, others forming in line or groups of fours and marching away.

"The Fifty-sixth are going," General Wheeler cried. "They're going to join in the mutiny."

Within a few minutes, only the 53rd remained in front of the huts. Wheeler rode over to Lieutenant Delacourt. The old Irishman's face was red with fury and mortification.

"Prepare to fire, Lieutenant!" he said. "I want to teach the Fifty-third that we mean business. Just to frighten them. I don't wish to see any casualties."

Delacourt saluted. "Yes, sir!"

Dudley turned away in disgust. It was not his place to tell the general what to do, to tell him that this was folly. He remained silent.

"Number-one gun," Delacourt shouted, "fire!"

"Fire!" a corporal repeated, and the 9-pounder on the right of the battery barked, jetting a long stream of smoke and flame. The gun leapt back on its trail. Dudley saw the dark iron ball as it hurtled towards the sepoy position.

The native soldiers had heard the report, but they made no move. They stood, perhaps in disbelief, as the ball struck the earth, gouting a great pillar of dust, and carried past them. Then the second gun fired, with the same result.

When the third gun fired, the sepoys scattered.

Wheeler slumped in his saddle. "I believe we shall be safe," he said. "I believe they will make for Delhi."

Dudley studied the general for a few minutes then turned his horse and began trotting back to the entrenchment. The Cawnpore mutiny had begun at last.

CHAPTER 15

Cawnpore
June 1857

Dudley stood on the low parapet to watch the looting and burning of Cawnpore.

So far, the rebels had ignored the entrenchment, preferring to plunder the city. Flames and dense columns of black smoke rose beyond the canal, and he realized he and his companions would not have been safe in Teecher's house. For all its inadequacy, he did not like to imagine what must have happened to the Europeans who had not sought shelter here in the little fortification.

The mutineers had not marched for Delhi as General Wheeler had assumed. Although a small group had begun to move in that direction, they had soon turned back. Since then, the rebel ranks had swelled as local landholders came in from the surrounding districts, bringing their personal guards. The land was in revolt, and now Wheeler faced several thousand hostile men under arms.

Dudley judged the number in the entrenchment to be just over nine hundred, about half women and children who had crowded into the barracks for shelter. Most of the men remained outside, positioned along the parapet and at the gun batteries. In addition to Dudley's squad were the men of the 32nd, a few invalids of Her Majesty's 84th Regiment, and almost a company's worth of officers from the rebellious sepoy regiments. About a hundred male civilians were also present, and a few sepoys who had remained loyal.

"At least we are well armed," he muttered to Captain Morrow.

Every man capable of fighting had ten loaded muskets, which rested in batches against the trench wall. Most of the muskets were smoothbore, for only Dudley's men had Enfield rifles. The artillery consisted of Lieutenant Delacourt's three batteries, each with three guns. The guns were all bronze 9-pounders save for one 24-pounder howitzer. The underground magazines housed plenty of ammunition for both the muskets and cannon.

"We may be few," Morrow said, "but General Wheeler insists that we must simply hold out long enough to be reinforced."

"Yes."

Wheeler and his closest aide, his son Lieutenant Godfrey Wheeler, had sent two messages to Lucknow, the nearest British garrison.

"Still, I wonder if the couriers could have made it through the sepoy lines. If they did, it seems probable that the European troops in Lucknow will soon have their own rebellion to deal with."

"Well, then, we wait for troops from Calcutta."

Dudley studied the burning city. Wheeler had requested troops from Calcutta weeks ago.

Captain Morrow trained his field glasses on the canal. Wheeler was inside the barracks consoling his wife and daughters, and in his temporary absence, Morrow had command of the fortifications.

"Hold on a moment," he said. "I think our rebels may be coming to visit us at last."

Dudley did not have the advantage of field glasses, but even without them, he could see narrow columns of troops beginning to cross the canal bridges. The sepoys still wore their red coats; the rebellious landholders' men were clad all in white.

"Second Cavalry," O'Ryan said from Dudley's other side. The Colour-Sergeant was pointing, but Dudley had already spotted the column of horsemen advancing behind the foot soldiers. The *sowars* were easy to identify in their pale-blue stable jackets. Like the sepoys, they no longer professed loyalty to Britain but continued to wear British uniform.

Dudley realized he was witnessing one of the greatest disasters in the history of British arms. One of the empire's own armies had turned against it. It was the equivalent of a major defeat, as if that army had met destruction in the field. India, once a place of such fascination for him, had become a place of fear and uncertainty. Even a place of horror. He thought of the massacres at Meerut and Delhi. The same could happen here if they could not hold the entrenchment.

He was at war again, and not even the ill-planned assaults on Sevastopol had seemed so precarious.

My duty will sustain me, he thought. *I can only do my best.*

He had often wondered how he would react to a situation such as this, and now he found that he did not fear for his own safety. In fact, he felt nothing at all. A soldier had to expect to face death or defeat, he supposed, had to fight on regardless, and he had learned that lesson well in the Crimea. But the safety of the civilians concerned him.

General Wheeler at last emerged from the barracks. With him was the Reverend Teecher, and together they approached Dudley and Captain Morrow. The general returned the captain's salute and asked, "How do things stand?"

"They've begun their advance," Morrow stated. "At least, that is how it appears."

Teecher wore a sun helmet and held his coat over one arm. He peered over the low wall at the approaching enemy.

"If I am to die," he said after a moment, "at least I go knowing that I have died in the service of our Lord."

"We ain't dead yet, sir," O'Ryan commented.

The rebel columns had begun to string out along the canal in no organized formation. Many were dancing and celebrating to the faint twang of music.

Maybe they will not attack today, Dudley thought. Or maybe they would let the defenders go. For a few seconds, he dared to hope that the sepoys were actually in the act of dispersing to their homes, that they had taken their revenge on the property of the Sirkar and that was enough.

Then he saw the cannon come rattling across the canal bridges. The guns pushed through the dancing infantry, the drivers lashing their teams. Within minutes, the sepoy crews had unlimbered their pieces and begun to ram home both cartridges and shot. They were about to attack.

"They've set their guns more than a thousand yards away," he commented. "They won't be very effective from that distance."

Behind the guns rode a man on an elephant and several officers on horseback.

"That's the Nana Sahib!" Wheeler exclaimed as he gazed through his field glasses. "He's thrown in his lot with the rebels. Damn him for a traitor!"

The first rebel gun fired. Dudley saw the puff of smoke, but the ball was almost upon them by the time the sound of the discharge followed.

"Take cover!" Morrow cried, and the defenders dropped behind the earthworks. The ball went wide, falling well outside the compound. It kicked up a spurt of dirt to the left then settled against a clump of bushes.

A second and third shot followed in quick succession. One ball also went wide, but the third struck the lip of the trench, bouncing high and hitting the wall of the larger barracks with a crash. Chunks of plaster flew from the impact, and high-pitched screams issued from within the building.

Dudley pressed his back against the parapet as Lieutenant Delacourt prepared his western battery to return fire. A gunner touched his linstock to the vent on the first gun, and white smoke blasted from the muzzle. The sharp report startled more shrieks from the barracks, and Dudley cringed. He imagined Charlotte huddled in fear and heated darkness.

As if reading his thoughts, Teecher announced, "I will return to Charlotte and her mother." The clergyman lurched to his feet and started running for the barracks.

"Keep your head down, sir!" O'Ryan shouted after him, but the rush and scream of a howitzer shell drowned out his warning. The defenders covered their heads with their hands, but the shell burst to the north, well outside the compound.

The colour-sergeant glanced at Dudley, managing a weak grin.

"Well, sir," he said, "at least now we know they're poor shots."

The firing ceased as night fell, and the next morning the rebels moved their guns closer. The mutinous infantry also edged forward, having abandoned their celebrations. As Dudley had feared, snipers took shelter in the unfinished barracks, while others hid inside nearby houses and behind trees and bushes.

Dudley had shed his wool tunic and waited in his shirt sleeves for the enemy to make its move. It was the second day of the siege, and he and his men were already filthy from lying and crouching along the low parapet. They had not moved all night.

"There she goes," O'Ryan muttered as a puff of smoke burst from a gun concealed in a nearby tope. The report came a few seconds later, and the ball struck the parapet, showering the defenders with dirt before bouncing over their heads.

O'Ryan cursed and rubbed dry earth from his eyes.

"Too close, sir. They're improving."

Several more shots roared overhead, the balls crashing against the barracks, spraying plaster and mortar dust. Dudley decided that fire was coming from at least two directions. One after the other, the iron balls struck the barracks, eliciting cries of terror as they had yesterday.

He again thought of Charlotte, huddled inside. She would not know what was happening, and he decided that it was not fair to simply ignore her and her mother, to let them languish in the barracks. Snatching a big smoothbore musket from the nearest stack, he turned to O'Ryan.

"I must see Charlotte and Mrs. Edwards," he said. "I must know that they're safe."

O'Ryan nodded. "Have a care, sir. It's grown hot out here all of a sudden."

Dudley held on to his cap and made a dash for the larger barracks. His dangling sword slapped his legs, and he almost tripped before reaching the nearest door. Once there, he tore it opened and ducked inside.

Fear-glazed eyes turned in his direction. Women and a few civilian men in sweat-stained clothes were crouching close to the floor and under the bunks. There was another crash and the walls shuddered. Two young girls began shrieking and clung to their ayah. Dudley ignored their horrible noise and scanned the room for Charlotte or Mrs. Edwards. He did not see them, so waded through the prone occupants to the nearest doorway.

The next room was in chaos. Several large eighteen-pound shot had smashed through the walls, and one had broken a window; the shot lay on the floor amongst bits of broken shutters, glass and masonry. Some of the women in the room were screaming. One was near hysterics, and had pushed herself into a corner, sitting with her hands over her eyes, fingers knotted in tangled hair. A native woman was writhing on a cot with a severe gash in her leg. A sweating army surgeon squatted next to her, fumbling in his instrument bag.

Doing her best to steady the wounded native was Mrs. Edwards. Teecher was behind her, seeming oblivious to the danger of incoming shot.

"Somebody fetch me some brandy," the surgeon demanded in a voice like gravel. White bone showed within the dark blood on the wounded woman's right leg, and her skin had turned a muddy gray. "I believe the bone is cracked. I'll need something to make a splint."

As Teecher scurried off, Mrs. Edwards turned to the woman in the corner.

"Charlotte!" she cried. "Stop your wailing and find us something to make a splint! We have to steady the bone and stitch the wound."

Dudley had not recognized Charlotte. At her mother's sharp tone, she suddenly ceased her cries but continued to gasp and moan as she lowered her hands to reveal a face covered in tear-streaked dust.

"I can't," she sobbed. "I can't look."

Blood had soaked the floor under the cot. Without further hesitation, Dudley set down his musket and snatched up two pieces of the broken shutter, then moved to help Mrs. Edwards hold the patient steady. Teecher reappeared with a bottle and some bandages.

"There is still plenty of wine and spirits left," Teecher declared. "Here are some of the bandages you made last night, Grace."

Sweat dripped from the surgeon's forehead as he examined the wound with a probe.

"The crack in the bone is minor. I shall stitch the wound as best I can, then splint it."

Dudley, Teecher, and Mrs. Edwards gripped the woman with tight hands as the surgeon worked. Dudley closed his eyes and listened to the thunder outside. He assumed the louder detonations were from Delacourt's batteries.

When the surgeon finished, he uncapped the brandy bottle and poured some of its contents over the stitching. The woman groaned, but she was only half-conscious. The surgeon covered the wound with the clean bandages then splinted the leg with the broken shutter and bound it with an old stocking.

"That will have to do," he said. "Undoubtedly, it will turn to gangrene in this heat, or she will die from loss of blood."

"You did all you could," Teecher said. "I will pray for her and the other wounded."

The surgeon passed the brandy bottle to Mrs. Edwards.

"I have other patients to attend."

"Of course," Mrs. Edwards replied.

As the surgeon moved off, Mrs. Edwards glanced at Dudley, then pressed the bottle to her lips and drank.

There was another loud crash as a ball struck the outside wall. Mrs. Edwards flinched, and a rivulet of brandy ran down her chin. In the corner, Charlotte again cried out.

"Be silent, girl!" Mrs. Edwards shouted. "You're just like your father was. Weak. I thought India would stiffen you."

Dudley released his grip on the now unconscious patient and went to stand over Charlotte.

"Are you all right?" was the only thing he could think to say.

"No, I am not all right!" she cried. "How could I be all right? We will all be killed here!"

"But you are not hurt," he offered. "You have to be strong, Charlotte. We aren't finished yet. This has just begun. All we must do is hold here until reinforcements arrive."

She glared at him as if he had lost his wits then shook her head and again covered her face with her hands.

"We should have left," she said. "We should have found a boat, or taken the horses. We should have left."

"I could not let you abandon your mother," Dudley insisted. "I could not abandon these other people."

"You may as well leave her, Ensign," Mrs. Edwards muttered behind him. "It's like speaking to a post. Your place is on the parapet. We have things well in control here."

Charlotte trembled as if in concert with the shuddering walls. Dudley stared at her, wanting to offer reassurance but stung by her hostility. He knew she would recoil from him if he tried to touch her.

Teecher was beside him.

"Ensign Dudley?"

Dudley tore his eyes away from Charlotte.

"Yes, Mister Teecher?"

"I was wondering if I could be of some use on the outposts. Are there spare muskets available?"

"Plenty, Reverend." He retrieved the smoothbore he had brought with him. "You may have this one, if you will follow me."

He gave Charlotte one last glance, but she was ignoring him. He turned away and moved towards the nearest door, with Teecher behind him.

As the siege progressed, Dudley and his men lived outside, eating and sleeping in the trench. Only the officers of the native regiments preferred to stay in the barracks, including General Wheeler, but they had wives and children to watch over. Dudley felt confident in Mrs. Edwards's ability to tend to her daughter and herself. He concerned himself with watching the enemy's movements. He could do nothing for Charlotte. She had no use for his comfort.

The mutineers sniped at the defenders, their artillery raining shot off and on during the day. For short periods, the fire was intense, making it impossible to leave the trench or the barracks. The well was a favourite target, and soon the *chabutra* was nothing but splinters.

But once the initial bombardment had ended, most of the firing was desultory and seemed half-hearted. The rebels had still not attacked nor attempted to storm the entrenchment. The bulk of their infantry remained on the edge of the canal, watching and letting the artillery do the work.

Delacourt's guns kept up a steady counter-fire of round shot and grape. Dudley's men also contributed to the defence. As the only ones armed with rifles, they could bring down sepoys who thought they were out of range.

"How do ye like the Enfield rifle now?" O'Ryan muttered after picking off a distant rebel gunner.

The Reverend Teecher carried the musket Dudley had given him, but he did not use it. He scurried back and forth between the barracks and the western side of the trench, alternately seeing to his sister and niece and watching the defence. Mrs. Edwards also left the barracks several times each day. At one point, she strolled across the open ground, scorning the shot that roared overhead. She carried tins of salmon, biscuits, and a jug of water for Dudley's squad.

"For heaven's sake, Mrs. Edwards," Dudley cried, running to her and taking the supplies from her arms. "You have to stay under cover when they're shooting at us!"

His concern did not impress her.

"If the Lord means for me to be struck down while doing his work, then so be it."

The men thanked her and sat against the trench wall to eat. O'Ryan pried open a salmon tin with his bayonet. Food supplies were still in abundance, although the civilians were consuming them at an alarming rate. Dudley knew they had no notion of rationing.

"How are things in the barracks?" he asked.

"Tragic, of course. The general has lost his son, and his daughters were unfortunate witnesses to the event. A shot took off the young man's head. You can see the stain on the barrack wall."

A round shot thumped into the parapet to their left, spraying dry earth. The men cowered; Mrs. Edwards stood her ground.

"Pretty soon we're all going to be stains on the walls," O'Ryan muttered.

The numbers of wounded and dead began to mount. Dudley's stomach had become a dead weight; and he founding eating difficult, signs that the strain was beginning to tell on him. He felt no overt fear, only resignation and a firm determination that he, like Morrow and Delacourt, had no option but to remain cool-headed. At night, he organized volunteers to carry away the bodies of those who had been killed in the barracks. An unused well south of the entrenchment had become a mass grave. The well was filling up.

Despite the growing list of casualties, when one of his own was killed it still came as a shock. The man was struck full in the body by an iron ball and died instantly. Dudley stared at the corpse, constricted by a sudden white-hot rage. But rage quickly turned to sorrow and frustration, then a renewed sense of resolve. The garrison would be reinforced. They just had to hold out.

Three more of his men were killed that same afternoon, struck down by a single howitzer shell that burst in the air, raining red-hot fragments. The 32nd was also losing men, but it was Delacourt's gun crews who had taken the heaviest casualties because of their exposed positions. One rebel ball knocked down three members of a gun crew at once, tearing the legs from two and disemboweling the other. Civilian replacements were now learning the procedures for loading and firing artillery.

The barracks were host to many panicked scenes. At one point, someone in the smaller building cried out that the roof was on fire. Dudley watched as the occupants, carrying their babies and dragging their children, fled outside and across the open ground to the larger building. No sooner had the fugitives filled it than a rebel round pierced the roof. He did not see what happened, but a moment later, a woman's anguished wailing filled the compound.

Soon it became obvious there had been no fire in the smaller building after all, and many returned. Not more than five minutes later, as if the earlier alarm had been a prediction, the thatched roof of the larger building began to burn. Bright flames consumed the thatch and everything in the rooms below, including the medical supplies and the khaki jackets of the 32nd. When the fire at last died, Dudley spied members of the 32nd poking through the hot ashes, perhaps looking for buttons or their lost service medals.

On the outposts along the trench, the defenders caught snatches of sleep between hours of vigilant observation, every man wary of sudden death from a musket ball, round shot, or bit of grape. As their numbers diminished, they took steps to create the appearance of strength. Top hats, sun helmets, shakos and exposed musket barrels were set along the top of the parapet. A few enterprising fellows had even draped jackets over frames of splintered wood. The ruse seemed to work, for soon the hats and jackets were filled with bullet holes.

On the fourth evening of the siege, Dudley was sitting under cover, his back to the parapet, facing the well in the centre of the entrenchment. Bullets slapped the dirt above his head. He was surprised to see a captain from one of the native regiments emerge from the smaller barracks with an earthenware jug in his hand. Crouching, the officer scurried towards the well. When he saw Dudley watching him, he gave a shy smile and said, "I promised a lady a drink!"

After lowering the bucket into the well, the officer let it fill then began drawing it up again. The tackle made a noisy squealing as it worked, a sound that must have alerted the rebels. Three shots rang out, and Dudley turned just in time to see a muzzle flash light up one of the windows in the unfinished barracks. One incoming bullet hit the dirt, and another ricocheted from the side of the well. The third hit the officer in the face, tearing away his entire lower jaw.

The man did not cry out. He simply rolled over, his back to the well, eyes blinking in surprise. He held one hand to the horrible wound, and dark blood sprayed through his fingers.

"Damn them for cowards!" Captain Morrow cried from his place beside the nearest 9-pounder battery. Heedless of the danger, he ran to the wounded officer's side. Dudley joined him, staying in a crouch. They each grasped a trouser leg and dragged the injured man into the trench.

The man's face was a red horror, his tongue dangling. Dudley had seen similar wounds in the Crimea, and he knew the officer would die. If the loss of blood did not kill him, the inability to eat would.

His rage returned, and he drew his sword, the metal scraping in the scabbard.

"I've had enough. I'm going to clear the bastards from those barracks. Colour-Sergeant?"

"I'll round up the lads, sir!" O'Ryan barked, having overheard.

"I'll come with you, too," Morrow declared. His eyes blazed.

The sun was setting. Along the canal, the rebel camp-fires had begun to flare, and music drifted over the plain. The enemy guns were silent and unmanned, but Dudley suspected the crews would return to fire a few random shots during the night. The unfinished barracks seemed empty as well, although the snipers had proven otherwise.

Having tended the wounded officer as best they could, Dudley and the other members of the scratched-together attack party loaded their muskets and formed a line along the western trench. O'Ryan had assembled his remaining eight men. Morrow had brought another dozen—soldiers and a few civilian engineers of the East India Railway.

Dudley carried an Adams revolver; the pistol had belonged to an officer who had died in the same manner as General Wheeler's son. Dudley loaded the revolver's five chambers and thrust the weapon into his belt at his back.

"If you will allow me, sir," he said to Morrow, "I will lead my men in a frontal attack if you circle around to the left."

"You're giving yourself the more difficult task, Ensign," Morrow said.

"And the greater glory, sir," Dudley replied, forcing a grin. "Though I suggest we also crawl along on our bellies. We will blend in with the dirt in this light. They won't see us until it's too late."

"Agreed."

Morrow nodded then slapped him on the arm. Dudley felt a surge of confidence. He had been uncertain about Morrow at first. The fellow carried himself with an air of superiority, and his open criticism of his commanding officers had made Dudley uncomfortable. But arrogance was common among men of Morrow's class, and he had found himself agreeing with the man more often than not. He was a fellow of courage and fortitude, and they had begun to work well together.

Making as little sound as possible, Dudley led the attack squad over the parapet. Outside the entrenchment, they dropped to their hands and knees. Morrow's party scuttled off to the left like shadowy crabs, while Dudley's went straight ahead. Dudley was in the lead, holding his drawn sword as he crawled.

His party had gone about ten yards when another series of flashes lit the barrack windows. Bullets hummed overhead, punching into the entrenchment behind them. The attackers froze, but when no further shots followed, Dudley decided the snipers had been firing blind.

He motioned for O'Ryan to continue. They slithered forward, and soon were close enough to hear men speaking, low voices coming from inside the barracks. He halted about four yards from the wall. The light was dim, but it surprised him the rebels had not seen the attackers.

To his right was the first doorway, the northern end of the building. He did not know how close Morrow's party was, but they could not be far from their objective. Gripping his sword, he leapt to his feet and charged for the wall. He heard O'Ryan and the others coming behind him, the shuffle of their feet, their panting breath.

He flattened against the rough brick just to one side of the doorway. O'Ryan positioned himself on the other side. The rest took similar cover between the empty windows.

Voices raised in alarm sounded within he next room. Shots rang out, and shouts of pain. Morrow's party had attacked.

Dudley did not like charging into a darkened building without knowing what was inside, but there was nothing else he could do. He had started this attack; he had to support Morrow. He drew the Adams from his belt.

"Onward, Colour," he said to O'Ryan and ducked into the doorway, bending low.

The light from windows in the opposite wall showed him the room was empty. A shot flashed beyond an inner doorway, and a man's voice rose in an enraged war cry. Dudley's squad leapt in through the windows. There was a clash of bayonets, gasps, the pathetic gurgle of a man choking.

Dudley and O'Ryan moved into the next room. Two rebels lay on the floor; one was still breathing, but his white frock was stained with dark blood. Dudley's men had moved on.

His party met Morrow's in the middle of the building. They had cleared the barracks of rebels, killing a few and chasing out the others. When Dudley and the captain emerged on the far side, they saw more rebels running from the next unfinished structure to the west.

"Cowards," Morrow spat. "Useless without their officers. You know, they should have taken the entrenchment in one day, completely overrun us. Yet here it is, almost a week later. They haven't the backbone for a proper attack."

"Let's hope nothing happens to stiffen their resolve," Dudley said, sheathing his unblooded sword.

"We can't let them retake these buildings," Morrow went on. "We'll establish a permanent outpost here. But

not you or your men, Ensign. I'll want you back at the entrenchment in case they do eventually attack."

Dudley nodded. He had long ago accepted Morrow
as the true commander of the defences.

The rebels assembled in force on June 11th, the sixth day
of the siege. Although Dudley had not taken part, the defenders had made another sortie the night before, this time
against two enemy batteries. They had spiked the guns
and ruined the carriages. In the morning, the rebels had
brought up fresh artillery. Behind the new guns, cavalry
scurried to and fro. Some of the *sowars* waved green flags.

"Calling the Mohammedans to battle again," Captain
Morrow commented when he saw the banners. "We'd best
get ready. I'll send a man to alert the general."

The defenders stood-to along the parapet. Dudley
sent the Reverend Teecher back to the barracks to tell
Mrs. Edwards and Charlotte to take extra cover. He suggested Teecher have them hide under a cot.

The rebels brought still more artillery forward, carriages and limbers rattling over the bridges. The infantry
began to move up, occupying the houses and other surrounding buildings, some taking cover behind barricades
they had erected between them. Dudley estimated the enemy infantry strength at more than two thousand.

General Wheeler appeared just as the three guns of
Delacourt's western battery opened fire in succession. One
shot scored a direct hit on a rebel cannon, dismounting
the barrel. The defenders cheered. Wheeler smiled and
congratulated the lieutenant, but the thunder of the enemy's reprisal drowned his cries of triumph. Every gun
and every musket leveled at the entrenchment seemed to
fire at once.

The rebels loaded and fired as fast as they could. Shot
and bullets tore at the parapet and pounded the barrack

walls. Dust from plaster and mortar filled the air in a dense choking screen. Two of Delacourt's western guns took hits, a shot sheering the muzzle from one, another smashing the carriage wheels on the second. The gunners abandoned the pieces and dove into the trench. There was nothing for them to do but press against the earth and wait for the rebels to storm their position.

But again no assault came. By early evening, the fierce bombardment and fusillade had slackened and, finally, ceased. The rebels began to slip away from their snipers' nests in the houses, as if disappointed that the defenders had not simply given up.

"Survived another day, Colour-Sergeant," Dudley said to O'Ryan as the sun began its descent. He tried to keep his tone light, despite his crushing fatigue.

The Irishman's eyes were hollow, his face sunken from strain and lack of sleep.

"Where are those reinforcements the general's been talking about, I wonder?"

Dudley could not answer him. For a moment, he questioned whether anyone even knew they were under attack. For the first time, he felt the edges of despair, and real fear, fear that he could not hold on. All he wanted to do was sleep—curl into a ball and burrow into the earth.

How does a man keep going, he thought, *in the midst of all this?* Then, he remembered how it was in the trenches during the siege of Sevastopol. *A man keeps going because he never truly believes he will be killed, even when he thinks, "I am going to be killed today." He never truly believes it. Death is an unknown country, no matter how much of it he has seen. It is inconceivable.*

He would not lose heart. Unless all of British India had fallen, help had to be on its way.

CHAPTER 16

Allahabad
June 1857

Sergeant Barker made his way across a small square in an Allahabad suburb. A group of local women had gathered at the well in the centre of the square, and he watched them as he filled his pipe, admiring their smooth bare arms and dark round shoulders. They wore white dresses or colourful saris, standing in clusters, filling their burnished brass and clay pots with clear water. When they spied Barker, some began to glower and turn their backs. They no longer cared much for the presence of British soldiers, it seemed. He sighed and turned away.

He wandered to a patch of shade and sat on the edge of a low stone wall. On all sides of the little square stood military vehicles and the materiel of an army on the move. Four elephants were tethered in the shade of a peepul tree. The great beasts tugged at tufts of dry grass with their leathery trunks while their mahout slept with his back to one huge hind leg. Barker wondered why the elephants were here. Maybe to haul heavy artillery, although he had not seen any big guns in the city.

Allahabad was the assembly point for the field force that would quell the rebellion in the Ganges valley. The small force was under the direction of Colonel Neill, the East India Company officer who commanded the Madras Fusiliers.

The detachment from the Royal Hants, with the Left Wing of Neill's regiment, had been one of the first formations to reach the city. Barker knew there were still too few of them here to do any good and suspected that Neill was awaiting the arrival of more units, perhaps some of the Queen's regiments that had been fighting in Persia.

"They better bloody well hurry," he muttered, sucking on his unlit pipe.

He thought of the tiresome and difficult journey from Calcutta. The men of No. 3 Company had traveled by train, bullock *dak*, and river steamer to Benares then made a hard overland march. Each day had seemed hotter than the last. A few times, thick bunches of clouds had formed in the searing sky, and then rain had pelted down. When the clouds passed, the air had become thick with sticky mist. Deaths from cholera and heatstroke had begun to mount.

"Same old story," he muttered. He was thankful that No. 3 Company had remained healthy, with only one fatal case of the fever.

He saw Private Geary approaching with Lazzy trailing at his feet. The beagle no longer needed a leash. Barker smiled. That was a good development, at least. Geary had trained the dog well.

Lazzy spied the elephants and began to bark.

"No, no, Lazzy!" Geary said. "Never mind the elephants."

The dog gave a final whine but obeyed his new master. The elephants watched with impassive dignity as they chewed their grass.

"You'll make a soldier of that creature yet, Private," Barker said.

"I've got a new trick, Sarge," Geary said. "Look! Lazzy, salute!"

The beagle darted a glance at the private then brought its right paw up to its ear, as if scratching. Barker laughed.

"Aye, that's good," he said. "Have him try that one on Captain Reed."

Geary's face lit up. "D'you think he'd like it?"

"No, lad, I don't." Barker knelt and rubbed Lazzy's neck. "And neither would Lieutenant Morris."

"Well, never mind. The captain don't have to like him. Lazzy'll march with me all the way to Cawnpore."

Barker nodded, but his uneasiness had returned. William Dudley and Aiden O'Ryan were in Cawnpore. He wondered how long they could hold.

During their march, Barker and his comrades had learned that the situation in northern India was worse than they had at first assumed. No native regiment could be trusted.

At Benares, on June 4th, the 37th Native Infantry had fired on its officers, initiating a skirmish that had resulted in several fatal casualties. On June 14th, General Hearsey at Barrackpore had been forced to disarm the grumbling native garrison despite the protests of their officers. The officers had continued to insist their men were loyal. Barker thought all such officers naive fools. The high regard the sepoys had for General Hearsey must have been the only thing preventing them from murdering every white man and woman in the Barrackpore garrison.

Everywhere in the Ganges valley there had been outbreaks of mutiny. There were rebels on the move only a few miles from Allahabad. "Pandies," the men were calling them now, in reference to Mangal Pande, the man now considered the first mutineer. According to the rumours, Cawnpore was under siege, and Lucknow would be threatened next.

Cawnpore would be the first objective for the field force, but it would be another week before they could reach it. Maybe longer.

"Mister Dudley would like Lazzy's trick," Geary suggested.

"Aye, that he would," Barker agreed. "I hope he gets a chance to see it."

He chewed on the stem of his pipe. Time was everything.

CHAPTER 17

Cawnpore
June 1857

The rebels opened another fierce bombardment a few days after their aborted attack; Dudley crouched in the shallow trench as a two-hour storm of artillery and musketry raged. When the storm had passed, the ground within the compound was pocked with shell craters, and the barrack walls were mottled and cracked with shot holes and scars.

The powder smoke continued to drift in white batches as the defenders stood-to along the trench, as ever expecting an assault but hoping it would not come. The remaining soldiers, ragged and filthy, alone crowded the parapet, muskets leveled, while civilians manned the artillery. Lieutenant Delacourt had so far survived, but only half of his guns functioned, two in the western battery and one in the southern battery.

Dudley watched as the rebel infantry gathered in long lines, bayonets glistening in the sun. They faced Wheeler's fortifications on three sides, while squadrons of the 2nd Cavalry galloped to and fro beyond musket range. He determined their strength to have grown to nearly six thousand men. If they chose to storm the entrenchment, they could not help but be successful.

Delacourt was supervising his citizen gunners in the load procedure when the rebel artillery opened up again. Guns to the north, south, and west fired as one. Once again Dudley dove for cover as round shot and a scattering of howitzer shells struck the barracks. Dust rained down into the trench, but after a few minutes, silence descended. The unexpected firing had ceased as suddenly as it had begun.

Dudley thrust his head over the wall to chance a look, expecting to see the start of a general advance. Instead, the mutineers had begun creeping forward as individuals, each man pushing a big bale of cotton before him as cover. Now and then a cotton bale would pause, and a puff of musket smoke would spurt from it. Then the bale would inch forward again.

He could not understand why the enemy did not attack in force.

General Wheeler, also observing this slow and scattered approach of the enemy, shouted encouragement to the defenders.

"Steady on, lads!" he cried. "Don't fire until they're in range. Let the enemy waste his ammunition. We must make every shot count. "

Three muskets leaned against the wall to Dudley's left. The first was a rifle that had belonged to one of his men, one of his casualties. The other two weapons were smoothbores. He picked up the rifle and pulled the hammer back to full cock. It was already loaded and primed.

Around him, the defenders began firing at the cotton bales, muskets booming, adding to the sulfurous stench of powder that already filled the air. Dudley chose a target—a rebel in the act of loading his musket behind his cotton bale. He could see the man's arms, the musket and ramrod in his hands. He could also see a part of the man's head. That was all he needed.

He let out a breath and squeezed the trigger. The rifle jolted against his shoulder, and for a moment, the smoke obscured his vision. When it cleared, he saw that his man was down. A clean shot.

He could not achieve that degree of accuracy with the two smoothbore muskets, so began reloading the rifle. He had placed a dozen cartridges in a depression in the wall for easy access, and now he took one, bit open the tail, and poured the powder into the barrel of his rifle. After pushing the remaining paper and its attached Minié bullet into the muzzle with his fingers, he withdrew the ramrod and thrust the charge home.

Removing the ramrod from the barrel, he replaced it in its slots beneath the stock, hefted the rifle, and pulled the hammer back to half-cock. He had attached a percussion cap pouch to his waist belt, and he opened it to take out a small copper percussion cap, which he then fitted over the breach nipple. Last, he pulled the rifle hammer back to full cock.

He was ready to choose another target, but in the time it had taken him to load, the rebels had already begun to withdraw. Many had run back, leaving their cotton bales behind.

Dudley sighted along the blued rifle barrel, moving the weapon to the left and right. He spied a man backing away at a crouch. Releasing a slow breath as before, he fired. When the smoke cleared, he was disappointed to see the man still standing.

Several defenders had already climbed the wall and rushed out to retrieve the cotton. In his indignation at having missed his target, Dudley dropped the rifle and drew his sword. It took no more than a minute for him to scramble over the wall and run the thirty paces to the nearest bale.

Something hummed past his ear, and he realized it had been a bullet. He grasped the cotton bale by the bits of hemp rope that held it together and started dragging it backward. When he neared the wall, O'Ryan and two others came out to help him.

Once back inside the entrenchment, Dudley and the colour-sergeant positioned the cotton bale on top of the parapet as additional cover. O'Ryan looked at it with his hands on his hips.

"Any more attacks like that," he said, "and soon we'll have a proper wall. "

Dudley shook his head. "Why don't they press their advantage? They could overwhelm us in a few minutes if they really tried. "

"Trying to wear us down, sir. Less costly for them. "

Dudley sat in the bottom of the trench, his sword held between his knees, point down. He thought of their slow casualties, the men he had lost, the gunners slain one-by-one.

"And they *are* wearing us down, Colour," he said. "They are. "

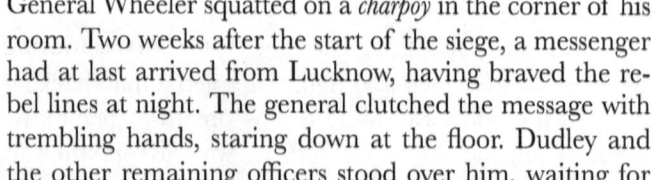

General Wheeler squatted on a *charpoy* in the corner of his room. Two weeks after the start of the siege, a messenger had at last arrived from Lucknow, having braved the rebel lines at night. The general clutched the message with trembling hands, staring down at the floor. Dudley and the other remaining officers stood over him, waiting for him to read the contents of the small scrap of paper.

"It is from Sir Henry Lawrence," the general said at last, "the Commissioner of Oudh." He glanced again at the paper then looked at his office, his gaze falling on each man in turn. Dudley saw defeat in those eyes. "Gentle-men, there will be no reinforcements from Lucknow. Sir Henry has assured me that, were success possible, he would brave any danger. But the enemy commands the river. With the small force at his disposal, he deems a crossing of the Ganges under fire impossible. "

None of the officers replied. Captain Morrow nodded, and another man took off his cap and slapped it against his filthy trousers. Dudley suspected every officer shared the same thoughts. The siege would go on. Their food was running out. It was difficult to draw water from the well, shot having smashed the tackle; the bucket had to be hauled up by hand. Ammunition was running low. There had been no word from Calcutta, no sign of fresh regiments from there. Yet the siege would go on.

"We will carry on the fight, gentlemen," Wheeler de-clared, although there was little force or conviction be-hind his words. Only weariness.

The officers filed out of the general's room. Morrow continued outside, but Dudley paused in the adjoining bar-rack. He saw men and women in tattered clothing, chil-dren in dirty frocks and bonnets. Against one wall lay a row of groaning wounded, their injuries bound with soiled dressings. A man in a suit that had once been white squat-ted on the floor. He held the hand of a middle-aged woman who had a strip of petticoat tied around her head. An-other woman lay on a bed, leafing through the pages of a prayer book, now and then glancing at the ceiling. A group of children who looked like London street urchins listened as an ayah told them a story. Others sat doing noth-ing, with vacant looks, hollow eyes. The stench of fester-ing wounds and unwashed bodies was appalling.

The rebel guns began to boom outside, and the build-ing shook. No one cried out anymore, but a few covered their ears. A woman pulled her ragged apron over her head.

A *baboo*, a native clerk, began rocking and mumbling to himself. The ayah's story continued in the corner.

Dudley moved into the next barrack room to look for Mrs. Edwards. He found her standing over a wounded soldier of the 32nd. She had somehow managed to keep a supply of fresh bandages—strips of torn petticoats, and she applied one to the man's injury. Next to her, the Reverend Teecher sat on a cot with a young girl in his arms. The girl was thin, her golden hair tied with a bit of faded blue ribbon. She listened, rapt, as Teecher told her the story of David and the giant Goliath.

"How goes the defence, Mister Dudley?" Mrs. Edwards asked, as if she were asking for the time.

"We are holding, Mrs. Edwards." Her strength reassured him, even though he knew it was bolstered by brandy. "The rebels have been unable to press their advantage. "

A few bits of plaster fell as another round shot struck the building. Mrs. Edwards glanced at Teecher and the little girl, then at Dudley.

"Lost her mother, the poor child," she explained.

Dudley nodded, not knowing what to say. He wondered for a moment where Charlotte could be, but then he spied her in the same corner she had occupied days ago. It was as if she had never moved. Her eyes were wild and staring, and she did not acknowledge him. He noticed that Wellington, the tin soldier he had given her for good luck, dangled outside the front of her ruined dress.

"Charlotte," he said, "why don't you help your mother?"

She looked at him, blinking. After a moment, she said, "I cannot. "

He stared at her. She was filthy and useless, he thought. Here were her mother and her uncle, trying to help while she sat alone and sulked. At that moment, he could not recall what he had ever liked about her. He remembered how she had said she longed for adventure. He wanted to laugh.

As he turned away in disgust, the wall to his left exploded. The blast threw him to the floor, debris and mortar spraying. He scrambled to his feet, brushing at the dust. He felt no pain and could find no blood anywhere on his body. He was all right.

"How is everyone?" he asked. Then he saw.

A shot from a rebel 24-pounder had smashed through the wall. The ball lay on the floor, motionless now; blood speckled the black iron. A few feet away, the Reverend Teecher held a small headless corpse.

Charlotte covered her eyes as she had done before and began sobbing. Teecher stared at the thing in his arms. Then he dropped it.

"Grace," he cried, "there is blood on my shirt!"

He began tearing at his shirt, pulling it out of his trousers. A few buttons popped. Mrs. Edwards leapt to his side. Taking hold of his shoulders, she began shaking him.

"Pull yourself together, George!" she commanded. "It's just one more death! The poor thing is with God now. "

Teecher looked at her, his chest heaving. Dudley glanced at the sad, headless body on the cot.

"I'll take her outside to the well," he said.

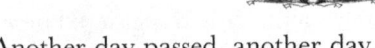

Another day passed, another day of misery made worse by the knowledge that no reinforcements were coming from Lucknow, and still no word from Calcutta. Dudley struggled with the notion Calcutta probably did not have troops to send. The mutiny may have encompassed half the subcontinent. Cawnpore would not be a priority in such a situation.

He wondered where the old Royal Hants had gone. Delhi seemed most probable.

The rebels became more aggressive, mounting small raids to recapture the unfinished barracks. A few times groups of sepoys rushed the main wall, each man firing his musket once before withdrawing, and the *sowars* of the 2nd Cavalry rode closer than they had dared before. At one point, a *sowar* rode within twenty yards of Delacourt's western battery, howling and aiming his carbine at a civilian gunner. The parapet erupted in musketry as the defenders tried to unseat the horseman. The *sowar* crashed to the ground, but within moments he had scrambled to his feet, unhurt. Every bullet had hit his horse. It lay in a growing pool of blood.

The *sowar* fired his carbine at the wall. The bullet rang as it struck the bronze barrel of a 9-pounder; then the *sowar* turned and ran. No one fired at his back. All eyes were on the dead horse.

"Fresh meat, lads," O'Ryan announced. "Who wants to fetch us some knives?"

Two men died in the attempt to carve up the horse. One was a member of Dudley's squad. Of the thirteen who had accompanied him to Cawnpore, only three still lived.

Later that same afternoon, Dudley slumped down in the meagre shade of a cotton bale with his back to the trench wall. The heat seemed to rise every day; Lieutenant Delacourt's pocket thermometer had registered more than one hundred and thirty degrees.

He sat with his eyes half-open. He tried to ignore the heat, his parched lips, the hunger in his belly and the growing weakness in his limbs. He tried to ignore the filth covering his body, the dust and encrusted sweat. He covered his nose and mouth with a grimy hand, for the compound stank of death, of powder smoke, blood, and rotting flesh. Vultures circled in the sky above. A few leafless trees stood inside the entrenchment, one just to the north of the larger barracks, and more vultures covered the splintered branches, hunched and waiting.

It seemed to Dudley that the scavenger birds were staring at him, their eyes intelligent, all-knowing. He reached for a loaded musket, brought it up to his shoulder, and fired in the direction of the tree.

The dismayed scavengers vaulted into the air on their massive wings, but as the small cloud of smoke dispersed, a strange apparition emerged from the barracks. Dudley blinked his burning eyes, wondering if he was really seeing the Reverend Teecher, stark-naked, running out across the parched ground. The clergyman's pale body seemed to glow in the concentrated sunlight.

"Have I failed in my great mission?" Teecher cried, stretching his skinny arms to the sky. "Have I failed in your work, oh, Lord? Oh, rebuke me not in thy wrath, neither chasten me in thy displeasure! For thine arrows stick fast in me, and thy hand presseth me sore!"

Mrs. Edwards came out of the building, arms reaching for her brother.

"Come inside, George! Come inside at once!" She took hold of one arm and began drawing him back to the building.

"What must we do?" he wailed at her, and then they disappeared through the doorway.

O'Ryan crawled over to Dudley's side.

"I think we've lost the reverend, sir."

"I'm afraid you're right, Colour-Sergeant," Dudley replied. He faced the Irishman. "We have to fight, all of us, to maintain our wits. There may be a way out of this yet."

O'Ryan looked doubtful. "As long as I go out fightin', sir, that's all that matters to me."

"That's fine for a soldier, but there are still women here, and children. There must be a way of getting them out safe. There must be. "

O'Ryan hesitated, then nodded. "Aye. You're right, William."

It was the first time the Irishman had used Dudley's given name since they had been sergeants together. It was an improper way to address an officer and would have been an affront at any other time. For some reason, it gave Dudley comfort.

The next morning, as Dudley peered over the edge of a cotton bale toward the enemy lines, the rebel guns suddenly fell silent. A few minutes later, a man with a white flag appeared on the edge of the maidan, having come from the direction of the canal. Behind him moved a palanquin carried by four stout bearers. The small procession approached the western edge of the entrenchment.

"Colour-Sergeant!" Dudley called.

O'Ryan had already seen them.

"Shall I fetch the general, sir?" he asked.

"At once!"

The procession halted yards from the edge of the wall, and the bearers set the palanquin down. A hand reached from inside to draw back the velvet curtains. Dudley stared in curiosity, for the single occupant was a woman with the creamy skin and eastern features of a Eurasian. He noticed that both of her earlobes were torn, as if someone had pulled out her earrings.

"I come with a message from the Nana Sahib," she shouted. "He wishes to parley."

Dudley clutched his rifle, half-expecting a trick. Captain Morrow moved over to stand beside him. Delacourt was a few paces to his left.

"Let her pass, Lieutenant," Morrow said.

Delacourt turned to the sentries he had posted before the gap of the western battery, waving them to stand aside. The bearers then hoisted the palanquin and carried it into the entrenchment.

"I believe that is Mrs. Greenaway," Morrow said to his companions. "Her husband was a local watchmaker, an Englishman."

The bearers set the palanquin down on the shell-pocked earth. Mrs. Greenaway emerged from its cover just as General Wheeler advanced from the barracks with a collection of Company officers.

Dudley, Morrow and Delacourt crawled out of the trench and joined Wheeler's party. Dudley studied the rebel envoy. Her handsome features wore a haunted expression, as if she had seen as much horror as the defenders in the entrenchment. She passed General Wheeler a piece of folded paper. He took it, bowed, and turned away to read. His officers crowded round him.

"What does it say, sir?" asked a young lieutenant Dudley knew only by his last name—Thomson.

Wheeler frowned. "'All those who are in no way connected with the acts of Lord Dalhousie, and are willing to lay down their arms, shall receive a safe passage to Allahabad.'"

"They're asking us to surrender?" Delacourt cried, incredulous.

"What do they take me for?" Wheeler said, face creased in annoyance. "Lord Dalhousie, indeed!"

Dudley remembered that Dalhousie had been the Governor-General of India responsible for the annexation of Oudh.

"We must reject the offer, sir," Thomson urged. "We still have plenty of ammunition, and they have not pressed their advantage."

"I agree," said the general. "I don't care for this insolence, after all we have endured. And I don't see what they have to gain by allowing us to leave."

There was a chorus of agreement from the surrounding officers, shouts of "Damn them!" and "Let them try and force us out of here!"

Delacourt exclaimed, "They're too cowardly to try and storm our wall! It must be a trick."

Captain Morrow cleared his throat, and the chatter died away.

"I beg your pardon, sir. Gentlemen, please allow me to speak. I understand the need for caution, but it may be hasty to reject the offer outright. If they promise us safe passage out, we may have a responsibility to take it, for the women and children."

"But can we trust 'em?" asked Delacourt. "They're traitors, after all. I've held my guns for twenty days! I won't leave 'em for an uncertain future."

"Captain Morrow?" Wheeler said. "Is it not our duty to defend our people to the last?"

"Yes, sir, if we can," Morrow replied, "but I must point out that the spring rains are long overdue. Once they set in, as they are certain to do any day, they will wash away our wall, flood the trench and the shell craters, and ruin our remaining powder. "

General Wheeler gazed at the sky, as if searching for the predicted rain clouds. Dudley considered Morrow's warning, but he could not decide what course he preferred. He had never surrendered before and found the notion revolting. It stank of failure, of the futility of those who had died over the past weeks. If they gave up now, they had fought for nothing. His men had died for nothing, foolishly hoping for relief. It would have been better if they had given up on the first day.

Yet he knew there was no hope of holding out much longer. In that, Morrow was right. They were not strong enough to escape, to break out. Perhaps the soldiers could do it, but not the civilians. All they could do was wait to die, one by one.

He pushed back his cap and rubbed his scalp. There was only one proper thing to do. They could not sacrifice the innocent for the sake of soldierly honour.

General Wheeler seemed to come to the same conclusion. He placed a hand on Captain Morrow's shoulder and said, "I will see what the Nana has to offer. You are right that we should at least make an attempt to achieve terms. I want you to negotiate, Captain. I would prefer it if we would be permitted to keep our arms."

Morrow nodded. "Yes, sir."

Dudley felt his rifle slip, the sweat-greased wood sliding through his fingers. At the last minute, he locked it in a tight grip.

In an instant, everything had changed. Asking for terms could only lead to one result. They would surrender.

CHAPTER 18

The long procession of elephants made its way from the entrenchment to the river. Every elephant carried a mahout and a British officer. The mahouts sat behind each massive head, switches in their hands; each officer perched behind his driver within the velvet shade of a howdah.

A scattering of sepoys and civilians lined the route, standing in silence, watching as the elephants moved past. The great gray beasts, gold balls on the ends of their tusks, moved in single file, their ears slapping at the flies.

This was the first time since arriving in India that Dudley had ridden an elephant. He found the rolling motion smooth and fluid compared to a horse, almost like riding in a small boat. His elephant was a mischievous creature and kept reaching out with its trunk to tug the tail of the elephant ahead. Dudley would have laughed and enjoyed the experience if not for the grim nature of the situation.

The officers were on their way to inspect the arrangements Captain Morrow had made with the enemy. The previous morning, Morrow had met outside the entrench-

ment with the Nana's negotiator, a man named Azimullah. He had agreed that the British would abandon their
position but had also insisted on several conditions.

The defenders would march out under arms. The rebels would provide transport for the wounded, women,
and children. The rebels would also provide the defenders with a sufficient number of provisioned boats to take
them down the river to Allahabad. Azimullah, a tall, handsome man in elegant native dress, had agreed. Now, he was
about to show the officers the chosen embarkation point.

From his high perch, Dudley could look behind him
and see the entrenchment and the barracks. He had fought
to defend that shabby compound for more than two weeks.
To continue the fight and eventually win had been his goal.
The option of giving up had never entered his head.

In the circumstances, he now accepted this as the best
solution—Charlotte and her mother would be safe. Yet he
remained uneasy. He hoped his concern was just a sign
of his exhaustion, and that the shame of defeat did not sit
well with him.

The elephants traveled down into a dry ravine. Dudley gazed up at the jagged slopes on either side. Broken
fences and clumps of prickly pear lined the crests.

The ravine widened, and at its mouth was a small Hindu
temple, it steps leading down to the sandy edge of the Ganges. Pulled up on the sand lay an assortment of small boats,
each with an awning of broken thatch. Opposite the temple, north of the ravine, lay a collection of whitewashed mud
huts. The temple, steps, and village were together known
as the Satichaura Ghat.

The villagers stood in clumps, watching as the elephants halted and lay down to let their human burdens
dismount. The British officers then gathered on the temple steps.

The state of the boats did not satisfy Morrow. He spoke to Azimullah, demanding that the rebels repair the thatch and place a bamboo lining in the bottom of each boat. Azimullah assented, and the officers waited as work crews began the task.

After about thirty minutes had passed, Morrow turned to Dudley and said, "What do you think?"

Dudley shrugged. He did not like the look of the ravine with its steep banks. It was too much like a pen, although he did not say so.

"I suppose there are enough boats."

Morrow nodded. "And they have agreed to my demands as to provisions. They have held true to their word."

Satisfied, the officers climbed back aboard the elephants and made their loping way back to the entrenchment. There they found the people out in the open, free at last from the stench and confines of the barracks. The wounded lay in the shade of one wall, while others made an attempt at celebration. A private of the 32nd had upended an empty keg, and was beating upon it while Colour-Sergeant O'Ryan whistled an Irish jig. Some of the soldiers danced and capered, and the children, starving, dehydrated and exhausted, managed to laugh.

General Wheeler, with his wife and daughters, stood beside the ruined western battery. As Morrow made his report, Dudley went to Mrs. Edwards. With her were Charlotte and the Reverend Teecher. Teecher wore an old blanket looped over his head and wrapped about his body.

Dudley described the arrangements, and Mrs. Edwards pursed her lips and said, "And can we trust these savages?"

"I think so," he said, fighting down his doubts.

There seemed no reason not to trust the Nana and his men. Some of the sepoys, recognizing their old officers, had approached the elephant delegation. They had apologized for all the harm they had caused.

"Now we are escaping in boats," Charlotte said. "As I asked many weeks ago."

Dudley glared at her, feeling a rush of anger. Anger at her, and anger at himself. She had been right after all. But defeat had been an option he had never considered. He wanted to tell her that they could not have known what the future held, but under the stare of her bleak and accusing eyes, he found he could not speak.

Then those eyes suddenly softened, and she added, "Oh, I'm so sorry, William. I'm so sorry." She shrank away, a hand to her mouth.

"You must excuse my daughter, Lieutenant," Mrs. Edwards said. "She was always a weak and selfish girl. But she does not mean to be. Her father indulged her, may the Lord have mercy on his soul."

"It's all right," Dudley said. He reached out and touched Charlotte's gaunt cheek. "It's all right," he repeated, fighting back tears. All at once, the anger had evaporated. Charlotte seemed just like a frightened girl. A girl who had seen and endured things no one should see or endure.

"We have all suffered for our sins," Teecher suddenly interjected. "We have committed the sin of pride in this country. Now we must face God's judgement."

Dudley ignored the comment, saying instead, "You must pack your things, whatever it is you want to bring. We leave here in the morning for Allahabad."

***

The defenders gathered whatever they could—bits of prized jewellery, Bibles and prayer books. Every soldier and armed man stuffed his pouches and pockets with ammunition.

The procession set out with Captain Morrow and an advance guard of the 32nd leading. The soldiers marched in fours in an attempt to maintain their military dignity.

The able-bodied civilians walked behind them, the men with slung muskets. After that came a long string of elephants and bullock carts bearing children with their filthy, half-dressed mothers. The wounded, their bandages made from petticoats and stockings, came last, riding in palanquins borne by officers and native servants who had remained loyal.

Dudley and the three surviving men of the Royal Hants came in the rear of the procession. Mrs. Edwards walked just in front of them, with Charlotte and Teecher shuffling along beside her.

A squadron of the 2nd Cavalry met the defenders near the head of the ravine. The *sowars* fell in to form an escort down to the river. Crowds of people had come out of Cawnpore to watch. Most stood in silence, while others hurled insults at these once-proud British overlords, now squalid and half-naked. Armed sepoys stood among the crowd. Some approached the column to ask after their former officers, as they had done the day before.

The procession filed through the ravine. On the sandy bank at the bottom, the bearers set down the palanquins, while the mahouts took the children down from the elephants. Morrow and the other men near the head of the column waded out into the shallow water to help the civilians into the waiting boats. It was a slow process. Dudley and his companions in the rear had to wait.

"Oh, let's go down to the boats, Mama," Charlotte wailed. Dudley noticed her hand trembling as she brushed a lock of greasy hair from her face. The chain holding the tin soldier still glistened against the skin of her neck.

"Patience," Mrs. Edwards said. "You must learn patience. We will go when it is our turn."

Dudley tried to dismiss his own anxiety and examined his surroundings. The *sowars* lined the bank, and more sepoys had gathered, melting out of the crowd. A group of four sepoys, all clad in white, began moving towards him. He clutched his rifle, wondering what they might want.

Then he noticed that one of the men wore a patch over his eye.

"Kesab," he whispered.

"That's your old servant, sir," O'Ryan said, but by then Kesab had halted in front of Dudley and brought his right hand up in a snappy salute.

"Good morning, Dudley Sahib Bahadur," Kesab said. "Will you please come with me?"

In his astonishment, Dudley did not return the salute. The other three sepoys took positions surrounding him.

Charlotte and Mrs. Edwards stared at Dudley's former servant while Teecher faced the river and mumbled to himself.

O'Ryan stepped towards Kesab and said, "Now, listen here. We have an agreement."

"Please, Sahib," Kesab said, ignoring O'Ryan. There was pleading in his eyes. "Please come with me."

Dudley glanced down at the river. The boats were almost full and ready to depart. He turned to O'Ryan.

"Colour-Sergeant, get the others into a boat. I'll be with you presently."

"Are ye sure, sir?"

"Yes. Please, get Charlotte and Mrs. Edwards to safety."

O'Ryan nodded, then turned to his charges.

"Let's be off then, ma'am."

"We will pray for you, Lieutenant," Mrs. Edwards said at last. Then she and the others began moving down to the sandy bank.

Dudley again faced Kesab. He was too surprised and weary to feel anger at the man's sudden appearance.

"What is it that you want?"

Kesab did not get a chance to reply. Dudley heard the unmistakable report of artillery coming from behind him, then a woman's shriek. Startled, he turned in time to see a sepoy charge at O'Ryan with his bayonet fixed. Before the Irishman could react, the bayonet had plunged into his side.

"What are you doing?" Dudley shouted. He dropped his satchel and rifle and darted forward, right hand grasping at his sword hilt. Kesab's men seized his arms and hauled him back. He struggled but could not escape their fierce grip.

Down in the river, people screamed as the thatched roofs of the boats burst into flames. The boatmen had fired them and now leapt into the water to swim for shore. In the village, sepoys had run two guns forward, two big 18-pounders. The first had already fired. As Dudley watched, the second discharged a blast of grape that blew one of the boats and its occupants to pieces.

He screamed a wordless cry and continued to struggle. Muskets were banging all around him as the sepoys fired into the boats. The *sowars* raised and fired their carbines. Dudley looked for Charlotte, saw her about twenty paces away, crouching with Mrs. Edwards. Teecher lay next to them on the ground, a pool of blood soaking the dust beneath his body. O'Ryan lay a few paces away.

"Murderers!" Dudley shouted. "Traitors!" He managed to free one hand, and his fist connected with one captor's jaw. The man cursed and backed away, but another kicked Dudley's legs out from under him. He crashed to the ground and lay there, gasping for breath, with Kesab lying on top of him.

"Be still, Mister Dudley," Kesab whispered, "if you wish to live."

Dudley lay on his side, facing the river. Sepoys fired at the boats from behind a pile of wood in the village, from behind trees and parked bullock carts. Shrieks and curses filled the air. A woman was screaming, "Don't leave me! Don't leave me!" Dudley saw two children, a girl and a boy, jump from a boat with their hair and clothes on fire. Many women had waded out into the middle of the stream where the water reached to their necks. Others hid under the high prows of the boats.

A scattering of men fired back. Dudley saw General Wheeler, standing in water to his waist, blazing away with a revolver.

The cavalry troopers drew their sabres and spurred their mounts into the water. Sword arms rose and fell. General Wheeler was the first to die, a *sowar*'s blade opening his neck. Many others followed, their screams cut short. The water and sand turned red.

The firing stopped, and Dudley heard the smack of clubs striking flesh, cracking bone. Some of the boats had drifted downstream. Perhaps they would escape, he thought. Sepoys were wading out to loot the remaining boats. Other sepoys herded the surviving woman and children onto the shore, where they gathered on the steps of the temple to shiver and weep. Dudley had lost sight of Charlotte and her mother.

Sepoy muskets cracked here and there as the rebels shot the remaining men. Dudley closed his eyes. His former servant was heavy, and the strength drained from his body. Kesab's breathing was loud in his ears.

"You're a lot of monsters," Dudley said. "A lot of murderous savages."

"I did not approve of this, Mister Dudley," Kesab said. "Many did not. But we have saved many of the women and children. The men were our enemies, but I have saved you."

"Damn you," Dudley muttered as his captors bound his hands and feet with tight ropes. Then he was lifted and carried, away from the river and the drifting powder smoke.

CHAPTER 19

Allahabad
July 1857

The roots of the banyan tree hung from its spreading
branches in pale wooden columns. In and among their
shady embrace, five bagpipers and their pipe-major tuned
their instruments. The pipe-major, a hulking fellow with
a massive black beard, moved from man to man, adjusting the drones on each set of pipes. Slowly, the discordant
screeching and whining became a unified music, the music of war.

Sergeant Barker sat on an upended cask and watched
them as they started into "The Atholl Highlanders." The
pipers were those of the 78th Highlanders, a regiment that
had arrived from the war in Persia. Four companies and
the headquarters had reached Allahabad; the rest were
still en route. The two companies of the Royal Hants were
now attached to this regiment under the command of its
colonel, Walter Hamilton.

Unlike the Royal Hants, the Highlanders had not yet
adapted their clothing to the climate. They had come in
dark Mackenzie tartan kilts and wool double-breasted dou-

blets, green for the pipers and red for the common infantry. The only alteration in their kit had been to their headdress. Their quartermaster had left their feather bonnets
in storage, issuing the men cotton covers and neck curtains
for their Kilmarnock-style "hummle" bonnets.

Barker rose from his seat when the pipers finished their
tune. Being attached to a Highland regiment with a reputation for fierceness in combat gave him some comfort.

"You lads were in Persia," he said by way of greeting.
"I hear you met with some success."

"Aye, that we did," one piper replied, a young man with
oval spectacles; he was the only one without a beard. "We
routed an enemy ten times our number at Koosh-Ab. And
we took no losses at all."

"'Least not from enemy bullets," another added.

"My name is Brian Barker," Barker introduced himself.
"Royal Hampshire Fusiliers."

"Barker? We have a Lieutenant Barker with us. Snotty
little bastard." The Scotsmen laughed. "You're no relation
are you?"

"If I am, I'm not snotty, and I ain't little, neither. But
I am a bastard."

The pipers laughed again, and the one with spectacles offered his hand.

"Roger Andrews, Ross-shire Buffs," he said. The Ross-
shire Buffs was the name of the regiment and was written in the circlet of each soldier's waist belt locket.

"I'm glad to be serving with you," Barker said. "The
enemy will be sorry to hear the pipes when we move up-
country."

The column was scheduled to advance the following
day, July 4th. Colonel Neill had already sent out an advance party under his subordinate, Major Renaud. Renaud's force consisted of detachments from the main column, together numbering about five hundred men. The
main column waiting in Allahabad was not much larger.

It included the remaining Madras Fusiliers, the Royal Hants and 78th Highlanders, the Queen's 84th and 64th regiments, and four 9-pounder guns.

Also with the column was the Ferozepore regiment of Sikh infantry, the Sikhs having all remained loyal to the Sirkar. They had no intention of joining the mutinous Bengal Army, which they had held in contempt since the two Sikh Wars more than a decade earlier.

General Henry Havelock, an old Indian campaigner, had come to Allahabad to take command of this tiny field force. The word on the station was that Havelock's arrival had infuriated Colonel Neill, who had hoped for the command himself. But Neill was a Company officer, while Havelock was a Queen's man; and according to another rumour, Havelock considered Neill something of a barbarian for having already hanged many suspected mutineers without trial. The two men detested each other.

As far as Sergeant Barker was concerned, any animosity between the commanders did not bode well for operations.

"Play us a tune, kilties!" someone shouted, and Barker turned to see a small group of Madras Fusiliers approaching. Their regiment was now known as the Blue Caps owing to the pale-blue forage cap covers they had received in Calcutta.

"We'll play when we have a mind to," shouted Andrews, "and no' before."

"Let's give 'em the 'Dornoch Links,'" the pipe-major suggested.

The pipers nodded then blew to fill their sheepskin bags with air. As the drones began to hum, Barker stood back to listen.

Tomorrow, that music would take him a step closer to battle.

CHAPTER 20

Cawnpore
July 1857

The rebel camp in Cawnpore straddled a road west of the canal. The camp was laid out according to standard British Army specifications—the tents in neat rows, the NCOs and officers on one side and the men on the other. Dudley's captors had bound his hands with a length of rope and led him along like a dog on a leash. They took him to a shallow *nullah* just outside the camp; Kesab secured the other end of the rope to a wooden stake.

No one spoke to him during his first hours of captivity. They fed him rice and bits of *chupatties* then built a small fire to prepare their own meals. That night he lay on the sand, hands still bound, with at least one guard watching him at all times.

He could not sleep. His pain and the memory of the day's events would not let him. O'Ryan was dead, Teecher was dead, General Wheeler was dead, and for all he knew Morrow and Delacourt were dead. His only hope was that Charlotte and Mrs. Edwards still lived.

He told himself he must not dwell on what had happened. If he did, he would lose his mind like poor Teecher. His immediate task was to deal with his own danger.

He was a prisoner. Kesab was keeping him here for some undisclosed purpose; Dudley had doubts his former servant had saved him out of some sense of loyalty. If that were so, the old sepoy would have simply let him go.

But whatever the reason for his capture, escape was his priority. He had to get away from the sepoy army. If he managed to reach the river under the cover of darkness, it might be possible to make it to Allahabad. If Allahabad was also in the hands of the rebels, he would go on to the next station. He would not give up.

He mulled over the problem through the night, sometimes dozing then starting awake. When the sun rose, he pulled himself to a sitting position with his back against the bank of the *nullah*. Every muscle in his body seemed to ache. His scalp and the fresh, unkempt beard on his chin itched. Fly and mosquito bites from too many nights in the open covered his body.

In the camp, bugles were sounding reveille as on any normal day in a British garrison. Kesab and his companions paid them no heed. Instead of rushing off to form on parade, they made breakfast. Kesab placed a small brass bowl of rice in front of Dudley then untied his hands.

"You must feed yourself, Dudley Sahib," he said, at last breaking the silence. "But do not try to run away. If you do, we will shoot you, or the cavalry will get you."

Dudley said nothing. He massaged his wrists then picked up the bowl and began scooping the rice into his mouth with his fingers. He did his best to maintain an appearance of dignity while eating with his hands, keeping his aching back straight, his fingers crooked like a spoon.

When he had finished, Kesab took the empty bowl.

"I will introduce you to my companions," the one-eyed Indian said. "These men served in my old regiment, the Fifty-third Native Infantry."

The three sepoys faced Dudley with their hands on their weapons. The eldest, Modhu, had a thick beard streaked with gray. The other two were brothers, each with a thin face and a prominent, overhanging nose. All three wore white undress jackets still bearing their brass regimental buttons.

In contrast, Kesab wore civilian clothing—a white caftan with red stripes along the hem. At his waist was an orange sash from which dangled a long curved sword. The sword hilt was decorated with curling gold quillions, each with a ruby at the end, and a polished emerald was mounted in the center of the scrolled pommel.

"I am sorry for having deserted you without warning," Kesab added. He began walking back and forth, hands clasped behind his back. "I met Modhu in the market, and he invited me to come to his house. There was a meeting. I had to decide where my loyalties lay. This is a difficult thing, in times of division. But I chose to stay with my old companions in arms."

He halted and fixed Dudley with his single eye. "But I am a man of honour, Mister Dudley, and it troubles me that I wronged you so. You were the only young gentleman on the Madras station who I felt I could trust. You remind me of the British officers I knew in my youth. They loved India and its people; they regarded us as their brothers, which is how it should be."

Dudley slowly got to his feet. He met Kesab's eye. In the circumstances, the apology meant nothing to him.

"What do you want of me, Kesab?"

Kesab rested his left hand on his ornate sword hilt.

"In good time. I will not tell you now."

173

"Why should I trust you after what you have done?" Dudley asked, unable to keep the edge of outrage from his voice. "Your leaders promised us safe passage, and they murdered the very—"

"I did not agree with what happened at the river," Kesab stated. "Many of us did not. We did not take part in it, electing to save you instead. But it is done. There is no use crying about it. And the ladies are safe."

Dudley took a deep breath. "How do I know the ladies are safe?"

Kesab untied the rope from the stake.

"I will show you."

The old sepoy bound Dudley's hands again then led him out of the *nullah*. The other three sepoys fell in behind them.

They walked through the streets to the canal then followed it through the outskirts of the city towards the river. The rough hemp bit into Dudley's wrists, and the climbing heat, combined with shock and fatigue, made him dizzy. He stumbled several times.

Kesab led him to the centre of the cantonments, to the street where the hotel and the assembly rooms stood. There, he halted under the shade of some date palms.

"The ladies are in that little house," he said, pointing.

Across the road was a low stone wall and two square gateposts. Beyond the gate was a wide yard with shade trees on three sides. The yard surrounded a small bungalow with a pitched tile roof and decorative etchings around the doors and windows. Several European women strolled about in the yard under the watchful eyes of sepoy guards.

"That is called the Bibighar," Kesab explained. "A British officer built it for his mistress. Your Miss Charlotte and the mem sahib are there, and are safe and well."

"How do I know that Charlotte's there?" Dudley said. "Let me see her."

"No, no one will see her," Kesab said. "You must accept my word. I do not lie."

Dudley stared at the little house. It struck him that there was no reason not to accept Kesab's word. It was true he had not taken part in the massacre at the river. He had saved Dudley's life.

There had been more than two hundred women and children in the entrenchment. Now they were all packed into that tiny cottage.

"Very well," he said, "I believe you."

That night, Kesab bound Dudley's feet and also bound his hands behind his back. Again the four sepoys took turns standing guard over him as he lay on his side on the floor of the *nullah*.

He slept a little, but most of the time his mind continued to sift through plans for escape. Kesab had unbound his hands at meal times to allow him to eat, and the knots in the rope were simple. If he worked at them, twisting this way and that, they would loosen. Getting his hands free, then his feet, would not be difficult.

It was obvious Kesab knew this but also knew that it did not matter. Were Dudley to break free of his bonds, he then would have to break free of his guards. Were he to accomplish that, he would have to escape from the sepoy camp, through its outlying pickets. Then he would have to cross the canal, somehow slipping past the guards at the bridges. Finally, he would have to escape across open country that was in the hands of the rebels.

It seemed impossible, yet Dudley still meant to try. He had a duty to return to British lines, wherever they may be, and report the things that had happened here. A relief force would have to be assembled to rescue the women in the Bibighar.

A bit of boldness, he thought, might be all it would take. Kesab was relying on Dudley's fear of being shot, of the difficulty of getting past the rebel guards. Perhaps he could, in turn, rely on Kesab's overconfidence. With a bit of audacity and an ability to recognize the most opportune moment, he could slip away.

Morning came. Kesab freed his hands and feet and gave him another bowl of rice. As Dudley ate, he listened to cheering and the firing of muskets in the camp to his left.

"They are cheering for victory at Lucknow," Kesab explained. "The British there are besieged in the chief commissioner's Residency. They will not last long, I think."

"They will last at least as long as we did," Dudley muttered.

Kesab stared down at him, a hand resting on his jeweled sword hilt. His one eye held a fierce glint.

"Allow me to show you something," he said. In a flash, he drew his sword. Crouching in front of Dudley, he pushed the point of the blade into the sand so Dudley could see the hilt.

"This is an ancient weapon, Dudley Sahib," he said. "It comes from the time of the Great Moguls, when they ruled all of northern India. That time is coming again. The British are no longer the invincible race we once thought them to be. They are finished here."

Dudley stared at the beautiful sword.

"But the Nana Sahib is a Mahratta, not a Mogul."

"It does not matter. India shall no longer be ruled by foreigners who do not respect our ways."

"You forget something, Kesab. The Moguls came from central Asia and Persia. They were foreigners themselves."

"Yet they became Indian."

Dudley could have reminded Kesab of Mogul oppressions, but said instead, "None of this excuses the behaviour of the sepoys."

Despite his captivity, he felt no reluctance to express his disagreement with his former servant. Kesab had not mistreated him, had not resorted to beatings or torture. They had discussed similar subjects during their old conversations in Madras. Kesab still seemed a reasonable man, despite having thrown in his lot with a pack of brutal traitors.

"This is a mutiny, not a rebellion against British rule. The sepoys have broken their oaths of loyalty to their commanders."

"The *sepoys* broke their oaths?" Kesab echoed.

He turned to look at Modhu and the brothers, who sat against the opposite bank of the *nullah*. None of them spoke English, and they remained impassive as they watched the verbal exchange.

Kesab pulled his sword from the sand, wiped the blade with the hem of his caftan, and slid the weapon into its scabbard. Standing over Dudley with his hands on his hips, he said, "It is the British who broke their oath first."

"How so?"

Dudley set down his empty rice bowl.

"Let me tell you a story, Dudley Sahib." The former servant began to pace again. "When I was a young boy, growing up not far from here, I wanted nothing more than to be a soldier. In Oudh, there was no more honourable profession. Soldiers were of an elevated class of people. The king would listen to our grievances under circumstances that would see a civilian ignored. When a soldier returned home on leave, all of the people of the village would rise at his approach. A soldier received much respect, Dudley Sahib.

"Although we were not British people, we gave our swords to the army of the Sirkar. Why not? The British were the most powerful people we knew, and they understood us in those days. Our white officers spoke our language; they came to our *nautches* and celebrations; they afforded us the respect our stature as warriors deserved.

"We could not understand why the white soldiers, men with whom we fought side-by-side, would allow themselves to be flogged, or forced to live in barracks, and not allowed to have families! We would not have tolerated these things. And our officers would not have tolerated them, either.

"Then comes your Lord Dalhousie to tell us the government of Oudh is corrupt. We cannot manage our own affairs, he says. Britain must step in to save us. So, Oudh becomes a vassal of the Sirkar." Kesab's one eye blazed, and he threw his hands into the air for emphasis as he cried, "Then everything changes!

"Our British masters tell the people of the country that they need no longer bow to their betters. Everyone is equal, they say. Thus, a soldier comes home on leave, and he finds that his privileges are gone. The lowest servant now refuses to move out of the way for him.

"But why should this be? Why should soldiers not have privileges, and a position of honour? Why should we not be regarded as great men and shown respect? Soldiers gamble with their lives every day! Have we not earned respect and privilege? This you know well, Dudley Sahib."

Dudley said nothing. He had expected to hear a lecture on the evils of the greased rifle cartridge, not this.

"Yes, everyone is equal now," Kesab continued. "There shall be no more bowing, oh, no! Not to Indian masters. Now, we must bow to British ones, to white men. When I was wounded, when I lost this…" He tapped his black eye-patch. "…the officers had already begun to change. No longer do they come to watch the *nautches*. Now they tell us that dancing girls are indecent. No longer do they speak our language, or attend our ceremonies. Now they sneer at us and tell us that we are superstitious, that we are silly.

"The British have changed. They have become arrogant and weak. They are finished here."

Dudley scratched at his short unruly beard, searching for something to say. He had seen some of the things of which Kesab spoke, had even felt shame at them. He could understand why the old sepoy was angry, even why he felt betrayed.

But Kesab was still an enemy.

"None of this excuses the mutiny," he asserted. "Your old comrades here…" He nodded at Modhu and the brothers. "…and their fellows have still rebelled. They still lied and slaughtered several hundred people, people they had promised to leave alone." He could not keep the bitterness from his voice. "That was a cowardly and despicable act."

Kesab stared at him for a moment. Then he said, "I see that you still do not understand. You must think on my words. Hold out your hands."

Dudley complied. Kesab took the length of rope and refastened it around Dudley's wrists.

The next morning it rained. The water came down in sheets, turning the *nullah* into a raging river. Kesab moved Dudley closer to the camp, to the shelter of a bell tent. On the way, Dudley noted that, even in daylight, the rain reduced visibility to only a few yards. His feet were free so that he could walk. If he ran for it now, he might actually get away.

Then he was inside the tent, and the opportunity was gone.

A circular ditch provided drainage, but an inch of water still covered the tent floor. Dudley sat on an empty ammunition crate with Modhu opposite. Kesab tied the length of rope to the tent pole and ducked back outside. Dudley did not know where the brothers had gone.

About an hour later, the rain ceased, and the canvas walls of the tent glowed with sunshine. Modhu stood and pushed through the tent flap, leaving him alone. At once,

Dudley began to think of escape again, although he realized the sepoy camp lay just outside the tent. He was alone inside, but surrounded.

A few minutes passed. At last, Kesab came into the tent and sat on the crate Modhu had vacated.

"You are wondering why I have not killed you," he stated.

"You mean to ransom me?"

"Ransom you to whom? British rule is ending in India."

Dudley shrugged. "Then why?"

Kesab leaned forward. "Just because British rule is ending does not mean there is no place for men like you, men who do not think themselves superior. I know that you do not; I sensed it in you at Madras. You are a just man, and I have chosen mercy in your case."

"So, what could be my place here? To join the rebels? I cannot do that, Kesab."

"That is not my offer." Kesab stood and again drew his sword. As before, he held it point down, displaying the jeweled hilt. "My old comrade Modhu has a cousin who once worked for a rich merchant in Lucknow, a man named Savada, who owns a very big house. This man was a supporter of the British, though he comes from a very old family, once vassals of the Great Mogul himself.

"In their cellar, they have a secret vault filled with ancient treasure. This sword belonged to it; it was a gift to Modhu from Savada, for a service Modhu performed for him. Now, Modhu has made it a gift to me.

"There are surely others like it there, in the secret vault. Dudley Sahib, Modhu knows the location of this vault. Savada showed him when he gave the gift. Soon, we will go to Lucknow and join the armies there. It is a city of great riches, and there will be much plunder. Savada, as a British supporter, is surely dead, and his house plundered already. But not the vault. Only we know of its existence."

Dudley blinked in surprise. "You want me to come to Lucknow with you? I don't understand."

Kesab smiled. "When the rebellion is over, we will open the vault and divide the treasure five ways. I do not ask you to take up arms against the British, but I offer you to join with my comrades. I give you the chance to live like a king here in India, or wherever you may wish to go, in time."

"But…but why save me to share treasure with me? Why not just let me go, Kesab, and divide the treasure four ways?"

Kesab sheathed the sword. "Then you will return to your army, which is certainly gathering to try to destroy us. They will surely fail, but even so, you would be there with them if I freed you. You would fight us, Dudley Sahib. Duty binds you to do so. But if you swear a new oath to me, an oath not to raise your hand against us, and so to share the treasure, I will let you live."

Dudley still did not see a rationale for the offer. He knew that Kesab respected him, but he could not see a reason for the man to reward him.

"Why not just ask me to swear an oath not to raise my hand against you in exchange for my life?"

Kesab shook his head. "Why are you making this difficult for yourself? I could ask that, yes. But I choose not to. You are a soldier, Dudley Sahib. We are the same, you and I. I knew that when I first met you, and you confirmed it by asking my name. I want you to show me that I was not wrong to put my trust in the British when I joined their army. Show me that there are still honourable men amongst your race!"

Dudley shifted on his crate. He did not know what to say. He had much sympathy for this man, and that was dangerous.

"There will be opportunities here," Kesab continued in a lower voice, "when the British are gone. Opportunities for men like you and me, soldiers who understand justice."

So, it was ambition, Dudley thought. Kesab was offering to share the power, as one soldier to another. He raised his hands to scratch his itching chin.

"What if I disagree? Will you kill me? That gives me no choice at all."

"You Christians believe that you go to heaven after death," Kesab said. "Why should being killed be so bad if that is true? There is a clear choice: join with us, or go to your paradise."

Dudley had not expected so frank a threat. He stared at the tent wall. For the first time, creeping fear began to rise in his stomach, a fear unlike any he had felt while defending the entrenchment. At least there he had been able to fight.

He swallowed, noticing how dry his mouth had become.

"May I…may I consider your offer for a while?"

Kesab nodded. "I will grant you this indulgence. But not for long. You must choose."

The sepoy left the tent. Dudley sat with the rope burning his wrists. He knew he could pretend to agree to Kesab's offer then make his escape. But to do that would be to break his word, to be no better than the rebels. And to betray Kesab's trust in him.

Kesab was right. His choice was clear.

Dudley did not know how many hours passed before Kesab returned. The sepoy said nothing as he ducked into the tent, untied the rope from the tent pole, and led Dudley outside.

It was still daylight, but the sky was dark with clouds. In the west, a strip of gold low on the horizon heralded the setting sun. There would be more rain before darkness fell. Dudley thought of what Captain Morrow had said about the rains washing away the entrenchment. Morrow had probably been right, at least on that particular.

Kesab led Dudley back to the *nullah*. Its bottom was now dark with half-dried mud. Modhu and the brothers were not present. Something about that and the look on Kesab's face turned his blood to ice.

"Where are your friends?" he asked.

"They are with their regiment," Kesab explained. "They have been away from it too long. They will march soon to face the enemy."

"I see." Dudley worked his wrists in their bonds. Beyond the rows of tents, the rebel battalions were forming for evening parade. He could hear the drums and bugles.

"The time has come, Dudley Sahib," Kesab said. "You must choose."

Dudley glanced at Kesab's sword, the only weapon the sepoy carried. The *nullah* was a lonely place, somewhat removed from the camp. A good place to commit murder.

A dark spot appeared on the sand behind Kesab. A raindrop.

Dudley said, "I have not chosen yet."

"No choice is a refusal," Kesab replied. "Or that is how I will see it. You must give me a clear answer."

More drops spattered, spotting the ground and tapping on the visor of Dudley's cap. The rain was warm, the drops the size of grapes.

Kesab shot a look at the sky then turned back for the tent, tugging Dudley along by his rope. Dudley knew that if he reached the tent he would have to choose. If he refused Kesab, he had about fifty paces to live.

He slipped his right hand out of the rope binding, the one he had loosened while waiting in the tent. Kesab, back to him, did not notice. Dudley's left hand was still stuck in the loop. He tried to pry it loose with his free hand.

The clouds burst, the rain coming down in torrents. Kesab hunched as the water soaked his clothing. Dudley pried the rope over his knuckles, and his left hand came free. The rope fell, but he had already turned and begun running along the muddy *nullah*.

"Stop!" Kesab shouted, his voice clear above the hissing of the rain.

Dudley knew the *nullah* ran to the southwest, towards the grand trunk road. He turned left before he reached the road, crashing through a small stand of bamboo and out the other side. He heard Kesab running behind him, but the old sepoy would be slowed by age and the wet skirt of the caftan about his legs.

As suspected, the rain and growing darkness made it difficult to see much more than a few paces in any direction. He hoped he would see the canal before he came to it.

Houses loomed on either side of him. He hurried past hunched pedestrians, a string of sodden camels, then crashed into a parked cart and fell into the mud of the street. He ignored the pain, worried more for the delay, pushed to his feet and ran on.

Ahead he saw the dark shape of one of the canal bridges. Beneath it, the canal seethed and fountained with the rain. A sentry stood on the bridge, musket at his side and a cloak looped over his head, his back to the railing.

Dudley slowed as he approached the sepoy. The man looked at him and said something. Dudley shook his head and raised one hand, as if in greeting. He knew the sentry's task was to watch the other side of the canal, not this bank. The man had little reason to be suspicious. In this light, with his tanned face and rough beard, the puggaree on his cap, Dudley could easily be a sepoy himself. And there was no sign of Kesab behind him.

When he came level with the sentry, Dudley smiled. The sentry smiled back. Dudley gave him a hard shove on the chest.

The sentry cried out in surprise and toppled over the railing into the water. Dudley lost no time. He ran for the open plain to the east.

Boldness, audacity, he thought. Kesab had not expected him to simply run away. It would not have been possible without the rain to cover his escape.

He risked a look behind him; he saw nothing but the dark shapes of buildings. Ahead was open country, the sandy plain, treacherous now with small rivers and forming pools. He had several hours of darkness to cross it.

His chest burned as he ran, and nausea almost overwhelmed him. He stopped and bent over, hands on his knees. Within a few minutes, most of the discomfort had passed. He knew he was in no condition to run for miles cross-country in the beating rain, but he had little choice. Kesab would wait for the rain to stop then come looking for him with a squadron of cavalry.

Or maybe he would not wait for the rain to stop.

Wiping his eyes, Dudley pulled his cap down low and angled to his left, towards the river. He would follow it to Allahabad and, he hoped, safety.

CHAPTER 21

The Ganges Valley
July 1857

Dudley crouched in the bamboo and studied the boat
stranded on the riverbank. It had an awning of scorched
thatch, a sign that it had been part of the doomed flo-
tilla. It had either drifted downriver by itself or its occupants had beached it and decided to take their chances
crossing open country.

Farther up the river lay a group of crocodiles with long,
narrow jaws. The massive reptiles were basking in the sun
not more than fifty yards from the boat. Their presence
made Dudley nervous, but he still planned to approach the
boat when darkness fell.

Even with the danger, finding the boat was an out-
standing bit of good luck. He could never walk all the
way to Allahabad. Already, his legs and feet were in heated
agony from the shuffling and stumbling of the previous
night.

He could not remember much from those frantic few
hours of running. At some point, the rain had ceased, and
a bright moon had emerged from behind the dark, drift-

ing clouds. He had followed the edge of the river, wading through flooded fields, skirting the villages and walled gardens. More than once, startled dogs had barked at his passage, but he had heard no human voices, saw no human form.

When the sky in the east had begun to fade to silver, then indigo, he began to look for a place to hide. He had chosen this stand of bamboo, making a nest among the tall stalks. It was then he had spied the boat lying a few yards downstream.

It was as if some unseen hand had guided him to it, and in his desperate need, he murmured a prayer of thanks, adding a plea that the enemy would not send cavalry to find him while he waited throughout the long hours of the day. There were no villages near this chosen hiding place, but still he feared someone would see the boat and alert the rebels.

As the hours passed, from time to time, he peered through the bamboo stalks to scout the lay of the land. Three times he spied horsemen ranging across the plain a few miles distant, and each time his heart leapt in his chest. At one point, the cavalry approached the river, but farther downstream from where he hid. He wondered if they were searching for him.

The most obvious route of escape for any prisoner was the river, but the horsemen were not following it. Perhaps, he thought, Kesab did not have the authority or ability to convince the rebel cavalry to chase a single prisoner that he had, after all, taken on his own volition.

Along with the fear of discovery, hunger gnawed at him. He had not eaten anything since his last bowl of rice, almost a full day ago. He tried to ignore the pangs and lie still in the tall green stalks. Insects crawled on his clothes and skin, and once a snake slithered past his feet. The dry fronds of palms rustled overhead, and parrots squawked.

He watched the sky, pale blue with growing cumulus. A kite soared in search of prey, trailing its forked tail. It was hot. His feet had swollen inside his worn leather shoes. He tried to sleep, repeating in his head, *I will survive this.*

It rained again during the day, but he could do nothing but let the water soak him. It was warm, but he shivered. Like hunger, sickness was also a danger, perhaps more immediate than the enemy.

At last, the sun began to sink in the west, and he was content to wait no longer. When he heard the crocodiles splashing into the water, one after the other, he knew it was time to go.

The high-prowed boat was heavy, and at first he could not budge it from the sandy mudbank. He fell against the hull and sat there, gasping, sweating, weak and nauseated. But he had to succeed. He tried again, and at last the boat began to slide backward on its low keel. When it was afloat, he waded through water up to his knees and scrambled aboard.

A long oar served as the rudder. Dudley steered the boat into the current and let it take him downstream. A short mast stood in front of the awning. The sail would provide greater speed, but he left it for now.

There were three baskets in the bottom of the boat, and he pulled one towards him. He wept with relief when he saw that it contained several loaves of flat bread. That was evidence the boat had drifted off unoccupied, or the provisions would not still be here. Another basket contained milk that had spoiled in the heat. He threw it overboard. The last basket held three army canteens—small wooden barrels painted blue. Each was full of warm but clean water. With the canteens were some army rations—tins of beef—but the water was more valuable than the food.

After a few bites of bread and sips from a canteen, he at last hoisted the small square sail and turned it to catch the light wind. With the moon again lighting his way, he kept a grip on the rudder and did his best to keep the boat in midstream. He was certain the river maintained a steady course for most of its length. Remembering the maps he had seen, he knew there were no major bends until near the town of Adong. That would mark the midpoint between Cawnpore and the town of Futtehpore.

When the sky again began to brighten, he lowered the sail and drifted to the northern shore. Thanks to the recent rains, the river ran high enough to allow him to beach the boat near some brush along the bank. There, he covered part of it with fallen palm fronds. He lay down a short distance from the boat and pulled more palm fronds over him like blankets.

Human voices awakened him. He froze in his nest until he realized the voices were coming from across the river. Sitting up, he crouched under the palms and squinted at the far bank.

Several women had come down to the water with their children to bathe. The children laughed and splashed each other under the watchful eyes of their mothers.

The naked bodies of the women made Dudley think of Charlotte. He had almost forgotten her in his desperate need to escape, but now he remembered that her situation was much worse than his. He now had a chance, while she was at the mercy of her captors.

Thoughts of Charlotte brought a host of conflicting emotions. Fear for her safety, joy at the memory of their first few weeks together, anger at her behaviour during the siege. What he had seen as her boldness of character, her daring, ultimately seemed to spring not from courage but a certain kind of self-indulgence.

Nevertheless, as he settled against a tree and dozed, his dreams were all of their earlier time, a fairer time, before the world had been turned on its ear.

When evening fell again, he pushed the boat back into the stream and hoisted the sail. After about an hour, he came to the bend in the river, a long curve to the left. He thought the course ran straight beyond the bend but maintained a sharp lookout nonetheless.

With morning, the rains returned. He lowered the sail but did not steer for shore, riding the current and using an empty basket to bail. The rain would provide some cover, as it had before. He passed several other boats, and villages with their *ghats* leading down to the water. No one took notice of him.

The rain ceased before midday. Soon after, Dudley spied another squadron of cavalry through gaps in the trees to his right. The squadron was riding on the plain, moving from the east.

He realized that, unless the troopers were members of a rebel patrol returning to Cawnpore, they had come from the opposite direction. They were clad in dark-blue tunics, but he could not identify them. From this distance, it was impossible to determine whether they were friendly or not.

He took a few deep breaths to stifle a sudden overpowering surge of hope and relief. If these were British troops, he was saved. If not, they might see the boat and decide to investigate. Although, he told himself, what was one little boat on the Ganges?

The cavalry came about in a wide arc, riding back the way they had come. Another group of horsemen faced them from a position on a low hillock. The members of this second group also wore blue coats, save one man clad in red. From the way they sat in their saddles, Dudley was almost sure they were British officers.

Almost.

He swallowed, wondering what to do. He would have to get closer. He turned for the southern bank.

With the boat safely grounded, he crawled through the river mud and paused on the edge of the fields. Between him and the road, the ground was a swamp at least two feet deep in water. The cavalry cantered through it, hoofs sending up small geysers. Atop the hillock, sunlight flashed from a raised pair of field glasses. In the east, a few columns of black smoke rose into the air.

One of the officers on the hill wore a conical sun helmet. Dudley had never known sepoys or native officers to have ever worn such a headdress.

He crawled to his feet and began splashing across the field with one hand raised above his head. Time seemed to stand still. His legs moved, carrying him forward as if of their own volition.

Taking off his cap, he waved it in their air. Several of the horsemen turned and broke away from the main body, coming toward him.

"I'm a British officer!" he tried to shout, but his voice came out not much louder than a whisper. "I'm a British officer!"

The horsemen surrounded him, forming a ring. He stopped running and stood on shaking legs in the swamp, swaying slightly.

"I'm a British officer," he repeated.

The officer with the sun helmet was suddenly there in front of him, staring down from his saddle.

"Good God, man," he said. "What has happened to you?"

Dudley met his eye.

"I've just come from Cawnpore," he croaked. "We have to go back there. We have to back at once."

A wave of nausea and weariness passed over him, washing away his joy at having been rescued; and he dropped to his knees in the muddy water.

CHAPTER 22

The Ganges Valley
July 1857

General Havelock's army snaked along the grand trunk road, the general and his staff riding in the van. The campaign was underway at last.

Behind Havelock rode Colonel Hamilton of the 78th Highlanders, with him the pipes and corps drummers of his regiment, marching and playing in the heat, stirring onward the long column of soldiers.

Barker walked alongside No. 3 Company. The men were formed in fours to the right, rifles sloped on their left shoulders. Sweat poured from under their covered forage caps and soaked the armpits of their white frocks, but no one drooped. The pipes and drums were enough to combat the heat and discomfort. When the pipes began to play and the drums beat in time, sagging heads and hunched shoulders stiffened and straightened. Hundreds of boots crunched as one on the hard road. The martial music put a bit of spirit into everyone's step.

Barker looked back along the column. Behind the Highlanders marched the Madras Fusiliers—the Blue Caps—

also sweating in their wool tunics. The 64th and 84th regiments were next, then the Ferozepore Sikhs. The field guns, bronze 9-pounders of the Royal Artillery, rolled along behind teams of draft bullocks, some on the road and some on the bare plain.

After the artillery came the baggage—camels bearing ammunition boxes, the long line of elephants loaded with provisions, the bullock carts filled with shot. At last, in the rear of the column, the great mob of civilians and camp followers straggled along. Natives still loyal to the British trailed the army to ply their wares and to curry favour in the event of victory.

It had been a swift forced march so far, despite its trials. Supply problems had delayed the departure of the column until July 7th. It had rained much of the time. When the sun had come out, it was broiling-hot, the temperature rising above a hundred and thirty degrees. Many men had fallen out of ranks with heat prostration, and there had been more small outbreaks of cholera.

The terrain was also difficult. The torrential rains had flooded the low-lying fields, while deep *nullahs* cut across other parts of the plain, sometimes bisecting the road. The guns had to pause at the *nullahs* while teams of men attacked the banks with spades, making earthen ramps. The artillery was then able to roll down one ramp and up the other.

Now and then, the column encountered evidence of the passage of Major Renaud's advance force. In the villages and along the road stood numerous burned and abandoned bungalows. In some places, bodies dangled from trees, their rotting limbs picked over by vultures.

"Not all of these fellows are sepoys," Barker had commented as they passed one grisly collection of native corpses.

"They're all Pandies, Sergeant," Private Douglas Marten said from the ranks.

"And you would know a treasonous rebel when you saw him, wouldn't you, Marten?" Barker snapped. "I highly doubt it."

It promised to be a war of immense cruelty, the sergeant thought. Although he supposed war might actually be the very definition of cruelty.

Cruel or merciful, Barker was glad to be on the march again. The mutiny was a terrible tragedy, but he was a soldier, and it was his task to fight wars. For him, war meant a personal challenge, a chance for distinction, for advancement. And it was good to get out of garrison with its dull and numbing routine. War was what soldiers trained for. Now they could put that training to some use against a hated foe.

And recent events had made this a foe more hated than most. This, Barker decided, would be a conflict of the righteous against the unworthy.

The massacres at Meerut and Delhi paled beside the news from Cawnpore. Garbled reports from scouts had spoken of General Wheeler's garrison besieged, then of its having been massacred. Then a trickle of survivors had come in, most having escaped down the river. They had confirmed everyone's worst fears with tales of the treachery at the boats and the imprisonment of the ladies.

Barker could only assume that Lieutenant Dudley and Colour-Sergeant O'Ryan were among the dead, and this made the war one of personal revenge. The column could not march fast enough for his liking.

At sundown, the little army halted to rest in a dry region of the plain. The men spread out on either side of the road to prepare a meal and bivouac. Their rest was short. At eleven o'clock, the column reformed, and the march resumed under moonlight. Barker marched in silence, ignoring his aches and pains, his fatigue. There was no time to lose, no time for further rest stops.

After about an hour, Captain Reed came riding along the perimeter.

"Halt the company, Sergeant."

Commands were ringing out ahead, the Highlander companies already coming to a standstill.

"Company, mark...time! Company...halt!" shouted Barker.

The men waited, steady and silent in their groups of fours. Insects buzzed and whined in the night air. From the head of the column came a tattoo of hoofbeats and the sound of voices raised in greeting.

At length, Lieutenant Morris reined in beside Barker.

"We just met up with Major Renaud's advance, lads. Our entire field force is assembled. Just let Pandy come out now!"

Despite his opinion of Morris, Barker felt like cheering.

Within a few minutes, they were moving again, the pipes and drums playing to wake the countryside. Barker forgot his sore feet and aching knees.

Someone was coming towards him on foot from the head of the column. He squinted in the moonlight; there was something familiar about the way the fellow walked, but he could not quite place it.

When the figure came closer, Barker saw a man of indeterminate age with a gaunt, clean-shaven face under the peak of his cap. He wore what appeared to be shining new summer trousers and a new white frock. A sergeant's yataghan hung from a private's belt at his waist, but he sported no other weapon or rank insignia.

"How are you, Sergeant Barker?" the man asked, falling in beside him.

Barker gaped in astonishment.

"M–Mister Dudley!" he stammered. "Sir...we thought we had lost you in Cawnpore!"

The gaunt face twisted in a smile that did not reach the eyes.

"I managed to get out. Just."

Barker said the next thing that came to mind.

"What of O'Ryan, sir?"

Dudley's smile disappeared.

"You'll be the colour-sergeant, now, I should think."

CHAPTER 23

The Ganges Valley
July 1857

The column marched throughout the night. Dudley rode a horse he had borrowed from the artillery, a slow and docile gelding more accustomed to working in a team; Major Renaud had given him a tent, a chance to bathe and to shave, to procure clean clothing

It felt strange to be going back to Cawnpore so soon. He knew he needed a rest of several days, but he refused to sit out the coming fight.

It had been with a mixture of joy and disbelief that he had joined Major Renaud's column. It had been like waking from a nightmare, like entering another world. Gone were the restless days and nights of waiting in Wheeler's entrenchment for death or relief. It was as if the journey to Cawnpore had never happened.

He would soon be with his regiment again, as safe for now as one could be in an army at war.

"Some of your friends in the Royal Hants are coming behind us," Renaud had said. "You'll soon be at home, Ensign."

He could have allowed himself to feel bitterness, even rage, for this force represented the very reinforcements he and the others had waited for in vain. Here they were, but too late. Too late to save the doomed garrison.

But not too late to save the women and children imprisoned in the Bibighar.

He had learned that, in many ways, it was a miracle a relief force had been assembled at all. The troops had come from afar—from Madras, Bombay, even Persia. More would be coming, but a major concentration would take time. Regiments would even have to sail from England—and they would, for the fate of British authority in India hung in the balance.

Now he rode beside his men in No. 3 Company. He still found it difficult to fathom that he was back with his friends and comrades. Sometimes it seemed that he was moving within a dream, and at any moment, he expected to wake in the boat beside the river, or in the *nullah* with Kesab, or in the entrenchment with O'Ryan and Captain Morrow. Strange waves of panic kept seizing him, and an unbearable sense of urgency.

He was in the midst of one such attack when Lieutenant Morris fell in beside him. Morris was smiling, his face aglow with excitement.

"So, you are real!" he exclaimed. "Not some rumour, as I half-expected. Damn me, William, if it's not good to see you!"

Dudley wiped sweat from his forehead with the back of his hand.

"Yes…uh, how are you, Trevor?"

Morris laughed. "How am I? I should ask the same of you. Captain Norcott told me the story, and I didn't dare believe it. How you escaped the massacre and how the advance column found you wandering through the countryside. A remarkable feat! You'll get the Victoria Cross for it, mark my words."

"I don't think one gets the Victoria Cross for saving oneself, Trevor. And surely I wasn't the only one to escape?"

"Well, no, there have been a few others." Morris's face took on a grim cast. "By God, I can't wait to get a crack at the damned rebels! You say they are holding the women prisoner?"

"Yes." Dudley swayed in his saddle as a wave of dizziness took him, but the panic was ebbing. "Yes. Mrs. Edwards and...Charlotte are still there. We shall have to rescue them."

"And rescue them we shall, William," Morris stated. "Rescue them we shall."

They rode together the rest of the night. Dudley found Morris's presence comforting, although he could not share the lieutenant's bright enthusiasm.

With the rising sun, the column marched on. They were now in the region of Futtehpore, a land of flooded fields dotted with dry hillocks, villages, and mango topes. The houses were of white-washed brick, many set within garden enclosures with high masonry walls. The gardens and orchards offered plenty of cover, had the enemy chosen to use it.

It was eight o'clock in the morning when the field force at last came to a halt.

General Havelock had chosen a low ridge on which to rest his men. Beyond the ridge, the road ran down between more inundated fields, broad expanses two to three feet deep in rainwater. Farther on was another ridge of brown earth and green trees, then the bright houses of Futtehpore itself.

The men stacked arms and began preparing fires to cook a meal; they had not eaten in almost twelve hours.

As Dudley and Morris prepared to do the same, Captain Norcott trotted towards them on horseback.

"Good morning, sir," Morris piped, saluting.

Norcott reined in, returning the salute.

"Good morning! Hope you are feeling better, Dudley. If not, perhaps my news will cheer you. Cavalry reports that the enemy is coming out of Cawnpore to meet us. We are to send a small reconnaissance force up to the high ground." He pointed towards Futtehpore. "Would you care to join it, Lieutenant Morris?"

"You know I would, sir!" Morris cried.

"Good. I'm sorry, Dudley. I know you're game as well, but after your ordeal, I don't want to use you up."

Dudley hesitated, wanting to protest. With reluctance, he had to admit that Norcott was right, and he was not strong enough. Not yet.

"Very well, sir."

This was just a reconnaissance. He would muster his strength for the main show.

Norcott and Morris rode off, joining a small force of infantry that had assembled about a hundred yards away. With its entourage of mounted officers, the infantry moved off through the swamped fields.

Dudley busied himself with his campfire. Around him, the men of the Royal Hants and the Highlanders were doing the same. Since little dry fuel was available, the firewood had come from the quartermaster's stores. Dudley got his small pile of kindling burning. He would have bacon and eggs for breakfast.

From Futtehpore came the dull thumping of guns. He stood, frying pan in hand, and gazed towards the town. The guns had sounded at least as large as 24-pounders.

His hand began to shake, and he set down the pan. He heard Sergeant Barker shouting at the men to form up. Fusiliers were snatching their rifles from the stacks and rushing to form in line. The Highlanders were also abandoning their breakfasts to prepare for battle.

Dudley clamped his hands under his arms and drew in a slow, deep breath.

So soon, he thought.

They would fight the enemy today.

CHAPTER 24

Futtehpore
July 1857

At the first shots from the rebel artillery, the reconnais-sance force withdrew, its members dispersing to their constituent units. Without orders, the entire British force assembled to meet the enemy. They faced northwest, along the road to Futtehpore.

The Grenadiers along with No. 3 Company of the Royal Hants formed up on the left of the Highlanders. Sergeant Barker bellowed at a final group of men who came running in from their abandoned bivouac.

"Fall in, two ranks!"

The men squeezed together, elbow to elbow, and they

One after the other, from the right of the line to the left, the men of the two companies stood at ease, as if forming on parade. Behind the ranks, Lazzy scurried to and fro, tail wagging.

"You know something's up, eh?" Barker said, and the beagle looked at him and bayed, ready for the hunt.

On the ridge across the flooded fields, a group of horsemen appeared, *sowars* in white turbans and pale-blue jackets. They paused, outlined against the sky, then spurred forward, riding down into the swamp. The *sowars* came to an abrupt halt, water spraying and churning around the legs of their horses. For a moment, they milled around in apparent confusion then turned and began riding back up the ridge.

"They didn't expect to find an army waiting for them, I warrant," Barker said.

Captain Norcott rode behind the companies with Captain Reed. The other officers—Morris and Dudley of No. 3 Company, Lieutenant Avery and Ensign O'Brien of the Grenadiers—took their positions on foot.

"We are to deploy to the right of the road," Norcott announced. "React to the commands of Major Mackay of the Ross-shire Buffs."

"Battalion will form fours right," commanded a strange voice with a Scottish burr.

Rebel guns had appeared on the ridge, two batteries of 24-pounders. The rebels unlimbered the guns under the mango trees as the British force began to deploy.

Barker marched with his men across the road and down into the adjacent field. Hundreds of booted feet splashed into the water; the Highlanders waded to their bare knees, kilts and hair sporrans brushing the surface. The pipes began to play, and the two companies of fusiliers halted and turned from fours back into line. The Highlanders continued to march, each company halting a few paces after the other.

"Deploy your company as skirmishers," Captain Norcott told Reed. "The rest of our battalion will form in extended order, at intervals."

"Sergeant Barker," Captain Reed said, "take the company forward and form skirmish order. Six paces between each pair of men."

The first 24-pounder barked as the company went forward in extended order. Three rebel infantry regiments suddenly appeared on either side of the batteries. Barker counted twelve guns and could see the rebel cavalry now moving behind the infantry. This could not be the main rebel army. It was just a small detachment.

The two little forces faced each other across the flooded fields.

A squadron of the Volunteer Cavalry anchored the British right flank. These were gentlemen volunteers, civilians dressed in felt sun helmets, blue tunics, and white trousers with knee-high boots. Next came the Blue Caps, then the 78th and Royal Hants, maintaining contact with the road. On the road itself, the Royal Artillery was bringing up six 9-pounders. To the left of the road stood the 64th, the 84th, and the Ferozepore Sikhs, with the Irregular Cavalry to cover their flank. The British outnumbered the rebel detachment two-to-one.

Captain Reed had dismounted and stood in the water with Barker, sword drawn. On their right, a company of the Madras Fusiliers had also deployed in skirmish order.

"Target their gunners, Sergeant," Reed said.

The 24-pounders were booming, and round shot came skipping across the water like stones, spraying fountains with each bounce. The skirmishers waded forward in pairs, and the rifles of the front-rank men began to crack. As they reloaded, the rear rank fired. Barker saw several enemy gunners fall. Raising his own rifle, he fired and brought the weapon down to reload, its butt in the water.

On Barker's right, the pipers were wading ahead of their battalion. They were too far apart to play together, and their music had become a discordant muddle of conflicting melodies. Piper Andrews was the farthest in front, moving in advance of the skirmishers.

"Move up, lads!" Barker shouted. He heard a strange wheezing behind him and turned to see Lazzy swimming toward him. As the dog paddled past, Barker shouted, "Follow Lazzy!"

The skirmishers fired as they moved, the regular popping of rifles audible above the wail of the pipes. On the left, the Royal Artillery had unlimbered their guns not more than two hundred yards from the rebel line. The 9-pounders began to bark, one gun after the other. Great gaps appeared in the rebel infantry battalions; the rebel casualties were sudden and substantial. The survivors began to edge back.

With the sound of a wave crashing against a rocky shore, the main body of Highlanders and Blue Caps came on behind the skirmishers. Barker raised a cheer. The rebel infantry battalions, already decimated by the close-range British artillery fire, broke and ran. One moment they covered the ridge, the next they were gone. They had even left their guns behind in their flight.

Piper Andrews gained the high ground, halting and continuing to play as his sodden kilt dripped. Lazzy clambered ashore next to him, barking as if to add encouragement. A bugle sounded, its notes telling the skirmishers to reform on the left of their battalions.

The men of No. 3 Company turned and went back into the water, hurrying to dress onto the Grenadiers. Then the entire battalion advanced as one, emerging from the water to join Piper Andrews. Lazzy yapped and followed his company, running at Private Geary's heels.

The rebel infantry ran back through Futtehpore, past the masonry houses and walled gardens. The Highlanders and Royal Hants halted to fix bayonets, watching in annoyance as a squadron of the rebel 2nd Cavalry drove off the Irregular Cavalry.

"Why don't the bastards fight?" Barker heard a voice, and realized it was Ensign Dudley. He stood behind the company, holding his drawn yataghan like a sword.

After its successful charge, the rebel cavalry withdrew. Beyond the houses, the rebel infantry had rallied.

"Company commanders," Colonel Hamilton cried, "dress your lines!"

"Company dressing," Captain Reed called out, "eyes… right! Dress!"

The companies seemed to shiver as the men shuffled closer, reforming a perfect straight line. The pipes had ceased playing, the pipers falling in behind the battalion. A bugle sounded the command for a general charge.

The field force advanced as one great line, closing the distance to the shrunken rebel ranks. A few sepoy muskets popped, but again the enemy began to edge back. The British halted, bringing their rifles to the ready.

The enemy did not wait to receive the British volleys. Their ranks disintegrated, the men turning to flee.

Barker watched them run with a mixture of satisfaction and curiosity. He hoped the main rebel force at Cawnpore was as easy to intimidate.

"They're nothing but a lot of cowards," he heard Private Geary sneer.

"No talking in ranks, boy," Barker snapped. Then he added, "This was just a skirmish. We had 'em outnumbered."

The British battalions remained in their ranks; Barker waited for the order to pursue, even though he did not relish the thought. Like everyone else, he was exhausted from the forced march. His stomach rumbled.

Behind him, at General Havelock's headquarters, a strange bugle call pierced the smoke-filled air.

"What's that call, Sarge?" Private Geary asked, ignoring Barker's earlier admonishment. Lazzy sat at his feet, ears cocked as if also awaiting the sergeant's answer.

Barker was smiling. He had not heard that particular bugle call for years.

"That's a rare one, boys," he said, "but welcome. The general must be pleased with us. That's the call for grog."

CHAPTER 25

Near Cawnpore
July 1857

Henry Havelock sat his horse before his army, sixteen hundred men who amounted to little more than a brigade. Each regiment was drawn up in two ranks, standing easy, the men eager to hear their general's words of encouragement.

Dudley stood behind the left flank of No. 3 Company. His friends were with him. To his right stood Sergeant Bell, then Lieutenant Morris, then the former Corporal, now Sergeant, Johnson. On the far right, beside the rear rank marker, stood Brian Barker. Barker now wore a gold crown above the three red chevrons on his right sleeve. As Dudley had predicted, Captain Reed had raised him to colour-sergeant.

"You have fought well over the last days," General Havelock declared, "though the true test still lies before us. The enemy, under the direction of the traitorous Nana Sahib, has entrenched before Cawnpore, across our line of march. They number some seven thousand men, sepoys trained in our own tactics."

The general shifted in his saddle. He wore a sun helmet with a neck curtain, a blue patrol coat, and white trousers. He was a handsome gentlemen of more than sixty years, with calm eyes and thick steel-gray side-whiskers.

"I have no doubt in your abilities," he continued. "Today, we shall meet the enemy. All reports tell the same tale— the women and children still live, and with God's help, we shall save them or die in the attempt."

The army cheered, the men waving their caps in the air. Dudley wished he could cheer with them but felt no exaltation at the anticipated victory. All he felt was the urgency of their task.

He adjusted his new sword belt, a baldric-style crossbelt hanging from his right shoulder to his left hip. From it dangled a sword he had borrowed from an officer of the Ross-shire Buffs he had met in Futtehpore the day after the battle.

The British field force had taken no casualties and had captured the twelve rebel guns. The following day, July 13th, they had camped just outside the village for a much-needed rest after the rapid advance from Allahabad. The Highland officer had approached Dudley after breakfast.

"Are you the lad who survived the siege?"

"Yes, sir."

The Highlander had grinned. He had large ears and close-spaced, merry eyes.

"I'm proud to have such a bold and enterprising young officer attached to the regiment. Allow me to shake your hand. I'm Captain Gabriel Mackenzie."

"Pleased to meet you, sir," Dudley said. "I just wish more could have been as fortunate as I."

"Well said." Mackenzie then glanced at Dudley's yataghan. "Is that the only weapon you have?"

"The rebels took my sword." He was sorry for the loss, the weapon having been a gift from a dying man. "I mean to sign out a rifle from the armourer."

Mackenzie had shaken his head in disapproval.

"An officer needs a sword. Come with me."

Mackenzie traveled with two native servants. By all appearances, he did not fit the model of the frugal Scotsman. In his tent stood a wooden rack holding three swords—an 1848 light cavalry sabre and two straight Highland broadswords. He took a broadsword from the rack and presented it to Dudley.

"I'll lend you this until you find a replacement. Some call it a claymore, though of course it's not a true claymore like those my ancient ancestors carried. A latter-day version, one could say. A might different from a sabre, with more heft."

Dudley slipped his right hand into the cloth-lined basket hilt.

"I don't know how to thank you, sir."

Mackenzie's blue eyes went hard and grim.

"Take your revenge on Pandy. That will be thanks enough."

That revenge had grown one step closer the next day when the field force resumed its advance. Dudley had begun composing a letter to his uncle describing the march. In time, if he survived the coming actions, he would begin rewriting his lost memoir and add these events.

"I have been over this ground before," the letter began, "but in a time of peace. Now, we fight one skirmish after another."

> Last evening, the 14th, we found the enemy entrenched near the village of Adong.
>
> In the morning, we advanced with our Volunteer Cavalry in the lead. Owing to their poor performance at Futtehpore, the Irregular Cavalry have been disarmed. Our small troop of Volunteer Cavalry will have to shoulder the burden of mounted operations from here on.

The enemy sent out their cavalry to capture our baggage, but the infantry guard
drove them off with their Enfields. Meanwhile, our main body went forward in skirmish order. The enemy was hidden amongst some thick trees. We could not see
them, but our Enfields did their work. Soon,
rebels came pouring from their positions in
flight. We followed them, again capturing a
few guns and some of their baggage.

After this brief action, we encamped to
cook our dinner. No sooner had we sat
down than scouts returned to report that
the enemy had taken up a position at the
Pandoonudda bridge. This stone bridge
spans a deep and flooded nullah. General
Havelock feared that, were the enemy to
destroy it, our field force could be delayed
for days.

We left our half-eaten meals and began moving again. We found a rebel 24-
pounder on the bridge, and two lighter
guns entrenched on either side. Our general turned and asked who would be the
first to the bridge, the 64th or the 78th?

A race was on, but the rebels did
not wait to meet our British bayonets.
They abandoned their guns, and all
agree that our two regiments reached the
bridge together, with a few of the Royal
Hants mixed in for the bargain.

The letter made it sound as if this was all business as
usual. Dudley did not mention his restless sleep, with its cha-
otic nightmares, nor the bouts of panic that still seized him.

After the capture of the bridge, the field force had made
camp within twenty miles of Cawnpore. The next morn-

ing, they had marched sixteen miles to the village of Maharajpur.

That had been three hours ago. While the troops rested in a mango tope, Dudley watched from afar as General Havelock spoke with some civilians and two armed men who appeared to be loyal sepoys. Soon after, the drums beat the assembly, and the regiments formed their ranks; and Havelock had begun his address.

"Gentlemen," the general said now, "bring your battalions to attention. We will form an open column, right in front, and advance according to plan."

Shouted commands rang out on all sides.

"Eyes…front! Atten…shun! Shoulder…arms!"

The army then changed from line to open column of companies. Each company swung to its right through an arc of ninety degrees, like a vast door on a hinge. The long column, one company after another, now faced Cawnpore along the grand trunk road. The artillery brought up its guns, sturdy bullocks pulling the bronze 9-pounders. The main battery of four guns rattled onto the road behind No. 3 Company and halted.

For a moment, there was silence. Dudley had lost his watch in Cawnpore, and he glanced at the sun. He judged the time at close to two o'clock.

Time for battle.

The Nana Sahib had drawn up his main army of seven thousand men in a long crescent. He anchored his right flank in a village, with infantry supporting three 9-pounders. In his centre was another village and two more guns. On his left lay a third cluster of houses and a low hill. Three 24-pounders crowned the hill, while the infantry waited in shallow trenches and behind garden walls.

Between the three villages ran the grand trunk and the branch road to the Cawnpore cantonments. The Nana's fire would be concentrated on the point where the two roads diverged. The British field force moved towards that point, the Volunteer Cavalry screening the advance. Behind the horsemen came the Blue Caps, then two guns, then the Highlanders and Royal Hants.

Dudley watched the Highland company marching twenty paces in front of him, pleated kilts swinging in time to the pipes. He could see the tops of their Queen's Colour and buff Regimental Colour, both hanging limp in the still, hot air. Behind him, the wheels of the four guns ground on the paved road, the bullocks snorting as they strained at their yokes. Far ahead waited the enemy, the same men who had besieged Wheeler's entrenchment. Kesab would be there, and Modhu and the two brothers.

A thick tope of mango trees ran off into the fields to the right of the road. Before the force reached it, Dudley heard the clear command, "Right wheel!" The Blue Caps turned off the road, moving along the edge of the trees, and the Highlanders and Royal Hants followed. The Volunteer Cavalry continued on their straight course, up the road to the Nana's firing zone.

The mango tope ran in a line parallel to the enemy's front, screening the British infantry that was now making its way toward the rebel left flank. The ground was still wet, so no dust rose above the trees to give away General Havelock's strategy. The pipes had ceased playing.

A gun banged away on Dudley's left, but the trees were so thick he could see nothing. More bangs followed, the deep-throated reports of 24-pounders. The Nana's artillery had engaged the Volunteer Cavalry.

The trees began to thin; then the head of the column emerged from behind the grove. A second tope began two hundred yards ahead, but for now the gap exposed the column to view.

"They'll see us," someone said, and Sergeant Johnson snapped, "Shut up, Private Geary."

Dudley looked to his left, across the muddy plain. The enemy line shimmered in the heat, the infantry entrenchments clustered between the brick bungalows, the flags of the various regiments hanging limp. The guns spouted white smoke as they fired on the cavalry. In the center sat a man on an elephant, the Nana Sahib. On the left flank, just below the hill, a squadron of the mutinous 2nd Bengal Cavalry waited.

Blue Cap skirmishers scurried onto the open plain just as the 2nd Cavalry spurred forward. The rebels had seen the column and had no doubt guessed that Havelock intended to turn their flank. Enfield rifles cracked, and one rebel horseman fell. The others hesitated before pulling back out of range.

The British column carried on, but the rebel gunners began trailing their cannon around to face the unexpected threat. Dudley watched the crews of the three left-flank 24-pounders sponging and loading.

One gun spat smoke. A few seconds later, the report followed, and a round shot sprayed mud and earth as it slapped into the plain just short of the column. Then the other guns fired. One ball again fell short, but the second skipped between No. 3 Company and the Highlanders. The field force was caught in the most dangerous of positions—an open marching column, its flank exposed to enemy artillery.

More shot roared towards them, and a howitzer shell burst in the air to Dudley's rear. He ducked, as did the men in front of him. General Havelock came riding back along the edge of the column, shouting, "Take heart, men! Another five hundred yards, and we will have turned their flank!"

The head of the column at last reached the next growth of trees. Round shot continued to crash through the branches, spraying leaves and bits of shattered limbs. But the rebels were firing blind, and soon the cannonade ceased.

The column marched on, having sustained little damage. When it again emerged from cover, it was within a short march of the village and hill on the enemy left.

They had done it, Dudley realized. They had turned the rebel flank. Sepoy artillerymen were struggling to redeploy their guns, and an infantry regiment was rushing to form a new line at right angles to its last position.

General Havelock's voice was clear as he shouted, "Column will reform line, for...ward!"

Without pausing in their march, the companies swung to the left, ninety degrees as before, to face the enemy flank. There, they halted as the British artillery came into action, its officers shouting, "Action left!"

"Madras Fusiliers, deploy as skirmishers to the right," Havelock cried as he rode behind the line. "The army will advance in echelon, right to left."

The 9-pounders had unlimbered, the gunners ramming home cartridge and shot. The rebels finished deploying the three 24-pounders, two in the open, one behind a low garden wall. The Blue Caps, armed with Enfields, went forward in pairs to engage the rebel gunners.

From behind the Highlanders and Royal Hants, Sergeant-Major Hart of the Ross-shire Buffs shouted, "Battalion will advance in line, by the centre, quick...march!"

The battalion stepped off, colours bobbing above the heads of the men. The pipes and drums marched in front, striking up with the regimental charge.

"*Caber feidh!*" the Highlanders roared in Gaelic. They were now leading the echelon attack, moving so as not to screen the British guns. Fifty paces behind them and to their left, the 64th and 84th would advance next in echelon. The last unit in the order would be the Ferozepore Sikhs.

The 9-pounders opened fire, one after the other. Dudley drew the great Highland broadsword and held it sloped on his right shoulder. He could see the 9-pounder balls striking in the village, three impacting against one rebel gun. The gun tipped over, a wheel smashed. The other two 24-pounders returned fire, blasting smoke. The shot howled as it rushed in, but Dudley did not see where it went.

He was sweating and clenching his teeth, eager to move forward, roused by the music of the pipes. The line advanced in perfect dressing, the men with rifles sloped on their shoulders, closing the distance to the enemy. The rebels sponged and loaded their two remaining guns.

The voice of Colonel Hamilton pierced the noise of the artillery.

"Battalion…halt! Take cover! Lie down!"

The line stopped, the men prone in the dust. Bagpipes honked and whined as pipers lay on top of them, squeezing air from the sheepskin bags. The two 24-pounders fired, belching grapeshot; the small iron balls puckered the ground where they struck, and Dudley heard a piece whistle close to his head.

The battalion rose to its feet, the line shivering as the men dressed without command. Then the colonel, still exposed on the back of his horse, said, "Forward, Sergeant-Major."

Hart's voice boomed again: "By the centre, quick… march!"

The pipes and drums started up, driving another tune. The feet of every man moved to the music, kilts and sporrans swinging. With a shouted order, Hamilton had every man in the front rank bring his rifle to the charge, bayonets leveled.

The village drew closer. A rebel infantry regiment fired a volley from behind a wall, but the smoothbore muskets had poor accuracy beyond fifty yards. One Highlander fell, blood streaming from his leg, and a man of the Royal Hants fell out with a smashed left arm.

In the rear, the 9-pounders continued to pound the enemy. Two rounds struck home on a second 24-pounder, flipping the gun barrel backwards off its carriage. The third gun was well concealed behind its wall. Shot struck the masonry but did no damage to the gun or crew.

"We will charge and take that gun!" Colonel Hamilton cried.

The men in the battalion increased their pace, eager to move forward up the slope of the hill. Hamilton at last released them.

"*Charge!*"

The remaining gun now lay to Dudley's right, and it fired as the men screamed and ran. Four Highlanders fell, but a moment later other kilted soldiers engulfed the gun position.

The rebel infantry lay in No. 3 Company's immediate front. Muskets boomed, but the rebels were firing too high. Two Fusiliers dropped, but the others leapt to the wall. Rebels began to stream away from their line. With a final rush, the British charged home. They hit the enemy with a crunch of colliding musket stocks and bodies, grunts and screams.

Dudley jumped onto the wall, sword raised. A rebel crouched against the brick and raised his musket to fire. Dudley brought the heavy blade down, howling. The sword bit into the man's shoulder and kept going, down into the breast bone. The body went limp, and he tugged at the blade. It stuck, and he had to place his foot on the man's chest to jerk the sword free.

All around him, Highlanders and Fusiliers were cheering. They had taken the gun and broken the enemy's left. Dead and dying rebels, their red or white clothes stained with blood, lay everywhere along the garden wall.

General Havelock rode amongst the cheering men as the sergeants were yelling at them to reform their ranks.

"Well done, Seventy-eighth," Havelock shouted, his voice little more than a hoarse shriek. "You shall be my own regiment! Well done, Fusiliers! Another charge like that shall win the day."

The battalion reformed a line across the road beyond the village. The 64th and 84th had already moved past them to engage the enemy center. The rebels were streaming away from that position, men running in small clumps. The Sikhs, massive turbans on their heads, went past in echelon, rushing to take the enemy's original right. Within a few minutes, the sepoys were fleeing that position as well.

Dudley knelt by a rebel corpse and wiped his blade on the dead man's clothes. He did not sheath the sword. The enemy would reform, and it would have more work to do.

The Highlanders and Royal Hants had wheeled to the right, and now they faced Cawnpore. The men stood easy as the other units formed around them. The Sikhs took up position on the left. On the far right, detached from the rest of the force, the Blue Caps still milled about in skirmish order.

General Havelock waited behind the Highlanders with his two buglers and his aide, his son Harry. The commander of the main battery of Royal Artillery, Captain Maude, approached him on horseback, saluting. Dudley noticed Maude was alone, the 9-pounders nowhere in sight.

"I'm terribly sorry, sir," Maude said, "but the bullocks are exhausted. We're trying our best, but they're moving at a crawl."

Havelock removed his sun helmet and wiped his brow.

"That is unfortunate, Captain. As you can see, the enemy is reforming not more than a thousand yards away."

Farther along the road, the rebel infantry was falling into line around two more 24-pounders. The 2nd Cavalry had also formed up on their left, facing the right of the British force.

"I could use your guns."

Maude's mustached face was set with determination.

"We'll have the guns up to support you, sir. It's just that it will take some time."

"I don't wish to lose the momentum." Havelock replaced his helmet. "The bayonet will suffice. I will leave the Volunteer Cavalry back to protect your guns while you bring them up."

"Thank you, sir. We won't disappoint." Maude then stared over the heads of the Highlanders. The Blue Caps were now forming a line beyond the village the Highlanders had taken. A few of them were still exposed on the plain, and the 2nd Cavalry had edged forward. "Looks like we're to see a charge, sir."

Dudley moved to a position on the right of No. 3 Company beside Colour-Sergeant Barker.

"Run, you buggers," Barker remarked as he watched the Blue Cap skirmishers scurry across the plain, the cavalry behind them, closing the distance.

The rest of the regiment began forming a square. The *sowars* raised their sabres, but one side of the square erupted in smoke. At five hundred yards, horsemen fell.

The skirmishers made it to the square, and their comrades made room for them. Another volley boomed. More horsemen fell, and the rest sheered off, galloping back for the rebel lines.

The Highlanders and Royal Hants cheered the Blue Cap victory. Dudley had never before seen a square formed in battle. It was a thing of beauty.

The infantry advanced in a single huge line of two ranks, in perfect order. Blue Cap skirmishers again ranged ahead, running out to meet the white shapes of their rebel counterparts. Rifles and smoothbore muskets popped, but soon the superior range and accuracy of the rifle told. The enemy skirmishers retired, leaving several of their number on the plain.

The two rebel guns fired from their new position amongst the white houses of still another small village. The shots plunged towards the British line but did no damage.

General Havelock rode near the centre of the marching battalions.

"Who shall take the village?" he suddenly shouted. "The Highlanders or the Sixty-fourth?"

The men needed no further command. Like the bridge the day before, the enemy position became the object of a race, the entire British line breaking into a run. The line snaked, the dust at last rising from many churning feet.

The rebel guns barked once more, but the crews and supporting infantry did not wait to meet the British charge. They fled again, a disordered mob pouring across the plain. They abandoned the two guns.

The British force halted in a shallow depression beyond the village. General Havelock halted with them.

"We will wait here. I think the enemy will rally again. They have one more reserve gun."

Dudley heard someone say, "We'd best take that as well," and the men of several units laughed. They were joking and smiling, exhilarated by their success. They had taken only a handful of casualties and routed a superior force from two positions.

They stacked their rifles and sat or lay on the ground. Dudley at last sheathed his sword and took a drink from his canteen. He had not realized how thirsty he was, how dry and cracked his lips had become.

Lieutenant Morris approached him, a huge grin on his face.

"Quite a race, isn't it? I haven't even used my sword."

Dudley pushed his cap back and pointed in the direction of Cawnpore.

"I remember this place from when I first arrived," he said, "riding in the Dak *gharis*."

"Ah, yes. With Miss Edwards."

About a thousand yards away, the sepoys milled around as they formed lines on either side of their reserve 24-pounder. They had no cover this time, no houses or walls. In their midst, the Nana rode back and forth on his elephant. A brass band stood to one side, the sun flashing from the polished instruments. The band struck up a discordant tune Dudley at last realized was "Auld Lang Syne."

The Highlanders laughed.

"That's it, Pandy," one said. "We're an old acquaintance, and we haven't forgot ye."

"Here come our guns," Morris announced.

Far to the rear, the 9-pounders were at last ambling up the road behind the weary bullocks. General Havelock stared at the guns then turned his field glasses back to scan the enemy.

"They are rallying," he said. "Not a moment is to be lost. I cannot wait for the guns. Up, men! Dress your lines and prepare for one more push!"

The men replaced the stoppers in their canteens and lurched to their feet. Morris went back to his position behind the center of the company as Colour-Sergeant Barker dressed the ranks. The companies shouldered arms and moved forward, up out of the depression. The single rebel 24-pounder fired, and the ball buried itself in the turf. The gun was in line with the 64th, to the left of the Royal Hants. In front of the Highlanders stood only infantry.

Dudley again pulled his sword from its scabbard. The ground was drier here, and dust began to choke his throat. He coughed. The enemy drew closer.

"Charge bayonets!" Colonel Hamilton shouted.

The front rank again brought their rifles down in a rippling display of steel. Smoke erupted from the rebel infantry as they began firing volleys by company. The 24-pounder also fired, grapeshot tearing a gap in the line of the 64th.

The men of that regiment seemed to cry out as one with anger and rushed forward. The Highlanders also began running, cheering a great roar of triumph.

The rebels fired another hasty and ineffectual musket volley then started to flee, but it was too late. The British line crashed into them with a collective grunt. Men fell with bayonets through their ribs.

Dudley screamed his wordless war cry and looked for someone to fight. He swung at a retreating back and missed then doubled over as pain stabbed his side. He thought for a few seconds that a bullet had found him, but it was just a stitch. He took even breaths, and the discomfort began to subside.

Rebel corpses littered the ground, and the rest were running. He straightened and sloped his sword on his shoulder. In the distance, he could see the riddled buildings of Wheeler's entrenchment.

A bugle call halted the British charge; the enemy had not reformed for a fourth stand. When the Highlanders were back in their lines, another bugle call sounded nearby—the officer's call.

Dudley made his way to the general's headquarters with the rest of the officers of the Royal Hants and Ross-shire Buffs. When they had gathered around, Havelock raised his hand and said, "I am afraid my bugler here has made a mistake, gentlemen. I did not wish to speak to you. But since I have you all here, I am glad to have the opportunity of saying a few words to you, which you may repeat to your men."

He removed his helmet and held it out to Colonel Hamilton.

"I am now upwards of sixty years old, and I have been forty years in the service. I have engaged in action about seven-and-twenty times. But in the whole of my career, I have never seen a regiment behave so well as the Seventy-eighth Highlanders this day. I am proud of you. And this, gentlemen, you hear from a man who is not in the habit of saying more than he means. I am not a Highlander, but I wish I was one."

"You do us a great honour, General Havelock," Colonel Hamilton replied.

Havelock beamed as he glanced at Captain Norcott.

"You fellows of the Royal Hants, I should think, are honourary Highlanders this day."

The Highland officers agreed and slapped their English companions on the back. Captain Mackenzie approached Dudley and wrung his hand.

"I hope my sword served you well, Ensign," he said.

"That it did, sir," Dudley replied. "I can't thank you enough."

"Keep it for now. I trust you'll have further use for it in the days ahead."

The field force camped within two miles of Cawnpore that evening. Before the battle, Havelock had left his field hospital, baggage train, and camp followers in a large walled enclosure in Maharajpur. These now rejoined the rest of the army.

"It's good to see you, Lazzy," Private Geary said as the beagle greeted him with tail lashing. "I didn't like leaving you there with the elephants."

Dudley grinned at the joyful reunion, the first true smile he had managed in many weeks.

"You must introduce me to this little fellow, Private."

A bugle chirped, again giving the officers' call. Dudley made his way to General Havelock's headquarters amongst a crowd of other officers.

The general sat on a camp stool before a small fire. Behind him were his buglers and aides, and two civilians. Orange light played about the general's grim features.

The officers gathered in a ring around their commander.

"I wonder what's up," Morris whispered in Dudley's ear.

Havelock stood.

"Gentlemen, these two men have just returned from scouting the city for me." He indicated the two strangers. "They are reliable men. They have brought news that the enemy is no longer there. They have fled to the Nana's city of Bithoor. Cawnpore is ours." Havelock held up his hands to stifle a cheer. He then turned to one of the civilians, an older man with a thick beard. "Tell these others," he said softly. "What of the ladies?"

Dudley felt his heart clench then sink inside him. There was something odd about the civilian's demeanour. He turned sad eyes to the assemblage.

"Sahibs," the man began, "it is most tragic. The ladies and children have all been murdered. This happened days ago, after you captured the Pandoonudda bridge. They are all dead."

The officers stood in silence. The flames of Havelock's fire crackled, orange light flickering.

"We will avenge them," Captain Mackenzie suddenly cried, and a great roar of agreement went up.

At that moment, the ground shook. Away in Cawnpore, a lurid pillar of fire rose into the sky. A few moments later, the clap of a great explosion struck the camp.

Dudley stared at the rising column of flame and black smoke. The rebels had fired the powder magazine, the last act of a defeated army. The British field force was victorious.

He crumpled, sagging to the ground to sit facing the city. Victorious, yet Charlotte and Mrs. Edwards were dead. They were too late.

CHAPTER 26

Cawnpore
July 1857

The 84th Regiment led the march into Cawnpore; the
Blue Caps brought up the rear. No bands played as the force
crossed the largest of the canal bridges and turned onto the
wide Street of Silver. The shops and stalls were closed, the
street quiet. Many civilians had fled the city with the Nana
and his broken army, perhaps fearing retribution at the
hands of the victorious British.

Dudley rode his artillery horse as if in a dream, passing sights and landmarks familiar from his brief time here.
There was a dull ache in the pit of his stomach. Part of him
refused to believe the women and children were dead,
killed as all the others from Wheeler's entrenchment had
been killed. He would not believe it until he saw the evidence.

Commands rang out, passed down from the head of
the column as, one by one, the companies halted. Dudley
brought his horse to a stop.

A sudden breeze stirred dust from the road. Several
minutes passed with no activity. He could smell more rain
on the wind.

At length, General Havelock rode along the column towards No. 3 Company's position. Behind the general and his aides came a squad from the Volunteer Cavalry. With the gentleman troopers was a civilian on foot. The civilian was gaunt and bearded, his linen jacket and trousers filthy and torn.

Havelock halted next to Captain Norcott.

"There is a lieutenant with you who was with Wheeler's defence," the commander said. "Kindly direct me to him, Captain."

A few seconds later, Dudley was facing the general himself.

"Good morning, Lieutenant," Havelock said, returning Dudley's bemused salute."I understand you are the young gentleman who was with General Wheeler but managed to escape down the river."

Dudley nodded."Yes, sir, I was. Ensign Dudley, sir."

Havelock swept a hand towards the scruffy civilian.

"This is Mister Shepherd, another who succeeded in escaping the massacre. Hid in an abandoned house here in the city; the Nana seemed to have forgotten about him. He says he can lead us to where the other prisoners met their end."

"The Bibighar," Dudley said."Yes, sir, I have seen the house as well."

Havelock's face wore a look of deep sympathy.

"The army will carry on, and the men will find their billets, but we are going to the Bibighar now. You may come with us, if you so wish. I will not force you to come, but it may be more inhumane for me to keep you waiting. It would, perhaps, be better for you to face this now rather than later."

Dudley tried to reply but found his throat constricting. The time had come.

"I think you're right, sir," he at last managed to croak."I'll come with you."

"There's a fellow," Havelock said.

The army resumed its march as Dudley followed the general's small detachment. He rode beside the general's horse as Mister Shepherd led the way. None of them spoke.

They came to a muddy street Dudley recognized. Kesab had brought him here to show him where the women were kept. Ahead, through the trees, vultures squawked and squabbled.

Then the Bibighar came into view, and Dudley saw why the vultures fought.

General Havelock's face went white, and he pointed into the yard.

"Get them down, this instant!"

Three cavalry troopers spurred forward and leapt their mounts over the low stone wall. The vultures scattered as the horsemen reined in beneath a tree where two young women hung from ropes knotted around their slender necks. The ropes had been thrown over one of the wide upper limbs then secured near the base of the trunk.

One trooper cut the ropes while the other two lowered the bodies, gently settling them on the ground. The rest of the detachment gathered around. A few men held handkerchiefs over their faces against the heavy stink of rotting flesh.

Dudley gazed down at the two dead things that seemed as though they could never have been human. Their bloated features were black and waxy, covered with flies; the scavenger birds had already plucked out the eyeballs. One corpse had long blond hair, the other brown. He did not recognize their shabby clothing. It did not match anything Charlotte had worn.

"There are sword cuts in the tree, General," one trooper said. The man's puffy face was flushed scarlet. "And there's blood and strips of hair within the cuts."

Havelock stared at the scars on the bark. Bullet marks pocked the lower trunk, and blood stained the ground between the roots.

"Let us see what they have left us inside," the general said after a minute.

A trooper held the horses in the yard as Havelock, his aides, the bugler, Shepherd and Dudley walked to the little bungalow. Harry Havelock opened the door, and the stench of an abattoir escaped into the heated air.

The men paused, collecting themselves, and then General Havelock stepped into the house. Dudley followed. He expected to find the place heaped with mangled bodies, but what he saw was somehow more terrible.

Inside was a single large room with no furniture. A lone column supporting two shallow arches partially divided the room. As with the tree in the yard, notched sword cuts covered the column and the walls, long hairs sticking to them. Clotted blood, dark red and as smooth as leather, coated the floor from one end of the room to the other. Strewn about in the gore were ladies' and children's clothing—bonnets, straw hats, slippers, torn petticoats, skirt hoops and stays. Here and there were tiny shoes, broken earthenware saucers, the covers of prayer books with the pages torn out.

The soldiers could not help stepping in the blood as they crowded in, boots sticking to the floor.

"What did those devils do with them?" Havelock whispered. "Where are they?"

Dudley stared at the scattered clothing, the shoes, the few half-nibbled *chupatties* in the corner. He looked for something of Charlotte's but saw nothing.

Then, with a start, he at last spied an object that he knew well, something he would never have wished to see. With two quick steps, heedless of the blood, he reached it and stooped to pluck it from the floor. He held the small tin soldier in his left hand, the chain dangling between his fingers.

"Wellington," he whispered.

"What was that, Lieutenant?" Havelock asked.

"General," a cavalry trooper called from the doorway."We've found 'em, sir! Outside!"

The tin soldier dug into Dudley's palm as he followed the general back into the yard. The trooper who had come to the door was the same puffy-faced fellow who had first noticed the sword cuts in the tree.

"The trail isn't hard to follow, as you can well see, sir. I don't know why we didn't note it sooner."

Leading to the back of the yard from the door was a track worn in the earth, as if someone had dragged many heavy objects that way. Farther on, a scrap of tartan cloth clung to a thorn bush, and more clumps of hair. A withered eyeball stared from the bark of a large tree.

Behind the house was a pukka well. It appeared to be unused, with no tackle for raising and lowering buckets. The men of the Volunteer Cavalry had gathered around it.

The track in the earth ended just in front of the well.

The puffy trooper pointed and said, "They're down there, sir."

The troopers made room, and Havelock peered down into the dark hole. Dudley hung back, taking in deep breaths through his nose, trying to bring the sickening pounding in his ears under control.

"The inhuman monsters!" Havelock cried. "Why would they do such a thing?" He pulled off his helmet and held it in his hand.

Dudley forced himself forward to stare down into the dark pit. At first he saw nothing; then he could make out a severed arm, a head, the dim corpse of a child. The well was stuffed with corpses and bits of corpses, like the well outside Wheeler's entrenchment. Bluebottle flies buzzed and hovered, and the suffocating stink rose in hot waves.

He staggered backward but felt hands on his shoulders, steadying him.

He clutched the tin soldier, looked at it, and noticed for the first time that the chain was broken. He had given the soldier to Charlotte because she had lacked courage, but it brought no memories of her cowering in the barracks, refusing to cooperate. He only recalled her bright face and quick laugh. He recalled the warmth of her lips, the scent of her skin, its smoothness as she lay next to him…

"We shall punish those who did this," someone was saying, and Dudley again felt the hands on his shoulders. He realized he was sobbing, tears dropping into the dust at his feet.

Then General Havelock was pulling him away from the well towards the front of the yard where their horses waited.

"I look forward to the wholesale destruction of the black-faced curs guilty of these dastardly crimes!" Lieutenant Morris cried. He stared across the yard to the Bibighar, the "House of the Ladies," as the men of the field force were already calling it. Two pioneers from the Madras Fusiliers were taking their axes to the tree from which the bodies had been hanging. The blades bit into the bark, perhaps echoing the sound the rebel swords had made a few days earlier.

Dudley sat on the wall, his back to the house, the broken brick rough through his thin trousers.

"Revenge is all anyone can think of now," he said, turning Wellington in his hand.

"And revenge we shall take, William," Morris stated. "Every man in the army should see that room, that abattoir. That's it, lads!" he shouted to a group of Highlanders who had just emerged, stony-faced, from the bunga-low. "Remember what you see here!"

"Aye, we wull, sir," one of the Highlanders replied.

Morris nodded and turned to Dudley.

"We have been in Cawnpore scarcely a few hours, and I have heard the Highlanders have already taken a solemn oath to kill a hundred Pandies for every one person slain here. And they shall reach their quota, I have no doubt."

"No doubt," Dudley repeated, watching as another group of soldiers approached, intent upon visiting the "massacre room." Since taking billets in the cantonments, the men of the little army had been parading through the Bibighar to see the enemy's latest atrocity.

With the report of the death of the prisoners, Dudley's panic—his uncontrollable bouts of trembling—had disappeared. The sense of urgency was gone now that the objective had evaporated. The field force had failed, and he would have to accept that failure. There had been nothing they could have done.

The Nana had killed the women and children in response to a British victory, a victory that had taken place days before the last battle of Cawnpore. He could not have saved Charlotte and her mother.

He tried not to imagine their final moments, the swords rising and falling, the screaming, the terror. He would not subject himself to that torment. It was better to remember the good things.

And there had been many things good about Charlotte Edwards. He would not idolize her memory, nor forget that he had not intended to carry on their secret affair; but logical reasoning had little to do with his feelings. Her death, and the death of all the others, had shocked and saddened him more than anything he had heard and seen in the Crimea. He wanted nothing more in the world than to see her again, to hold her and know she was all right.

He would never see her again. Her body lay among more than two hundred others, rotting in the well.

His horror at this fact had already evolved into a calm, cold anger. It was an anger so intense he had to keep it hidden away, waiting for the proper moment of expression. That would come on the battlefield. His assessment of the enemy had altered, his sympathies for men like Kesab obliterated in the blood of the House of the Ladies.

Whatever the British had done to bring about the mutiny, however insensitive they had been to their sepoys' ways and beliefs, there could be no justification for the things that had happened here at Cawnpore.

———————

The field force settled in to rest for a few days. Cawnpore would become the headquarters from which General Havelock would direct all operations against Oudh. While the artillery gathered the captured rebel guns, and the surgeons tended the wounded, the commander would plan his advance on Lucknow.

On the second day of rest, July 18th, Havelock decided to move the force to the western end of the cantonments. A few rebels still lurked west of the city, in the vicinity of Bithoor, the location of the Nana Sahib's palace. The British redeployment would help thwart an attack if the Nana somehow managed to regroup his forces.

The new barracks were adjacent to the suburb of Nawabganj, near the Reverend Teecher's house. After establishing his billet in the junior officers' quarters, Dudley walked to the place where he had waited for the mutiny to begin.

The house was gone. The servants' quarters and the carriage house remained, but there was nothing but a rectangular strip of ashes and charred timbers where the bungalow had stood.

The rebels had looted and burned many houses in the suburb. The home of a Christian must have been a tempting target to the mutineers and the many *badmashes* who had joined their ranks.

Dudley hovered for a while on the edge of the ashes, kicking at some bits of broken earthenware.

He made his way back to his quarters, passing a group of Highlanders and Sikhs chatting and chuckling at each other's jokes. He was somewhat gratified to see that the men could still laugh at something.

That afternoon, he and Morris visited Wheeler's entrenchment. As Captain Morrow had predicted, the monsoon rains had washed away much of the trench. Morris wanted to go into the barracks, but Dudley would not accompany him. He did not think he could bear another reminder of the tragedy he had escaped.

"Quite a harrowing sight," Morris said when he at last emerged from the larger of the riddled buildings. "I hope the general can contain our men. They're about ready to slaughter any Indian in sight, whether civilian or sepoy."

"I think the measures taken have been adequate," Dudley replied.

Havelock had issued a general order calling for the hanging, in uniform, of any British soldier found guilty of plundering or otherwise molesting the civilian population. The sepoy prisoners taken in the recent battles were also safe, housed in the garrison cells. Under the circumstances, such orders could have caused resentment, but Havelock had been loud in his praises for his tiny army. The men had come to love him, and to respect his judgment.

On July 19th, the general issued further praise in his latest general order. The company commanders read the order to their men during morning parade. It began with the grandiose statement, "Soldiers, your General is satisfied, and more than satisfied, with you. He has never seen steadier nor more elevated troops."

Captain Norcott recited the general's words to the combined Grenadier and No. 3 Companies of the Royal Hants.

> "But your labours are only beginning," the order continued. "Between the 7th and the 16th you have, under the Indian sun of July, marched one hundred and twenty-six miles and fought four actions. But your comrades at Lucknow are in peril. Agra is besieged. Delhi is still the focus of mutiny and rebellion. You must make great sacrifices if you would obtain great results. Three cities have to be saved; two strong places disblockaded. Your general is confident that he can effect all these things, and restore this part of India to tranquility. If you only second him with your efforts, and if your discipline is equal to your valour."

Later that day, General Havelock sent a detachment to Bithoor to probe the Nana's position. The detachment consisted of a few companies of Blue Caps, Sikhs, and Volunteer Cavalry. They found the town abandoned, the Nana and his household having fled. Under orders, the detachment plundered and burned the Nana's palace then blew up the powder magazine. They returned to Cawnpore with twelve more enemy guns.

The Nana's power seemed broken, but not all the rebels who had supported him had perished. There was concern that some might even have gone to add their strength to the rebel forces now besieging the Lucknow Residency.

"We must not become preoccupied with what happened here in Cawnpore," Captain Mackenzie said to Dudley after dinner. They had left the mess and wandered outside to take the evening air, fresh after another rain. "Lucknow is where we will next strike the enemy."

"I will never forget what happened here, sir," Dudley said. "Nor, I think, will many others."

"I do not mean to suggest that, lad," Mackenzie assured him. "Not for an instant. But we can't forget that, this minute, another group of men, women, and children are in the same situation you had here. Shall we let them meet the same fate? I think not, Lieutenant. I think we must make every effort to prevent it."

Dudley nodded. Mackenzie was right. At Lucknow, the army could redeem its failure.

On July 20th, the newly promoted Brigadier-General James Neill arrived from Allahabad. Neill brought close to three hundred troops with him—a small reinforcement—and a determination to make the rebels suffer for their crimes. General Havelock was to leave Neill in command at Cawnpore while the field force pushed on for Lucknow. The bad blood between the two men had not abated, and it was rumoured that Havelock had told Neill not to issue a single order until Havelock had left.

But Neill, like much of the army, was seeking vengeance. While Havelock was busy with preparations to cross the swollen Ganges, Neill began devising his punishment for those rebels already in British hands.

Dudley received an invitation to witness that punishment. It came while he and Morris were in their quarters, deciding what baggage to take with them on the next leg of the campaign. They planned to travel light, with little more than their weapons, a blanket, haversack and canteen.

"Roughing it," as Morris said.

There was a knock on the door. Dudley answered and found himself facing an unknown lieutenant. The man introduced himself as one of General Neill's aides.

"General Neill has tried a number of rebel prisoners," the lieutenant explained. "They are about to receive their just desserts. The general thought that, as a survivor of the massacre with a personal stake, you may be interested in witnessing the punishment."

"So, I am privileged to observe horrors again," Dudley replied, although he did not refuse the invitation. He turned to Morris. "Shall we both go and see what General Neill has devised?"

The aide led them to the House of the Ladies. In the yard, a new gallows had replaced the tree. The gallows was a simple wooden frame with no rope yet attached. Next to it stood a pair of elephants and a guard of Blue Caps keeping watch over five sepoy prisoners.

As Dudley drew nearer to the prisoners, he stopped and stared. One of Kesab's companions, one of the two brothers, was among the condemned. The other sepoys stared back with pride and defiance, but the brother smiled in recognition, as if he expected Dudley to grant him a reprieve.

"So, the British are finished in India, are they?" Dudley cried, taking a step toward the man he knew. At his anger, the sepoy's smile vanished. The man shook his head; Dudley remembered he did not speak English.

"At least we got one of you," Dudley continued. "I wish you were Kesab, so I could tell him a thing or two. I'll find him, you know."

"You know this creature, William?" Morris asked.

"One of the fellows who kept me prisoner. Now the shoe is on the other foot."

"He'll be strung up afore long, sir," a guard said. "Beggin' yer pardon, sir."

"What he deserves, Private," Dudley said, "and all those like him."

"I say, Lieutenant Dudley?" Neill's aide called from the house. Dudley had grown accustomed to being referred to as "lieutenant," although he had received no such promotion. "The general is here."

Neill stood beside the door with a native servant—a sweeper, an untouchable. The servant held a bucket of water and a rag. Dudley approached the general and saluted.

"Ah, Lieutenant," Neill said, "I believe you will take satisfaction in these proceedings. I have prepared a task for each miscreant, and vowed that it shall be as revolting to his feelings as possible."

The general smiled. He had an arrogant, indifferent face, Dudley thought. It was thin, with a long, straight nose, a fine upswept moustache, and thick side whiskers. The flesh under his cruel eyes drooped.

Neill motioned for the guards to bring one of the prisoners forward. The captive sepoy moved with little compulsion, although he paused to salaam the gallows by touching his hand to his forehead. Then he halted before Neill. Behind him came a Blue Cap sergeant carrying a cat-o'-nine-tails.

"You were a *havildar* of the Fifty-fourth Bengal Native Infantry," Neill said to the man.

The sepoy still wore his white shell jacket with its three chevrons and regimental buttons. He nodded.

"Yes, Sahib."

Neill pointed at Dudley.

"Tell this officer what you told me this morning. Tell him what you said of the murders."

The sepoy looked at Dudley.

"When you took the bridge," he began, "the Nana was frightened, Sahib. He had expected to hold the bridge. He ordered the prisoners, all of them, killed.

"But no one would do it. The guards refused and fired their muskets into the ceiling. At last the Nana found volunteers, but many of them were *badmashes*, Sahib. It was the *badmashes*, Sahib."

Neill feigned astonishment.

"Oh, so it was the *badmashes* who committed this crime! Did you try to stop them?"

The sepoy frowned and shrugged.

"But Sahib, the Nana had ordered it."

"Quite right. Carry on, Sergeant."

"In you go, mate," the sergeant said, propelling the sepoy towards the door.

General Neill, the servant, Dudley and Morris followed them into the house. At first it seemed to Dudley as if nothing had changed. The clothing and other debris still lay on the floor, soaked in clotted blood.

With his rag, the servant moistened a patch of floor, about a foot square. The sepoy watched, and sweat began to bead on his forehead.

"Perhaps you expected mercy," Neill said. "Perhaps you expected us to believe that you are not guilty of the crime committed here. Look hard on these walls, at the blood here that is on your hands!"

The sepoy glanced at the moistened patch of floor; then, with a nervous flickering, his gaze darted over the scarred walls. Dudley examined the room as well, once more taking in the sword cuts, the strands of hair. He was surprised to suddenly notice markings that had not been there before, messages scrawled in the plaster.

"Revenge! Revenge! countrymen, for the lives of your country fellows," one urged.

"O God," another began, "take us into thy Holy Tabernacle. Signed Miss C.S., aged 18 years."

The most elaborate message read, "Country men and women remember 15th July 1857. Your wives and families are here in misery and at the disposal of savages, who has ravished both young and old and then killed us. Oh! Oh! my child my child.Countrymen revenge it."

Dudley knew the messages had to have been written within the last two days. Perhaps meant to enrage. Although he wondered why anyone would think such hoaxes necessary when the reality was so powerful.

"Now, on your knees, sir!" Neill barked.

The sergeant placed a hand on the sepoy's shoulder and forced him down. The Indian looked at Neill, confused and horrified. Before the prisoner lay the moistened square of bloody floor.

"Right, lick it clean, you damned Pandy," the sergeant said, pushing down the sepoy's head.

"But, Sahib…" the sepoy cried.

Before he could say another word, the sergeant struck him across the back with the cat. The man flinched, and the sergeant struck him twice more. Hands now on the floor, the sepoy leaned forward. His tongue protruded then touched the moistened blood. It went no farther. The sergeant used his cat once again.

"Lick it up, damn you!" Morris suddenly cried, stepping forward.

Dudley watched in revolted fascination. At last, the sepoy began to lap up the blood, groaning in disgust. Dudley glanced at Morris, but the lieutenant seemed transfixed.

"Sir," Dudley said to Neill, "I don't believe I can bear to breathe the air in here any longer."

Without waiting for the general's response, he moved outside. He sat on the low garden wall, removed his cap, and massaged his scalp. Perhaps the sepoys did deserve this, he thought; he could not be sure. But somehow, he saw no value in torturing the guilty. He would prefer their simple destruction.

After about fifteen minutes, Neill, Morris and the prisoner emerged into the afternoon sun. The sepoy no longer walked with chin up and shoulders straight. Now, his feet shuffled, his head drooped. There was blood in his short beard and on his lips. Like most of the sepoys, he was probably a Brahmin, and now his caste was broken. He did not seem to notice as the sergeant bound his hands behind his back then led him to one of the elephants.

A mahout made the elephant sit, and the sergeant and a private hoisted the sepoy onto the animal's back, behind the massive head. Another private looped a noose about the sepoy's neck. The elephant rose, its mahout leading it across the yard until it stood beneath the gallows. The sergeant cast the end of the hanging rope over the crosspiece then secured it to one of the uprights.

"Carry on," Neill said.

With a flick of his long switch, the mahout urged the elephant forward. The huge animal took three steps. The rope dragged the sepoy off the broad back, and the man hung choking, his feet gyrating in the air.

Long before the first prisoner was dead, Neill pointed to the next. Kesab's companion, one of the brothers. Dudley had wished this man dead for many days and nights, but now he did not stay to witness what followed.

CHAPTER 27

Oudh
July 1857

There were certain things Barker cared about and cer-
tain things that he did not. For instance, he cared that the
advance to Lucknow had been delayed.

The delay was initially due to there being no way for
the army to cross the river, the rebels having destroyed the
bridge of boats and most of the ferries. The native boatmen were also in hiding, fearing punishment from either
side. For days, a single steamer plied to and fro, gradually
assembling the field force on the north bank, one squad
of soldiers at a time.

What Barker did not care about was the change in the
political situation.

"Lucknow is as important as Delhi now, perhaps more
so," he overheard Mister Dudley say to Lieutenant Morris one day as they stood on the riverbank watching the
overworked steamer. "It has given this rebellion a new focus both for the enemy and for us. The Pandies will be
fighting for this new king of Oudh."

"That makes it a proper war," said Morris. "Not just
a mutiny. Though I hear this so-called king of Oudh is noth-

ing but a child, a spoiled brat with a crown. A puppet of the Begum of Lucknow."

"Perhaps," Dudley said. "He is, after all, the son of the Begum, Huzrut Mahal. But he is fourteen, not a small boy. Did you know that his name, Birjeis Kuddr, means 'As exalted as the planet Mercury?'"

Barker listened with something like wonder—wonder at the interest officers displayed in irrelevant things, even Dudley. He did not know what Morris meant by a "proper war," for war was war, men killing men, with innocents caught in between. And it did not matter who was in charge of the enemy, whether a Begum, whatever on earth that might be, or a boy king. Barker just wanted the next campaign of this war, proper or not, to get moving.

"General Havelock is in constant communication with Colonel Inglis," Dudley said next, "the commander of the Lucknow garrison. Our couriers seem to have no trouble crossing rebel-held territory. I was speaking to one of the general's aides this morning—his son Harry. Puppet or not, the *zemindars*—the biggest landlords—have all declared for the king. I think their matchlock men will fight us with more determination than our rebellious sepoys. They wish to undo Lord Dalhousie's annexation. At least in this theatre, we are now fighting a war for Oudh's independence."

What that really meant, as far as Barker was concerned, was that enemy numbers would be even greater than before. It meant that the longer the delay, the harder the coming fight.

At last, after days of scrounging, the members of the field force managed to find twenty boats. With these and the reluctant help of a few old boatmen, the little army finally assembled on the north side of the river on July 25th. The force consisted of fifteen hundred infantry, ten guns manned by invalid gunners, and a mere sixty sabres of the Volunteer Cavalry. About three hundred men would remain in Cawnpore with most of the baggage and the camp followers.

They camped on the riverbank for one more night. In the morning, the men awoke to the pipers of the 78th playing "Hey, Johnny Cope" to signal reveille. After a quick breakfast, they formed ranks and changed from line to marching column. In a golden haze of heat and rising dust, the column stepped off along the Lucknow road, moving north.

"About bloody time," Barker muttered to himself.

The country they marched through was one of deserted and ruined hamlets. The plain lay like a sea of yellow sand, the square plantations of sugar cane and groves of tall palms like islands. Overhead rode the broiling sun. On the eastern horizon, deepening cloud promised more rain by noon, and that caused Barker some concern.

The field force had no tents; every man carried his blanket, full haversack, canteen, sixty rounds of ammunition in his cartridge pouch, and twenty rounds in his expense pouch. They were prepared to fight, but there were no tents, no shelter from the continuing monsoon. They would have to establish their camps in the deserted villages.

Barker saw Mr. Dudley approaching on horseback; he touched his rifle sling with his left hand, and the young officer returned the salute.

"I never had an opportunity to congratulate you on your promotion," Dudley said, turning his horse about to walk beside the new colour-sergeant. "You'll wear the flag and sabres on your tunic." The badge of a colour-sergeant, as worn on the dress tunic, was a single chevron surmounted by an embroidered union flag, crossed sabres, and a crown.

"Thank you, sir," Barker said. He thought of the badge as a tangible symbol of his success. "How are you feeling, sir?"

"Fine, Colour."

Any other officer would resent a personal question from an enlisted man, even a senior NCO, but Barker and Dudley had long since accepted a friendship that transcended rank.

"I am no more or less outraged than anyone else. The entire thing saddens me, of course, but I just wish to focus on our present task."

Barker nodded. He felt true sympathy for the young officer, for his having lost his lady friend in the massacre. Barker was sorry to have lost O'Ryan, who had been a true friend and an excellent senior NCO.

But such things happened in war. He supposed that, like Dudley, he detested the rebels as much as anyone; but now that the army was on the move, he had reason to be optimistic. With his promotion, he was a made man. If he managed to survive the fighting, he could retire with a proper pension and some respectability.

The army had come through for him, and war had again propelled him up the ladder of success. Each of his promotions, from his first during the Second Sikh War in '48 to his next in the Crimea, had been due to casualties in battle. As far as Brian Barker was concerned, war meant not just destruction and murder but a chance to rise in the world.

Dudley continued to ride beside him as the day wore on. The rain began to fall then stopped then blew in again with greater force. At six o'clock, the column halted in a village, the men seeking shelter in the empty houses. Even with the wet, bivouac fires appeared in the courtyards and enclosures.

Barker messed with Sergeants Bell, Johnson, and a sergeant of the Grenadier Company. When he had eaten his field rations of biscuits and salt beef, he reclined against a vine-covered wall to smoke his clay pipe. A gecko crawled across his shoulder and down his arm, and he flicked it off with a finger.

A few yards away, Private Geary was feeding scraps to Lazzy and entertaining some Highlanders with the dog's tricks. The Scotsmen laughed as the beagle begged, rolled over, and "saluted."

Not long after, a lone piper played "Sleep Dearest Sleep," the signal for lights out.

The march resumed at first light. The dusty plain on either side of the road had again become a swamp from the previous day's rains. More dark clouds loomed, choking the sun but not lessening the humidity. By noon, men began to drop out of the column. Barker knew the sickness was not just from heat but from the old enemy—cholera.

Evening brought the field force as far as the large village of Mangalwar. The village sat on a ridge of dry ground commanding the countryside. Some of its inhabitants had stayed to protect their homes, and they regarded the British with uneasiness.

In the fading light of dusk, Barker stood on the ridge and watched rebel horsemen galloping about farther north. Then another curtain of rain descended, blocking his view.

The next day, the fourth of the march, the field force advanced to meet the enemy in battle.

Three miles from Mangalwar lay the town of Unao, a cluster of walled gardens and tall, shivering palms. No doubt hoping to delay the drive on Lucknow still further, the rebels had placed an advanced force in a large enclosure in front of the town. Beyond the advanced force waited the main rebel body, several thousand men hidden in the gardens and houses. Improvised loopholes dotted the walls, while swamps protected both flanks, the fields flooded and impassable.

The British column deployed in two lines across the road, one behind the other. In response to the move, the entrenched rebel guns opened fire. General Havelock ordered his artillery forward, and the bronze 9-pounders unlimbered on the road not more than a hundred yards from the rebel advanced force. The British guns blasted smoke and flame, sending solid shot plunging through the garden walls. Within minutes, the rebels came streaming out of the enclosure, making for the town.

The British lines advanced, the drummers beating cadence. Barker marched on the right of his company, rifle at the shoulder. The town grew nearer, the rebel guns keeping up a steady roar, the round shot thundering as it raced past. Shells burst, and musket volleys poured from behind the walls. Soon, sulfurous smoke settled in a dense fog. Barker heard the wet smack of bullets striking flesh, and some Highlanders on his right fell. It was then that the pipers filled their bags and began to play.

The battalion halted; Colonel Hamilton was screaming commands. Barker brought his rifle to his shoulder, sighting into the smoke. He fired with the rest of the men, the volley crashing out. Then they surged forward, into the village.

The line lost all formation in the dense smoke. Muskets fired from windows, but groups of Fusiliers and Highlanders stormed into the buildings to clear them of rebels. Barker crouched behind a low wall and rammed a bullet into his rifle barrel. In the road, the British guns had moved up, unlimbered, and were lobbing shells into the town. Barker crouched low as the shells began to burst just yards away. Some exploded in the air, raining hot fragments, while others blew holes in the walls and roofs of the houses.

He did not see the enemy withdraw but heard a bugle from beyond the town calling the signal to reform. He searched for the men of his company and began pushing them into line as the guns limbered up and again advanced.

Captain Reed walked along the back of the line.

"We took a few casualties, Colour," he said, his thin faced strained.

"Did we, sir?"

Reed nodded and wiped his brow with a handkerchief.

Smoke was billowing from the town, the houses on fire from the shelling. Ahead on the road, the hot air was clear, the swamps on either side glistening with reflected sunlight. A heavy column of rebels, many still in red coats, was advancing, drums beating.

Colonel Hamilton rode up on the back of his black charger, calling, "Captain Norcott, Captain Reed! Form your combined companies in skirmish order. Deploy on the right of our line to flank the enemy."

"In the flooded fields, sir?" Reed inquired.

"Yes, Captain," Hamilton snapped. "You heard me."

The guns lumbered forward again, the invalid gunners defying whatever maladies they had to swing the cannon into action, loading with grape. The men of the Royal Hants prepared to enter the swamps, shortening their haversack straps, tying them in knots, then removing their cartridge pouches and holding them in their hands.

"In we go, lads!" Barker cried, leading the company into the water on the right of the road.

After only a dozen steps, the water had already reached to his waist. Barker was more than six feet tall and heard curses as shorter men soaked their powder.

In pairs, the men waded in an arcing course around to the right.

"We'll take the Pandies in the flank!" Dudley shouted. He was wading out in front, his broadsword sheathed and a rifle in his hands.

Back on the road, the British guns barked, firing grape into the rebel column. Barker saw sepoys dropping in mangled heaps. The rebels tried to deploy from column to line, but the water on either side of the road hampered their movements. When the Highlanders and Blue Caps began firing volleys of musketry, the rebels about-faced and began an orderly retreat.

"Fire into them!" Captain Reed was shouting. "Don't let them fall back! Nip their flanks."

Barker raised his rifle and fired. Other rifles banged around him. Then there was a lull. The skirmishers paused, trying to reload without plunging their rifle butts deep into the water that swirled about their legs and waists. On the road, the British guns began sending shells after the retreating enemy. With that, the rebels broke and ran.

Barker abandoned his attempt to reload. *First victory*, he thought as he turned to wade back to the road.

The field force bivouacked for three hours and took a meal then marched on for six miles. Ahead loomed the crenellated medieval walls of the town of Bashiratganj, another rebel stronghold. The high road to Lucknow passed through a gate in the town wall. Lying across the road was a new earthwork housing four heavy guns. Beyond this battery, loopholed turrets flanked the town gate on both sides.

They halted, and the Volunteer Cavalry spurred forward for reconnaissance. The gentleman riders soon returned with news that the ground to the left was passable. Behind the town was a *jheel*, or sheet of water, six to seven feet deep, spanned by a bridge and narrow causeway. The bridge emerged from the town's back gate.

The infantry lay down as the rebel battery opened with solid shot. Colour-Sergeant Barker sucked on his unlit pipe and watched as the 64th Regiment stood then detached itself from the column. The regiment moved off the road to the left, marching steady with drums beating. Barker assumed they were to flank the town, perhaps to come in at the back. Flanking seemed to be General Havelock's favourite maneuver, and so far, it had worked every time.

A minute later, three British 9-pounders unlimbered in the road and returned the rebel fire, throwing round shot at the battery and the gate. The round shot buried itself in the enemy earthwork but struck the thick gate with the deafening noise of splintering timbers.

Barker stuck his fingers in his ears and watched the rebels scurrying to and fro on top of the wall.

"We'll be with you in a minute, boys," he muttered. "Just you wait."

The fire from the enemy battery slackened, and Barker heard the cry, "Rise up and prepare to advance!" He grunted as he stood, looking to his left and dressing onto the company. A few seconds later, Colonel Hamilton shouted, "Battalion, by the center, quick…march!"

Barker stared at the black muzzles of the rebel guns, waiting for them to fire. The British artillery was still sending round shot into the ruined gate, pitching the cast-iron balls over the heads of the advancing infantry. The rebel guns drew nearer, and Barker found himself gritting his teeth. If the guns fired at this range, he was a goner.

Someone shouted the charge, and the tension released all at once. Barker started running, cheering; then he and his men were climbing the face of the earthwork. They found the rebel gunners huddling under cover from the British artillery fire. The gunners stared upward in astonishment then snatched whatever weapons lay at hand. They defended their guns with savage resolution, striking out with rammers and worms, sword bayonets and *tul-wars*.

Barker ducked a blow then thrust his fixed yataghan bayonet into the chest of his assailant. He yanked the blade free and whirled about to find someone else to fight, but there were no more rebels in the battery.

Sepoy muskets fired down from the wall, but the range was too great for the smoothbores to have much effect.

"Come on, lads!" Barker cried, waving his arm and rushing for the broken gate. The company came on, cheering; then the whole battalion was charging. General Havelock rode behind them, shouting encouragement.

The sepoys did not hold. Swarming down from the walls, they fled for the back gate. The British followed but got no farther than the causeway. The charge came to a sputtering, exhausted halt. General Havelock, with a small cavalry escort, alone pursued the rebels to the next ridge. There, he stopped and took out his field glasses.

Spent but jubilant, the infantrymen gathered on the bridge and causeway, gasping for breath and leaning on their rifles. The bodies of dead sepoys floated below them in the waters of the *jheel*.

Private Geary, with Lazzy in his arms, turned to Barker and said, "Did you see Lazzy charge at the battery, Colour-Sergeant? He's a real hero!"

"No doubt he is," Barker said.

Then the cry went up from ahead: "Clear the way for the general!"

The soldiers shifted to either side of the causeway, making room for Havelock as he returned from his surveillance. The pale light of evening lit his stern face as he rode along the improvised corridor.

But then he smiled. "You have cleared the way for me already, men!" he shouted.

Barker took up the cheer as Havelock rode past.

"God bless the general!" the soldiers of the little army cried. "God bless General Havelock!"

CHAPTER 28

Oudh
July 1857

The clamor of battle still rang in Dudley's ears, the stench of powder clogging his nostrils. He sat with his back to a stone wall, the tin soldier dangling from his hand on its broken chain. He swung it from side to side as he listened to Captain Norcott explain their orders. After the two short but furious skirmishes, the field force would be withdrawing in the morning.

"It's the cholera," Norcott said. "There's too many men down with it now."

They had twelve men killed and seventy-six wounded, but close to three hundred lay sick with intestinal cramps and fever. Lucknow was still thirty-six miles away.

"Colonel Hamilton has also informed me," Norcott went on, "that a courier came in from Brigadier-General Neill this evening. The Nana Sahib has returned to Bithoor. He has sent cavalry to harry our rear. And that is not the worst news." He poked at the bivouac fire with a stick, sending orange sparks spiraling skyward to mingle with the stars. "There has been another outbreak of mutiny, this time at

Dinapore. The reinforcements Calcutta promised us have gone to deal with that situation. We can't expect them for weeks, perhaps months."

"So," Dudley said, leaning forward, "our campaign is already a failure."

Norcott's face clouded, and he snapped, "Of course it's not a failure! Haven't we thrown the enemy out of two strong positions, killing at least six hundred of the devils? That's no failure, Dudley, and I'll hear no more talk of that nature.

"Besides, we'll only be withdrawing to Mangalwar. We'll send our sick back across the Ganges, and General Neill will send us as many men as he can spare. We'll be going forward again in a few days. You'll see."

Dudley just nodded. Around him, the other officers were already rolling into their sodden blankets and resting their heads on their haversacks. The fire snapped, and bats fluttered overhead.

The night was warm. Dudley thrust Wellington into the inside pocket of his frock then snatched up his blanket and began folding it.

Morris squatted beside him.

"I shot a Pandy with my revolver," he boasted. "It was at Unao. Confusing fight, that was."

Dudley lay back with his head on the blanket.

"I'm glad you managed to bag yourself a Pandy." He covered his face with his cap and closed his eyes.

"You're in a surly mood tonight," he heard Morris grumble. Minutes later, he was asleep.

The "army" that returned to Mangalwar numbered just over eight hundred able-bodied men. From the Cawnpore garrison, General Neill managed to send more than three hundred replacements, including a fresh company of the 84th that had just arrived from Allahabad. With the infantry, he also sent a half-battery of Bengal Artillery with three horse-drawn 9-pounders and two 24-pounders.

On August 4th, the fourteen hundred-man field force turned and again marched for Lucknow, just as Norcott had predicted. That night, as the rain pounded down, they bivouacked at Unao; in the morning, they marched to find the enemy again in possession of Bashiratganj.

General Havelock adopted the same plan of attack as before, although he changed the deployment. The heavy guns moved up the road to pound the earthwork battery and repaired gate. Supporting them went the Blue Caps and the 84th Regiment. The honour of the flanking movement fell to the Highlanders, the Royal Hants, and Captain Maude's battery of Royal Artillery. Colonel Hamilton, riding his black charger, had command of the flanking brigade.

Bullets hailed down from the town's high wall as the brigade moved to the left in fours, the men half-running, ducking their heads. Dudley again carried a rifle, keeping his sword sheathed. He did not like having an exposed flank and kept glancing to his right at the town. Smoke from the main frontal assault, which was already well underway, drifted high over the walls, blowing away in long white ribbons.

Colonel Hamilton rode along the edge of the brigade, broadsword aloft; he alone of the Highlanders wore a feathered bonnet. He shouted something, but then his horse fell, screaming. A moment later, and the colonel was back on his feet, but the animal lay dead, shot through the heart.

"Brigade will advance in line!" Hamilton roared, ignoring the downed animal and continuing on foot. "Halt... front!"

The formation halted then faced to the right and formed line. Dudley's combined battalion, Highlanders and Fusiliers, stood in two ranks, rifles loaded. Dudley squeezed in on the right flank of his company next to Colour-Sergeant Barker.

"At sixty yards, ready!" Hamilton shouted.

Every man adjusted his feet, taking a ready stance, then fumbled in his percussion cap pouch. They fitted the caps over the breech nipples of their rifles and pulled the hammers back to full cock.

Rebels were now streaming through the back gate, crossing the causeway as they had in the last battle here. They saw the British lines waiting to fire into their flank and began a hasty re-deployment to face the threat. Their movements were confused and uncertain as more of their comrades emerged from the gate at a run, pushing into them.

"Front rank," Hamilton ordered, "pre...sent!"

Dudley aimed. The command to fire came, and jetting smoke obscured his view. A second later, the rear rank fired its volley. When the smoke cleared enough to see, rebels lay sprawled on the causeway and floated in the *jheel*. A few had managed to form a line beyond the *jheel*, across the road, but then the Blue Caps emerged from the back gate. At the sight of this second threat, the rebels broke, as they had broken so many times before.

Victorious again, the field force bivouacked north of the town that evening. At midnight, a bugle sounded the officers' call to report to headquarters.

The force was so small that every officer in it was able to gather around General Havelock's bivouac fire. Dudley squeezed in next to Morris, sensing something ominous. The meeting reminded him of another such gathering, when they had received the news of the Cawnpore massacre.

"Gentlemen," Havelock began, his face creased with worry, "we have fought as gallantly and with as much success as could have been hoped. But we have more sick and injured. Our artillery have expended one-quarter of their ammunition. Between here and Lucknow lie several strongholds." He held up a piece of folded paper with a broken wax seal. "I have received another letter from Colonel Inglis at Lucknow. He estimates that the country is held by at least thirty thousand rebels."

He paused to allow the significance of these facts to sink in.

"I have consulted my staff," Havelock continued. "Inglis claims to have ample supplies in the Residency, and a good defensive position. Losing this force will not help him. Therefore, I am resolved to wait. My reinforcements will arrive, in time. For now, I will retire to Mangalwar to strengthen communications with Cawnpore. We depart in the morning."

There was nothing more to be said. Dismissed, the officers returned to their companies to spread the news to the men.

For four days, the force sat at Mangalwar. Work commenced on a new bridge of boats connecting the Ganges islands. Other work parties repaired portions of the road the rain had washed away.

When the first section of bridge was complete, Havelock sent what baggage he had and his spare ammunition back to Cawnpore; the field force would follow in a few days. Threats now faced Cawnpore from three directions. The Nana Sahib was in Bithoor, the Dinapore mutineers had yet to be contained, and there was a new contingent of mutineers at Gwalior. All northern India was in arms against the East India Company and British rule.

During the evening of August 10th, cavalry scouts reported a large force of the enemy again assembling at Unao. An attack upon Mangalwar seemed imminent. The following morning, the field force formed for parade and set out for the enemy position. They made contact with a few small rebel outposts, but brief skirmishes saw these dealt with. They then bivouacked for the night just outside Unao.

At dawn, the force advanced and found the enemy drawn up at a village beyond the town. The rebel infantry stood in extended lines on either side of the houses. In the center, several heavy guns were positioned behind new earthen mounds.

Havelock formed his army in line, with two wings. The wings then advanced in echelon from the right. The right wing included the Highlanders, Royal Hants, and Blue Caps.

The rebel artillery opened the fight, firing round shot at long range. Blue Cap skirmishers ran ahead of the advance, while the British artillery attempted to pull three guns across the muddy fields to the right of the road.

Dudley marched in his place behind the shrunken company, with Sergeant Bell and Morris on his right. The rebel guns drew closer. Every time one fired, the concussion jarred his teeth. A ball passed through the ranks, carrying away two men in a red spray.

"Close up," Sergeant Bell shouted, and then a second ball passed through the same spot. Bell screamed as the shot tore away his legs.

Dudley shouted, "Close up!"

Smoke blew past them as the front rank brought their rifles and bayonets down to the charge. The rebel gunners switched to grape, blowing a gap in the Sikh battalion to Dudley's left, then a similar gap through the Highlanders on his right. Morris glanced back at him; he was marching at a crouch, his eyes wide, his mouth a tight line.

Ahead, two shells burst above the rebel battery. Dudley felt a surge of excitement. The British artillery was at last in action on the right flank. He felt like running, the wild excitement of battle surging in him.

Then, as if reading his wishes, the Highlanders rushed forward as one, cheering, charging for the battery.

The sepoy gunners remained at their pieces as they had before, but the infantry broke and fled. Dudley leapt onto the earthen mound before one gun, a 24-pounder, and hacked down with his broadsword. His blow was wild, off-balance, slicing down to sever a man's ear then glancing off the man's shoulder. The sepoy fell, clutching the wound. Dudley jumped into the battery, Fusiliers and Highlanders surrounding him, stabbing down with their bayonets.

"Turn the guns!" he cried, and Morris was beside him, screaming and firing his revolver after the fleeing rebel infantry. The Highlanders grabbed the trail handspikes and wheels of the guns, spinning the pieces around. A garland of quilted grapeshot stood between two guns, and the Highlanders loaded, primed, then touched linstocks to the vents. The guns roared, scattering iron into the scurrying enemy troops.

Dudley turned to Morris, who was scowling and dabbing a small scrape on his cheek.

"Hot enough for you now, Trevor?" Dudley asked.

"Their infantry are most cowardly," Morris said in disgust.

"Thankful for that we should be," Colour-Sergeant Barker said from the other side of a rebel gun. "We'd be in a pickle if their foot sloggers were as good as their artillery." He kicked at a dying sepoy gunner.

"Keep your comments to yourself, Colour-Sergeant!" Morris snapped.

Dudley opened his mouth to chastise the lieutenant, but Barker laughed.

"Very good, sir!" he said then marched forward into the smoke.

The Ganges crossing was now secure, and the field force returned to Cawnpore for three days' rest. There, the Highlanders received their No. 4 Company as a reinforcement. With the two companies of the Royal Hants, the improvised battalion now numbered two hundred and sixty men.

Wounds and sickness had taken their toll. The rest of the field force was in a similar state, yet Havelock was determined to complete the secondary task of dispersing the Nana Sahib's remaining army with what men he had.

On the morning of the 16th, the field force, not more than a thousand men, marched west up the river for Bithoor. At noon, they came within sight of the enemy, some four thousand strong.

Before the town stretched fields of sugar cane and castor, the green stalks as high as a man's head. Through the middle of the plantation ran a flooded *nullah* that drained into the river. A single narrow bridge provided a crossing, although a rebel breastwork guarded it. Beyond the *nullah* waited the sepoy infantry, drawn up in line. Behind them, new earthworks protected the town.

The British did not pause in their march. The horse teams and gun carriages crashed through the sugar cane; then the guns were unlimbered and firing on the waiting rebel lines. The sepoys retired behind their earthworks. Their two remaining guns belched smoke but were not enough to prevent the British from easily crossing the bridge and forming on the far side of the *nullah*.

Havelock rode along the front of the line, watching the fall of the shot as his batteries kept up their pounding. The iron balls threw up clumps of dirt when they struck but did little damage to the earthwork. He turned in his saddle and shouted, "Soldiers! We will have recourse to the bayonet!"

The tiny army cheered him; then the commands began to ring out and the drums to beat. The British again advanced in echelon from the right, the Highlanders and Fusiliers marching alongside the Blue Caps. The two rebel guns lay straight ahead.

"Down!" Colonel Hamilton shouted, and the shrunken companies fell flat in the sugar cane. The rebel guns fired, and Dudley heard the bits of grape crashing through the stalks. He turned to Morris with a grin.

"Like someone throwing cricket balls at us!"

They stood and advanced again, the line wavering in the tall cane, the officers slashing at it with their swords. Twice more they lay down and got up again to resume the advance. The sugarcane screened the view ahead, and Dudley did not see the enemy earthworks until a rebel volley burst ten yards in front. Bullets hummed overhead, fired too high; none found a target. With a cheer, the Fusiliers and Highlanders rushed the works.

By the time Dudley stood on top of the earthen rampart, the two ranks that had charged before him had already killed the sepoy gunners and were rushing through the town. He jumped down into the captured battery and stopped, his breath rushing in his ears. He was suddenly very tired. He wanted to sit down.

"Hot work, eh, Lieutenant?" someone said, and he turned to see Captain Mackenzie. The Highlander had somehow managed to keep his uniform in spotless condition. "Five battles and five victories. So ends our first campaign against Lucknow."

"A failure, I'm afraid, sir," Dudley said between gasps of air.

"Nonsense. We've killed plenty of Pandies, and that's all that matters." Another cheer rose in the town, amid the popping of muskets. "Well, we must go and see what the lads are up to."

The Highlander strode into the sounds of fighting. A moment later, Dudley followed.

CHAPTER 29

Cawnpore
September 1857

"Whilst we were stumbling back and forth on the road
to Lucknow…" Dudley wrote,

> …Brigadier-General Neill was very busy.
> Upon our return to Cawnpore, we found
> part of the trunk road lined with hanging
> men. From the clothes the corpses wore,
> it was obvious that not all were sepoys. A
> warning to those who support the rebel-
> lion, I suppose. It was like some terrible
> scene from ancient Rome. The majority
> of my comrades seemed to approve of it,
> and I must admit I take some satisfaction
> in it myself. Forgive me, Uncle; forgive
> me, Aunt, and dear cousin Jane, but our
> anger is causing us to sink into base cru-
> elty.

He paused in his writing. He sat at the table in the quarters he shared with Morris. The rooms were similar to those

in Madras—two bedrooms and a sitting room, sparse furnishings, and a punkah shuttling back and forth overhead.

He dipped his metal nib in the ink bottle then continued:

> The civilian population has begun to return from wherever they were hiding, but they are not friendly. Women gather round the wells and stare at us with contempt, and we stare back with the same. This is what our rule has brought us. Cruelty breeds cruelty. How the Indians must hate us to have done the things for which we condemn them. And now how we hate them.

This was the latest in a series of candid letters. He had written about the Cawnpore massacres, the failed attempt at Lucknow, and subsequent events with as much clarity as he could manage. He had not mailed any of the letters yet, and they lay before him now on the table.

The remaining companies of the 78th Highlanders have arrived, one letter began, a page he had written a month ago. *However, there has been no word from the siege of Delhi, no word of the rest of the Royal Hampshire Fusiliers. I wonder for the fate of my old comrades.*

Another letter opened with the sentence *Horrible news! Most heartbreaking!* It explained that Sir James Outram, who had commanded in Persia, was coming to replace Henry Havelock as commander of the field force.

> This is how the Government in Calcutta rewards our gallant general for one victory after another.

Outram had marched from Allahabad on September 5th, bringing with him two fresh regiments—the 5th Northumberland Fusiliers and the 90th Light Infantry. The regiments were part of a larger contingent that had arrived

in India with Sir Colin Campbell, the old hero of Balaclava
in the Crimea. Campbell was now Commander-in-Chief
of Operations in India.

It had taken Outram and the reinforcements ten days
to reach Cawnpore. When they arrived, Dudley had written:

> The Northumberland Fusiliers look like my
> own Royal Hants, dressed in white frocks
> and cotton trousers, though the 90th, or
> Perthshire Volunteers, wear a sort of rig I
> have never seen before. They have come
> dressed in standard blue Oxford mixture
> trousers, with the red seam stripe, but their
> tunics are tea coloured, with red facings.
> These "brown coats" are very sensible in
> this climate and terrain.

A day later, Outram had stunned and pleased the field
force with his first division order.

"The important duty of relieving the garrison of Lucknow," the order had read, "had been first entrusted to Brigadier-General Havelock, C.B., and Major-General Outram
feels that it is due to that distinguished officer, and to the
strenuous and noble exertions which he had already made
to effect that object, that to him shall accrue the honour
of the achievement."

Outram went on to state that he would waive his rank
and accompany the force to Lucknow in his civil capacity—with the death of Sir Henry Lawrence at Lucknow,
he was now Chief Commissioner of Oudh. He would ren-
der his military services as a volunteer.

Dudley's opinion, in another written account, said, "This
is a fine and popular move, but I foresee a conflict. It will
be difficult for General Outram not to issue orders, as he
is accustomed to doing."

He read over this and the other unmailed letters, sorting the pages according to date. One day they would make a fine addition to his memoir. He would have to remind his aunt and uncle to not throw them away.

He again took up his pen and began a fresh page.

> We shall be setting out soon, with not a moment to lose. In his messages sent through enemy lines, Colonel Inglis at Lucknow estimates his stores as good until the 25th. It is now the 17th. Despite a rash of cholera, our men are more than ready to go. Now we are an "army of relief," with two proper brigades of infantry and one of artillery.
>
> The First Brigade is under Brigadier-General Neill, our hangman. It contains the 5th Fusiliers, 84th Regiment, Madras Fusiliers, and a company of the 64th. The Second Brigade has the privilege of Colonel Walter Hamilton as commander. In it we have the 78th Highlanders, our two shrunken companies of Royal Hampshire Fusiliers, the 90th Light Infantry, and Ferozepore Sikhs. The Artillery Brigade holds three full batteries, and with them are the Volunteer Cavalry and a few engineers. Then there is the ammunition train, the bullocks, camels, elephants and such, and the camp followers.
>
> I do declare that Pandy won't stop us this time. This army is not large enough to recapture Lucknow, you understand, but is to provide relief to the besieged. Once there, we will no doubt become be-

sieged ourselves. However, Sir Colin Campbell will not be far behind. Our troops and
supplies will enable Lucknow to hold
for another month until an even larger
force can be gathered from England and
abroad.

He finished the letter with: "I will write to you again
from the Lucknow Residency. I assure you that I am in excellent health. The sickness has not touched me, nor shall
it. God bless you all. Yours, etc. William."

An advanced party of infantry secured the Oudh bank of
the Ganges while the engineers completed the last section of the bridge of boats. The majority of the relief
force crossed on the 19th, while the heavy guns, ammunition camels, and elephants followed a day later.

The two depleted companies of the Royal Hants made
a single unit as the second advance on Lucknow began.
Dudley rode in front of them, and Colour-Sergeant Barker
marched on their right flank. With Barker walked Private
Geary's little dog.

The army halted just after noon outside Mangalwar.
The enemy had fortified the village, and Havelock decided
it would have to be taken. A battery of British 24-pounders
deployed across the road and in the field to the right. The
5th Fusiliers moved forward in skirmishing order, with the
rest of the First Brigade following in line. A moment later,
and the Second Brigade also advanced, moving off the road
to the left through a shallow swamp to assault the rebel
flank.

Dudley rode his horse through the swamp, ducking low
in the saddle. This was his ninth battle in India. In the road,
the 24-pounders began their work, their heavy shot smash-

ing through the sepoy breastworks. Before Dudley's brigade could reach its objective, the rebels were already in retreat.

Sir James Outram put himself at the head of the Volunteer Cavalry, and the horsemen charged after the retreating sepoys. The British infantry reformed in open columns and followed. Some time later, Outram returned triumphant, sword bloodied, one of his companions carrying the captured Regimental Colour of the 1st Bengal Native Infantry.

Rain pelted down as the army pursued the enemy through the old battle ground at Unao. There the force halted for half an hour, the men digging in their haversacks for something to eat. When the rest period ended, the army pushed on for Bashiratganj.

This time the walled town was empty of all save the mouldering corpses from the battles of a month ago. The army halted for the night, the men crammed into the shelter of a large serai.

The rain fell in steady sheets the next morning as the march resumed. Colour-Sergeant Barker tried to perk up his men by having them sing marching songs. A few voices had joined his powerful baritone when Geary's dog began to bay. This served to lift spirits perhaps more than the colour-sergeant could have hoped.

After fourteen miles, the column crossed a long masonry bridge over the Sai River. On the far bank sat a gun emplacement built of sand, earth, and planks. Two bronze guns pointed from the embrasures, but they were abandoned. The enemy had not waited to meet the British force.

Beyond the guns squatted a collection of dilapidated brick huts. There, the soaked and weary soldiers took shelter, although shelter so inadequate that Dudley led his horse to a grove of tall slender teaks, their even tiers of branches offering a little cover. Morris came with him. In the distance, over the hissing of the rain, came the deep-throated pounding of artillery.

"Lucknow," Morris said. "We must be close."

"We've done it, then," Dudley stated. He shook his head. "It seemed so simple this time. The enemy hardly made an effort to delay our advance."

"I admit that I'm disappointed, too. Our little force gave them such a toweling last time they fear this larger army."

As Morris spoke, a splashing of hoofs heralded the approach of a 9-pounder battery, the teams dragging the six guns to the edge of the road. The curious infantry officers watched as the gunners deployed their pieces and began loading them with blank cartridges. General Havelock and Outram sat their horses not far away, heedless of the foul weather.

Under the eyes of the commanders, the artillery battery fired a Royal Salute—twenty-one guns.

"Ah, we're signaling the Lucknow garrison!" Dudley said. "Colonel Inglis will know we're coming."

Morris nodded. Dudley shivered as the powder smoke drifted by, hanging close to the ground.

"We won't fail them this time," he murmured. "Not this time."

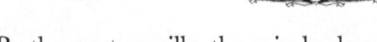

By the next reveille, the rain had ceased. The army of relief set out, marching for ten miles without encountering opposition, finding no rebels hidden in the topes that dotted the sandy plain. At two o'clock in the afternoon, the force came within sight of the village of Jalalabad, a cluster of white cottages far to the right of the road. Standing over the village was an ancient and crumbling fort.

A mile from Jalalabad stood the Alam Bagh, the "Garden of the World." This was a large and fanciful enclosure with an octagonal tower at each of its four corners.

Within the enclosure was a palace for the royal family of Oudh.

Arrayed in line, its left flank against the Alam Bagh, stood the rebel army.

The British infantry halted in column within sight of the enemy while the cavalry ranged ahead to reconnoiter. The rebel center, situated across the road and in a series of hillocks, was concentrated around six guns. A flooded field anchored their right. Beyond their position, the plain rose to the crest of a wide ridge. What lay behind the ridge was invisible, but Dudley knew it was Lucknow. He could hear the guns, the ongoing struggle between the rebels and the besieged garrison in the British Residency.

Tall on a new horse beside the regiment, Colonel Hamilton called to his regiments, "The army will advance along the road until it passes the swamps on either side. The First Brigade will carry on, while we in the Second Brigade will turn to the left and attack the enemy's right flank." He then spurred forward to the head of his brigade.

Dudley gripped the hilt of his sword. He wondered if he should dismount. Save for the unnecessary attack at Mangalwar, he had never fought on horseback. It made him feel exposed.

The sudden screech of mortar shells made him duck in the saddle. This was a reflex he had acquired in the Crimea, but he could see the shells, two dark smudges rising about five hundred yards forward. The purplish smoke lingered in the air after the shells had fallen, hanging in black tendrils. He did not see where they burst, but as more screeched towards them, the command to march rang out.

Two explosions rocked the head of the column, and then Dudley heard the deeper roar of round shot. A ball thumped along the sandy ground to his right. His horse shied to the left, but he steadied the animal before it could knock over Colour-Sergeant Barker.

Barker glanced at him, and said, "First Brigade's getting it hard up ahead, sir."

The column had still not passed the swamps when the head of the Second Brigade wheeled left. Again the men waded in filthy water. Far forward, on the road, the First Brigade infantry was swinging from open column into line. A field battery deployed to support them, horses and limbers rushing to the rear.

Dudley remained dry in the saddle and kept his eyes focused on the enemy right flank as it drew nearer. Some sepoys had seen them and were struggling to trail two guns around to meet the flanking movement, but too late. A British battery whirled into action first, and Dudley saw a black ball hurtle toward the enemy, striking a gun wheel, shattering it and spraying the sepoys with splinters. The second rebel gun jetted smoke, and a ball came skipping over the water, like a stone pitched by a boy. It fell somewhere behind the column, in the rear of the Sikhs.

The sepoys did not have a chance to fire the gun again before the British column had overlapped their flank. The companies wheeled to the right into line, the Royal Hants now on the right of the Highlanders. They halted and prepared to fire.

"File firing by companies," Colonel Hamilton cried, and a second later, Captain Norcott shouted, "Two rounds independent fire, commence firing!"

The men in the rear rank of each file waited as their front rank counterparts aimed and fired. As the front rank men reloaded, the rear rank men took their turn. Sepoys a hundred yards away began to fall as they scrambled to form a new line at right angles to their old position.

Meanwhile, First Brigade had advanced and begun firing volleys by company, rifles roaring in unison. The enemy was caught in a crossfire.

"Cease firing!" Colonel Hamilton cried as the rebel line began to crumble, sepoys making for the rear in ones and twos. Second Brigade prepared to advance.

When the brigade stepped off, the pipes and drums struck up with "Caber Feidh." The sepoy right and center disintegrated, and Second Brigade began to rush forward as a body.

"Steady!" Dudley shouted with the other officers. "Keep your cadence with the pipes!"

They drew closer to the Alam Bagh, small puffs of musket smoke appearing at the loopholes cut into its outer wall. To Dudley's right, the Northumberland Fusiliers were charging, raising a cheer that became an enraged growl; a gun in one of the octagonal towers belched flame and grape into the Northumberland ranks. Men and bits of men were thrown left and right. At the sight, the Highlanders shouted as one and surged ahead.

There was no point in trying to hold back the Highlanders this time. Dudley dug his heels into his horse's flanks and charged with them. With his sword over his head, he dashed for the enclosure.

A bullet whined past his head, and then he was falling, his horse collapsing beneath him. He rolled in the dust, losing his grip on his sword. He came to a stop lying on his back. For a moment, he just lay there, gasping for breath but unable to find any. The sky filled his vision, patches of deep blue behind racing bunches of white-and-gray cloud. He could hear the noise of battle, a roar of shouting, rifles and guns, but he could no longer see it.

He did not know how long he lay, but eventually his breathing steadied. When the noise turned to cheering, he rolled over and pushed to his feet. His sword lay in the dust a few yards away. His horse lay closer, on its side, motionless.

Checking his limbs and feeling his ribs, he decided he was unhurt. As he stooped to retrieve his sword, he saw the Highlanders on the walls of the Alam Bagh, brandishing their rifles and cheering. Beyond the walled garden, the Volunteer Cavalry was disappearing over the ridge at a gallop. The only sign of the enemy was the abandoned guns and hundreds of their dead sprawled on the plain.

Dudley rode his remount to the top of the ridge; the horse was a spare he had taken from the supply train after the Alam Bagh battle. He stroked its neck as Morris pulled up beside him. Below, in a shallow river valley, lay a city sprung from the pages of a fairy story.

In the distance ran the silver trace of the Gumti River. Closer to the ridge, crossing the road, was a long canal. Between canal and river, the morning sun glinted off an expanse of golden domes, cupolas, minarets, terraced roofs, colonnades, pillars and archways. On a bluff above the river stood a huge temple or mosque, its three gold domes rising in a cluster.

Nearer the canal was the Kaiser Bagh, or king's palace, a tall gate and two storeys of archways and columns. Away to Dudley's right, in the east, lay a wide green park, a small forest, lawns as green as any in Ireland—the Dilkusha Park, a vast oasis on the stoney plain.

The sight of Lucknow brought with it the pleasure of discovery. This was all he had ever imagined India to be.

Then a gun fired, and he remembered he was at war.

"We'd best get under cover from those cannon," he said, reining his new mount about.

Five hundred yards before him was a two-storey house of yellow stone, an elegant building resembling a small French manor. The rebels had placed a battery there. Far-

ther on, the road bent to the left, passing through a village until it reached the Char Bagh bridge over the canal. Rebel infantry lined the canal, while another battery
of six guns commanded the bridge.

The Char Bagh bridge, with its strong defenses, was
not the best route into Lucknow, but it was the one General Outram and Havelock had agreed upon. Havelock
had wanted to cross the canal farther east, march through
the Dilkusha Park, then cross the Gumti and come at the
besieged Residency from the north. Outram had agreed
that such a plan would limit British casualties but claimed
the ground near the Dilkusha was too wet or flooded for
cavalry, artillery, and supply vehicles. He was impatient
to relieve Lucknow immediately, unwilling to wait to see
if the ground would dry.

The time was ripe, as he had told his army. In an address to the troops in the wake of the capture of the Alam
Bagh, he had explained that Delhi had fallen to the British relief force on September 20th. The men had cheered
the news, understanding its significance. Lucknow was now
the key to the entire rebellion.

The planned attack would be difficult. Once the infantry had crossed the canal, they would not be able to continue straight into the city and to the Residency. The rebels
had dug trenches across the road, and every house would
be loopholed. Instead, the army would turn right, following the north bank of the canal, then turn left again near
the eastern end of the city. From there, they would move
up the streets, following the Gumti, passing between the
river and the Kaiser Bagh. The besieged Residency stood
on the river several streets west of the king's palace.

The attack was already underway. A few hours earlier, the relief force had left the sick, wounded, and many
of the beasts of burden and native followers at the Alam

Bagh. Guarding them were detachments from the various regiments under Brevet-Lieutenant-Colonel M'Intyre of the 78th. The rest of the army had eaten a hot meal then begun its advance just after eight o'clock.

The First Brigade was moving up the road now to force the Char Bagh bridge. To the right, three British 9-pounders covered the attack. The guns fired in quick succession, scoring direct hits to silence the rebel battery at the yellow house. When the firing ceased, the gunners cheered. The route to the bridge was clear.

Dudley and Morris moved aside as the First Brigade went past, the Blue Caps in the van. The Second Brigade would follow. The Highlanders and Royal Hants had orders to bring up the rear and secure the bridge for the passage of the supply train. Dudley and Morris sat and watched the advance. They would be among the last to enter the city and had time to wait.

Past the yellow house, the regiments of First Brigade tramped along the bend in the road; the bridge and its six guns lay two hundred yards away. The guns, one a 24-pounder, opened fire with grape, and musketry poured from loopholed houses on the north side of the canal. British soldiers began falling in clumps at the head of the column. Smoke and dust swirled in the air. Officers scurried on foot, having had their horses shot from under them, calling for the troops to halt and lie down.

Two of Captain Maude's 9-pounders rolled up to the bend in the road and halted. Rebel fire continued to pour in, but the gunners ignored it, unhitching the trails while the drivers pulled the horse teams and limbers to the rear. As the gunners loaded, the 5th Fusiliers moved at a crouch to the right, heading for a clump of trees on a low hill. From there, they could drive flanking fire into the rebel battery. Meanwhile, a company of Blue Caps formed skirmish order and advanced to line the canal bank left of the bridge.

Maude's two guns managed to fire a single round each, but they would not fire another. Grape shot savaged the gun crews, and soon their mangled bodies lay sprawled in the dirt. On the left, the skirmishers were having no effect, while the 5th Fusiliers had yet to reach the hill.

General Neill rode to the head of his old regiment, his Blue Caps, and shouted, "Madras Fusiliers will advance and take the bridge!"

The men stood, dressed their line, and marched forward. They were still a hundred yards from the bridge when their skirmishers, without orders, charged along the canal towards the rebel battery. Their officer ran in front, sword in one hand and revolver in the other. The rebels let them reach the bridge, let them form a dense clump of men. Then, all six guns fired as one.

Not one man survived the charge. Severed arms and legs twirled in the air while broken bodies fell into the muddy canal.

The sepoy gunners began to sponge their pieces and ram home fresh cartridges. In the lull, the enraged Blue Caps rushed to avenge their fallen company. The sepoys hurried but could not load fast enough. The fusiliers surged over the battery like a wave taking a sand castle. Bayonets stabbed downward, rifle butts crushed skulls. Within seconds, the bridge had fallen.

The rest of the First Brigade rose and doubled forward, the Second Brigade following. The 5th Fusiliers provided covering fire as the other regiments spread along the far side of the canal and began breaking into the houses.

Dudley and Morris dismounted and passed their horses to a *syce*. It was time for them to join their company, and they would continue on foot.

CHAPTER 30

Near Lucknow
September 1857

Three Highlanders put their shoulders to the wheel of a gun carriage, pushing until it slipped over the bank of the canal. The long bronze 12-pounder splashed into the water and at once sank to the bottom. The Highlanders retrieved their Enfield rifles and ran to join their comrades, who were engaged in a fight to capture a second gun.

Lieutenant Morris stood to one side of the Char Bagh bridge and observed the little action with envy. The rebels had brought the two guns forward to harass the British rear guard and the supply train. Colonel Stisted, now in charge of the 78th, had ordered only two of his companies forward in skirmish order to engage the guns. The rest had to stay in the village and at the bridge while the main body of the army plunged into the city.

"There lies a chance for glory," Morris said to Dudley. "Enemy guns to capture, and I must stay here and guard this great circus."

Dudley had learned to ignore Morris's now routine complaints. He was looking the other way, watching as the last of the cattle and commissariat carts lumbered over the bridge. The long line of camels, ammunition boxes strapped to their backs, was already moving along the rutted canal road into the city.

"It's fine for you," Morris went on. "You already captured your Russian battery."

The Highlanders were returning from the village now, having spiked the vent of the second gun and left it where it stood.

"It's time to go, Trevor," Dudley said.

A company drummer was calling the assembly on his bugle. Pipe-Major MacLean and his pipers had been sitting on a patch of grass, and now rose to their feet, brushing off their ragged kilts and straightening their sporrans. The battalion was scattered, a few men near the bridge, others in the houses of the Char Bagh village. In pairs and small clumps, they came running, forming around the Colours and the corps drummers.

Dudley's company took its usual position on the left. As Colour-Sergeant Barker dressed the ranks, Dudley listened for the sounds of battle in the city. The main army was long out of sight, but the noise allowed him to follow their progress. The army had traveled east at first then had turned west, moving through the streets. Now it seemed to have stalled beyond the Kaiser Bagh.

Colonel Stisted positioned himself behind the battalion then shouted, "Battalion will form fours right! Form fours…right!"

In response, the men faced to the right; then, every even number stepped to his right and forward, making a long column of men in groups of four. The officers took positions on the flank nearest the canal.

The battalion advanced, the men stumbling in the ruts the guns and supply carts had left in their passage. Dudley heard a shuffling and shouting behind him and turned in time to see a large body of rebels swarming over the Char Bagh bridge from the south. They had come out of hiding places within a territory the British had thought secured. More were running along the south bank of the canal, where a long stone wall offered some protection. They wore powder horns and carried matchlocks. These were *zemindars'* men, not mutinous sepoys.

Norcott saw the unexpected threat and shouted, "Company...halt!"

The Royal Hants halted; the Highlanders carried on. With quick commands, Norcott brought his men back into line and wheeled the formation on its center until it faced back down the road.

"Volley fire at fifty yards," he shouted. "Ready!" When the men had pulled back the hammers on their rifles and adjusted their rear sights, he cried, "Front rank, pre...sent! Fire!" A volley boomed. "Rear rank, pre...sent! Fire!"

The smoke from the second volley cleared, revealing a street choked with downed rebels, the still dead and the stumbling wounded. The survivors darted into the houses for cover.

Captain Norcott turned the company, formed fours, and shouted, "By the right, double...march!"

The men ran to catch the Highlanders, who were already more than a hundred yards away. There was no sign of the supply train, nor of any of the other troops that had gone before.

A squad of the Volunteer Cavalry suddenly appeared from a side street near the front of the Highlanders. Their officer pointed to the left, to the west.

"This way!"

Some of the *zemindars'* men followed, using all the cover they could. Rebel muskets appeared in the windows and loopholes of surrounding houses. Shots rang out, and two men in the running Fusilier company fell, their comrades stumbling over their prone forms. Other men broke ranks to assist the wounded.

The Highlanders followed the cavalry, moving along another narrow lane. The Royal Hants charged after them, at last catching up, the men breathless and harried.

The battalion began to lose its formation in the narrow streets, flowing between the modest dwellings. Fusiliers mixed with Highlanders, all stumbling west, towards the continuing sounds of battle. When they reached a small square and crossroads, they halted, a shapeless mass of armed men.

"Which way do we go?" someone demanded. Officers looked this way and that, but no one answered. The supply train seemed to have disappeared, engulfed by the embattled city.

"The Residency has to be over yon," Captain Mackenzie said from the back of his horse, "in the west."

"We can follow the sound of the guns, sir," Dudley suggested to Colonel Stisted. The noise of artillery was loud, seeming to come from only a few blocks distant.

"We'll go this way, then," Stisted said, spurring his mount towards a beckoning street.

Sergeants began bellowing at the men, pushing them into fours. Without a command to march, they followed the colonel.

The street was wide, lined on both sides with fine houses, many with colourful frescos and scenes painted on the walls. Trees and flowering shrubs towered over garden enclosures, although jagged loopholes in the masonry marred the beauty of the scene.

The battalion was not alone. Dudley saw a flash of white through a gap in a wall, then another. Sepoys had occupied the gardens and were moving to keep pace with the Highlanders. Muskets began to protrude from the loopholes, fire, then disappear. A few more men fell. Casualties began to mount, the wounded men helped along by their comrades, the dead left where they had been shot.

Colonel Stisted held up his hand, and sergeants shouted for the men to halt. The street terminated at a small plaza. Dudley could not see what was happening, so he pushed through to the front. Morris trailed behind him, saying, "You'll not leave me behind!"

On the far side of the plaza stood a pointed archway. Over the arch, carved in stone, were two fishes facing each other, the royal crest of Oudh. Through the arch, the wheel of a gun carriage was visible side-on, with sepoys scurrying to load and fire. The gun's target lay across the street, to the right. It was a long rectangular palace with rows of arched windows. British soldiers were returning fire from those windows. The battalion had at last caught up to the main army.

"There's your battery, Morris," Dudley said, nodding at the gun. Three more cannon lay behind it. "And we have them in the flank."

"Who shall be the first to take the guns?" Colonel Stisted called.

The Highlanders needed no further prompting. Their battle cry was an enraged howl. Morris went with them, but when he reached the battery, the gunners were already dead.

———◆———

The reunited army of relief paused in the courtyard of a palace called the Moti Mahal. The wounded, baggage and animals would stay there. The rest of the force reformed and pushed along the street to the next palace, the Chattur Manzil. This was a tall building, each storey smaller than the last. Near the top was a roof balcony and a smooth golden dome.

South of the Chattur Manzil stood the great edifice of the Kaiser Bagh, its every archway an emplacement for rebel guns. To the west, on the riverbank, stood the long walled compound of the Residency. From the rooftop of the main Residency building, the besieged defenders were waving rifles and handkerchiefs.

Sight of the defenders gave Dudley an unexpected thrill; he had almost forgotten why they had come to Lucknow. It was to reinforce these people, to prevent their destruction. To prevent a repeat of Cawnpore.

All around him, expectation lit the faces of the Highlanders. Dudley searched until he found Colour-Sergeant Barker, then said to him, "Here we go, Colour."

Barker grinned. "Good luck, sir."

Round shot continued to come in from the Kaiser Bagh, some striking the wall of the Chattur Manzil, spraying bits of shattered masonry. Heedless of the fire, the relief force formed a column of companies in the street. At the head of the column stood the Highlanders and Sikhs. The honour of becoming the first to enter the Residency would go to the regiments that had been the last to enter the city.

Sepoys began running along rooftops on either side of the street, taking up sniping positions. Every few seconds a bullet found a target, a man grunting and falling, bleeding. Still the calm dressing of ranks went on. British skirmishers moved out to the flanks to provide covering fire, their Enfields shooting up at the rooftops and windows.

Pipe-Major MacLean and his men took their place at the head of the regiment. The musicians tuned their drones as the bullets hummed about their ears, then MacLean said, "Let's give 'em 'The Campbells are Coming.'"

The pipe-major steadied and waited for the command to march. Outram and Colonel Hamilton maneuvered their horses to stand in front of him. Then Hamilton shouted, "Brigade, by the center, quick...march!"

The pipes and drums struck up. The column stepped off, the skirmishers running along the flanks. Ahead lay a broad plaza. Sepoys leapt along the rooftops to follow, and Outram rode here and there, pointing them out as targets for the skirmishers.

The pipes and the two lead companies marched to the other side of the plaza, passing the head of a street on their right. Outram chased after them, shouting, "No! The turn is here! Back here!"

The center companies did not make the mistake. The colour-sergeants ordered, "Right wheel!"

A slight breeze stirred, and the buff Regimental Colour of the 78th unfurled as the battalion turned down the street. At the end was the stout gatehouse and tall archway of the Bailley Gate. Right of the gate was a long banqueting hall and, in the rear, the main Residency building. From the left of the gatehouse ran the yellow brick wall of the compound, its doors barricaded.

Realizing their error, the pipers turned and marched back to the proper street, not missing a note. The rifle companies parted to let them pass then followed in an unformed mass. The relief force began to lose its cohesion, becoming a vast crowd of men making for the Bailley Gate and the Residency. The noise of musketry had become one long continuous roar.

Dudley drew the Highland sword and chanced a look at the houses to his left, at the muskets protruding from the loopholes, the jets of smoke and flame. One after the other, bullets whined past his ears, rushing between the ranks.

But no one broke step, no one faltered in the urge to move forward. He saw the Regimental Colour fall, but then another man grabbed the pole and raised the flag again. That man in turn passed the colour to another.

At the gate, the center companies crammed together to push through the arch. The companies behind them, unable to penetrate the congestion, turned and began firing at the swarms of rebels who had appeared on all sides.

Dudley shoved his way through his men, pointing at targets with his sword. The music of the pipes had stopped, and he noticed two pipers who had set down their instruments to help a wounded rifleman. One of the pipers was Roger Andrews. The rifleman lay at his feet.

A group of rebel *sowars* milled about on some broken ground to the west, drawn *tulwars* in their hands. When they saw the pipers standing alone, they spurred forward.

"On your left!" Dudley shouted. Riflemen broke from the mass of the relief force, kneeling to fire at the oncoming threat. Two *sowars* fell in the dust and rubble. A third carried on.

As Piper Andrews threw the wounded man over his shoulders, the other piper lifted his instrument and pointed the drones at the horseman. The musician gave one mighty, tuneless blast on his pipes, and the *sowar*'s mount reared. With fear and alarm, the *sowar* reined about and galloped the other way.

"Well done! Well done!" Dudley shouted, joining the pipers as they ran for the Bailley Gate, the entrance to the Residency. The gate was clear now, and defenders lined the top of the wall, their rifles spitting fire; Dudley recognized the khaki shell jackets of the 32nd Regiment.

Then he was through the gate and standing in the courtyard.

Everywhere, Highlanders and Sikhs were cheering and embracing the defenders. Men, women and children spilled from the main building. The battle continued to rage outside as rough, bearded Highlanders and turbanned Sikhs lifted up the children and laughed. Soldiers were shaking hands. The sound of musketry seemed to fade, drowned by the noise of triumph.

Dudley sloped his sword on his shoulder, gazing around in amazement. It was like coming inside after the fury of a storm.

A pretty young woman with hair the colour of ripe chestnuts was walking towards him with open arms. She embraced him, weeping into his shoulder, repeating the words "Thank you."

He encircled her with his left arm, rocking her gently. They had succeeded at last. He closed his eyes, but tears began to roll down his cheeks, making streaks in the grime.

"You're welcome," was all he could say. "You're welcome."

CHAPTER 31

Lucknow
October 1857

"I'd make it seven hundred yards, Tom," Barker said.

His companion, Tom Gillespie of the 78th, adjusted the rear sight of his rifle to the seven hundred-yard mark then raised the weapon and sighted along the blued barrel. With Barker and another Highlander looking on, he aimed at a trio of rebels across the street from the Residency.

The rifle spat smoke and flame, the butt plate jarring into Gillespie's shoulder. Barker saw the distinct jet of mortar dust as the bullet struck the wall next to the rebel's head. The sepoy and his two comrades quickly ducked back into their trench.

Barker laughed. "Like picking off Russkies in front of Sevastopol."

Gillespie and the other private, MacIntyre, both chuckled, even though the shot had missed.

"You're still two up on me, Brian," Gillespie said.

Barker slapped him on the shoulder.

"They'll poke their heads out of their holes again soon enough, and you'll get another chance."

The two Highlanders began loading their rifles, ramrods rattling in the barrels. Their white cotton frocks were stained at the right shoulders from days of sniping; the frocks had replaced their tattered doublets, cotton being more practical than the heavy wool. Some members of the Ross-shire Buffs had even abandoned their kilts for cotton trousers, making them resemble the few Fusiliers in their ranks.

Barker peered over sandbags piled on the edge of the balcony, searching for another target. His sniper's nest was on the roof above the second floor of the Residency. The first two storeys made a square block, but the third was in the shape of a cross, leaving a balcony in each corner. From here, he had a clear view of the rebel trenches, rifle pits, and batteries surrounding the defences.

The Residency had been turned into a stout fortress. An octagonal tower on one corner served as another observation post, while each of the tall rectangular windows framed a rifle position, the defenders having piled sandbags behind the shutters and Venetian blinds.

The siege had left the interior of the building a complete wreck. The offices, mess, and billiard room were filled with shattered furniture, *doolies*, empty crates and ammunition boxes. Women and children crowded every room with nothing but a few stained *charpoys* for bedding. Barker found the accommodations superior to some he had endured, but he knew it must be a trial for these fine ladies of privilege.

He had tried to imagine the scene in General Wheeler's doomed entrenchment, thinking it must have been much the same as this. Mister Dudley had assured him it had been worse.

The siege had settled into something of a routine after the initial breakthrough; casualties from the mad charge through the streets had been high, and detachments had spent the following few days venturing out to bring in the wounded. They had braved a murderous fire, loading the injured into *doolies* and taking more casualties in the process. They had also collected the dead, including the body of General Neill. Neill had fallen only a few streets away from the Residency. His old regiment, the Madras Fusiliers, "Neill's Blue Caps," had mourned his passing.

Infantry squads had also gone out to retrieve the supplies and equipment left in various places in the city. The 78th had provided an escort to bring in the heavy artillery, moving in silence at night. The rebel sentries at the Kaiser Bagh had discovered the escort, but too late; the entire train of artillery had entered the besieged compound without mishap.

For days after that, the troops had cleared the enemy from the buildings nearest the Residency. They had taken the palaces along the river, almost to the walls of the Kaiser Bagh, for barracks. The Highlanders had established their quarters in the domed Chattar Manzil then began constructing a tunnel through to the adjacent houses—General Outram planned to evacuate the civilians to safety and had ordered the establishment of physical communications with the Alam Bagh and Cawnpore.

The little army had gone from house to house with crowbars and pickaxes, knocking holes in the walls to build a physical corridor through the city. The work had been nearing completion when Outram changed his mind; the defenders had more food and ammunition than he had originally believed. With the arrival of so many beasts of burden, such as the supply bullocks, the garrison had enough food to last more than another two months. Conferring with Havelock, he decided not to evacuate. He would wait for Sir Colin Campbell.

Since then, the men of each regiment had stood guard for three days out of four. Every fourth day found them improving defensive positions, digging new rifle pits, making loopholes in walls, and erecting barricades. It was while on guard in the rifle pits that Barker and Private Gillespie had begun their sniping contest. So far, Barker had a score of fourteen hits to Gillespie's dozen.

"Maybe it's tha' short sergeant's rifle," the Highlander offered as a possible explanation as they sat behind the sandbags on the Residency roof.

The door behind them squeaked open, and Private Geary crawled out onto the balcony. Lazzy was with him. The dog went at once to Gillespie, tail thrashing.

The Highlander grinned and said, "You'll no' find any scraps here, Lazzy. I'm sorry I did na' think to bring any."

"What's up, Sarge?" Geary said then added, "I mean Colour?"

"Potting Pandies, lad," Barker explained. "Take your place on the wall, if you'd like."

Geary knelt behind the sandbags next to Gillespie. Below to the west stretched an expanse of stoney ground that ended at a series of rifle pits. Leading away from the rifle pits were trenches covered with plank awnings. A few men in white clothes were milling about under the awnings and among the houses to the rear.

"Pandy don't dare get too close, what with the range of our rifles," Geary said. "Should have thought twice before rejecting the greased cartridge. Now they're paying for it, right, Colour?"

"Aye, lad," Barker agreed. "But don't worry. They don't know the true range of the Enfield rifle in a steady hand. We can send a bullet farther than the rear of those trenches over there. See if you can give the fellows in those houses a surprise."

Geary smiled and began loading his rifle. He had leapt at any chance to please Barker since becoming Lazzy's keeper. Barker watched him and thought what a tough little bugger he was after all. He had survived the Crimea and had made it through all this hard marching and fighting without a scratch. Maybe he would even make corporal one of these days.

Geary sighted by resting his rifle on a sandbag. He squeezed the trigger, and the rifle bucked. One of the rebels standing in the shade of the houses whirled and fell. His two companions ran for cover.

Barker laughed and slapped the private's back.

"Quite a shot, lad. You'd do Sergeant Johnson proud, and he's the best shot in the regiment."

Gillespie whistled in admiration.

"Must ha' been nigh on seven hundred yards, as ye said, Colour-Sergeant. A fine shot, indeed. Cut a notch in your stock." He winked at Barker. "We'll have ta let him in on our wee contest, eh, Brian?"

"Not with shooting like that," Barker said. "He'll pass my score in no time, and then where will I be?"

CHAPTER 32

Lucknow
October 1857

With the poor range and accuracy of their smoothbore muskets and matchlocks, the rebels turned to undermining the walls of the British outposts; the defenders spent much of their time lying on floors, ears to the brick, listening for the sound of pick and shovel. They also dug countermines, stacking them with powder and igniting the charges before the enemy could do the same. In this way, by digging mines, sniping, and making the occasional sortie, they held the rebels at bay.

Dudley had become a miner. He crouched in a new tunnel holding a small brass lantern to illuminate the head of the sap. Two men worked on the sap with picks. Waiting behind them were others with planks, pegs and mallets, ready to brace the ceiling. The tunnel was one of three branching out from a house two streets over from the Residency. The work was under the direction of an officer of the Bengal Engineers.

This was a different siege from the one at Cawnpore. Dudley sensed no underlying desperation here, no horrible uncertainty. Communications with the base at Alam Bagh, and thence with Cawnpore, were strong. The defenders knew that Sir Colin Campbell was not far off with a second relief force.

There was hope of escape and ultimate victory, although the garrison was not yet out of danger—there were still casualties, both from random enemy fire and from disease. Dudley avoided the civilians in the Residency, not wishing to know those people, the women and children of the station. As in Wheeler's entrenchment, he preferred to spend his time on the outposts, visiting the men in the sniper's nests, the pickets, and helping with the digging of the mines.

It was hot in the tunnel, the air damp and close. The men working as sappers, Private Marten and a fellow named Tailor, were coated in sweat and dust, rags tied over their noses and mouths. When they had made some progress with the picks, they took up their shovels and passed the earth back to the mouth of the tunnel. Other shovel men then scooped it into a pile.

Private Marten took up his pick, swinging it with great force and stumbling as it bit deep into the wall—the tool had gone farther than he had expected. When he withdrew it, he turned to Dudley and whispered, "I've broken into open space here, sir."

Dudley shuffled forward with the lantern. By the dim flickering light, he could see the dark gap where Marten's pick had encountered so little resistance.

"Listen," he said, and each man cocked his head. Only silence met them from beyond the hole.

They had found the head of a rebel mine. The tunnel seemed unoccupied.

"Dig it out," he commanded, and as the picks resumed their work, he turned to the shovel man behind him. "Pass the word for Lieutenant Morris."

Soon, Morris was crouching next to him. Sweat beaded the lieutenant's smooth brow.

"Don't much care for these dark, constricted places," he muttered. "I'm not a mole, you know, nor a rabbit."

"Then lend me your revolver," Dudley said. "We've encountered the end of an enemy sap. I'm going to take a look."

Morris squinted as the sappers cleared away the debris in front of the rebel tunnel.

"But it could be ready to blow," Morris objected.

"There are no powder charges," Dudley insisted. The floor of the tunnel was visible now, sloping upward. "Hand me your revolver."

Morris bit his lip as he slowly drew his heavy Adams. Then he jerked his arm forward, and Dudley took the pistol.

"Tell Lieutenant Langley to have the powder charges ready when I return," Dudley said.

Morris nodded.

The tunnel was clear of obstructions now. Dudley transferred the lantern to his left hand so he could hold the revolver with his right. He checked the Adams to see that the percussion caps were in place behind the five chambers. Then he shuffled forward.

"Be careful," he heard Morris whisper.

He paused, watching for movement ahead. He saw none, nor the dim shape of powder barrels. A few picks and shovels lay in the dirt, and scraps of wood from the support beams.

He turned down the lantern flame, extinguishing it, then blinked in the darkness. His eyes adjusted, but still he could see little but a few vague outlines. Alone in the inky black, he inched forward like a crab until his head brushed the low ceiling, knocking his cap askew. He adjusted it and carried on, his hoarse breathing loud in his ears.

The floor of the tunnel suddenly became level, and he stopped. Pale light glimmered ahead, the square mouth of the tunnel not more than five yards away. He saw movement, and a voice speaking, a low murmur.

His trigger finger tensed. There was more movement, and now he could see a man's legs framed by the square of light. Taking two more shuffling steps, he waited. The man did not move, and he heard the voice again, the words in Hindustani.

He raised the revolver, aimed, and squeezed the trigger.

The report was loud in the confined space, the flame blinding. A man screamed, a high-pitched shriek of surprise and pain. Dudley turned and began scrambling back to the British end of the tunnel as fast as he could.

When he reached it, Private Marten was there with Morris. Marten brandished his pick like a battle axe.

"What happened?" Morris cried. "Are you all right?"

Dudley glanced behind him, but there was no movement, no pursuit. The shot had taken the enemy by surprise. He turned back to Morris.

"Let's have our engineer pack the charge in Pandy's tunnel," he said.

Lieutenant Langley, the engineer, directed the men to pile the small powder barrels and bags in the enclosed space. The enemy made no appearance to stop the work.

"I hope you enjoyed your little adventure," Morris remarked as Langley began stringing a length of quick fuse from the charge.

"I did," Dudley admitted. He had been frightened at the time, uncomfortable in the dark mine. But it had also been action, a release. "Better than the frustration of doing nothing, waiting for Sir Colin to get here."

"Time to go, gentlemen," Langley said.

Marten and the other privates had refilled the tunnel mouth with dirt. The fuse running out of the packed earth looked like the tail of some gargantuan rat.

The officers and men took cover behind a wall on the other side of the house, closer to the Residency. Langley lit the fuse, and it hissed away through the doorway. Seconds passed. At last the ground shook, and a great mushroom of smoke, flame, and debris burst from the buildings in the next street.

Dudley gazed up at the smoke and dust rising into the clear sky. A light autumn breeze took it, snatching it into dark ribbons that streamed away to the south.

CHAPTER 33

Lucknow
November 1857

In early November, a British force advanced from Cawn-pore and encamped about six miles from the Alam Bagh. Six days later, a second force arrived under the Commander-in-Chief, Sir Colin Campbell. A semaphore station sprang up on one corner tower of the Alam Bagh, the long arms signalling the besieged garrison. General Outram ordered a similar station erected on the roof of the Residency, and the communication continued all afternoon.

Sir Colin requested information regarding the layout of the city, and Outram soon obliged him. A clerk in one of the civil offices at Lucknow, Thomas Henry Kavanagh, volunteered to carry a letter and map through the streets to Campbell's camp. It was a dangerous task, but vital. Outram's letter suggested the commander adopt General Havelock's preferred route of approach through the Dilkusha Park and along the river. He had marked the route on the map.

With Kavanagh's mission a success, the relief force began its approach. The defenders crammed the palace balconies and other high places to watch. The force opened its assault according to Outram and Havelock's wishes, first occupying the Dilkusha then capturing a large building known as the Martiniere. The force then worked westward, smoke and the din of battle marking their progress. For a while, the advance stalled at the Shah Najif, a large domed mosque and garden. Campbell then brought up the Naval Brigade, a battery of sailors detached from their ships with their heavy guns. Taking horrible casualties, the sailors at last blew a large hole in the mosque wall. The 93rd Highlanders then stormed the building, taking it after another savage struggle.

With the relief force on its way, General Outram decided to fight through the streets to meet it. On the morning of November 16th, every able soldier who could be spared from picket duty mustered in the courtyard of the Chattar Manzil beneath the towering pointed dome.

The assembled troops presented a motley appearance, the 32nd in their khaki shell jackets, the Sikhs in tunics of a darker tan. Mixed in were the brown coats of the 90th Light Infantry, the dirty white frocks of the Fusiliers, and the few surviving doublets and kilts of the Highlanders. The men and officers also sported a variety of headgear, from covered forage caps to straw hats, white or colored puggaree, and sun helmets. All went armed with swords, pistols, rifles, bayonets, and native *tulwars*. Many had improvised "grenades" by attaching lengths of quick match to small bags of gunpowder.

Dudley carried a rifle in addition to his broadsword in its shoulder sling. He also wore a waist belt with an expense cartridge pouch. Tied next to the pouch were two grenades for use in clearing rebels from houses. Like the others, he was determined to fight his way along the river from building to building to make the link with Campbell's men.

Earlier that morning, the relief force had opened an assault on the next rebel stronghold, a two-storey building with Roman columns called the Sekundar Bagh. The defenders planned to begin their assault with an attack on a walled garden adjacent to the Chattar Manzil. Sappers had dug mines under the wall and stacked them with powder charges. When the garden wall came down, it would clear the range of fire for a large battery: four 18-pounders, four 9-pounders, an 8-inch howitzer, two 24-pounder howitzers, and six 8-inch mortars. The batteries would bombard and shell the riverside houses beyond the garden; then the infantry would move forward.

The infantry waited, standing easy and listening to the clamor of the assault on the Sekundar Bagh. On the opposite side of the courtyard, Outram and Havelock conferred with their engineer officers. The sun rode high overhead, heating the flagstones. The rainy season was over, the air parched, the morning breeze stirring small clouds of dust. The men spoke in low voices, offering each other encouragement for the coming action. This would bring a release from the frustration of living under siege.

Dudley noticed Private Geary clutching his little dog, the company mascot.

"You stick with me, Lazzy," Geary was saying. The dog turned in the private's arms and licked his ear.

Morris strode up with a sun helmet perched on his head and a half-nibbled *chupatty* in his hand.

"Here we are, about to leap into the fire again."

"I should have thought you would be pleased," Dudley replied.

"Oh, I am, certainly. I was just thinking that since we set out from Cawnpore it's been one long, unending battle. There hasn't been a let-up. I can't imagine it was like this in the Crimea." He took a bite from the *chupatty* then asked as he chewed, "Was it?"

"The siege of Sevastopol was a long, unending battle. Plenty of waiting and sniping back and forth. Like here."

Morris slapped his forehead.

"I forgot to tell you! Speaking of sniping, when I was on picket yesterday, I should have sworn I saw your old one-eyed servant amongst the rebels. You know, the fellow who ran off?"

Dudley stared at him. "Are you certain?"

"A beard streaked with gray, an eye patch, white puggaree. He smiled at me, a most vicious smile. I tried to fire my revolver at him, but the cap didn't spark. Then he laughed and ran away, the insolent knave."

Of course, the rebel army was vast, a hundred thousand men strong. The odds of Morris having encountered Kesab seemed slim, but many of the Cawnpore mutineers must have come to Lucknow; and Dudley realized Kesab wanted to find his treasure, his secret vault.

"Where, exactly, did you see him?" he asked.

"Captain Lockhart's outpost," Morris said, pointing south towards the Kaiser Bagh.

"And you say he laughed at you. Maybe he recognized you?"

Morris nodded. "I assumed so at the time. I'm sorry I didn't mention it before. I was so wrapped up in worrying over the relief force."

Musketry rattled in the east, a sputtering volley. Dudley wondered if it would be possible to find Kesab among the rebel horde. Find him, and, perhaps…kill him. Yes, kill him.

It surprised him how certain he was that he wished to kill another man—not a nameless enemy soldier but a man he knew. A man who had been present when the women in Cawnpore had met their terrible fate.

"Looks like we're ready," Morris said.

The generals had concluded their conference with the engineers, and now the battalion commanders were riding out to face their men. The battalions came to attention then fixed bayonets and shouldered arms. Morris moved away to his position behind the center of the company. Dudley took his more senior place on the left.

His heart was hammering with the desire for revenge, but he had to push that need away for now. It was time to look to his duty.

The infantry filed out of the courtyard and lined the street east of the Chattar Manzil, behind the batteries. The senior officers divided the troops into five storming parties, each with an accompanying engineer and men armed with tools and powder bags. Downrange from the guns lay the long garden wall. Slender ornamental palms rose behind it, their fronds quivering with each discharge of the cannon pounding the distant Sekundar Bagh. Beneath the wall, the mine shafts waited for ignition.

The engineers lit the quick fuses. Trails of smoke and flame hissed away before disappearing underground. A moment later, that ground heaved upward. There was no rising flame, just rupturing earth, sections of the wall falling inward, collapsing in heaps of brown rubble and yellow dust. But when the dust cleared, much of the wall still stood.

The 18-pounders opened fire to finish the task, to smash away the remaining brick. On the left, closer to the river, the engineers prepared two more mine shafts for detonation. The infantrymen sat or lay down in ranks to wait. Many broke into their haversacks to eat what might become their final meal.

It was past noon when the new mines exploded, sending up twin pillars of smoke, earth, and rubble. This time, when the air had cleared, the section of garden wall was gone.

At once, the British guns began to pound the houses. The sepoys and matchlock men stayed under cover as howitzer shells burst and round shot smashed through the masonry. Now and then a man ran, crouching, from one building to another. Others showed themselves in windows for brief seconds, firing their muskets and then ducking back.

The cannonade ceased, dust and sulfurous smoke swirling amongst the sweating gunners. Infantrymen coughed and fidgeted where they lay.

"On your feet!" Sergeant-Major Hart of the Highlanders suddenly shouted. The men rose, adjusting their belts and dressing their ranks. "Second storming party, we'll go in after the Perthshire lads."

Dudley watched as those Perthshire lads—the brown coats—rushed into the gap the mines had made. A few muskets flashed from windows. The brown coats began screaming and shouting as they charged into the houses. Grenades exploded, and there was the sound of steel striking steel.

Colonel Stisted scurried forward on foot. He drew his sword and pointed at the breach.

"Forward!" he cried. "Will we let our comrades fight alone?"

"Stay together," Colour-Sergeant Barker shouted at his company.

The section rushed ahead in a ragged clump, scrambling over the bits of fallen brick and masonry. Dudley saw Private Geary's dog running with them, charging into battle with his master.

The Perthshire lads had already cleared the first house in the garden. Dudley ran into the street beyond and turned left to face another building where muskets protruded from jagged loopholes. Barker followed him with a dozen men, including Geary and his dog. The muskets in the loopholes fired, three at once. A Fusilier went down with a curse, blood spraying from his right elbow.

Dudley dashed to the side of the house, throwing himself against the wall beside a window. Barker squatted next to him. Dudley slung his rifle over his shoulder then took a box of lucifer matches from a pocket in his frock. He removed a single match, passed the box to Barker, and pulled a grenade from his belt. Striking the match on the stone wall, he lit the fuse and cast the powder bag into the house. Voices cried out in alarm, and a second later the grenade burst. Smoke boiled from the window.

Dudley's men hammered on the door with their rifles. The wood splintered and gave way, and the enraged Fusiliers poured into the house. Rifles flashed and boomed. Dudley and Barker climbed through the window, joining the Fusiliers as they stormed the rooms, stabbing with bayonets, leaving the house heaped with dead and wounded. In one chamber, they encountered a civilian couple, an elderly man and woman. The Fusiliers would have butchered them in their frenzy, but Dudley was there to shout, "No! Keep going to the other side!"

They emerged into another street. A wave of British soldiers was sweeping east through the houses. Ahead, puffs of smoke spurted from the top of a stone wall as rebels fired from the far side of another garden. Dudley and his followers took cover against the near wall. Ramrods clattered in rifle barrels as the men reloaded. Behind them, Lazzy darted here and there, tail bobbing.

The beagle suddenly barked and howled, dashing up the street to the left. From the opposite direction came a group of men carrying small brass shields and drawn *tulwars*. Somehow, they had escaped the British wave. Now they advanced on Dudley's flank.

When they saw Lazzy, the rebels came to an abrupt stop, the man in the lead flinching away from the charging dog. Lazzy stood in the street and continued to bark and howl. At the garden wall, Barker primed his rifle, pulled back the hammer, and fired from his seated position. The lead rebel fell, *tulwar* spinning from his hand. More rifles fired, Minié bullets slapping into soft flesh. The remaining rebels turned and ran.

"Here, Lazzy, here!" Geary shouted. The dog gave the fleeing swordsmen one last glance then rushed into the private's outstretched arms.

"The dog's a regular hero!" Barker cried, laughing with the others. "Better than a squadron of cavalry."

Dudley chanced a glimpse into the garden opposite. The sepoys who had lined the wall were gone.

Every house beyond the Chattar Manzil had fallen. The Moti Mahal was now the only rebel stronghold between the besieged garrison and Campbell's relief force.

Generals Outram and Havelock rode forward together, each on the back of a white charger. The artillery brought their 18-pounders up and trained them on the palace. The sky was darkening, the sun beginning to set. The bright flash of the guns reflected from many a ruined façade of cracked plaster and broken brick. Soon, the fighting sputtered to a halt as night fell.

The men slept in their captured positions. When dawn came, bringing enough light for the gunners to see their targets, the fight resumed. Campbell's relief force, now just a street away, joined in the fray from the other direction, the Naval Brigade hauling up their big guns.

The Royal Hants and Highlanders waited in reserve as a company of browncoats formed to make an advance against the Mahal. When the holes in the wall were big enough, the light infantrymen stormed in, shouting and firing. The palace was, within a few minutes, again in British hands.

The rebels retreating from the Mahal took up more secure positions in a long, low building adjacent. This was the old mess house of the 32nd Regiment. Havelock and Outram moved their forces forward, their riflemen covering a party of sappers who made holes in the wall with picks and sledgehammers. Meanwhile, the relief force pummeled the building from the east.

With the wall breached, the Perthshire Light Infantry again stormed inside. Soldiers of the relief force joined them, and the two forces met in the middle, laughing and greeting each other over the bodies of the slain.

Dudley watched as Havelock and Outram met Sir Colin Campbell, shaking hands amidst the rubble. Campbell was a small man with a pinched face, a thick mustache and goatee, and a head of curling hair. He made a contrast to Outram, who was a handsome figure with a thick black beard.

Of the three, General Havelock seemed the least impressive. He did not look his usual self, his face pale and shoulders hunched. His son Harry held his arm to brace him. Dudley wondered what could have happened. No one had mentioned that the beloved victor of Cawnpore was sick.

At noon, the triumphant troops sat on their hard-won ground and ate what rations they had with them. A few long shots continued to come in from enemy positions in the Kaiser Bagh, but no one paid them much attention.

As Dudley shared a few crumbling biscuits with Barker, Captain Reed approached him and said, "Orders have been filtering down from the top, Lieutenant. We are to evacuate Lucknow tonight."

Dudley stopped chewing. "Tonight, sir?"

"Yes. Our company is to provide a guard for a mortar battery that will shell the Kaiser Bagh to keep the enemy occupied. They are building the battery now and getting the mortars in place back in the Moti Mahal."

"Evacuate?" Dudley repeated. The order seemed an outrage after all they had done. "Abandon the city to the enemy?"

Reed glared at him. "Those are our orders. I expect you to carry them out." He turned to walk away then paused and looked back. "We must think of the civilians, Mister Dudley."

Dudley nodded.

———◆———

There were only a few hours to prepare, and much work to be done. The civilians gathered what few belongings they wished to take while soldiers loaded the wounded into *doolies* for transport. The entire route of evacuation was then strengthened with strong points made of sand bag barriers and rifle pits.

The route would follow the course of the recent fighting, a long corridor along the river to the Dilkusha Park. Dudley's company worked all afternoon helping to build the new barricades and strong points. As they toiled in their shirtsleeves piling sandbags, they joked and laughed about Lazzy's heroic charge. Many declared the dog should receive a medal.

By evening, the weary Fusiliers had taken positions in new rifle pits along the south face of the Moti Mahal. Behind them lay a new battery of 13-inch mortars. The evacuation route ran along the front of their position.

Dudley slumped behind a sandbag parapet as darkness fell, snapping awake every few moments when his head nodded. Morris was on his feet beside him, smoking a cheroot to keep away fatigue. The mortars began to fire one after the other, each sending a luminous cloud of smoke high into the evening air. The big shells whined and trailed flame as they arced towards the Kaiser Bagh. Some burst on impact, while others exploded in the sky like fireworks.

The mortars kept up their deadly rain for two hours. There was no enemy activity.

A few minutes after midnight, the vanguard of the evacuees came within sight. Two regiments moved in open column, and behind them shuffled the long procession of families, civilian men and officers of the mutinous sepoy regiments with their wives and children. Pairs of soldiers carried the sick and wounded in doolies. A few bullock wagons carrying grain and the contents of the treasury followed. Last in file was a train of ammunition camels.

Save for officers on horseback and gunners riding limbers, most of the people went on foot. Vehicles of various types waited in the Dilkusha Park to take the women and children to the Alam Bagh. From there they would continue to Cawnpore and thence to Allahabad.

Dudley noticed the woman with the chestnut hair who had embraced him in the Residency courtyard. She was holding a child with each hand, a little girl and a little boy. She seemed to have no husband with her. Tears streaked her face, and she flinched each time a mortar fired.

"Some of these people have had enough," he remarked as the woman receded into the darkness. "Perhaps it's best to evacuate them."

"I don't like leaving the city to the Pandies," Morris said. "The Chief will regret it later. When they realize what happened, the damned rebels will call it a retreat, a British defeat. They'll say we couldn't recapture Lucknow after two attacks, and that now we're running with our tails between our legs."

Dudley watched the bursting shells over the Kaiser Bagh. Getting the civilians to safety was important, but he shared Morris's dislike at leaving this place in rebel hands.

He saw no need to evacuate the entire garrison with the civilians.

"We'll be back," he said.

CHAPTER 34

Dudley sighted through the brass telescope, twisting the eyepiece to focus on the rebel trenches that faced the Alam Bagh. His horse wandered a few steps to crop a tuft of grass, causing the image in the telescope to dance and bob. One hoof struck something with a crunch. A bone.

He lowered the telescope and stared down at the white skulls that littered the ground. Several complete skeletons, their gleaming fingers clutching weathered muskets, lay in the remains of sepoy uniforms. Others lay amid heaps of plain cloth that had once been white, now turned gray, brown, or yellow.

The skeletons were those of the rebels who had died in the first battle for the Alam Bagh. It had not taken the scavengers long to pick the bodies clean.

Dudley had seen so much death, the bones gave him nothing more than a grim sense of satisfaction. He again raised the telescope, turning his attention from the dead rebels to the greater number of living ones half a mile away. Sepoy regiments and matchlock men were spreading in long columns from west to east. The enemy appeared to be massing for an attack, the first they had mounted on the British defences here.

The Alam Bagh had become a British redoubt with gun batteries at each of its four corners. Another battery stood to the left of the enclosure, then a long abatis of thorns and sharpened stakes. This was the British forward line. Half a mile to the rear was a second line, a series of rifle pits, gun emplacements, and another abatis. The ancient Jalalabad fort anchored the right, while the left lay west of the Cawnpore road. A large *jheel* protected the left rear.

Behind the defences, a city of tents had risen where the British regiments were camped one beside the other. Here sat Sir Henry Havelock's original field force, left to watch over Lucknow and keep the rebels at bay. James Outram commanded, for Havelock was no longer there to over-see his rugged little army.

After the evacuation of Lucknow on November 23rd, his aides had carried him to the Alam Bagh in a *doolie*; he had been weak and delirious with dysentery. His son Harry had placed him in the shade of a private's bell tent, but there had been no improvement in his condition. General Havelock, who had received a knighthood just weeks before, died a few hours later.

Havelock's body had gone back to Cawnpore with Sir Colin Campbell. With the greater part of the relief force at his disposal, Campbell would use Cawnpore as a base for operations against the Gwalior contingent of mutineers. Meanwhile, Outram would guard the Alam Bagh and keep the Cawnpore road open. There was still a further campaign to wage against Lucknow.

The Lucknow rebels had constructed a network of long trenches just south of the canal, parallel to the British defences. Thus, the two enemies had faced each other for many weeks. A few times they had clashed, although the

British had been the most aggressive. The largest sortie had been in late December. Sir James Outram had led the attack himself, returning with several captured guns, elephants, and wagons of ammunition—Christmas presents for his army.

Dudley moved his telescope left and right, scanning the rebel regiments as they spilled from their trenches to dress in line on the plain. The sepoys were all clad in white jackets and *dhoties*. They presented a frontage of almost two miles, overlapping Jalalabad on the British right. Dudley trained his glass on their faces, searching for a man with an eye patch.

He spied a dignitary in a gilt palanquin, then another figure riding an elephant within a silver howdah. Officers galloped here and there on their horses, waving swords and pistols.

Dudley collapsed the telescope and thrust it into a saddlebag. He had seen no sign of Kesab.

Taking up his reins, he urged his horse westward. His battalion had formed a few hundred yards left of the road, behind the forward abatis. The men had loaded their muskets and now waited in two ranks. He rode along the rear of the Highlanders, halting behind the shrunken Fusilier company.

Private Geary's dog eyed Dudley's horse but stayed behind his master. Lazzy wore an English shilling on his collar, his medal for bravery.

"Did you see him?" Morris asked as Dudley halted. He, too, was on horseback, as were most of the officers, the elevation allowing them a clear view over the heads of their men.

Dudley shook his head, then took the telescope from his saddlebag and passed it to Morris.

"There must be thirty thousand of the devils. Little chance of finding a single man in that crowd."

"Perhaps you will find him some day." Morris opened the telescope and peered through the eyepiece. The enemy had completed their dressing and now waited on the stoney plain. Drums were beating, bugles sounding. "It appears that crowd is about to move forward."

The vast rebel army had begun its advance. The battalions moved as one entity, a solid wall of men. Dudley had never seen a moving line so massive, not even when he had faced the Russians. He watched in fascination, if not apprehension. Had he not known better, he would have thought them unstoppable.

The rebels had more than half a mile of open, broken ground to cover to reach the position held by the Highlanders. The northern corner of the Alam Bagh was much closer. Its guns spat fire, smoke engulfing the sepoys on the British right. Morris shifted his telescope. Dudley knew the sepoys would be falling in heaps, and within minutes, he saw their left flank begin to unravel. The attack was already finished in that sector. There would be more whitening bones in the dust outside the Alam Bagh.

The regiments on the rebel right ignored their unfortunate comrades and continued to advance. The defenders prepared to fire volleys by company. Captain Norcott gave the command.

"At one hundred yards, ready!"

The men adjusted their sights to one hundred yards, primed their weapons, and pulled back their hammers, making a staccato rattling up and down the line.

"Front rank," Norcott shouted, "pre...sent! Fire!"

The volley sounded with a high-pitched crack. The smoke cleared at once, and Dudley could see that gaps had already appeared in the enemy line.

More volleys rang out, company after company firing up and down the length of the abatis. Rebels fell in ranks, but others continued to advance into the accurate Enfield fire. Some passed through a large tope, gaining its cover for a time. The Highlanders and Fusiliers adjusted their rifle sights to seventy yards, then sixty.

In the noise and excitement, Lazzy ran back and forth behind the company, dodging in and out of the horses' legs. Dudley's mount shied, and he shouted, "Lazzy! Stay! Stay here!"

The dog stopped and stared at him, ears twitching as if considering whether Dudley had any authority over him. In the ranks, Private Geary continued to load and fire as if at the shooting range. The volleys came in regular, calm, controlled intervals.

A scant fifty yards from the British line, the remaining rebels broke and ran. The defenders raised their hats and cheered. Lazzy howled along with them.

"Here, now, stop your noise," Lieutenant Morris said to the dog. "Sergeant Johnson, tell Private Geary to tie this animal during alarms and raids. He will end up getting shot, and we will have lost our mascot."

"Sir," Johnson responded. Geary turned to gape at the officer from his position in line as if he had never considered this possibility.

Morris pointed his telescope at the fleeing sepoys.

"See how they've broken up completely? Their men running in scattered clumps? There's an opportunity here for anyone who wants to grab himself an enemy colour."

"Just mind the cavalry, Morris," Dudley said. A regiment of *sowars* had formed on the enemy right to discourage pursuit.

Morris grinned. "Something I have been considering. They're bound to attack again. And when they do, I shall be ready."

Dudley was no longer listening. He was watching the broken enemy, thinking of a one-eyed man.

Weeks passed, and the enemy did not attack again. The war had become static in the Lucknow theatre, a stalemate much like the opposing trenches at Sevastopol. It was a period of routine morning parades, supply escorts to Cawnpore and back, and the occasional small raid or sortie. Dudley started riding on the plain every afternoon as he had done in the Crimea and at Madras. The rides allowed him to pass the time, to think, to clear his head. He even considered writing his memoir again.

He approached the camp from the south after one such ride, letting his horse slow to a walk. A formation of snow geese passed overhead, flown in from a colder clime. It was January, a hot southern winter. He rode for the stable lines, passing a group of grass cutters swinging their scythes. Before he reached his regiment's position, his *syce* scurried out to meet him.

He dismounted and passed the reins to the *syce*. One of his *bhistis* also waited, offering a drink of water from a ladle. Dudley took the ladle and drank.

When the British had evacuated Lucknow and encamped here, men from the local villages had come in seeking employment. Now, every officer again had his entourage of servants; Dudley had five, all of them hard-working and uncomplaining.

His *syce* worked the hardest. After every one of Dudley's rides, the servant would hand-rub the horse, wash out its nostrils, ears, and hoofs, water it, soak its grain and feed it. After that, the man would clean the saddlery and bits before even thinking about sitting down for a rest and a pipe.

"Thank you," Dudley said, returning the ladle to the *bhisti*. The native bowed. Dudley made his way towards the tent he shared with Morris.

He passed the tents of the Highland officers, noticing Captain Mackenzie sitting under his awning on a camp stool. Mackenzie was sifting through some newspapers. He raised his hand in greeting.

"I was about to have my tea," the captain announced. "Care to join me?"

Dudley accepted the offer. A servant unfolded another camp stool for him while a second placed a tea tray on a low camp table. The second servant filled a cup, added milk and sugar, then offered the china cup and saucer to the Highland officer.

"Thank you, Raseem," Mackenzie said then added to Dudley, "I still prefer a hot cup of tea in the afternoon, no matter the climate. Tell me how you like yours, and Raseem will prepare it."

"Milk and one lump of sugar would be fine," Dudley said.

When Dudley held the steaming cup in his hands, Mackenzie said, "The Indians brew a fine cup of tea. Truth be told, they do many things well. It is a great shame, the general hatred we now direct against them."

"Most things about this war are a great shame, sir." Dudley said.

"Quite true. Though I mean to say that the Indians do not deserve to be blamed for the actions of our treacherous sepoys. And yet, they are."

"I have observed the same phenomenon, sir. At times, I have even felt that hatred myself."

"Ah, well. I suppose that's natural, given your experience. It's all so unfortunate. We have let things get out of hand. The mutiny was nought but a great misunderstanding, as I suppose all wars are."

Dudley tested his tea, but it was too hot to drink. He held the saucer on his lap and said, "My experience aside, I agree with your assessment. Though I think the general hatred stems from the perceived support the population gives the rebellious sepoys. It is as if they supported the... the massacre at Cawnpore."

"Aye, but I think it unwise to make such a judgment." The Highlander sipped his tea. "I despise the Pandies, but I know the Indians, having served here in the thirties and forties. You have to understand that they don't see women and children in quite the same light as we. They should not have killed the prisoners, of course—a civilized army should not do that. But I know that many of our sepoy prisoners were telling the truth when they claimed to have protested, and that the Nana had some difficulty finding men willing to do his dirty deed."

Dudley again tested the tea as Mackenzie leaned back and stared into the distance.

"There is great beauty in this country," the Highlander continued, "a fine history, fine art, philosophy. My regiment has a long association with India. As does yours, I believe."

Dudley nodded. "It does, Captain."

Mackenzie narrowed his eyes and grinned. "Do you know the tale of Assaye?"

Dudley returned the smile. "I know it well, sir. I have known it since I was a child, reading of Wellington's exploits."

"Ah! Then you know why we wear an elephant on our badges, and on our buttons. That the Ross-shire Buffs are one of the Assaye regiments." He turned and passed his empty cup to Raseem, who refilled it. "Tell me the tale, if you know it so well."

Dudley thought for a moment.

"From what I recall, Wellesley's army of six thousand faced a Mahratta army of some thirty-two thousand, and a hundred guns. The Seventy-fourth Highlanders were on the right of the British line, your regiment on the left.

Wellesley advanced in echelon from the right. The Seventy-fourth were cut up quite badly, but your regiment captured a number of enemy guns."

"Aye, you do know it, then! Then you'll recall that when the Seventy-eighth passed the enemy guns, the gunners rose from the dead, or seemed to. Shamming, they were. Our lads had to turn back and finish 'em." He took the fresh cup from his servant. "Thank you. Aye, that was how we earned a third colour, the Assaye Colour. All the Assaye regiments received them. My father was at Assaye."

Dudley was impressed.

"Was he, sir?"

"Aye, but serving with the Seventy-fourth, despite being a Mackenzie through and through. The Ross-shire Buffs are a Mackenzie regiment, you see. We may almost be called the Mackenzie Highlanders, or at least Seaforth's Highlanders, our founder having been Lord Seaforth. We owe a great deal to the Mackenzie clan. Not just the tartan sett, for we also share the clan motto. *Cuidic n' Righ*. The only Gaelic motto in the army."

Dudley's curiosity was genuine.

"What does it mean, sir?"

"'Help the King,'" Mackenzie explained. "Another legend, from the thirteenth century, though no one is certain of its truth. The clan chieftain was riding with the king of Scotland on a hunt. The king cornered a stag and wounded it. When the enraged beast charged, the chieftain raised his claymore, shouting, 'Help the king,'" Mackenzie raised his fist as a demonstration, "And with one blow he severed the stag's head. He then presented the head and horns to his monarch. Thus, we have the emblem of the deer's horns, or *caber feidh*."

Dudley smiled. "I don't think we have any stories quite as dramatic from the history of the Royal Hampshire Fusiliers."

"No matter. Your regiment must be a fine one if your two companies are anything to go by. A fine and honourable set of men." Mackenzie again passed his empty cup to Raseem, this time waving his hand and saying, "That will be all, thank you. Are you done there, Lieutenant?"

When the servant had taken Dudley's cup, the Highlander added in a softer voice, "There must be honour in war, Lieutenant. The Bengal sepoys no longer have it, for they have broken their oaths. They do not stand and fight when we meet them in battle. They have lost their spirit, as if they believe they deserve their fate. They are a lot of bad apples, and must be eradicated to a man, lest they spoil the whole barrel.

"The other rebels, these matchlock men and so forth, at least fight us for a just cause, or a cause they consider just. The *zemindars* of Oudh, the king and his family, all fight against a situation to which they never agreed. In that, they have a right, so I will think of them as an honourable enemy.

"And I honour our men, of course. They have fought against indescribable odds, risked great danger, and done so without complaint." He leaned forward with a jerk. "But one set I grant no honour to is our government here in India, the government of the East India Company. They have blundered from start to finish! They did not heed the warnings, even after the initial mutinies. One bad decision after another, and trying to place blame on others. Relieving our General Havelock when he had shown nothing but great skill and enterprise. They broke his spirit, Lieutenant, sent him to his early grave. Like the sepoys, they broke faith."

The Scotsman slumped in his canvas chair, as if his outburst had left him drained of strength.

Dudley folded his hands and said, "I agree with you, sir. Though I find it an uncomfortable subject, I admit to being disappointed with the government's actions."

"Aye," Mackenzie responded. "It pains me when I know my own people have done wrong."

The two sat in silence for a moment. Then Mackenzie stood, saying, "Well, I suppose I will see you again at dinner."

Dudley also rose from his camp stool.

"Thank you, sir. You will."

"Good afternoon, then."

Calling for Raseem, Mackenzie turned and entered his tent.

CHAPTER 35

Alam Bagh
February 1858

Late in February, word came from Cawnpore that Sir Colin Campbell would soon be on the move. He had defeated the Gwalior mutineers in December, and since then, regiment after regiment had been pouring into India from England and other parts of the empire. An army of more than twenty-five thousand British troops was mustering to deal with Lucknow once and for all.

Perhaps knowing they were running out of time, the Lucknow rebels attacked the Alam Bagh defences again on February 21st. As before, the artillery and Enfield rifle fire cut through the sepoy ranks, repulsing them with heavy losses. Three days later, a bugle again pierced the morning air, calling the familiar notes of "stand to your arms." The rebels were massing for a third attack.

Dudley and his company had not taken part in the last repulse, but now they and the Highlanders found themselves at the forward abatis. The 90th Light Infantry took up a position on their left.

Dudley and Morris sat on horseback, watching as the rebels spread out, flags waving and drums beating. As before, the attack would involve mostly infantry, although several regiments of enemy cavalry were drawn up in column near the British right.

"See all those flags, William?" Morris said. "If I get my hands on one of those I will have made my mark."

"If the chance presents itself, by all means," Dudley replied, wondering how this defensive action would provide such an opportunity. "Though I'd advise against doing anything rash."

"Rash?" Morris shrugged. "What's rash? Are you saying I shouldn't take a chance even if it might lead to fame and a field promotion? I would have thought you would give me encouragement rather than warnings."

Dudley sighed. "Just do your duty, Morris. No one can ask more of you."

"My duty is to take a bite out of the Pandies. Capturing a colour would surely have a demoralizing effect."

A sudden pounding of artillery, far-off and regular, sounded from their right rear. A cheer arose, a distant roaring of many voices.

"They're attacking Jalalabad," Dudley said.

As he spoke, the rebel cavalry spurred forward. In a moment, the horsemen had galloped beyond the Alam Bagh and out of sight.

The minutes went by. Soon they stretched into an hour. The noise of battle continued on the far right flank, but the rebel infantry in front made no move. The Fusiliers and Highlanders began to slump in ranks, the men leaning against the edge of the shallow trench behind the abatis. They talked in low voices to pass the time. A few had produced playing cards and pocket chess sets.

"Maybe we'll be left out of this one, too," Dudley suggested. Morris frowned and chewed his bottom lip.

Captain Norcott and Captain Reed approached the two junior officers.

"Dismount and send your horses to the rear," Norcott said. "Our company is to deploy as skirmishers level with that clump of trees." He pointed to a mango tope about two hundred yards forward and left. "We will advance in twenty minutes. For now, rations will be served out to the men."

Silence had settled over the battlefield when the company at last extended into skirmish order and advanced from the abatis. The battle on the right flank had ended with the rebel cavalry in withdrawal. The defeated horsemen were now milling around, reforming north of the Alam Bagh.

"Dig in here," Captain Norcott called when the Fusiliers had reached their position. Under direction from the sergeants, the men began scraping at the earth with their bayonets, throwing up low barriers. The rebel infantry opposite had still not made a move.

Dudley had not thought to bring a rifle when the stand-to had sounded, and his only weapon was his sword. He kept glancing at the tope, now just a few yards to his left. The trees would make decent cover if for some reason the company became cut off from the main body.

Something moved to his right, and he turned to see Lazzy bounding over the plain towards Private Geary. The dog trailed a length of frayed rope from his collar. The men greeted the beagle with cries of joy, although Geary said, "No, Lazzy, go back! It's too dangerous out here."

The dog jumped and licked the crouching private's face. He did not seem intent on obeying. He began to dart here and there in his excitement, snuffling the dusty plain. Now and then, Geary would glance in the beagle's direction, but there was nothing he could do. He could not leave his post and carry his pet to safety.

The sun had begun to descend behind the tope when the sound of trumpets and drums suddenly blared from the rebel lines. The Fusiliers straightened and readied themselves, priming their rifles and kneeling behind what little cover they had made. Distant rebel infantry, their images distorted in the late-afternoon heat, began to pour out of the trenches to form lines. Rebel skirmishers moved out in the van.

"Look sharp, lads!" Norcott shouted. "Remember to trust in your better range and aim for their legs."

Dudley sloped his sword on his right shoulder. The rebels were advancing. At sight of that wall of men, a tingling sensation flared along his neck and scalp. He counted more than thirty enemy flags, each one representing a rebel battalion.

The sepoy skirmishers came within rifle range, and the Enfields began to crack. The men loaded and fired with calm precision. With their smoothbore muskets, the sepoys could do little more than hold their positions. Soon, the opposing skirmishers began to withdraw to the main rebel lines.

The sepoy infantry was about seven hundred yards away when the Fusiliers adjusted their sights and aimed. Here and there, bullets found their marks. Dudley saw two mounted officers fall and pointed out another target to the skirmishers nearest him.

Colour-Sergeant Barker came to crouch beside him.

"They're getting close," Barker said.

As if to confirm this statement, a whistle blew somewhere to their left, beyond the trees. The 90th Light Infantry was recalling its skirmishers.

"Cease firing!" Norcott shouted.

The sepoys had halted and were bringing their muskets to the ready. A few seconds later, their line spat a volley. The range was still too great, but a bullet struck the dirt next to Dudley's toe.

Then the rebels were coming on, having reloaded faster than Dudley thought possible.

"Time to go," he said.

But the men were already moving. The speed of the rebel advance was disconcerting, more determined than it had been in the past. Behind the abatis, the main British line stood with rifles at the ready. The skirmishers made for a gap to the left of the Highlanders. Before they reached it, the front rank of the 78th brought their muskets to the shoulder. The volley blasted. Although the bullets passed to their left, the Fusiliers threw themselves to the ground. There they stayed as the rear rank volley rang out.

Sepoys were falling, but their battalions had reached smoothbore musket range and were preparing to fire. Dudley turned to find himself staring back at the dark faces of his enemy, men in white jackets beneath a flag emblazoned with the twin fish of Oudh. He reached down and hauled a man to his feet. Colour-Sergeant Barker was with him, and together they began pulling the men up, pushing them into a rough line among the wooden stakes of the abatis. Lazzy danced in and out of the hurrying men, yelping with excitement.

A sheet of flame and smoke spat from the rebel battalion; a bullet hummed by Dudley's ear while others tore chips from the abatis stakes. Still others struck home, smacking into flesh. Men grunted and fell while others thrust ramrods into their rifle barrels. On the right, the Highlanders began firing volleys by company, but the sepoys were returning volley for volley. Smoke hung in the space between the combatants.

"Independent fi—" Captain Norcott choked. Bright blood sprayed between his fingers as he gripped his throat. He crumpled to the ground, eyes glazed.

"Let every shot count!" Dudley shouted. He stooped to retrieve a musket from a dead man on his left, also taking a cartridge from the man's pouch. He watched the enemy as he bit the cartridge open. Then he froze in astonishment.

Through the smoke, a tall sepoy was waving his arms, encouraging his men to stand and fight. The sepoy's comrades were falling all around him, victims of a superior weapon, but the rest were holding. The man wore an orange sash, a thick beard streaked with gray...

And a black patch over his left eye.

"Kesab!" Dudley shouted, the paper from the cartridge jetting from his mouth.

The sepoy turned, although Dudley doubted his cry could have been heard over the roar of musketry.

Smoke drifted and eddied. Kesab looked from side to side. The Enfield was having an effect. The rebel line stood in fragments, some men kneeling to fire, others beginning to edge back, fire, then back some more. The colour bearer fell dead, and another man took his place.

Then the entire sepoy line began to give way.

"William," Morris shouted, "do you see it?"

Dudley saw Morris's mouth move but just barely heard the words with his deafened ears.

"Yes," he cried. "I saw him right enough, the blackguard."

"Saw who? I mean the colour!" Morris pointed with his sword. "I'm going to get it! The moment is right. God himself has placed this opportunity before me." He rushed out in front of the company, his sword over his head. "Who is with me?" he cried. "Who will help me take the Pandy colour?"

He ran. Two men followed him, but the rest hung back. The sepoy colour bearer was a hundred yards away now, running with the remnants of the shattered battalion. Riding fast to cover the retreat was a squadron of *sowars* from the waiting enemy cavalry.

"Damn it, Morris!" Dudley threw aside the rifle and turned to look for Barker. He spied Captain Reed lying on his back, eyes closed, his trousers red with blood and his face ashen; a bit of puggaree was tied as a tourniquet around his left thigh.

"Colour-Sergeant!" Dudley shouted. "Bring some men!" He pulled the broadsword from its scabbard and raced after Morris. The lieutenant was thirty paces away.

The three leading *sowars* spurred forward, angling between Morris and the colour bearer. The lieutenant skidded to a halt in a cloud of dust, the two accompanying privates coming up short behind him. Morris raised his revolver as the *sowars* bore down on him, with fifty more behind. The revolver blasted smoke, but with no effect. The lead *sowar* raised his curved sword.

"Trevor!" Dudley yelled.

Then Lazzy ran past him, moving like a cannon shot. The lead *sowar*'s horse reared in fright at the barking dog, unbalancing the rider's sword blow; the blade caught Morris on the wrist. The lieutenant fell, his revolver tumbling to the ground.

The other two horsemen galloped after the privates. One foot soldier went down, his cap and skull split in two. The other dodged aside at the last second, avoiding a sabre aimed at his neck.

Lazzy darted amongst the hoofs of the lead *sowar*'s horse, snapping and growling. Morris was clutching his bleeding arm as Dudley reached him and scooped the heavy Adams revolver from the dust. He heard Lazzy squeal in pain, raised the revolver and fired. The lead *sowar* toppled backward from his saddle.

Dudley turned as one of the other two horsemen bore down on him. He fired the revolver a second time, and the horse screamed and fell, its rider tumbling forward. Rifles began to bark from his left, and he saw Barker had brought a squad forward from the abatis. The men were kneeling and firing, knocking down more cavalry. Rifles were also firing from the line of Highlanders.

Dudley grabbed Morris by the arm and dragged him to his feet. The nearest cover was the tope, twenty paces away. He pulled Morris after him as he ran, expecting the bite of a *sowar*'s blade at any second. Horses and men were screaming.

When he reached the trees, he chanced a glance to his rear.

A horse and rider lay on the ground ten paces back. The man was motionless, while the animal was attempting to rise. The rest of the cavalry were turning back, their charge checked by accurate long-range rifle fire. One of the privates who had gone forward with Morris was scrambling back to the main line. Barker's squad still loaded and fired.

Lazzy lay on the ground, twitching, his tongue protruding from his mouth.

"William," Morris whined, "I need a bandage. God, I think my arm is severed!"

"Quiet," Dudley snapped. "I told you not to do anything foolish."

"I didn't see the cavalry," Morris protested. "I hadn't noticed they had moved forward."

"It doesn't matter," Dudley muttered.

Lazzy had ceased his convulsions. Dudley assumed the horse had dealt the dog a kick hard enough to kill him.

He unwrapped a length of puggaree from his cap, cutting it with his sword blade. With this, he bound Morris's wound. As far as he could tell, the glancing blow had only cut the flesh, leaving the bone intact.

When he finished, he discovered Captain Mackenzie and Colour-Sergeant Barker standing over him.

"Is the lad all right?" Mackenzie asked.

"He's fine," Dudley replied. "His arm will be good as new after a few stitches."

"Aye." Mackenzie nodded. "Pity about the wee dog, though."

Barker sighed and pushed back his cap.

"A pity, indeed, sir."

Geary, weeping without inhibition, held Lazzy's little body curled in his arms. Rough Highlanders and Fusiliers stood around him, offering sympathy and cursing the enemy.

"He was a wee hero, that one," Private Tom Gillespie stated. "He died a hero's death."

The men muttered and nodded.

A day after the rebel attack, Lazzy was laid to rest in the soldiers' graveyard behind the camp. Barker made a wooden marker for the grave, inscribing it with the words:

PRIVATE LAZARUS

A faithful soldier and mascot

Born: unknown

Died: February 24, 1858

As men piled dry earth over the little body, a squad of seven Fusiliers raised their rifles into the air to fire three volleys in salute.

Geary kept the dog's medal.

CHAPTER 36

Lucknow
March 1858

A native servant helped Morris on with his frock. As the man slid the shirt over the lieutenant's outstretched arms, he jarred the stitching, causing Morris to cry, "Be careful, you damned nigger!"

Dudley glanced up from his camp desk, pursing his lips in disapproval.

"Colour-Sergeant Barker told me that Private Geary has taken ill," he said. "Some sort of fever. He thinks losing his dog may have broken the boy's spirit."

"I suppose you will blame that on me as well," Morris snapped as the servant fastened his collar buttons.

"I'm not blaming you, Morris," Dudley said, although that had been his intended implication. "Lazzy chewed through his rope."

Morris sat in silence for a moment, then muttered, "Well, perhaps I blame myself. It was a damned foolish thing to do, trying to take that colour."

"It might have been possible," Dudley suggested, pleased by Morris's humility. "If there had been no cavalry ready to interfere."

Morris stood, and the servant fastened the sword belt around his waist. From outside the thin walls of the tent came a great rumbling of field drums and the squeal of fifes. The tune was "British Grenadiers."

"What's all that noise?" Morris wondered, fumbling to fit his right arm into a white cotton sling.

Dudley closed the lid on his lap desk and set it aside.

"Let's go see."

Together, they ducked outside and followed the sound of the music. Many officers and men were moving through the camp in the same direction. When Dudley and Morris reached the edge of the Cawnpore road, they saw the source of the music. Sir Colin Campbell's army was approaching.

"Well, I'll be damned!" Morris exclaimed at the sight.

The general rode at the head of the army in front of the fifes and drums. Behind the musicians came the pipers of the 93rd Highlanders, then a column stretching along the road as far as the eye could see. Regiment after regiment of infantry marched, stirring up dust, while artillery rolled along and cavalry rode with lance tips gleaming.

Far in the rear came a horde of ammunition camels; elephants had tent canvas, chairs and tables piled on their backs, others hauling big siege guns. Then came the bullocks, flocks of goats, sheep, a dark mass of civilian supports, commissariats, sutlers and prostitutes. All had returned to Lucknow to punish the enemy.

As the head of the column came level with the camps, the fifes ceased their martial music. The drums began a roll as the pipers filled their bags, drones humming, and broke into the tune of "Sir Colin Campbell's Farewell to the Crimea."

"Hurrah!" Morris shouted. "There are our lads, William! Our dear old Royal Hants, returned from the siege of Delhi."

The Royal Hampshire Fusiliers marched two regiments behind the Highlanders, Lieutenant-Colonel Willis at their head, the Queen's Colour and blue Regimental Colour flying. Dudley and Morris shouted and waved, and Willis raised his cap in greeting. The men in the ranks stared straight ahead, steady with their rifles sloped on their left shoulders.

An officer broke from the column, riding towards Dudley and Morris. When he pushed back his cap, they saw it was Tom Carlisle.

"Hello, gents," he said in greeting. "We're here to get you out of this mess." Then his brow furrowed, and he added, "I say, Trevor, whatever happened to your arm?"

"We've been fighting the enemy here, Tom," Morris quipped.

"Oh, I see." Carlisle's face kept its grim expression. "Well, William. I saw the House of the Ladies in Cawnpore."

"So have we all," Dudley replied.

"It's caused quite a stir. I understood you were there? Must have been a frightful experience. A wonder that you escaped." He straightened, affecting a proud stance. "Do you know how we executed Pandies at Delhi? We tied them to the muzzles of field guns, wrists against the carriage wheels. Then, of course, we fired the guns. We performed many such executions on the road from Cawnpore."

Dudley said nothing, but Morris made a face.

"That sounds quite disgusting," he said. "Though I suppose it's what they deserve."

"Quite. Don't you agree, Dudley? After Cawnpore, that is?"

Dudley held Carlisle's gaze. "I don't see a reason to torture our enemies, whether with fear or by any other means. Eradicate them, yes, but why these elaborately revolting methods of punishment?"

"Oh, come now, William. It's just like you to object. We didn't invent it, you know. It's a native form of execution. The untouchables come along afterwards and pick up the bits. The heathens believe this means their souls have to wander about before they can be reborn in the same caste, or some such rot." He shifted in his saddle and pulled his horse's head to the right. "Well, I'll be off to find where they are putting us. I will see you later, I suppose." His face brightened. "We shall be messing together again."

With a final wave, he rejoined the marching column. Dudley watched him go and remarked, "He wanted to ask me about Charlotte Edwards, maybe even lay some of the blame for her death at my feet. But he lacked the courage."

"Why on earth do you think that?" Morris exclaimed.

Dudley shrugged. After a moment, he murmured, "Perhaps, like you with Lazzy, I do blame myself. A little bit, anyway."

"Oh, I'm sick to death of this sort of talk," Morris whined. "We're all to blame for something, it seems. Let's forget it and go see where the regiment is making its camp. We shall be saying farewell to the Seventy-eighth Highlanders, I suppose."

When they reached their tent, Colonel Willis was waiting outside to greet them, having broken away from the column. He had been speaking to a few of the Highland officers, among them Mackenzie. He smiled when he saw Dudley and Morris then shook each of them by the hand.

"It is such a pleasure to see you both well," he cried. "Or well enough, in your case, Lieutenant Morris. 'Tis a pity to hear about Captain Norcott and Captain Reed. Am I to understand that you are acting captain for the combined Grenadier and Number Three Company, Mister Dudley?"

"Yes, sir," Dudley replied. "That is, until Lieutenant Morris or Captain Reed recover. The doctors think they can save Captain Reed's leg."

"Wonderful news! Pandy put up quite a fight here last time, it seems. At any rate, the regiment is waiting in ranks at the moment. We are to encamp next door to you this evening. In the morning, we will advance as one battalion again. I want your company to march in the place of the Grenadiers."

When Willis had remounted and ridden back to the road, Morris said, "We're too short to be Grenadiers, the two of us. You have to be six feet or more."

"We were honorary Highlanders," Dudley reminded him. "Now we are honorary Grenadiers."

That evening Dudley visited Captain Mackenzie's tent to return the borrowed sword.

"I would like to thank you again for the honour of using your fine weapon," Dudley said. "It was a privilege to serve with your regiment."

"And a privilege to serve with yours as well," Mackenzie replied. The two men shook hands; then the Highlander produced a flask of a liquor "resembling Scotch," as he put it.

When the flask was empty, Dudley said his farewells and made his way back to his old regiment.

Dudley wandered through the Dilkusha Park, enjoying the green shelter of the ancient trees. Scores of langurs—sacred white monkeys with black faces and long tails—raced along from branch to branch, chattering and scolding him. In the east, a small herd of antelope grazed on a wide lawn.

The peaceful parkland was a prize of war. Sir Colin Campbell's great army had seized it after marching east, bypassing the rebel trenches facing the Alam Bagh. Now the army was encamped here in the pleasant shade—four divisions of infantry, one of artillery, one of engineers, and one of cavalry. Sir James Outram was in command of First Division; the Royal Hants, with the 78th, 90th, and Ferozepore Sikhs, were now part of his 2nd Brigade. These regiments would get a rest when the main assault began. All had fought hard at Delhi or Lucknow and had earned a respite. The fresh regiments, those arrived from Britain or elsewhere, would pitch in first.

Dudley moved between groups of Fusiliers lounging about, some reclining under awnings made from blankets or greatcoats. It was past noon, and enterprising native boys were tending small fires, earning a few rupees by preparing meals for the men.

Colour-Sergeant Barker came across the lawn carrying a small langur in his arms like a child.

"Are you up to what I think you are, Colour?" Dudley said.

"Just a thought, sir," Barker replied as the sacred monkey pulled at its long white whiskers. "I rescued this little fellow from a few of the lads who were using his comrades for target practice."

"I see. How is Private Geary?"

Barker hesitated, his jaw working.

"Not well, sir. I feared it was the cholera, but the doctors say it ain't. Some sort of fever." He shrugged. "One more man in the sick tents. He has plenty of company, sir. We've lost a lot of good men that way, never mind to Pandy bullets."

"But Geary has always been somewhat special to you, hasn't he? Almost like a son, of sorts, I would say, or a younger brother. You were inseparable for some time. You were quite an influence on him. For better or worse."

Barker's deep-set eyes were bleak.

"Didn't see much of the lad after my promotion, sir."

"No, of course you wouldn't. You spent your time with fellows like me, and the other sergeants." Dudley reached to take the monkey's hand, but the creature hissed and drew back. "Ah, well. You had a spot of trouble with Geary recently, did you not?"

Barker struggled to calm the monkey as it wriggled in his strong arms.

"That I did, sir."

"Perhaps he feared you had turned your back on him," Dudley ventured. "Was trying to cause a stir."

Barker nodded. "Aye, I think so. That's why I gave him Lazzy after Colonel Willis let us keep him."

"Maybe he'll appreciate the monkey. Help him rally."

"What I was thinking, Mister Dudley."

Dudley smiled. "Good luck, Colour-Sergeant."

"Thank you, sir." Barker hesitated, then added, "And for what you said here, too."

"You're welcome."

Dudley left the colour-sergeant and wandered north, through the trees and towards the river. He wanted to be alone with his thoughts this afternoon.

He came to the place he was seeking, a botanical garden where tall cypresses and elegant tamarinds bordered orange plantations. A covered walk led to an open space with a platform for an orchestra and dancing. It was a place of peace and beauty, now gone to neglect. Vines covered the statues in their alcoves, and weeds choked the irrigation canals. The flowerbeds had grown wild, overspilling their once-careful borders. The fountains were dry.

Dudley came to a flight of steps that led down to the low-riding Gumti. On the broad landing, he found an iron bench that gave a view across the river at the plain on the far side. A pair of peacocks strutted across the lawn, trailing their luminescent tails.

From the groves, the warm, sweet scent of orange blossoms washed over him. The scent brought with it, for a moment, some of the joy he had felt when he had first arrived in India.

"There you are," Morris's voice boomed from behind him. "The colour-sergeant said you went this way."

He sighed as Morris dropped onto the bench beside him. From somewhere on his left came the sudden concussion of artillery.

"Pandy chucking a few shot our way," Morris said.

Dudley stood. "I'm afraid you've spoiled my peace. You and the guns, that is. Why don't we go and take a look at what's happening? We can get a clear view from the roof of the palace."

The Dilkusha palace stood on the north side of the park not far from the river. It resembled a small French chateau, with a flat roof and Roman colonnades on its front and rear faces. A few Highlanders from the 79th Camerons, dressed in kilts, pale-blue cotton frocks, and feather bonnets, were loitering in the yard. They steadied to attention, and a corporal saluted as Dudley and Morris approached the palace door.

A wide flight of steps ascended from the main hall. The two officers made their way up, stepping around the ruins of a smashed chandelier on the landing. Other debris lay in their path as they climbed—broken mirrors and picture frames, chairs, crumpled tapestries.

The stairs at last brought them to the rooftop balcony. On its western edge, they joined another group of officers, a few Sikhs and Highlanders. Morris had his telescope but was unable to use it with his injured right arm. He passed it to Dudley.

From here, they could see the entire city, the sun glinting on its domes and spires. Just below the Dilkusha ran a flat expanse of ground that ended at a ruined brick wall, shelter for a regiment of men in red tunics. Beyond the wall, a chain of rebel rifle pits and gun batteries lay under the lee of the Martiniere; the building had been a school for half-caste boys. Convoluted wings surrounded its square central tower, and statues perched on every corner and ledge—lion's heads, eagles, and human figures in various poses.

"They're very close to us, aren't they?" Dudley said.

A Sikh near him snorted.

"We will sweep them away like flies."

Beyond the Martiniere, the enemy had prepared three heavy lines of defence. Each looked like a railway embankment running through and marring the appearance of the fairy-tale city. The first followed the canal where it turned to flow into the Gumti. The second ran across the city level with the Moti Mahal. The third lay at a right angle to the others, across the north face of the Kaiser Bagh. About one-hundred and fifty thousand armed rebels manned those defensive lines and the houses between them.

"I think we can break those defences without much trouble," Dudley mused. "We've done it before, and now we have heavy siege guns, ten-inch shell guns and mortars, and this professional little army of experienced soldiers. Sir Colin Campbell is also a fine general, though I hear he is cautious."

"Then there is the force of Gurkhas," Morris added, "that are coming to join us from Nepal."

Dudley surveyed the city with the telescope.

"It's a wonder they let us watch from up here—the Russians would have knocked this palace to dust under our feet long ago. But I don't see many big cannon." He lowered the telescope. "We captured most of their good artillery in the previous fights. Now they have nothing to oppose us but their numbers."

The Sikh officer came over to stand beside them.

"Their numbers will avail them nothing. The sepoys were never a match for the Khalsa." The Khalsa had been the Sikh army before the British annexation of the Punjab. "They are worse now that they are faithless to their salt."

"Hear, hear," Morris said. "Though one did give me a nasty cut."

"You will have your revenge," said the Sikh. "There will be much destruction when the assault begins. Lucknow is a rich city; there will be plunder for all. Sir Colin will allow it." He shrugged. "So I have heard."

Dudley leaned on the flat stone railing and stared at the city. A city to plunder. He remembered Kesab saying the same thing.

All was quiet now, save for the occasional rebel cannon shot from the Martiniere. Another storm of death awaited this place, more rushing from street to street, house to house. And much of the army was men new to this conflict, who had just seen the House of the Ladies in Cawnpore. Men whose cries for vengeance had not diminished with time and many struggles with the enemy.

Soon, the streets would flow with blood.

CHAPTER 37

Lucknow
March 1858

The hospital tents in the Dilkusha Park were filled to bursting when Barker at last visited Geary. The assault had begun, and the wounded had been streaming to the rear for days. They lay crammed together under the canvas, lying on the ground or on blood-soaked *charpoys*. Bluebottles gathered and hummed in clouds while the surgeons worked, the air stinking of blood and corruption. There were no female nurses here as there had been in the Crimea, just native servants who came to bring food and collect the dead.

The sick lay in the last tent. A native orderly tried to stop Barker from entering with the monkey in his arms.

"You cannot go inside, Sahib Bahadur," the man said, shrugging and apologetic. "You will catch sick."

"No, I won't," Barker said. "Get out of my way."

The orderly shouted as Barker pushed past him but would not follow.

Barker knew where Geary lay from having almost come into the tent several times previous. He had always turned back, but now he made straight for the private's location. There were no doctors in the tent to stop him. They were all tending the wounded.

He knelt next to Geary and set down the monkey. The creature did not try to escape, having learned to sit on Barker's command. Geary's face was pale and slick with sweat, his hair matted to his forehead. He had been like this for days, getting neither better nor worse.

Barker shook him, saying, "Private Geary. Wake up, lad."

Geary's eyelids fluttered open. He stared sightless for a moment, then blinked and croaked, "Colour."

"How are you, boy? I've brought my new mate, Morris the monkey. Named him after our lieutenant."

The monkey scratched its arm, looking from Barker to Geary. Geary's eyes flickered over the creature's furry shape, then back to Barker.

"I can hear the fighting. Have we got Lucknow yet?"

"Not yet, lad, but we're making progress. Sir Colin's split the army in two, given our own Sir James Outram one half. Outram crossed the river and came at the Pandies from behind their first line, while Sir Colin took the Martiniere in a few hours fighting. Now we're almost to the second line." Barker sighed, suddenly uncomfortable. "Look, Geary. You haven't died yet, so I figure you ain't going to unless you want to. We all miss Lazzy, all of us. But he died like any soldier, like any soldier should want to. You've got to rally, lad."

Geary shifted on his filthy charpoy but said nothing.

"I saw my wife die like this, boy," Barker said. "I don't want the same again with you. We never had children, she and I, but I tell you…" He swallowed. "…you've been like family to me, here in the army. I don't want you to die, boy. Do you understand?"

Geary was staring at him. Then he nodded.

"You mean it?"

Barker lurched to his feet then scooped Morris the monkey up with one arm.

"Aye, I mean it," he said. "I'll leave you now, let you get some rest. But I'll come back later."

He turned and ducked back through the tent flap, embarrassed at what he had said. The monkey squirmed, and he shouted at it to be still.

It wasn't true, he thought. Geary had just been a young soldier he had been able to influence. He had needed to gather power to himself at the time, to prove his superiority over an army administration he had loathed. There had been nothing else to it.

Or so he told himself.

CHAPTER 38

Lucknow
March 1858

The Royal Hants deployed as a reserve force for the at-tack on the rebel second line; the regiment waited in camp for the word to march. To the west, the rattle of musketry and thud of artillery announced the beginning of the assault. Now and then a distant cheer would rise, a sign of British success.

Civilians had been coming out of the city in large groups, entire families seeking asylum. Many had instead received beatings and insults.

"We're missing out, by the sounds of it," Colour-Sergeant Barker said as the company at last formed in line.

"I believe I've had my fill of fighting, Colour," Dudley admitted. "I don't mind missing out."

When the battalion was assembled and ready, it moved off in fours, marching north to the Dilkusha. There it turned left towards the Martiniere, where it halted. Dudley wondered at the reason for the delay but did not care. He brought the rifle he carried down to the order and examined the signs of the recent struggle around them.

Patches of blood had dried black on the ground amidst parts of discarded uniforms, accoutrements, and weapons. Bloated sepoy corpses lay heaped in the ditch in front of the Martiniere; coolies were removing the bodies one-by-one, stacking them for burning. Stiff arms and legs stuck out at all angles from the grisly pile they had made.

An aide reined in before Colonel Willis, saluting.

"General Outram's compliments, sir, but you may move forward now. Just a mopping up, I'm afraid. Their line gave way all along the front, and the Moti Mahal is already in our hands."

"Thank you, Captain," Willis replied. "We shall do some mopping up, then."

The battalion stepped off, crossing the canal by the Dilkusha bridge. On the other side ran the old rebel first line. Here were more corpses, broken gun carriages, discarded artillery stores and muskets. Farther on, the regiment entered a street of fine houses, all covered in gilt and stucco, windows with Venetian blinds. Many of the houses had small courts with fountains and aqueducts, kiosks, and small temples, all strewn with bodies and shards of broken glass.

The noise of the fight grew louder. Ahead, Dudley saw men running to-and-fro, British soldiers in many forms of dress chasing rebels clad in red or white.

When the battalion crossed the remains of the rebel second line, it deployed from fours into two ranks and halted. Colonel Willis rode along the front.

"It seems we are hunting fugitive rebels. We will break off by companies and hunt the enemy house-to-house."

Dudley still had command of the acting-Grenadier company.

"Colour-Sergeant," he said, "divide the company into squads, each under a junior NCO. We will begin with this block of houses. And move with care."

"A damned strange way to fight a battle," Barker commented as the battalion began to spread out.

The men broke in doors and windows, leapt over walls into courts, seeking the enemy. It soon became apparent the only true battle still raging was in the south, where British artillery pounded the Kaiser Bagh.

Dudley held his rifle at the ready, stepping from a courtyard into a boulevard lined with elegant lanterns. A body of Sikhs was scurrying about, the men holding boxes, pictures, clothing and other loot. A young woman emerged from a doorway and ran into the street. She screamed as three Sikhs caught her, laughing.

"You, there," Dudley called. "Take that woman to the rear!"

The Sikhs looked at him, puzzled expressions on their faces. Dudley realized that he did not look much like an officer. He wore plain white clothes, no sword, and carried a rifle, bayonet, and expense cartridge pouch.

"You heard him," Barker snapped from Dudley's side.

The Sikhs bowed their heads, one saying, "Very good, Colour-Sergeant." They began leading the terrified woman away, now and then glancing behind them at Dudley and Barker.

"Let's move on, Colour," Dudley said, and they resumed their progress up the boulevard.

Groups of Fusiliers moved on either side of them, now mixing with other regiments as they entered the battle front. Another group of Sikhs came rounded a corner chasing a group of sepoys. A squad of infantry in red tunics fired their rifles into the windows of a large house then threw in a powder bag grenade. Here and there, sepoy muskets still fired from behind cover. More sepoys lay dead or wounded in the courtyards. Blood and bits of brain were spattered on walls and statues. Not a structure stood that did not have bullet scars.

Dudley and Barker entered another street, the pavement covered in broken furniture. British soldiers came out of every door laden with tapestries, jewel-encrusted swords and muskets, silk dresses, wooden caskets, blankets and bolts of cloth. A pair of men from Dudley's company appeared in an arched window, china vases in their hands. They raised the vases above their heads and cast them to the ground, where they shattered.

As the Sikh officer at the Dilkusha palace had predicted, the commander-in-chief had given his tacit approval to the looting of the city.

"Take a good look at this scene, Colour-Sergeant," Dudley said. "You are witnessing the final punishment of Lucknow."

The Royal Hants had lost all cohesion, intermingling with the other victorious regiments that had gone before them.

Dudley and Barker wandered along an alley and ducked under an arch bearing the twin fish of Oudh. They found themselves in a narrow court. Along the right side was a row of plain wooden doors bound with iron bands and padlocks. On the left were open sheds filled with elegant carriages, harness, palanquins hung with velvet, and spare wheels and axles.

"Looks like a government storehouse of some kind," Barker said.

On their right, the nearest door hung open, hinges twisted. They moved inside, finding the room packed full of wooden crates. Barker pried one crate open with his yataghan bayonet. It was full of china cups packed in straw. Another crate contained saucers, while a third held spoons.

Outside in the court, there was a scuffling of feet and an excited shouting. Dudley and Barker emerged from the storeroom to find several men of their company attacking the locked doors with the butts of their muskets. Each man's frock bulged, the pockets already stuffed with plunder.

At last, one man put the muzzle of his rifle against a padlock and pulled the trigger. The lock shattered, and the men rushed into the room.

"They'll come out with a bunch of knives and forks," Barker said, chuckling.

A cry of triumph went up from in the room. To Dudley and Barker's surprise, the men rushed out carrying wooden caskets and iron boxes, their lids broken open to reveal jewels and gold coins.

Dudley and Barker entered the room. It was packed from floor to ceiling with similar boxes, crates, and two iron safes with combination locks. Barker pried open a crate. It was filled with jewel-encrusted daggers.

"King's ransom, sir!" he cried.

Dudley used his bayonet to break the tiny padlock on a beautiful sandalwood box then threw back the lid. Diamonds sparkled in the dim light of the room, segments in a necklace. The box held brooches, armlets, rings, all covered in rubies, emeralds, gold and silver.

This could just as well be Kesab's treasure, he thought, *the riches of the King of Oudh himself.*

There had been fish over the archway, meaning that these rooms were the property of the royal family. Dudley could fill his pockets now, taking his share of the plunder, the soldier's pay down through history.

But despite Sir Colin's implied consent, he did not approve of looting, on principle, for it usually involved taking from noncombatants and simply felt like thievery. Granted, now that he stood here, he wondered why he should make a distinction between stealing from these people and knocking their houses down left and right.

"Spoils of war, sir," Barker was saying as he filled his pockets. "It might all be forfeit to the bloody East India

Company if we don't take it, and the Company's what got us into this. I figure they don't deserve it like we do."

"If the Company takes it, then there will be prize money for us," Dudley said, but he had already settled on a compromise. He took the diamond necklace and a gold armlet studded with jewels and stuffed them into the pocket where he kept the toy soldier Wellington. Then he closed the sandalwood box and marched out of the storeroom.

The final wing of the Kaiser Bagh fell later that day. The Begum and her boy king fled, the rebels retreating west through the streets to a hastily constructed line of flimsy barricades. The British settled in on conquered territory, each regiment slowly gathering its scattered troops as evening fell.

Dudley's company bivouacked in a small courtyard, the men building cooking fires with broken shutters and shattered furniture. The other companies in the battalion occupied the adjacent buildings. Colonel Willis had made his headquarters on the other side of Dudley's garden wall.

Just after sunset, Morris came into the enclosure. He had been left behind, watching the battle progress from the roof of the Dilkusha.

"I'm here, and I'm not leaving," he announced. He had discarded his sling, although a bulky bandage still covered his hand and arm. "I don't care what the surgeon says. I won't sit out tomorrow's fight, and that's that."

"It wasn't much of a fight, Trevor," Dudley said.

On the other side of the court, Barker laughed and added, "A fight to see who gets the best loot."

Morris glared at him, but a chorus of raised voices interrupted any further comment. A group of men, all civilians, had gathered around Colonel Willis. They clasped their hands before them or gripped their belongings, imploring the officer to protect them. Willis faced them with his hands behind his back and his chin in the air.

"Bloody curs," Morris commented. "We should shoot the lot of them! This city is nothing but a nest of rebels. They all agreed to rebellion and should be punished for it."

Dudley studied the civilians. Ever since he and Barker had discovered the storerooms, he had been thinking about Kesab's treasure house and where it might lie.

"Excuse me, sir," he said, approaching the wall that partially divided him from Willis. "May I ask these gentlemen a question?"

"By all means," Willis said, looking exasperated.

Dudley turned to the men, who regarded him with a mixture of fear and curiosity.

"Pardon me," he said, "but do any of you fellows know where the Savada house is?"

The men all spoke at once, waving and pointing. Dudley held up his hands.

"Please, one at a time!"

"Excuse, please, Sahib Bahadur," a man in the front said. "Savada is a very rich man in Lucknow. Everyone knows his house. It is the big yellow one south of the Chattar Manzil."

Dudley smiled and shook his head. He was certain that he knew the house well—he had stared at it almost every day for over a month, although he had never gone inside. It lay a good distance from the river and had not played any part in the earlier fighting or mining.

"Thank you," he said to the civilians, then added "Thank you, sir" to Colonel Willis.

He slept in the open court that night, and in the morning, the noise of guns awakened him. He assumed the guns were British, for the enemy no longer possessed much artillery.

One of General Outram's aides brought orders, and soon the regiment was formed and advancing again through the streets. When the battalion split into companies, Dudley took his in the direction of the Chattar Manzil. Before they reached it, he heard a rattle of musketry and shouting from the streets ahead.

"So, there are still some Pandies about!" Morris said with a note of glee.

"Mind the men stay under cover, Colour-Sergeant," Dudley called to Barker.

Moving in loose order, the company came to an avenue strewn with stiff corpses, some British, most those of sepoys. Living sepoys occupied the houses on the other side, and a few muskets flashed from the windows. Dudley's men threw themselves flat against the dusty street, but the bullets went wide.

"Right," he shouted, "let's get them out of there!"

His men rushed forward, some firing as they ran. Soon they were repeating their work of the previous day.

The Chattar Manzil was close—two streets north and west. Dudley and Morris led the company from house to house, clearing one building of rebels after another. Within minutes, the sepoys were running, abandoning their strong positions. The British pursued.

Dudley halted under the cover of a broken brick wall to catch his breath. It had not taken long to penetrate the enemy line, although in taking the first houses, his and other regiments had already resumed the spree of looting and vandalism.

In a courtyard opposite, he saw a squad from another regiment, men in blue tunics. They had lined a group of civilians against a wall, three men and a boy. The soldiers raised their rifles, and the civilians fell on their knees, clasping their hands and pleading. Before Dudley could shout, the volley rang out, and the victims fell in a quivering heap.

Dudley's shoulders slumped. He looked left and right, saw men from various units mixing with his own. To the north was a mosque of white plaster. Standing on the balconies of its two slender minarets were Highlanders from the 93rd. They were firing down at sepoys in a tall house twenty yards away. The tall house was yellow, and beyond it was the Chattar Manzil.

Dudley carried his rifle at the port, running across an alley and then along the base of the mosque. A squad of his men were already there, hammering at the door of the yellow house. The door burst inward, and the men followed it. Dudley heard a scream, and glass breaking. The sepoys who had been firing from the arched second-floor windows had already disappeared.

He ran to the shattered door and stepped inside. The house was once very fine, but now it was a shambles. Soldiers from his company were racing through the rooms, smashing the furniture, tearing down pictures and mirrors. A corporal ran past carrying a wooden box, and a private had a silk shawl draped over his shoulders. From what seemed like a long way off, he heard harsh laughter and glass breaking. He followed the noise, discovering an open door and stairs leading down.

Kesab had told him there was a secret vault in the cellar. Dudley descended the stairs with careful steps.

The cellar was a wide room filled with large casks and a stack of shelves containing bottles. Wine bottles. Two men were busy gulping down their share. One of the men was Private Douglas Marten.

Marten held a fine curved native *tulwar*. The sword had an ornate hilt with rubies at the end of each quillion and an emerald in the pommel. Dudley had seen it before. It was Kesab's.

"You, there," he shouted. "Private!"

Marten dropped his wine bottle, and it smashed on the flagstones at his feet. His companion did the same, and the two stood abashed like guilty schoolboys.

"Where did you get that sword, Marten?" Dudley demanded.

Marten's shoulders relaxed. He quickly pointed to the far corner of the room.

"'Twas over there, sir. In this little room behind a big barrel. Someone had pushed the barrel out of the way, but the room was empty, sir. 'Cept for this sword, that is."

Dudley reached into his pocket and took out the jewelled armlet.

"I'll give you this for the sword."

Marten's eyes widened, and he grinned.

"I think I get the better half of that deal, sir!"

When they had made their exchange, Dudley said, "Now, take a bottle each for yourselves and get out."

The privates obeyed, although not without a few forlorn glances at the shelves.

When they were gone, Dudley considered destroying the wine, but there were hundreds of bottles and several casks. It would take too long, and there did not seem to be much point.

He moved to the corner Marten had indicated. A massive wine cask sat at an angle. Behind it was a low opening in the brick wall, little more than a crawl space. When Dudley knelt and peered inside, he saw a small room about ten feet square. A shaft of light shone down from a slit at the top of one wall. The room was empty save for a simple wooden table.

He straightened and looked at the sword in his hand, wondering how it could have come to be in that room. Setting down his rifle, he grasped the hilt and drew the sword from its scabbard. The blade was very fine, the steel unmarked by blemishes.

Was this a mockery, he wondered, or a challenge of some kind? Had Kesab been here, retrieved the treasure and left the sword for him to find?

He thrust the blade back into its sheath. Picking up his rifle, he climbed the stairs to where the destruction continued.

CHAPTER 39

Rohilkund
April 1858

The regiment marched west from Cawnpore, moving up the Ganges into Rohilkund. Night was falling, the air filling with the buzz and hum of insects. Dudley rode with Kesab's Mogul sword hanging at his side. Colour-Sergeant Barker walked beside him.

"I see that Private Geary has rallied after all," Dudley said.

"Aye, a bloody miracle," Barker growled. "Though I'm pleased to see him hale and well."

Geary marched three sets of fours ahead in the column. The private had left his new pet, Morris the monkey, riding on top of a regimental baggage wagon.

"One's spirits may play an enormous role in one's health," Dudley suggested. "Losing his little dog was quite a blow, I imagine."

"I think I raised those spirits somewhat, sir. If he wants to see me as his elder brother or some sort of father, that's fine with me."

Dudley smiled. "You're the colour-sergeant. You *are* the father of this company, Mister Barker."

Barker chuckled. "I suppose so."

They marched in silence for a while, listening to the crunch of boots, the grinding of gun-carriage wheels, the snorting of horses, the creak of harness. The army had entered the province of Rohilkund to begin a new campaign, leaving the further pacification of Oudh to others.

The days had been hot, the men in the column calling for the *bhistis*, some falling out with heatstroke. Many had already died. Now, the sun was dipping, but the march would continue. To avoid further casualties, the army would move in the cooler air of night.

Events were drawing to a close. After March 16th, General Outram had offered to pursue what was left of the enemy forces that had fled Lucknow. Sir Colin Campbell had declined, asserting that the remaining rebels would simply go home to their families. With the fall of Lucknow, the rebellion was, in essence, at an end.

Yet pockets of resistance remained. Many of the rebels had fled with their weapons, and many had gone west to join a new force gathered there. The force was under the direction of a man named Khan Bahadur Khan, whose stronghold was Bareilly, the principal city in Rohilkund.

The Hindus of Rohilkund professed loyalty to the British, and they needed protection. Under orders from Lord Canning in Calcutta, Bareilly would become the next target. Thus, Campbell had created the Rohilkund Field Force. It utilized a third of the troops that had been at the final capture of Lucknow. Another third would remain in Oudh, while the rest would pacify Azimghar.

The Royal Hants and the 78th Highlanders were both detached to the Rohilkund Field Force. They had left Lucknow for Cawnpore, arriving on April 2nd to begin a two-week rest period. After that, they had escorted a siege train upriver to the city of Fatehgarh. There, they had made the river crossing, and now they moved along the north bank, marching under the last rays of another day's campaigning.

The sky of brilliant gold-and-scarlet faded to a deep purple, then a velvet blue sprinkled with stars. Two regiments of men, horses, bullocks pulling heavy guns, a trail of goats, sheep, ponies and camels—all stumbled along in the dark. The hours passed. Dudley continued to ride in silence, sometimes dozing in the saddle.

The morning sun ascended into a haze of dust thrown up by many hoofs, wheels, and feet. The Royal Hants tramped through a village where the people lay on *charpoys* in the small square, having slept outside during the night. A few rose up on their elbows at the passing of the military column.

But many soldiers had passed this way in recent months and days, and the curious soon went back to sleep.

Beyond the village, a flock of vultures marked another sign of the passage of British troops—the bodies of six men in sepoy uniforms dangled in a tope. Their legs were bare, the word *rebel* having been branded into their flesh with hot irons.

Voices in the column cried their approval, but Dudley felt sickened at the sight. From Lucknow to Cawnpore, Cawnpore to Fatehgarh, they had passed one display of hanging corpses after another. And there had been worse sights. He thought of an incident in Lucknow, on the last day of the assault. He had been with Tom Carlisle.

A native boy had approached Carlisle, leading an aged and blind fakir by the hand and asking for protection.

"Have you been here all this time, supporting the king?" Carlisle demanded.

When the boy did not reply, the lieutenant drew his revolver, put it against the old man's head, and pulled the trigger. With the old man lying in a pool of blood and brains, Carlisle said, "That is my protection."

Dudley had stormed away in disgust, shouting a variety of unflattering names in Carlisle's direction. Carlisle had been astonished at both Dudley's reaction and that of the private soldiers who had stood nearby, crying, "For shame, sir! You are nothing but a bully to kill a harmless old man!"

The outrage of the private soldiers had given Dudley some comfort, but he had seen others shoot down unarmed civilians that day.

The column halted at noon to take shelter from the heat and have a meal. As native workers pitched the tents, local inhabitants began to arrive from the surrounding villages. Dudley watched them gather around Colonel Willis's headquarters—Hindus and Mohammedans, asking for protection, swearing faith to the British cause.

These are our people, Dudley thought. All were subjects of the British Queen. He thought again of the killings, the hangings. British soldiers had done things here that would have sparked outrage at home had the victims been Europeans.

He remembered how he had condemned and hated the Russians for bayoneting British wounded at the battles of Alma and Little Inkerman. Now, the British were behaving in a similar fashion, justifying it as revenge for the Cawnpore massacres. Yet the British were Christians, and Christians were meant to forgive.

There was little sign of forgiveness here. Dudley did not expect to see any for a very long time.

The march resumed at sunset. After crossing the River Ramgunga in the dark, the Royal Hants and 78th Highlanders joined the main Rohilkund Field Force under General Walpole. It was the 26th of April.

Dudley realized it had been just over a year ago that he had met and danced with Charlotte Edwards.

In camp the next day, he heard the tale of what many were calling "Walpole's Folly." A corporal of the 79th Cameron Highlanders described the event to Barker, and Dudley paused to listen.

The general had made a foolish frontal assault against a rebel fort. The loyalty of the landholder in charge of the fort had been wavering between the British and the rebellion. When Walpole discarded diplomacy and deployed his troops, he had made the landholder's choice for him. Then the general had advanced a portion of his force in a charge against a high stone wall.

"Many of our Sutherland men went to the slaughter for naught," the Highlander told Barker, referring to the 93rd Highlanders.

The Highlanders had little use for General Walpole, but they need not have worried for the future of the campaign. That day, the commander-in-chief arrived to take command in person. Sir Colin would allow no more follies.

At dusk, the column moved in the direction of the city of Bareilly. The enemy made no opposition, its cavalry patrols retreating before the British advance. Two more small British forces were converging on the same spot.

By daylight, the column reached the town of Shahjehanpur, where it halted to establish a command post. Two days later, the other forces arrived. The combined army now amounted to five regiments of cavalry in two brigades, five batteries of field artillery and a siege train, a detachment of engineers, and ten regiments of infantry.

Sir Colin arranged the infantry in two brigades. The Royal Hants, the 42nd and 93rd Highlanders, the 4th Punjab Rifles and a Ghurka battalion comprised the First Brigade. The Second Brigade consisted of the 78th and 79th Highlanders, the 64th and 82nd Regiments, and the 2nd Punjab Infantry.

It was the 4th of May. In the morning, the little army would advance on Bareilly.

On the eve of battle, a duty corporal came to Dudley and Morris's tent with a summons from Colonel Willis.

"We are both to report to the colonel?" Dudley asked.

"No, sir," the corporal said. "Just Mister Dudley, sir. That is, yourself."

Dudley arrived at Willis's tent wearing a new pair of white trousers, a new white frock, and a sun helmet wrapped with tan puggaree. Kesab's Mogul sword dangled from his waist belt. He pulled off the bullet-shaped helmet, tucked it under his arm, and ducked inside the tent flap.

Colonel Willis's moustached face lit with joy when he saw him.

"Ah, Mister Dudley. Good of you to come, good of you to come."

Dudley had not had a choice but to come.

"You wished to see me, sir?"

"I have good news for you, Ensign." Willis swept his hand towards a camp stool. "Please, sit." As Dudley sank into the canvas stool, the colonel lifted a piece of paper from his mahogany camp desk and cleared his throat. "I have been hearing some good things about you. You are mentioned in General Outram's correspondence from the defence of the Alam Bagh."

Dudley felt a bright surge of pleasure. He had managed to subjugate his soldierly ambitions during the recent brutal and desperate struggles, but those ambitions were never far from the surface.

"I am happy to hear that, sir."

"That is not all. I am pleased to inform you that the general has recommended you for the Victoria Cross. For your rescue of Lieutenant Trevor Morris during the rebel assault on February twenty-sixth." The colonel stood. "Allow me to shake your hand, sir, and offer my congratulations."

Dudley shook the offered hand in a daze. The Victoria Cross was Britain's new highest medal for valour. It was a simple bronze Maltese cross on a bit of crimson ribbon. The bronze used in the casting of every cross was said to come from the Russian guns captured at Sevastopol.

"I don't know what to say, sir."

"Nothing is final, of course," Willis replied. "The War Office doubtless has yet to hear of it, let alone approve it. Nevertheless, the simple recommendation stands for something. You bring honour on the whole regiment, Ensign." He grimaced, and in a lower voice added, "It is about time that you purchased your lieutenancy, is it not?"

When Dudley left the colonel, he was quivering with excitement. The recommendation had not come because he had destroyed something, but because he had saved someone. He was sick of destruction.

He began running towards his tent. Then he stopped, suddenly wondering how Morris would take this. Not very well, he decided.

He changed direction, making for Colour-Sergeant Barker's tent instead.

CHAPTER 40

Bareilly
April 1858

The enemy deployed before Bareilly with their center on some hills of sand. There they had placed their guns. The rebel infantry stood in lines on either side, with the cavalry waiting on the flanks.

Behind this first line ran a narrow river, the Nattia Naddi, and beyond that the old British cantonments. A second line of rebel infantry stood along the cantonment parade ground. It was a sound position, a strong position.

The Rohilkund Field Force faced its opponent with a similar formation, centering on a battery of 24-pounders. The Highland regiments changed from column to line and moved up to the left of the guns, while the Sikhs and Royal Hants did the same on the right. Cavalry and the Royal Horse Artillery moved around to take positions on the flanks.

Only the first infantry brigade deployed. The Second Brigade waited in reserve, protecting the baggage and siege train from enemy cavalry.

In the Royal Hants, the officers sent their horses to the rear. Dudley's company was now the right flank of the regiment, the place of honour. He watched the Light Company skirmishers range forward while the regimental fifes and drums squealed and pounded behind the ranks.

"One final push," he said as he turned to Barker, who stood directly behind him. "And may I live to see the afternoon."

"May we all, sir," Barker said. "It would be a shame to get this far and bite the dust now."

The fifes and drums suddenly ceased, and for a moment all Dudley could hear was a rushing of wind in his ears. Then, with a pounding of hooves and a rattling of harness and trace chains, the Horse Artillery began moving forward on the right.

At that moment, two of the rebel guns spat smoke from behind their sand mounds. The deep boom followed a moment later, and the iron balls plowed into the dirt fifty yards short.

Shouted commands filled the air, and Dudley strained to hear Sergeant-Major Maclaren's voice above the din.

"Royal Hampshire Fusiliers, by the center, quick… march!"

Every man in the battalion shot his left foot forward, and they were moving. The Punjab Rifles were also advancing, with the heavy guns trailing a bit to the rear. Dudley could hear pipes as the Highlanders stepped off far to his left. The entire British line was advancing as one wave.

The rebels served their artillery well, loading and firing with rapid precision. Two round shot crashed through the Royal Hants, leaving four men twitching on the dusty plain. The battalion closed ranks and kept going.

"Battalion…halt!" Sergeant-Major Maclaren shouted. The skirmishers were withdrawing, having made short work of the enemy light troops. "Volley fire as a front and rear rank standing, prime and load!"

The men pivoted on their heels and brought their rifles down, priming with percussion caps then dropping the rifle butts to the ground. Hands reached to pull cartridges from the expense pouches. Then the troops were biting the cartridges open, pouring the powder in the muzzles of their weapons, drawing ramrods, and pushing the bullet and the infamous greased paper home.

The rebel cannon were still firing two hundred yards away, although their infantry, armed with smoothbore muskets, could only wait at this range.

The sergeant-major gave the next required commands.

"At two hundred yards, ready! Battalion, pre…sent! Fire!"

Six hundred rifles crashed as one, the blast stirring dust from the ground to mingle with the smoke. Colonel Willis was shouting, "File firing by company."

Now it was Dudley's turn to give commands. The smoke and dust were clearing, showing the murderous effect of the Enfield rifle. Even at two hundred yards, the battalion volley had plucked away a good fifth of the sepoy regiment opposite. The survivors were closing ranks.

He marched around to the centre rear of the company, filled his lungs, and shouted, "Independent fire, at two hundred yards, ready! Commence firing!"

Sergeant Johnson had moved around to stand next to Barker, and his was the first rifle to fire. Private Geary was the next; then the files were blazing away, front rank to rear rank, as calm as on the shooting range.

"Can't see a damned thing," Morris complained. The smoke and dust made a dense screen.

"Cease firing!" came the voice of Colonel Willis. "Prepare to advance."

The wind cleared the smoke as the men shouldered arms then stepped off, taking their alignment from the Colour party. The sepoy infantry had decided to retire, crossing the shallow stone bridge that spanned the river.

The rebel gunners were also trying to pull out their guns, but the carriage wheels had become stuck in the sand. The sepoys gave frantic heaves on their handspikes and flogged the bullocks, but the guns would not shift. The British drew closer.

With an angry shout, the 93rd Highlanders surged forward, and within seconds they had engulfed the battery. The Royal Hants carried on past them, advancing to the river.

The Nattia Naddi was little more than a wide *nullah* with a few feet of water in its bottom. Its banks were steep. The Royal Hants marked time then formed a column to cross the bridge.

Left of the bridge, the Highland regiments remained in line along the riverbank. They had taken the enemy guns and were now firing to cover the advance of the right wing.

The enemy did not contest the river crossing.

On the far bank, the Royal Hants reformed their ordered line, the men slipping and stumbling in the loose sand. A few hundred yards away, the sepoys had also reformed and waited to receive the next attack. The Horse Artillery was already sending round shot into their ranks.

"Fix bayonets!" Colonel Willis suddenly cried, and Sergeant-Major Maclaren relayed the order, shouting, "Battalion will fix bayonets! Fix!"

Every man grasped his bayonet socket in his left hand. "Bayonets!"

The men drew their bayonets and slid the sockets over the muzzles of their rifles, thumbing the locking rings into place.

The heavy British 24-pounders had crossed the river and unlimbered, the gunners already ramming home cartridge, wad, and shot. As the Royal Hants started forward, the artillery rained a steady fire on the enemy reserves in the cantonments. The Punjab Rifles, with the Royal Hants, continued to bear down on the rebel first line.

"Right into their teeth!" Colonel Willis was shouting. "Into their teeth!"

The enemy grew nearer, and Dudley felt his heart begin to race. He held the Mogul sword sloped on his right shoulder as he marched behind the center of his company. He could see the faces of the enemy now, the sepoys raising their muskets to their shoulders, preparing to fire. When they did, their volley roared like waves lashing a beach, the smoke billowing outward.

One man in Dudley's company grunted and fell. But only one. The rest kept going. Dudley glanced at the fallen man. He sat clutching his left arm and grimacing in pain.

The battalion halted, and again Willis gave the order for independent fire. The enemy was so close that every shot would count, perhaps on both sides.

"Commence firing!" Dudley cried when the men had loaded and primed their rifles. As the firing began, he returned to the right flank of the company, the flank of the battalion.

Gaps were opening in the enemy ranks, but the sepoys stood and fought with as much determination as they had shown outside the Alam Bagh, their steadily shrinking line closing on the yellow Regimental Colour that hung motionless above their centre. A few of the sepoys began to edge back each time they loaded their muskets, giving ground slowly. A big NCO shouted at them to hold, and even grabbed a few men by their clothing to push them forward. Dudley watched the NCO, a man with a thick beard and a patch over his right eye.

He at first assumed the *havildar* was not Kesab, but another man who looked very like him. The blowing smoke was partly obscuring his vision, and this fellow was wearing a white uniform jacket. Then the man met his gaze.

Kesab held up his fist and shook it. He tilted back his head and seemed to laugh.

"See that one?" Dudley said to Barker. "That big fellow with the eye patch? Shoot him!"

Both Barker and Johnson primed their short sergeants' rifles and pulled back the hammers. Kesab had turned and was waving at something. As the sergeants brought their rifles up, dark shapes loomed in the haze beyond the fraying sepoy regiment. A large body of men appeared, charging through the gaps in the line, making straight for the Royal Hants. They wore green turbans, had grizzled beards, and carried round brass shields on their left arms.

"Ghazis!" someone shouted.

Dudley felt a fleeting moment of terror. The Ghazis were radical Muslims, and their life mission was to gain paradise by killing infidels. They charged with gritted teeth and crazed looks in their eyes, gleaming *tulwars* raised in their right hands. It was the first true enemy charge Dudley had faced in the entire war.

Barker and Johnson fired as one. Two Ghazis went down, but several hundred others came on. Smoke and flame spat from the two ranks of Fusiliers as every loaded musket fired. More Ghazis fell, tumbling over each other.

But there was no time for the Fusiliers to reload and fire again. The Ghazis did not pause in their attack. The Fusiliers brought their bayonets down to the charge then dropped into the guard position, feet twenty-four inches apart and legs bent for thrust.

The Ghazis crashed into the British line, crying, "*Din! Din!*" Fusiliers stabbed with bayonets or received *tulwar* blows to the head, arms, and shoulders. Some fell backward under the weight of their assailants. Bayonets, swords and shields clashed; men grunted and screamed.

It was not a time for emotion, but a time to fight or die. Dudley parried a blow with his Mogul sword then kicked at his adversary's knee. Sergeant Johnson slid his flat yataghan between the ribs of another man, while Barker blocked a *tulwar* with his rifle stock. Dudley hacked down at his fallen enemy, feeling the blade slide from the flesh of the man's neck. He then stabbed the point at the belly of the man Barker held at bay.

The Fusiliers fought the Ghazis in line of ranks, stabbing, kicking, ducking sword blows. Officers pushed into the fray, firing their revolvers. One by one, the Ghazis fell. They would not break and run. They fought to the death.

Dudley struck at another man, cutting him on the wrist. The fellow dropped his sword but snarled and rushed forward. Barker hit him in the side of the head with his rifle butt. The man collapsed in a heap.

The Ghazis were almost spent. The sound of the melee had slowed, the groans and cries growing weary. Dudley glanced towards the sepoy line, saw that the opposing regiment had rallied around its single yellow Colour. Kesab was shouting, calling out commands. Dudley felt a wave of anger, a surging rage washing over him.

He turned to his left, saw Morris standing back and fumbling to reload his revolver. A gash on the man's forehead was spilling blood into his eyes.

"Trevor!" Dudley shouted. "Do you want another opportunity to distinguish yourself?"

Morris blinked in surprise. Less than twenty yards away, the sepoys had raised their muskets to their shoulders. Dudley fell flat as the volley thundered. Bullets struck flesh. Men crumpled.

He looked for Colonel Willis. All he saw was a confused mob of men in a rough line. Jumping up with his sword above his head, he cried, "Come on!"

Then he charged.

The rebels were loading their muskets, ramrods rattling in hot barrels; they were unprepared to meet a charge. Dudley ran, heard Barker bellowing behind him. In a great mob, the remains of the battalion surged forward.

Dudley saw Kesab through the drifting smoke, made for him. He did not care for the danger, had not even considered it. Sepoys were fleeing, dropping their muskets and running. Fusiliers ran after them, including Morris, who was screaming and holding his pistol stuck out in front of him.

Kesab alone stood, facing Dudley.

Another sepoy darted between them, and Dudley recognized Modhu. Modhu swung his musket like a club. Dudley ducked and slashed sideways, cutting into the sepoy's legs. Modhu grunted, staggered, but did not fall.

Dudley recovered from his swing, brought the sword back. The edge bit into both of Modhu's elbows, and the sepoy dropped his musket. Dudley shoved past him.

Kesab threw down his musket and drew a curved *tulwar* similar to the one he had abandoned to Dudley. The two men faced each other.

Kesab struck.

Dudley was not a skilled swordsman, but he assumed he was more than a match for a former *havildar*. And Kesab had reduced vision. He parried the first blow high in the air, pushing forward to unbalance his foe.

Kesab grasped Dudley's left arm in an iron grip as their swords scraped together. Dudley hooked his left leg behind Kesab's right shin. He jerked forward, smashing the crown of his helmet into his enemy's face. Kesab fell backward but did not release his grip. Dudley fell with him, landing with his sword still in contact with Kesab's, pinning it to the ground.

Dudley bent his left leg, bringing his knee into Kesab's belly. Kesab was a bigger man, and stronger, but Dudley was younger, faster. He put his weight on the knee, forcing himself up off the ground, at the same time scraping his sword blade sideways. The tip of the blade came to rest against Kesab's neck.

The old sepoy grunted from the pressure of Dudley's knee then froze. The tip of Dudley's sword just pierced the surface of the skin.

Kesab tried to talk, but the knee in his belly would only allow him to gasp. Dudley stiffened his right arm, prepared to push the sword blade home, but he could not finish the deed. He had won, but he could not simply cut a man's throat when the frenzy of battle had died. Images of hanging men flickered in his head, of Carlisle shooting the fakir, of General Neill making prisoners lick blood from the floor.

He was better than that. He had been recommended for the Victoria Cross for saving a fellow officer.

"Why don't you finish that 'un, sir?" a voice said.

He glanced up, saw Fusiliers standing around him. The man who had spoken was Private Marten.

Dudley released his grip, pushed to his feet. Much of the battalion had advanced towards the Bareilly cantonments, and the firing had ceased. The infantry, cavalry, and artillery had moved up. This section of plain, littered with the silent dead, the stumbling, writhing wounded, was now the rear.

"This man is a prisoner," he said, pointing to Kesab. He looked for Modhu but did not see him. "And any others you find alive."

His helmet had come off when he had struck Kesab with it, and he stooped to pick it up. A private took Kesab's sword and pulled the old sepoy to his feet, saying, "Get up, ye damned nigger."

Dudley whirled and pointed at the man who had spoken.

"I will not hear that sort of talk in this company!" he shouted. "Do you understand me?"

The soldiers all stiffened to attention.

"Y–yes, sir," one stammered.

Dudley sighed. He did not think the man really understood.

Replacing the helmet on his head, he faced Kesab. The one-eyed sepoy stood with squared shoulders, his face expressionless.

"Thus I find I should not have let you live, Dudley Sahib," he said.

"The tables have turned, haven't they? I'm afraid the British are not finished in India after all."

Kesab shrugged. "Maybe you were not so weak as we thought. Perhaps we have forced you to find your strength."

Dudley wondered if that could be true.

"It's a pity," he said, "about your plans for Lucknow. I believe most of the loot went to our lot."

"Not all of it, Dudley Sahib. I succeeded in my plans. My treasure is buried in a secret place far from here. No one will ever find it now."

Dudley was unimpressed.

"I think our men got their fill of gold and jewels. And I found your sword."

Kesab nodded. "I doubted that you would find it but am glad that you did. My little jest, Dudley Sahib." He smiled in his defeat, smiled as the soldiers surrounded him. "And it means I was not bested by a British sword."

CHAPTER 41

Bareilly
April 1858

The battle had lasted six hours in broiling sun and chok-ing dust; by noon, it was over.

The Highlanders had seized the suburbs and can-tonments in their front. There the troops halted, seeking a place to rest in the shade. For the remainder of the day, the soldiers hunted rebels through the suburbs, killing some and rounding up others. Sir Colin Campbell would wait to enter the city proper until the next day. Flocks of Hindu civilians came out to cheer the British troops.

That evening, the army encamped outside the canton-ments. The tents and other baggage had not yet arrived, so the men had to roll themselves in their blankets and sleep in the open. There was also no wood for fires, and the last meal of the day was cold rations.

Colour-Sergeant Barker squatted in the dust with Ser-geant Johnson, each chewing a navy biscuit. When Pri-vate Geary approached, Johnson snapped, "This is the ser-geants' mess, Private."

"It's okay, Johnny," Barker said, standing. "I asked the lad here."

Barker took Geary by the elbow and led him away a few paces.

"What's up, Colour?" Geary asked.

Barker's expression was stern.

"It's just this—we both came through this alive, and there's not much left to do but chase the few that got away. Thing is, we'll be back in garrison at Madras before you know it, or bound for England or Canada or some place where there's little to do. I don't want to see you slipping into your slovenly ways."

Geary's face was downcast.

"I won't, Colour. I promise."

Barker nodded. "You want to be a corporal some day? A sergeant? You may think you have to wait ten years to be sergeant, but I didn't, and neither did Mister Dudley. But slackin' off, like I used to do, won't get you anywhere."

"I…I might want to be a corporal some day."

"That's the spirit, lad." Barker grinned. "You just listen to what I have to say from here on. Then you'll be all right."

"I will, Colour," Geary promised. "I will."

CHAPTER 42

Bareilly
April 1858

Its baggage and siege train finally having arrived, the field force marched into the cantonments and encamped on the brigade parade ground. The regiments pitched their tents in ordered rows, anticipating several days of rest.

Meanwhile, the sepoy prisoners were the subject of a series of courts martial. Every court found its man guilty of mutiny and the murder of his officers, of *nimuck harami*— being faithless to his salt. The prisoners were to receive the native punishment. They would be blown from guns.

Three days after arriving in Bareilly, 1st Brigade formed three sides of a hollow square—a horseshoe—to witness the punishment. The Royal Hants was on the right arm of the formation, standing easy. In the open end of the horseshoe, six 9-pounder field guns faced the formed troops. The hot morning air carried the scent of smoldering slow match.

A guard detachment escorted ten sepoy prisoners from the cantonment lockup. The sepoys formed a line in front of the guns, facing the gunners and the commander of

1st Brigade, Brigadier-General Herbert. Four of the sepoys still wore their white uniform jackets. One was a native officer with a fine white beard and curled mustache. On his chest hung the medal for the Sikh campaign, and round his neck was the Order of Merit.

How did a soldier of such standing, Dudley wondered, come to mutiny against his commanders?

The native officer stepped forward from the ranks, leveling his right hand in a salute to General Herbert.

"Sahib," the officer said, "I have often faced death for the *Sirkar*. Let me show my children how to die."

Herbert's expression showed no emotion when he replied, "Yes. A pity you did not show them how to live like loyal soldiers."

The aged officer said nothing more but faced right and marched to halt before the muzzle of the first gun. He saluted the gun then touched the muzzle with the tip of his right hand. Last, he touched the caste mark on his forehead.

The guns were not shotted, the cartridge alone being sufficient.

"Number-one gun," the battery-sergeant-major cried, "fire!"

"Fire!" responded the corporal behind the first gun.

A gunner touched his linstock to the igniter tube in the vent. The blast of smoke engulfed the sepoy officer, and his body fell backward. It lay on the ground, a heap of bloody ruin, flesh and clothing smoldering. Two untouchables stepped forward to pick up the body and carry it away.

"Now, men," said General Herbert, "follow your officer."

The next man in line alone stepped forward. It was Kesab. He also saluted the general.

Herbert returned the gesture, asking, "Have you anything to say?"

Kesab turned his head, surveying the ranks lined up to watch his death. His single eye found Dudley where he stood on the right of his company. The two men stared at each other across the parade square.

Kesab turned back to the general.

"Sahib, I have chosen my fate."

"Then accept it," Herbert declared.

Kesab faced right as the officer had then marched to stand before the next gun in line. He turned to look at Dudley again. He brought his hand up in a salute.

Dudley slowly raised his hand until his fingers touched his right eyebrow.

Kesab nodded, saluted the gun, and touched the muzzle and his forehead. The commands rang out again. When the gun jetted smoke, Dudley flinched, but he did not close his eyes or look away.

The sweepers took away Kesab's body, and the gunners reloaded.

The general asked who was next, but not one man stepped forward. The sentries seized six and propelled them towards the guns, turning them so their backs were to the muzzles. The sentries then stretched out the arms of each man and fastened his wrists to the carriage wheels.

All six guns fired at once. Pieces of bodies flew across the square. An arm landed at Dudley's feet, and blood splattered across his face. He pulled a handkerchief from his pocket and wiped the blood away.

"Perhaps the service charge is too much, Sergeant-Major," the artillery officer suggested. "Reload with a re-duced saluting charge."

The bits of bodies did not scatter so far next time.

The executions went on all morning. When the brigade was at last dismissed, Dudley wandered to the edge of the cantonments and sat on a parked gun limber.

Fifty paces away lay a graveyard where the British dead of Bareilly had been laid to rest. He looked at the graves— fresh mounds of earth and rows of wooden crosses. He did not move for a long time.

At length, he reached into his pocket and pulled out Wellington. As he examined the tiny tin soldier, he heard footsteps and saw Morris approaching. There was a wide bandage around the lieutenant's head where he had taken the cut from the Ghazi *tulwar*.

"Is it true?" Morris cried, halting next to the limber. "You were recommended for the Victoria Cross for rescuing me at Alam Bagh?"

"Yes," Dudley said, his voice hollow. "I'm sorry I didn't mention it."

"Sorry you didn't mention it?" Morris repeated. He shook his head then sagged onto the limber beside Dudley. "Bloody hell!"

Dudley let Wellington dangle from the broken bit of chain.

"I have been thinking, Trevor. We say that our enemy is cruel, and that is true. But we condemn him and then emulate the same behaviour. We have nothing to teach these people."

Morris covered his face with one hand.

"Oh, you're not on about this again, are you?"

"Why shouldn't I?" Dudley snapped. "I wonder why I'm fighting here. I am a professional soldier. I always wanted adventure, to see the world, to seek glory, to test my courage, and I have done that.

"But I want one thing more. I am a British soldier sworn to uphold British justice. And I don't see British justice here. It has been subverted by hatred. We have forgotten who we are."

"Oh, nonsense," Morris said.

"It's not! We must learn something from this great mutiny, Trevor. We must study its lessons and not repeat our mistakes."

"Fine. I fight to uphold British justice, too, you know. And, like you, I am a glory seeker. But what do I do? I make a fool of myself and, in so doing, give more glory to you." His face was red with mortification. "God must be laughing at me."

Dudley clasped Wellington in his hand.

"I think God may be weeping," he muttered. "For all of us."

"What do I have to do?" Morris went on, as if he had not heard. "If I don't seek laurels, how will I ever find them?"

"Just do your duty," Dudley told him. "And you have done your duty, Trevor. You fought bravely in every engagement of these campaigns. You never once flinched. Don't you realize that?"

Morris sat in silence for a moment, lips pursed. Then he turned to Dudley with a hopeful expression.

"You really think so?"

"Don't be foolish, Trevor. Perhaps if your decent actions didn't stand out, it was because you never found an opportunity."

"Is it luck, then?" Morris asked.

"Yes." Dudley stood. "Excuse me, Trevor. There is something I must do. Alone."

He left Morris on the limber and wandered towards the new graveyard. He thought of a similar burying ground in the Crimea, near the hospital where he had spent so much time with Elizabeth Montague. Would she read of this war in the Boston newspapers? What would she think of the things her former patients had done here?

In his mind, Dudley saw the faces of the dead. O'Ryan, Teecher, Mrs. Edwards. Charlotte. And now Kesab.

Near one row of graves grew a stand of oleanders in bloom. He knelt between the crosses and dug with his hand, scooping out the soil with his fingers. He placed Wellington in the center of the small depression and covered him with earth. Straightening, he packed the earth down hard with his foot. Then he took two paces pack, steadied, and saluted.

He held the salute for a dozen heartbeats then turned on his heels and went back to where Morris was sitting.

END

GLOSSARY

GLOSSARY

Badmash	Hooligan
Bagh	Garden; Habitation
Bahadur	Champion
Begum	Muslim woman of high rank
Bhisti	Water carrier
Brahmin	A member of the Hindu priest caste; the highest caste
Cantonments	Military station or barracks
Caste	Hindu hereditary class, with members socially equal but having no social intercourse with people of other castes
Chabutra	A wooden seating platform
Charpoy	A low four-legged bedstead
Chupatti	A flat patty of coarse unleavened bread
Coolie	Unskilled labourer

GLOSSARY

Dak   Postal service, or transport by relays of horse or bullock drawn vehicles

Dhoti   A loin cloth worn tucked between legs and fastened at the waist

Din   The faith of a Muslim; his party cry

Doolie   Small covered litter or stretcher

Fakir   Poor person, usually religious mendicant living on charity

Ghari   Cart or carriage

Ghazi   Radical Muslim devoted to killing infidels

Griffin   A new arrival in India, usually a young army officer

Hackery   Bullock drawn cart

Havildar   Indian Army sergeant

Jheel   Swamp or shallow lake

GLOSSARY

Khaki   Literally, dust-coloured; a yellow-brown or ash grey colour when first unofficially adopted for uniforms

Mahal   A house or palace, or a queen; also, a palace built for a queen

Mahout   Elephant driver

Maidan   An open plain near a town, or parade ground

Naik   Indian Army corporal

Nautch   An exhibition of professional dancing girls

Nullah   Small ravine, stream, or ditch

Palanquin   A covered litter carried by four or six men

Puggaree   A light turban, or wrapping of cloth around a hat or helmet

Pukka   If referring to a house, burnt brick instead of sun-dried brick; tile roof instead of thatch

Punkah   A swinging cloth fan on a frame operated by pulling a rope

GLOSSARY

Sahib	Title of respect; "sir"
Sepoy	Infantry private in Indian Army
Serai	An inn, or place to accommodate travellers
Sirkar	British government in India
Sowar	Cavalry private in Indian Army
Suttee	The custom requiring a Hindu widow to cremate herself on her husband's funeral pyre
Talookdar	The holder of a talook, a member of the landed gentry in Oudh
Tiffin	Light meal or luncheon
Tope	Grove of trees, most often in reference to mangos
Untouchables	Hereditary class of people outside of the Hindu caste system; contact with them was presumed to break or destroy one's caste, even after death
Zemindar	Landholder

ABOUT THE AUTHOR

HAROLD THOMPSON was born at the end of the 1960s and grew up in the prog rock era, surrounded by the music of Genesis, Pink Floyd, and Yes. His favourite TV shows as a child were the original *Star Trek*, freshly syndicated *Gilligan's Island*, and *Space: 1999*.

He studied neuroscience and cognitive psychology, running two independent labs for his honours degree program (a sort of mini-Masters). He had his eye on med school but at some point made a left turn and ended up in law school.

That was a critical decision, because his dislike of law school caused him to quit to become a "serious" writer. Within five months, he had sold a short story and two non-fiction articles, and in October 1994, he wrote the first draft of *Dudley's Fusiliers*, the first book in the best-selling Empire and Honor series.

Thompson's love of history stems from his work with Parks Canada at the Halifax Citadel National Historic Site in his home town of Halifax, Nova Scotia. In his current position, he creates interpretive programming for visitors to the site.

He is also an avid amateur filmmaker and founded his own studio, Rec Room Movies, in 2007. Rec Room Movies has actually produced several real films, short pieces for Parks Canada, but is most proud of its no-budget feature *A Tale of Bloody Creek*.

Thompson continues to write short science fiction and historical fiction in his spare time. He lives with his family in Nova Scotia.

ABOUT THE ARTISTS

For nearly twenty years, **FRANÇOIS THISDALE** has worked as an award-winning freelance illustrator, creating images for children's books, news magazines, annual corporate reports, and book covers on behalf of North American and European clients. His trademark multi-textured images are the product of a unique blend of traditional drawing and painting techniques with digital imagery. An experienced musician, he has also composed soundtracks for short films and art exhibits.

TAMIAN WOOD is currently based out of sunny South Florida. Using art, photography, typography and digital collage techniques, she creates book covers that appeal to the eye and the mind, to entice the book browser to become a book reader. She holds degrees in computer science and graphic design and is a proud member of Phi Theta Kappa National Honour Society.